WHY IS THAT GODDAMNED RADIO ON?

WHY IS THAT GODDAMNED RADIO ON?

ESSAYS AND STORIES **JIM CORY**

RADIATOR PRESS *

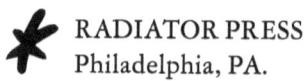 RADIATOR PRESS
Philadelphia, PA.

WHY IS THAT GODDAMNED RADIO ON?
Copyright © 2024 Jim Cory
Printed & Bound in the USA
First Edition
ISBN 978-1-7328145-4-7 (PB) | LCCN: 2024933957

Edited by Marion Bell and Ryan Eckes
Design by Kim Gek Lin Short

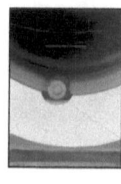 Cover art:
Revolution 2020-21
by Jonathan Eckel

www.radiatorpress.com

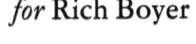

for Rich Boyer

Contents

WHERE'S THE HOTBOY GOING TONIGHT?

This thread would be 1,000 times more interesting if some of you old fucking queens did more than just list a bunch of old bars. Tell us stories, cunts!

—Anonymous

In the late 1970s, on the 1500 block of Spruce Street, in the City of Brotherly Love, there was a bar so raunchy, seedy, and disreputable that it seemed less a commercial establishment than a cave for miscreants licensed, probably by means of the usual Philadelphia payola, to serve drinks. A sign—"Roscoe's"—alerted those unfamiliar with the neighborhood to its presence, but if the purpose of a store sign is to call attention to the business, this one was discreet to the point of timidity. It was as if only a select few were to know the bar was there, and since obviously they already did, the demure marquee existed mostly to satisfy some ordinance requiring liquor licensees to post signage.

To call what was served in Roscoe's "drinks" is at best a stretch and at worst a delusion, since almost no one who went there ever ordered an actual mixed drink. In that bar, wine was highbrow and all beverage of foreign manufacture pretentious. It was a place where a jigger of whiskey dumped in a glass of Rolling Rock and quaffed in a half-dozen gulps between pulls on a Marlboro was considered righteous consolation for the accident of an unfair existence.

I offer the cave metaphor for two reasons. In the first place it was always dark. Sunlight spilled in only when someone opened the front door, which happened infrequently until about 10 at night. Rumor had it that a window existed adjacent to that door until a body went through it, after which the opening was bricked in.

And then there was the smell, an odor of Neanderthal leavings, of unventilated space with its own special atmosphere of alcoholic exhalations, discreet farts, indiscreet burps, cigarettes alive and dead, the funk of wet coats on rainy days, the whiff of unwashed masculinity.

That this was a male establishment was clear enough on entering. What woman would bother coming in? Even fag hags rarely went into Roscoe's. So, the drinkers consisted of drag queens, hustlers, vintage drunks, horny pensioners, spiritual has-beens and bar circuit regulars, including suburbanites who wandered in out of curiosity. There among the meth-addled prettyboys from Kensington or South Philly you might meet Hustler Johnny or, among the slummers, High Speed Jimmy, a barrel-chested blond from Cherry Hill across the river who would've been sexy except that he was always half in the bag, known for his trademark of exiting the bar, after a certain number of drinks, to stand in the middle of Spruce street screaming *STELL-AAAAA!!!*

Still, even with all that testosterone flowing, some ingénue watching the nightly proceedings from the lobby of the Drake Hotel across the street—that'd be me before I worked up the courage to go in—might've initially imagined the place as a *seraglio* for particularly noisy and overly made-up ladies, until it became clear that these were…not that. Roscoe's attracted as regulars a dozen or so "female impersonators," a dreary term, which manages to beat out "homosexual" for sheer sterility and impartial contempt. Roscoe's was where drags who did shows at Center City bars went when the show was done. Their size, scent, splendor, wit and especially the ingenuity of their names—Brandy Alexander et al.—fascinated. Among these, easily the most well-known and self-possessed was someone called "Sarah Vaughan."

"Where are you going?" my mother wants to know.

"The city."

"The *city?*"

In Philadelphia's Main Line suburbs, where I caught the train in, "city" was code for certain things. It meant crowding and crime, crime meaning (but not stating) Black crime, the sort of unpleasantness that causes petty bourgeois sensibilities to rear back in extreme fright. And there was also—not as often articulated but no less present—the notion of vice, which I equated with a kind of joyous squalor. It was that, primarily, that drew me. I wanted all I could get of drunkenness, exotic drugs, squalid sexual adventures with strangers no doubt leading to exotic friendships.

On the 1100 block of Filbert Street one night a friend and I stumbled through the doorway of a tappy where three quarters of the stools were occupied but only a single person was conscious. The bartender. The rest slumped, foreheads on forearms. Wiping a glass with a moist rag, he looked us over.

"You guys sailors? Whuddaya having?" We told him we were—lies were thrills seemingly without consequence—and he served up shots of Scotch and Schaeffer on tap. The beer was flat but for a quarter, who cared? What magic, I wondered, had transported me onto the set of *The Iceman Cometh* in real time? A month or two later I felt the thrill of newly acquired sophistication at the sight of a man in his 40s, thoroughly sozzled, toddling up the sidewalk on Broad Street in the middle of the afternoon, fly open and a thumb-long dick bouncing side to side while passing eyes shifted to avoid the sight. It never occurred to me that I could be looking at some version of my own possible future. I had arrived!

Of course once Roscoe's was located, I rarely went elsewhere. It served as a one-stop shop for urban entertainments. It was a place where lines of coke were vacuumed off the acrylic tops fastened to wobbly tables; where the Ladies Room had been repurposed as a blow job chamber and where, who knew, love might saunter through the door any minute.

One night, in blond form, it did. Love that is. His name is Pete and he's from one of the South Jersey river towns. It's a first love, full of letters, gifts, whispered phone calls, soulful tete-a-tetes among empty beer mugs and infinite cigarettes. We consummate this torrid affair in the mom-and-pop motels that line I-95, where we arrive around midnight with a large cheese pizza and a six-pack and where we can hear the moans and howls of lovers through the walls and floors as easily as they hear ours. This goes on for some months. Years later time has erased all those motels and I'm sitting in the rotunda at Penn's Landing by the Delaware River listening to the singer Chris Connor, a big band songbird (she fronted for Stan Kenton) who went out on her own and stayed there. She's thin, a bit weathered, short blond hair, wears a white linen pantsuit. Her voice sounds like an entire warehouse of tobacco has passed through it, but carries unshakeable conviction:

If you were on my mind, all night and day,
Blame it on my youth
If I forgot to eat, and sleep and pray,
Blame it on my youth...

"Chris! Chris!" someone in the crowd yells. "'You don't know what love is'!"

"Chris! Chris! 'These Foolish Things!'"

"'Ten Cents A Dance', Chris!"

I'm there with a boyfriend who was, then at least, not a fan of jazz. We're the only ones in the crowd under 40. Maybe under 50.

He leans in and whispers: "Blame it on Vermouth."

The fans are all pushing 60 and Chris is well past it.

Standing at the mike, nearing the end of a long set and what must be a long day and an endless career, a breeze pushing at her clothes like a tailor adjusting the cut, Chris Connor takes a sip of water and bows her head slightly, better to make out what they're yelling. She nods, smiles and looks to her left. The bass player thumps a note. Confidence contains a grace that vanquishes every disqualifying detail.

Roscoe's was one of those places you go to meet the people who'll change your life, without knowing who they are or that they will.

Still, anyone under 25 is assumed to be wearing a sign that says: *Ass For Sale.*

"Are you hustling?" an older man asks one afternoon, out of politeness, I then supposed. It was one of those occasions where flattery and embarrassment occupy the same emotional space until evicted by confusion. I shake my head. He nods to the barkeep, Russell, and buys me a Rolling Rock anyway.

My status as suburban interloper is evident to all but me. I look, sound and act like Bryn Mawr or Radnor. And green? There must be a particular shade of it that equates to my naiveté then. Fern, perhaps? "My sense," a friend said the other day, when one of us raised the subject of John Dos Passos' mysterious passage from virulent leftist circa 1932 to John Birch crypto-Nazi and Goldwater supporter in 1964, "is that the more naïve you are, the more conservative you become."

If that's the case, I'm grateful to be an exception to the rule. At the time, my utter lack of life experience bequeathed to me an intellectual vanity stunning in its arrogance and vacuity. Was that little half-in-the-bag poseur babbling about Celine or Hart Crane or Henry James really *moi*? On more than one occasion I was shoved out the door of some party or bar (but never Roscoe's) for being a pain-in-the-ass drunk, the type who insists on attention without even the possibility of delivering anything in the way of wit or conversation. It made a certain sense, even then, but later when the drinking days receded, I wondered from time to time why no one had ever busted a bottle over my head or tossed me in front of a train for the Anna Karenina death I had, at that point, probably earned?

The reason, I suspect, was that the life I was living did not differ much from anyone else's on that frenzied circuit. Bedding hotties was the object, youth the currency, liquor or quaaludes the marital aids of choice. Every other activity or ambition—family, work, hobbies, career—was on maintenance.

"See that one there," says Russell, nodding toward a dreamy little blond who came in nights, looking for clients. "He's trouble."

Russell knew "trouble" from troubled. He was an Italian from South Philly with a lust for wounded innocence. One after another he fell for the rent-boys, often giving them keys to his apartment

5

so they could crash between tricks. Later I wondered if it wasn't a chicken (no pun intended) and egg situation. Was this obsessive pursuit of rough (rumpled?) trade the byproduct of his job—you take what you can get?—or was he working at Roscoe's to facilitate this passion? His was a generous nature joined to a sympathetic disposition, distinct disadvantages in that little world. Select clientele hit him up for free drinks and soon enough came to expect them. They borrowed money with no thought of repaying it and turned to him in every emergency. Some I don't think he even had sex with. A medieval saint, in flannel, he wanted only to shepherd his flock past all the many wolves lying in wait.

Soon enough he befriended me. Age—I was in my early 20s—overrode various considerations. Besides, we had something in common, namely a passion for rock 'n' roll and classical music. In his spacious apartment overlooking 11th and Spruce at least 500 LPs leaned against the wall. You could spend a few hours going through them, begin in ecstasy and end in exhaustion. He kept the fridge stocked with bottles of Budweiser to quench the thirst of strumpets who visited. Big apartments in lovely old buildings were cheap then. But he had been too free, trusting and less than careful.

On a certain afternoon, one of his loveboys, with accomplices, parked a van at the curb and emptied the apartment, including the refrigerator, of everything but the butcher block kitchen table. It was probably too heavy to carry. They left the empties on top of it. Meanwhile up the street, Russell poured beer, rinsed glasses, dumped ashtrays and lent an ear to someone's tale of woe.

Nature's movements bend to the logic of beginning, middle and end but at Roscoe's the beginning was somewhere in the middle and the end could be anywhere or anything, a fiery finale or a tawdry disappearing act. Russell's was the latter. He vanished soon after the burglary. High Speed Jimmy vanished too, only his disappearance took place in increments.

Jimmy left the bar one night at closing, bellowed *STELLA!!!!*

three or four times and lurched a block north toward the Locust Street entrance to the PATCO (Port Authority Transit Corporation) high speed train line running between Philly and the Jersey suburbs. On the train he was arrested and run in for public intoxication by PATCO cops. No big deal, except that the following night, with half a load on, Jimmy chose to make it one, boasting of his arrest in terms alternately defiant and indignant. By the end of the evening he was High Speed Jimmy. Instead of fun, or derring-do, the bar crowd viewed his escapade as a textbook example of Dumb Things Drunks Do. The nickname took hold. The "Stella!" thing ceased. Jimmy became quiet, appeared less frequently, then not at all.

People came, hung around a few months, and went, which is always the way it is with a dive bar. The dramatic finales were few, but being few grew to proportions of legend. There was that late afternoon when Hustler Johnny, elbow on bar, beer in hand, lost his mind in a kind of Primal Scream seizure. He sat up straight, glanced left to right, raised his arm and hurled his empty beer glass at the barkeep. The glass smashed, then silence. Face livid with rage, Johnny grabbed another glass and flung it at the queens watching from the end of the bar. Everyone dove for the floor. When he ran out of glasses, Johnny grabbed beer bottles and when the bottles were gone, he went for the ashtrays. Mirrors shattered, the falling shards knocked bottles off shelves and on to the floor. It happened like a holdup and was done just as quickly, at which point Johnny snapped to, looked around like someone waking from a dream, and bolted.

You'd think drag queens would take the lead when it came to outrageous and profane behavior but if anything, they were a stabilizing force, way more grounded than the rest of the nits in that place. Roscoe's regulars offered a broad sampling of dysfunction. All of it flowed from identity, or its lack. Drag queens, on the other hand, knew who they were and what they were all about. They comported themselves with a dignity drunkenness would've thoroughly despoiled. Some did drag for money on raucous stages but most were not so much performers as guys daring to live the life they wanted at a time when the tweaking of gender roles, deliberate or inadvertent, triggered annoyance or fury in many, especially straight males. This was the age of fag-bashing, when a half dozen suburban high school kids or 20-somethings would pile in the family station wagon and cruise Center City on a Friday night looking for someone drunk, alone, and obviously queer. I had a friend, Richard S., later lost to AIDS, who, one unfortunate evening, got beaten bloody by just such a posse. He described how they'd circled the vicinity a time or two, parked, and divided into teams that appeared suddenly at opposite ends of the block where he was walking.

"Hey faggot!"

They knew not to fuck with drag queens, who were well-prepared to defend themselves. Some I knew opened purses to show me Bowie knives and stilettos. To say that, when crossed, they 'had their knives out,' is not a figure of speech. They came equipped with a kind of courage originating as anger tamed to the point where it can be unleashed and directed on command. One minute sweet as punch, the next minute ready to punch your lights out. They were angry satirists, characters without a proper stage. But all satire begins in sincerity. You must have valued or even desired something or someone to lampoon it, or them, effectively, which explains why no contempt can measure up to the hatred between enemies who were once close friends.

In the *casbah* of Center City's back streets and colonial alleyways the drag queens of the day had constructed a demi-monde, and in that world within a world "Sarah Vaughan" held the apex position. She got respect, even deference. Why was apparent. A certain poise, an imperturbable demeanor, explained it. With ram's horn bouffant and pale blue-green eyeshade, her entrance was always news, her movement from bar to tables and back tracked by every eye.

What puzzled me was the name. Others of less renown took on monikers steeped in irony and pun. Helen Damnation. Tara Dactyl. Jenny Talia. But Sarah Vaughan? The name sounded, to me, like that of a nobody who's just won the Lotto.

Everyone knew who she was. She'd been around a decade and a half, at least. A poem in a gay magazine from 1965, "remembrances of rittenhouse square," by Adrian Stanford, describes how in Philadelphia's premier public space, that jewel of a park, "black sarah ruled."

A decade and a half after the poem's occasion her reign continued, though her scene's shifted, a nightly tour of watering holes such as The Allegro, The Westbury or Steps, where she's about the only Black person who comes and goes unchallenged by the racist protocols of doormen charged with screening people of color via chickenshit demands for i.d.

I knew her only as one who admires style from afar until the evening she sidled up to the table in Roscoe's where I was seated.

"Sarah Vaughan," said Sarah Vaughan, extending a pinkish palm moist in the pressing. The sort of gesture you'd expect from a new colleague at the office or someone running for one. Now we'd acknowledge each other with a nod, even a wave, from opposite sides of the room.

Roscoe's in the afternoon and Roscoe's in the evening, same dive but different. In the afternoon, squandered disability checks and devil-may-care wisecracks among drinkers who'd survived every stage of disgrace. At night, sexual telepathy and cutting for advantage.

At night the door swings back and forth as suburbanites, circuit queens, bands of yacking falsettos and various wrecks push their way in and through while the bartender, now the genial but street-smart Woody (later to open a different sort of oasis four blocks away called, what else, Woody's) quietly keeps an eye on who's where and doing what, via the mirrors behind the bar and on the opposite wall. Sometimes the place was shoulder to shoulder, toasting in its own heat. If typical conversation produces about 60 decibels of noise, the sound in Roscoe's on a Saturday night felt like 120 decibels. You screamed to be heard.

On that sort of night once the door opened and a pair of

Marines in Dress Blues—pressed white slacks, deep blue jackets, gold braid delineating white hats from snappy black brims—presented themselves. They step inside. In five seconds, the place goes silent, which is about how long it took the Jarheads to figure out they'd marched right into a trap. Unlike that bar in San Diego I once entered, packed with shaved heads who only had eyes for each other, this pair had different ideas about what might constitute entertainment in the City of Brotherly Love. They stood there a moment, taking it all in. Their eyes darted back and forth. Then, having exchanged baleful glances, the Leathernecks turned and beat a hasty retreat, even as Roscoe's resumed its nightly roar and the door swung shut behind them.

Jammed, it was easy to pick someone up. The ticking clock forced a decision. Around the corner from Roscoe's at Steps the final 15 minutes before the place closed, its bartender once told me, was known as "the Funeral March." Past two o'clock you could repair to The Penrose or the DCA—after hours clubs oozing hormones and bumps of cocaine—checking caution and all sense of propriety at the door. "I saw you in the DCA last weekend," spat some queen on the street, whom I didn't know and had never met but who nonetheless had arrogated to himself the role of not just judge and jury, but prosecutor and embittered eyewitness. "There you were, DRUNK AND MAKING OUT with some guy in the corner! TWO WEEKENDS IN A ROW!"

I had no memory of it—blackouts being an every-other-night occurrence then—but it sounded in character. I waved him away thinking: if only it could've been three.

Of course, if you were too soused to be admitted to either of those venues—which would be approximately at the *delirium tremens* stage—there was always The Merry Go Round, AKA The Block, AKA The Carousel, bounded by Spruce and Pine north and south, 20th and 21st east and west, where cars circled, slowed, and circled again. After midnight it became a river of brake lights, a place so notorious that the Philadelphia Streets Department posted a sign consisting of a black, left-turning arrow encircled in red with a red line through the center. Under the circle it read: "MIDNIGHT to 5

AM Daily." Forbidding left hand turns from Spruce onto 21st Street during posted hours might have put a stop to the cruising circus except that the Philadelphia Police Department had no more desire to enforce that law than they did, or do, any other.

Odd creatures turned up there. Someone I knew once performed an unauthorized exit from the substance abuse rehab in West Philly where he was then in residence, commandeered a cab on Market Street and directed its driver to 21st and Spruce. He was standing there, in hospital gown and boxer shorts, hoping to cop drugs, get laid or—jackpot!—both. A car door opened and closed. *Poof!* Gone. Another acquaintance, known to the demi-monde as Crazy Bill, showed up there one night, wildly ogling drivers of every other vehicle while he propped himself up with a stop sign. Intoxicated by equal parts lust and pills, he staggered up to a blue BMW. The driver leaned out the window, looked Bill over and hissed: "Keep walking, sister!" It became his mantra and punch line, repeated for laughs in any situation of frustrating circumstance. My roommate, Tim, arrived back at our apartment late one night to relate how a car had slowed as he crossed 20th Street at Pine, the driver regarding him with a look of unconstrained desire. A block later, crossing 21st, the same car, window down, comes to a near-stop.

"Where's the hotboy going tonight?"

"Home," Tim said.

"So why didn't you get in?" I asked the next morning.

A shrug. There were more suitors then than you could shake your dick at.

One night, before things have gotten crowded, I take a seat at the bar. I don't see anyone I know, which is probably for the best, since I haven't slept in two days. Some kind of nerve cell clusterfuck consisting of multiple nights of blackout drinking sits in the middle of my brain, wrapped in insomnia and emitting the most toxic vibrations. I'm working my way toward the next blackout, but beer after beer, nothing. "Had enough to sink a battleship, but the ship won't sink," is how Jamie puts it in *Long Day's Journey Into Night*.

Meanwhile after four months of bliss my country bumpkin boyfriend Pete has given me the gate. ("I think I need to see other people.") Now I slide without resistance into that state of mind where separation from all humanity is not so much desired as preferred, even insisted on, a first prescience of old age and its inevitable misanthropy. I'm alone. I feel alone. I look alone.

I sit at the bar, smoking a Lark. *Richly rewarding, uncommonly smooth.*

When you get thrown over, everything in life is reconfigured into terms of hopelessness. Nothing gets you anywhere. Jobs, for instance. Between unloading trucks in a warehouse (day job) and bugging people on the phone with market research surveys (night job) I "can't keep two cents" in my pocket (how my mother would've put it). I've published a few poems but re-reading them only reminds me of how turgid and obvious they are. Forget about a mid-life crisis, what about a pre-life crisis, the one you have before you've seriously entered adulthood and can't seem to find the knob on the door that admits? And now I can't even get drunk?

Someone leans onto the bar adjacent. I don't bother to glance. It's a troll looking for sexual hired help or some delusional letch who believes you can see through the wreckage and waste to the beauty he once was. Then I notice gold, bangles and baubles bunched and gathered at the narrow wrists of dark arms.

"Honey, you're lookin' a little peaked tonight," she says.

Oddly, it's exactly the word—*pee-kid*— my mother would've used.

I nod.

"You look like you could use some rest."

I tell Sarah Vaughan that my lover had dropped me two days before, that I hadn't slept, couldn't sleep.

She slides onto the barstool adjacent.

"That blond number?"

I nod.

"Lovers come and go. You'll find someone else."

She frowns.

"Now how come you can't sleep?"

Frantic, overlapping streams of doubt and dread get activated the instant I awake, I more or less explain.

A scent. What is it? *Promise her anything, but give her Arpege.* Sarah Vaughan leans closer. This presence I knew as simultaneously regal and flip became in an instant brotherly and empathetic.

"Honey, I got just what you need."

A wallet appears and in the instant it splits into halves I glimpse a driver's license with a name that is not the name "Sarah Vaughan." Sarah Vaughan sees that I see. I say nothing. I had less sense than a bowl of soup but I knew enough to shut up.

She snaps the change purse open. Three yellow pills spill on the bar.

"Take these," she says. "You'll sleep."

Some months later, around 11 o'clock on a Saturday night, a troupe of middle-aged white men with flipped up collars and cashmere arms languidly draped across shoulders come flying through the door.

"I'll take a Vodka Tonic!"

"Make mine a Manhattan!"

"Gin Fizz! TANQUERAY, MARY, IF YOU'VE GOT IT!"

I'm seated in the same spot I was the night three Valium finally doused the coalmine fire in my brain. How much time has elapsed? In your 20s time stops, starts, sputters, leaps, and every now and then takes a nap. The sweater queens, already tipsy, had squeezed in next to me.

Why are they here? I think.

"We were just at the Academy of Music," Gin Fizz turns to me suddenly and explains.

"Who was there?" I say.

"Sarah Vaughan."

Seeing the dumbfounded expression on my face, and no doubt believing he'd made an impression, he begins to convey details of the performance. But I'm hardly listening. You mean all this time that drag queen was famous and no one ever told me?

"Wherever I am," Maria Callas once said, "it is hectic." Ah, the frenzy that issues from a star's imperious presence. Such tumult may characterize the atmosphere around operatic divas, but I can tell you now that it's not normally to be found in a venue where jazz is performed. There, cool's almost always the rule. Hectic would come across as out of control, unseemly. Unless the diva you're talking about "outshines every star."

Fast-forward a decade if you will. I'm standing on the steps of the aforementioned Academy of Music with Pete. Two blocks away, Roscoe's is now JP's. Still a bar but the new owner has gambled on respectability, without realizing that being a dive is what the place has to offer and all it has to offer. Pete and I have dated, parted, made up and somehow stayed friends. "Just friends, lovers no more..." I've stopped drinking. I have a job with benefits and commute to the suburbs each morning, sometimes with buddy Devon. I live in a '20s apartment building on Center City Philadelphia's western fringe, a fun, friendly place where upstairs neighbor Doug is forever on the fire escape smoking as his boyfriend won't let him light up in their apartment. Daily we wave and exchange pleasantries. The neighborhood at 23rd and Pine is two blocks from the Merry Go Round where, within yet another decade, the suburban BMWs and Mercedes, instead of circling the block, are parked in its parking spots and their owners walking designer dogs on once super-cruisy Delancey Street at 11 PM. They look up as they round the corner of 21st and Spruce, wondering why in the world that sign is there.

But tonight I'm at the Academy of Music because Devon has told me I *have* to be. "She rules!" he explains, on the train out to the office. Besides toiling at this dreary suburban publishing company where we both work, Devon plays trumpet and reviews jazz for the weeklies. Not to hear Sarah Vaughan, he says, is tantamount to committing intellectual suicide.

"They don't call her The Divine One for nothing."

The crowd surges through and past the doors of this fabled opera house, modeled on La Scala, that opened before the Civil

War. It's utterly unlike a crowd at the Philadelphia Orchestra, which also performs here, and hardly resembles anything I've seen in a rock palace, when there were rock palaces. Working class Black folk from North and West Philly, jazz snobs, queens, intellectuals, intellectual queens, gay Black jazz intellectual snobs, this strange human brew is in and of itself entertainment. Is Sarah Vaughan, Roscoe's Sarah Vaughan, here? I don't see her. Queens blow kisses and wave or, spotting enemies, sneer. One gentleman who writes dog food commercials and from whose embraces I had drunkenly and deliberately departed in mid-coitus some years prior, lifts his lip's corner in the perfect if unwitting imitation of a cornered canine's snout. *You? Here?*

A crowd is to performance what water is to swimming: the force against which strength, energy, strategy, presence—'talent' is a given—are deployed, then continually tested. This one means business.

Against the norm, the vibe *is* hectic. It's the place—equal parts pomp and poetry—as much as it is the performer. Imagine Tchaikovsky or Mahler conducting on this stage; or Horowitz in its center, offering his marvelous Chopin to a similarly long-sold-out crowd. Picture Walt Whitman tucked in some velvet box, shedding his own secret tears over "Una Furtiva Lagrima" in Donizetti's *Elixir of Love.*

If you're up there in the amphitheater, where the sheer verticality makes you believe you're about to pitch forward into the abyss, what you see are tiny creatures on a platform, bathed in kliegs. But we're not in the Nose Bleed section. I've wrangled tickets in the Parquet, 30 or 40 feet from the stage, where now sits a drum kit, a vintage double-bass leaning against a chair, a grand piano with its bench and, in front of the piano, a barstool with a box of tissues on it. A few feet away from all these is the mike stand from which The Divine One will extract said mike and drag its cord across and around the stage all night. Every seat has a body in it.

On my left, Pete, already craving a cigarette, and on my right an African American woman in late middle age. The purse in her lap's so big if she were trying to board a plane today, they'd make her check it.

There are performers for whom the audience is a necessary inconvenience. Glenn Gould, for instance, grew to loathe the fascinated crowds that came to hear him play until he quit live performance at 31. He was certain they were only waiting for him to fail. Betty Carter, on the other hand, watched her career wane in the 60s when, in the face of the rock n' roll onslaught, jazz became passé and she elected to get married and raise a family. Toward the end of the 60s she launched a comeback at The Village Vanguard. I heard her at a club in Germantown maybe 15 years later. Her vocal stylings, which suggest musical cubism, make her not an easy singer to get right away. At intermission she came down off the stage in a floor length blue gown with sequins that caught every stray ray of light in the room and plunged through the packed house, bowing, shaking hands and exchanging pleasantries.

"Miss Carter, your dress!" said my friend Ron, as she arrived at our table and we, all of us, stood. He extended a hand and, if I remember right, uttered a small gasp. Her raiment was as fabulous as the performance, but neither was as fabulous as her response to the compliment: that magnanimous, unforgettable grin.

Sarah Vaughan's deportment will be somewhere in between.

Now her trio takes the stage. The tension feels like the moment before a significant exam or maybe the aftermath of something dreadfully expensive tumbling off a shelf. It's in the air. You can't escape it. The room quiets.

"Ladies and gentlemen, tonight we bring you, the divine Sarah Vaughan! MISS SARAH VAUGHAN!"

It would take a quarter-page dictionary entry crammed with adjectives and similes to describe Sarah Vaughan in performance. And if you were reading it, you'd think whoever wrote it was describing five people, not one. Her stage patter between songs is girlish, even coy. When she's not those she's composed, commanding, sometimes even regal, but when regal, also peevish, like a monarch handed an imperfect martini. She appears on the edge of pissed off. She wants to be funny but she's only funny because she's a distracted person going about some serious business. If you had to pick one word, the word would be tough. And a woman that's tough is twice as intimidating as a man.

I saw a man trying to escape from a woman who clearly would've killed if she could've gotten to him. They were in the middle of Lombard Street, at about 3 o'clock in the morning, Between the two of them was a bicycle. Gripping the frame, he wielded the bike horizontally like a lion tamer uses a chair, for distance, and it was barely doing the job. A crowd circled them. Street crowds in Philadelphia are usually of a piece with the hooting, jeering mobs at Philadelphia sporting events. This one wasn't making any noise. They were waiting for whatever would happen to happen.

Sarah Vaughan had inside her something of that woman's fury. You sensed it. Her springy Afro wig, eyelids shaded bluish green, the frown—that stamp of permanent dismay that arrives in middle age—the whole take-no-prisoners affect she gives off. She projects a certain ambiguity that says: keep your distance. She's equally capable of innocence or cruelty. Still, it's hard to prepare for the contradiction between her demeanor and what happens when she opens her mouth to sing. The moment a note sounds, complete concentration ensues. If you're in the room, her voice pulls you into the center of that energy, whatever it is she's doing, because nothing short of a missile strike could compete with it.

Then, the song over, she's yucking it up, giggling like a schoolgirl busted for passing notes.

"Requests?" she says. "Requests?"

"BODY AND SOUL!"

The Divine One looks up toward the Nose Bleed section. She scowls, snorts and rolls her eyes. Later I realize it's just not on the set list. If you've ever seen or heard her on video singing it—the best version was recorded in 1969—what she pulls off makes this impudence from the chandelier region totally understandable. She turns this 1930 lament—message: "take me I'm yours"—and transforms it into something so sensual and intimate that hearing it is more like eavesdropping than performance. But you're not going to hear it on the Academy of Music stage tonight, this song that, as a teenager, launched her career at the famous Apollo Theater. What performer gets away with this sort of imperiousness? No matter. The woman to my right extracts a tissue, dabs her eyes, drops the Kleenex in her open purse, and reaches for another.

I might've prepared myself by listening to a few of her records, but I had no knowledge of her repertory, even its most polished gems—"Misty," "Tenderly," "Send in the Clowns" or "Body and Soul" for that matter—the songs she'd staked out as her own at varying points. Before Sarah Vaughan I had never heard jazz singing in performance and no one had briefed me about the three-octave range, her infamous vibrato, the coloratura attack that's unlike anything, *anything*.

My ignorance deprived me of the opportunity to weigh each song against recordings, or compare her performance to that of others. I had neither context nor specifics. I knew only that she was famous enough to be emulated by a drag queen who was no doubt present but had the good sense not to show up looking like Sarah Vaughan.

That, however, held a certain advantage. Arriving with zero expectations left me fully exposed and vulnerable to the effects of her artistry, which leans toward the emotional rather than the intellectual. Had I known more, the experience would've been different. Not necessarily better, just different.

Did she sing Shania Twain's "From This Moment On?"

> *From this moment life has begun*
> *From this moment you are the one*

Or am I only remembering the excitement of the versions I've watched on video, since the song wasn't released until ten years later? Was "Time After Time" in the line-up, or am I thinking about a documentary I've watched probably 50 times (*Live at the 1984 Monterey Jazz Festival*) in which The Divine One introduces the next number by telling the audience, "I haven't sung 'Time After

Time' *since* time after time," a typical faltering effort at comedy, then proceeds, of course, to kill it.

The woman next to me lifts another tissue, dabs her eyes, drops it in the purse.

By the fifth or sixth number, Sarah Vaughan is sweating like a fighter in Round Ten. Her body is at pains to contain her. Onstage, she's back and forth to the Kleenex box, mopping her face, neck and forehead. She shuffles over, plops the box on the piano and hoists herself onto the stool, giggles, and soon slides off again.

The open purse to my right is piled with crushed and wadded tissues.

In his *Jazz Encyclopedia* critic Leonard Feather called Sarah Vaughan's voice "completely different from that of Billie Holiday, Ella Fitzgerald or any of the other great jazz stylists before her" and notes that she "brought to jazz an unprecedented combination of attractive characteristics: a rich, beautifully controlled tone and vibrato; an ear for the chord structure of songs, enabling her to change or inflect the melody as an instrumentalist might; a coy, sometimes archly naïve quality alternating with a sense of great sophistication." Listen to the live sets she recorded at the Tivoli club (*Sarah Swings the Tivoli*) in Copenhagen in 1963, where she'll have you running for some Kleenex of your own (though not to mop sweat) reprising that Sammy Fain/Irving Kahal weeper, "I'll Be Seeing You," or, marveling at the depth in her bag of tricks as she turns every word in the title/line "Fly Me To The Moon" into its own short sentence, a technique she reprises from time to time. She wasn't just a singer of tunes everyone knows and just about everyone at some point performs, she built them out into independent and incomparable constructions, hers alone.

I found this out later when, in the aftermath of that performance, I set out to hear every jazz singer that I could, live, starting with the most famous. Comparing one to another is like comparing a warbler to a whippoorwill. Yes they all sing but that's not the point. The Tivoli Club live sets make something else clear as well. Among the distinctions separating Sarah Vaughan from her peers was her power to set a room on edge with one note, an asset you can hear on live recordings but which being in the room rendered transcendent.

"No one cruises anymore," Doug says. "On the street. Even in Rittenhouse."

As expensive cars of foreign manufacture began to fill every available parking spot in the neighborhood, we all eventually got crowbarred out of that apartment building at 23rd and Pine and were scattered in different directions. But I run into Doug at a party after a half-dozen years and we start making these road trips to the backwaters of the tri-state area in search of colonial iron forges, modernist architecture, and Revolutionary War battlefields, plus birds—which love battlefields—if they're around.

We're driving back from one of our expeditions, talking about our storied youth.

Was he saying they don't cruise, or rather that they don't cruise *us*. With his gray hair and my white mane, fishing vest, pressed khakis, cameras and binoculars slung from necks, we look like two old queens who went out on a safari and landed in a tea party. Where exactly would be the temptation? What he meant was that hot guys don't even cruise each other. Online dating sites do it all. Why bother with eye contact when you can text someone a dick pic and be fucking 20 minutes later?

Doug's stopped smoking but only after a scary episode that happened a year or two before. We're in the woods. I'm moving along a trail at a fair clip and hear him call my name. Serious alarm. I turn. He's nowhere. I bound back down the path to find him leaning against a tree fighting for breath.

Doug's exactly my age and moved to the city six years before I did and it turns out we slept with some of the same guys, most of them long dead. You forget that being old means people you know die fairly regularly. Soon, he would as well.

No, he never went into Roscoe's, it was "a little too skeevy." We both laugh at this interesting turn of phrase. By straining for politeness, the two adverbs that qualify the adjective effectively negate themselves. Skeevy's like scumbag. You're either a scumbag or you're not. He wasn't about to set foot in the place.

Meanwhile, on the phone, Pete remembers the tables that wobbled and the acrylic sheets screwed atop the wood and that under the acrylic were photos of the period's porn stars in every compromising position and then some.

"I forgot about that," I say.

"Ass under glass," he says.

He's on his cell in the break room at the nuclear plant where he's worked for what, three decades?

"Were you there when that hustler went berserk and started throwing ashtrays?"

He was not. At this distance, what happened and who witnessed it are slipping from testimony into myth.

"A lot of outrageous shit went down but I don't remember anybody ever getting thrown out," he says.

"Of course not," I say. "They never had a bouncer. Besides, what exactly would constitute out of line behavior at Roscoe's? There was no line."

"My mom lived on the next block when she was in school," he says. "Her apartment was right across the street from the Allegro, where the Kimmel Center is now. She told me when she was there Roscoe's was a Rexall drug store. She used to go in all the time."

"For what?"

Shampoo. Conditioner. Feminine needs."

"A good thing she didn't come in 30 years later. Instead of Tampons and Prell, she would've found you on a barstool."

I pass that address once or twice a week. It's a Rita's Water Ice at the moment and always empty, even in July. Its next incarnation will probably be a yoga studio for pets.

Everything material changes endlessly, so our lives and moods change whether we want them to or not. Sometimes they change by not changing, which is to say we find ourselves blindsided by the forward motion of events. Often they change in ways we're helpless to control or avoid. A loved one leaves not just you but the city you both live in. Your new boss is a scheming monster. A close friend's dying of AIDS.

"What did you do?" I asked Richard S., when he told me he'd been diagnosed after the bathroom mirror revealed Kaposi's lesions at the base of his back.

We were both 35 then.

"I went to the park and cried," he said. And the way he matter-of-factly stated it told me that that was exactly what he needed to do to find the strength to get through what came next, which was dying, and a hard dying. In those days, before 'the cocktail,' people were gone within a year or two.

One of the things that changed, and not because I willed it to, but because it just did, was my taste.

If on that evening I'd heard not Sarah Vaughan but some second tier singer, I never would've spent the next decade trying to replicate the thrill of it. My compulsive nature meant that after experiencing her performance I had to hear all the singers and then all the pianists and then all the tenor saxophone players of note and the alto players and the trumpet players and the trombone people until finally it became clear to me, via six and a half minutes of uninterrupted bliss delivered in the form of a solo by Ray Brown in the Jazz Showcase in Chicago (when it was located behind the lobby of the old Blackstone Hotel, a place so old Sinclair Lewis mentions it in *Babbitt*) that the double-base, that lowly, cumbrous object, that bloated lyre that cannot ever, somehow, be made glamorous, an instrument I had conceived of as useful only for background noise, keeping time, could yield aural pleasures as exquisite as Miss Vaughan's. She'd delivered me to the threshold of a world I knew existed but had neither emotional nor intellectual access to. She was one of those artists who not only make you feel glad to be alive, which is what art should at the very least aim to accomplish, but grateful to have lived when they did.

Of course that didn't stop me from taking her for granted, like you take love or prosperity for granted.

I was in Chicago, in August two years later. There, in the *Tribune*, I read that The Divine One is booked for a four-night run at a local club. How not to go? By this time I owned a shelf of her recordings.

But I was in the city on business, a job that required me to be on my feet all day. In the evening I'd taxi back to the hotel exhausted. The first night of her gig passes. I resolve to go the next night. That goes by too. The last day of her gig I'd been walking or standing for 12 hours. Fuck it, I thought, I'll catch her the next time she's in Philly.

Less than a year later—April 4, 1990—it's a sunny spring afternoon. I'm driving in a suburb close enough to the city that the car radio picks up WRTI, a college radio station that plays jazz. *Ladies and gentlemen, we have some very sad news to report today and...*" There immediately followed her up-tempo version of "I'll Remember April." The song was introduced in a 1942 Abbott and Costello comedy called *Ride 'Em Cowboy*. Everyone from Eydie Gorme to Red Rodney recorded it. Sarah Vaughan spits out the first line of the second verse one syllable at a time. That old trick.

Be. Con. Tent. To. Love. You. Once. In. A. Pril...

As I was leaving the Academy of Music that afternoon, I looked around again for the drag queen known as Sarah Vaughan, hoping to see her so that I could wave. It was later it occurred to me how doubtful it was she'd ever appear in drag at this concert. Someone dressed and moving like the singer, an impersonator in the same wig and eyeshade, risked danger from this crowd. It would be like shouting blasphemies at a human sacrifice. But I wondered then how The Divine One might've responded had she slipped into a bar near her hotel for a quiet glass of brandy (her preferred beverage, a preference she shared with poet Jack Spicer). Would she have yanked off her wig and backhanded her across the bar? Actually, it occurred to me that The Divine One would probably have laughed and lit another cigarette. Being all too aware of the scope of her talent, my guess is she would've viewed this doppelganger as an act of sheer flattery, if not adulation, which is what it was. We're not talking Diana Ross or Cher, popular drag acts of the time. We're talking Sarah Vaughan. That must've taken work. And love.

"Oh yeah, she's still around," says Darius, who's cut my hair for two decades now. "Woody gave'er a job working in the kitchen."

"In drag?"

"Oh yeah. She'd be back there makin' sandwiches for those queens. But she wasn't always in drag. You know Joe Z___?" he says.

Snip. Snip. I tell Darius I do. He pauses.

"Well, he's in there one night in the bathroom at the urinal. And suddenly there's this Black man standing next to him. And honey, she whips out this monster meat. And Joe's eyes are all popping out of his head. 'Joe?' she says. 'Yeah,' he says. 'You don't know me?' she says. 'If we'd met before, I'd remember *that*,' he says, looking at the monster meat. 'Actually, we've met a number of times,' she says, raising her eyebrows. And then, tongue tip flicking her upper lip, says: 'Sarah Vaughan?'"

SO WHAT DO YOU THINK ABOUT CONCRETE?

On the eve of her 90th birthday, my aunt Dorothy invited several dozen people to a celebratory dinner at the Holiday Inn in Fargo, North Dakota. It was there, while she was picking at a plate of fried walleye between sips of iced tea, that someone much younger asked her what it was like to be that old.

Dorothy, who greatly enjoyed answering questions as well as asking them, looked as if she'd caught a sudden whiff of insecticide. Her eyes narrowed and dropped to the placemat. Her mouth worked back and forth. The placemat advertised, in alphabetical order, 28 varieties of pie, most of them fruit. Dorothy studied the pie drawings for a moment and looked up.

"Every day I'm more convinced I shouldn't be here," she said.

Then went silent.

The silence was unnerving since my aunt liked to talk. Actually, she lived to talk. "Blue streak" only hints at the storm of opinions and quips, declarations and pronouncements that typically issued in the course of one of her conversations. In Fargo, where she spent most of her life, people knew her as an irrepressible talker. Seated shotgun in someone's car, over scrambled eggs in a booth at The Frying Pan, or ensconced on the plaid sofa in her living room, from whatever perch on which she'd landed, she fluttered from topic to topic, a Swallowtail disposing itself blissfully among summer's weeds. Encountering diffidence or a reluctance to engage, a favorite tactic was the blind-siding stem-winder of a question, originating so far out in left field it left the listener reeling for response:

"So, Jim, what do you think about Franklin Delano Roosevelt?"

Of talkers there are types, and some are types to avoid. What separates the gabber from the blabbermouth, the windbag from the gasbag? Only volume, duration. All view anyone unlucky enough to fall within their purview as simply a receptacle for the endless quantities of words they generate. Whether stolid or distracted and fidgeting, to them you're simply a foil, preferably on Mute. Their aim is not an exchange of views, but to activate the vocal cords. For this purpose, an audience of one is not only better than no audience, it's the best possible audience. They want a passive but responsive listener. They would talk to a parking meter if a parking meter had ears.

Who hasn't, at some point, been trapped in a car, bus, bar booth or elevator with the drunk who won't shut up, the embittered complainer about a job or lousy marriage, the monomaniac with a subject, the more arcane the better? A man in Center City, Philadelphia, for instance, will buttonhole strangers on city busses and hold forth at length on the comparative strengths and weaknesses of various supermarket chains.

Of course, a drunk has nothing on the sober monologist. These are infinitely more tedious. You can't simply change seats or push them in a cab and bellow Good Night. Talkers are level-headed creatures, cool to the glance, imbued with a sense of purpose, which is to limit conversation to subjects on which they can prevail as minor authorities. What they do is seize control of social interaction using time-tested methods for foiling interruption. Male, mostly, if that needs saying. I recall the silver-headed savant who was a fellow guest at a late afternoon "tea." His monologue on European, then German, history, had gone on for approaching two hours when it became clear that he had no intention of ending it. As polite interest gave way to boredom, boredom to exasperation, then torture, there was, on my part, a moment, but only a moment, of total awe. How, I thought, could any human being be this self-absorbed? At which point I gathered my coat while the rest of the party exchanged glances as our poor host squirmed.

And then there are those with a cause. Loquacity being a matter not of accident but intention, their methods tend to be more polished, making escape more difficult. A man I knew, for instance, had spent most of his adult life collecting sheet music. In middle age, his apartment was a labyrinth of paths laid out between banks of filing cabinets. One path led to his bed, another to his desk, a third to the kitchen, and so forth. His knowledge was vast, internationally recognized, and he felt compelled to share it, whether on sidewalks, in drugstores or in the middle of social occasions. Parties were a favorite. He would back the unwitting into corners, where there was little choice but to, at some point, bolt. Singles of the naïve sort were his preferred quarry.

Motormouths turn up often enough that your chances of encountering one at a dinner party are statistically significant. One in eight? It's always wise to have an exit strategy.

My aunt, to be clear, was neither a blusterer nor a blowhard. She had little in the way of ego and no actual expertise in anything besides survival. She aimed to fill time and space with talk that was always essentially mutual and to that end had long since established herself as a raconteur of trivia, the mistress of the mundane. Her sources consisted of women's magazines (*Redbook*, etc.), television, gossip and *The Fargo Forum*, North Dakota's largest paper, located around the corner from her apartment.

"So..." or "Oh, say!" is how she'd get her schtick rolling. There might follow some utterly quotidian visual detail (thimble-shaped flowers, of purple hue, appearing mysteriously in a window box), then a fact or anecdote of disarming pointlessness, followed by three or four non-sequiturs. Like a poet—a good one—she could coax an idea from topics or details most wouldn't give a thought to.

Once underway, she improvised, resorting to every manner and means in the effort to sustain the energy level. She worked her way outward rather than down—preferring broad to deep—reaching always for connection. She had a genius for linking the most seemingly disparate topics—bone spurs and bunions, for instance, with the effectiveness of sandbags in municipal flood control efforts—without anyone ever noticing a seam. She could talk all afternoon and into evening, and did.

It helped, of course, that, being curious by nature, everything seemed to surprise her, most often to pleasant effect. She once dispatched me to pick up a pair of pumps from a shoe repair shop at a strip mall, which—like an archeologist removing treasure from a tomb—she extracted from their polish-spattered bag as if they were gem-crusted items of antiquity.

"I don't see how they do it," she said, sincerely floored. She shook her head, perusing a row of stitches. "I just don't!"

Dorothy never married.

That's how someone—another aunt—once explained her to me. Implying that all that chatter concealed an emotionally threadbare existence, a stunted life.

"Oh, that Dorothy," a Fargo cousin said, somewhat later, "she just goes on and on."

This seemed to be, I gathered from his tone, my father's view. It was the fall of 1962, and Dorothy, accompanied by my grandmother, was visiting for the first time. The two of them traveled via train from Fargo to New York, a journey of several days, grueling by coach.

My siblings and I knew Aunt Dorothy as the author of mysterious notes inside birthday cards that also contained checks for five dollars. A fortune in the '60s. We demanded to know what the benefactress was like, imagining Garbo-esque sunglasses, a leather coat, lapels of lustrous mink.

"Dorothy has her ways," my mother, her youngest sister, said.

Her cards were signed: *Birthday Luff, DoDo.*

My father, a high-powered sales executive, spread the twin wings of the evening paper before him and remained silent. He regarded Dorothy as frivolous, insubstantial.

"What do you mean, 'her ways?'" my sister asked.

"Oh, you'll like her."

Dorothy was, in that year, 53, her brown hair flecked with gray en route to a pearl-like whiteness. She wore pink lipstick, pendant earrings, glasses remarkably like those worn by the nuns in our school and a slender wristwatch set in a glittering silver ribbon. She seemed nearly as tall as my father, perhaps taller. She asked endless questions.

"What grade are you in?"

"Are you good at math?"

"How's the piano going?"

She'd frown and nod, listening.

It being October, in Connecticut, what my aunt wanted, more than anything, was to see "the color." After a day or two of catching up, my mother scheduled an afternoon road trip from Stamford to New Haven and back. Six of us scrambled into the station wagon, my mother at the wheel, Dorothy riding shotgun, the Merritt Parkway weeping orange.

"Gorgeous," my aunt said, as we sped past a copse of maples.

"Gorgeous," she repeated, as the yellow Ford sailed by melancholy ponds, granite outcroppings.

"Gorgeous," she said, under an Art Deco bridge.

"Gorgeous," my sister repeated, as we sped past a gas station/ rest stop.

In the rear-view mirror, my mother's eyes registered alarm.

"Gorgeous," I said, as the station wagon whizzed past a barnyard where an old horse chomped on hay.

"Gorgeous," echoed my little brother, in the back seat.

"Alright, God damn it, that's enough," my mother said.

Thereafter, the pale blue birthday checks, loyally dispatched, served as regular reminders of Dorothy's existence. These and long distance calls. A few months would pass and there we were, gathered at the kitchen table, trying to divine, from my mother's end of the conversation, which of our mysterious relations was under discussion. Death, drunkenness and disasters popped up regularly. Who could they be talking about? Lives moving forward or, for whatever reasons, plunged into free fall.

One by one—there were eight of us—we were put on the line and ("Say, is this Jim?") Dorothy's questions began. How did she remember which of us she was speaking to when my mother could barely manage it? She asked about friends, pets, hobbies, and vacations. ("So, did you like Fort Ticonderoga? I'll just bet!") Was

Judy continuing to volunteer at the Stamford Museum and Nature Center? (Her growing responsibilities there included feeding meat scraps to eagles.) Did Debby still babysit?

"You must be a Yankees fan?" she said, on one occasion, when my turn came. What could I say? Sports, all sports, struck me as only slightly less tedious than cleaning the garage.

"You know Roger Maris?"

I'd heard the name and grunted, neither agreeing nor denying.

"He's from Fargo!"

Sensing no real interest, she switched tacks and asked what I was reading. *Martin Chuzzlewit*, I informed her.

"Charles Dickens?"

"Umhmmm."

From the other end of the line came a long, low whistle.

"Oh, land'a living," she said.

The '60s seemed like a decade on Fast Forward, at least when it came to style. In a few years, boy's hair went from crew cuts sculpted in place with wax out of cans to Louis XIV tresses; the girls, meanwhile, morphing from bouffant and beehive to flowing locks of Rapunzel-like length, secured by beaded headbands.

Whether and in what form any of this reached Fargo, I have no idea. But when Dorothy visited again, a few years later, things had changed and the changes were evidently a bit unsettling. The last time she'd seen us we wore blue and white Catholic school uniforms (polyester knit tie, fat throbbing knot). Suddenly—this is 1969 now—here are these teenage hippies, responding with cannabis titters to her endless reminiscences and remarks.

At one point she directed a glance at my brother's blond ponytail, then to the yellow-and-black striped bellbottoms that I rarely removed, and finally at my mane of knotty curls.

"Say," she said, with a wink, "that's quite a haircut."

A few minutes later my sister walked in. Granny glasses, knee-length moccasins, buckskin jacket rich with fringe. Dorothy's gray eyes narrowed.

"Who're you," she said, "Annie Oakley?"

It's October, 1985. I'm at Dorothy's kitchen table, in Fargo. My mother, discovering that work was about to take me to the Twin Cities for the first time, points out, not subtly, that the timeline for my trip coincides with Dorothy's birthday. Surely a visit would be in order?

Fargo's somewhere I had never imagined setting foot. And—fast perusal of the atlas—it's not a quick ride. But I liked driving then. If you don't own a car, which I didn't, it can be like a toy that gets you places. I call the night before I fly.

"Judas Priest!"

She immediately offers her foldout couch. I demur, pleading that I'll need space to work, though the issue, of course, is privacy. It can be weird enough staying with friends, but your aunt?

She suggests a hotel downtown, informing me that it's "right across the street!"

At 18 stories, the Radisson is twelve stories higher than any other building in Fargo, and Fargo is, or was then, not so much a city as a scaled-up version of all the small towns between Minneapolis and Spokane.

I'm not in my room a minute when the phone rings.

"Oh, joy! So you got in safe?"

Safe?

In Fargo, you're more likely to be mauled by an angry tree than you are to be mugged. Jaywalking draws indignant stares. Litter and graffiti are nowhere to be seen. This was the 80s, the lawn of about every third house sported a flagpole from which the indigo blue-fimbriated-on-white cross, set on a field of red—*Norway!*—fluttered and snapped.

Her building—a four-story brick structure that looked to have been built in the 20s—sat exactly opposite the hotel. It's clean but spare, inside and out. I step in the brown-paneled foyer with its bank of recessed aluminum mailboxes.

Number 41 reads: "Dorothy Brantseg."

Bzzzzzzzz.

Five steps down, and to the right. I hear fumbling at the door's big spyhole.

"Well, I'll be the son of a sea captain!"

Her apartment is dim, small, carpeted, subterranean and smells of air freshener, brand undetermined. In the dining room/living room windows, above the sofa, bare and trousered legs swing past. The bedroom itself is a little bit bigger than just big enough, but not by much, for a bed and chest of drawers.

"Let me take your coat."

Closets strain to contain this infinity of coats, scarves, boots, shoes and hats.

She'd lived there long enough—at least 60 years—to transform the place into its own, well-tended museum, a personality manifest as objects. There, for instance, among the sofa, chairs, table, and TV sits an organ, its presence in this junior one-bedroom a miracle of engineering. A pewter Viking ship makes its way across the lid. *Uff da*, reads a knitted wall hanging. "Sensory overload"— one definition of this amorphous and appropriated Scandinavian expression—indeed.

Near the top of the late '60s paneling on the wall, a man in chest-length beard of rolling curls and a woman with her hair in a bun as severe as that of any Shaker eldress, gaze across the room. Either they're watching you or you simply can't avoid looking at them. I try to imagine what those late 19th century photographic portraits must've cost this pair of immigrant Norwegian farmers? Plenty.

Pictures set in small frames arrayed on dust-less end tables. An aunt or two I recognize, the rest strangers. More photos on the wall, teens with the bored, upturned lip endemic to yearbooks. The menagerie's oddest item is a homemade montage. Into this Dorothy has inexpertly pasted scissored heads of all sizes at all angles. They float in the frame. *Oh Christ.* My own pinched visage from 20 years previous features Tiny Tim tresses and an adolescent snarl.

"Um, who are these people?"

"That's your cousin Bob. You've never met him? A pistol! Oh, and over there, your cousin Barb, and..."

Dorothy gave a sudden start and glanced at her watch.

"Oh," she says. "Land'a living! We're meeting your Uncle Arne for lunch."

At age 65, the same year my grandmother died, Dorothy retired from the Burlington Northern Railroad. Its corporate offices were blocks from their apartment. For 40 years she took dictation, typed reports, answered phones. There weren't many perks, but there was one. Travel. Employees could ride, coach, for free, anywhere the rails went. That got grandfathered in when Amtrak took over the passenger lines.

Dorothy boarded trains to visit Texas and the Twin Cities. She rode to New Orleans and to New England. She went west to Montana, on the Empire Builder, and farther west still, to Seattle. She was one of those people you get to know if you spend time riding long-distance trains. Their mode of travel is more than mere conveyance. They're romantics. They have dreams left in them. (I note, on the envelope enclosing one of her inimitable letters, the stamp with a mid-19th century locomotive towing a far smaller coal car.) She couldn't afford a sleeper—they're expensive—but she became adept at getting a good night's rest in coach, a knack for which experience, and fatigue, are the only teachers.

My aunt traveled light. She brought along packaged snacks and an extra pillow. Her luggage consisted of two suitcases in sky blue vinyl, the smaller for essentials, its parent for all else. She made a point of getting up regularly to stroll to the observation car, the bar car or onto the station platform, if the train was stopped more than 10 minutes, somewhere. Meanwhile, of course, she is talking.

In the days before Androids, laptops, Nooks, Kindles, and phones smarter than their owners, there were three ways to pass time on a long train trip: read, talk or take in the scenery. But restlessness can make the greatest scenery seem as interesting as someone else's X-rays, and turn a great book into a box of stale cigars.

So along comes this stranger whose conversation must've seemed like a great relief. Barriers came down. Dorothy talked to everyone. She was unfailingly pleasant and polite, inquisitive but not intrusive, and could work up an interest in just about any topic or anybody's story. By the time she got off the train, she'd inevitably added a few names to her address book. All received Christmas cards. Some became correspondents. A few invited her to visit. She was not a difficult guest.

One year, on the day before her birthday, I dropped by her apartment for a few minutes after settling in at the hotel. On her dining room table, there's a shoebox.

"Birthday cards?"

Arranged end-to-end, they filled the box.

"Oh, yah."

"You haven't opened any?"

"Well, it's not my birthday yet!"

There were two boys among my grandmother's five children. The older—Donald, known as Red—was a taciturn family man and resolute teetotaler. Arne, second to last and nearer my mother's age, had always, I gathered, been a hell-raiser, and was sometimes referred to as the black sheep, though the more I came to know him, the more he seemed like an ornery buffalo stuck in a pen in some roadside zoo.

They had a saying in that family: *Red never touched a drop, and Arne never dropped a drink.*

That seemed to be the case. Arne liked to fish, and imbibe. He also liked to do both at the same time, which brought on difficulties with the authorities. You can't always fish when you're drinking but you can always drink when you're fishing, if you remember to bring the whiskey, which Arne never forgot. The state took away first his drivers' license, then his truck. Someone in that family told me that Arne was the oldest person in the history of North Dakota to get a DUI, but even if not apocryphal I'm guessing that the record's been bested at this point.

Hard drinking bubbled up like swamp gas in that gene pool. In the '30s, Olander Brantseg, Dorothy's father, painting contractor and binger of legend, would arrive home so sozzled and out of control that my grandmother and Donald had no choice but to subdue, then lock him, raging, into the coal cellar, where he'd pound and scream till he passed out. If that hadn't shocked Red into swearing off, then the cause of his father's death certainly would have. One cold night, in December of 1934, my grandfather, age 49, left a bar. He became overwhelmed with fatigue, and decided to take a nap in a snow bank, which is where they found his body.

I heard this story from my mother, who told it once and only once. I sought more details from Dorothy, but she wouldn't get near it. Nor would she talk about the family's various suicides. Her only comments had to do with the great crisis that ensued in the wake of his death.

"Mom worked like a Trojan after Dad died."

Pause.

"We all went to work."

Pause.

"Oh, say…"

And off she went on something completely unrelated.

The banner on the wall, in blue, reads: *Willkommen!* Arne sits in a red vinyl booth at the end of a row of them. We've just walked into the Sons of Norway, Lodge 25, Kringen Klub, a fraternal organization in downtown Fargo.

Arne has the broad family face, masculine version. Ski slope nose, eyes quick to narrow. A shock of gray hair, straight and solidified in gel, sweeps straight back, like a sheet, from the hairline.

Dorothy orders a chicken salad sandwich and a glass of iced tea. She's quiet. When the food comes, she nibbles. She's leaving the field to Arne but Arne looks from one of us to the other. Thunderstorms gather behind that face. Has he already had a few? His idea of conversation is to ask questions ("So how's your Mom?") the answers to which he is mostly indifferent.

"How many cards ya got this year?" he says to my aunt.

"Oh, I don't know, Arne."

35

Arne stares at his Coke.

"Last year I sent out 200 Christmas cards," he says. He pauses. "Signed every last one of 'em."

"Two hundred?"

She says this in a tone that is supposed to register admiration and amaze.

Arne nods and looks away.

"How many ja get back?"

"Not a goddamn one."

My aunt waves to this table and waves again to that booth over there. In 15 minutes, the place fills. The Sons of Norway is the hot spot for a low-cost lunch downtown. Chicken and dumplings is today's special. At one point, I turn to my aunt. A dab of mayonnaise has somehow found its way onto her face. It resembles a tiny rhinoceros' horn.

Arne is talking about something. She leans forward, listening intently, and while she nods the horn bobs.

Arne squints.

"Ya got somethin' on yer nose, Dot," he snaps.

A few years later, when half his leg's removed for diabetes, she goes to visit him in the veteran's hospital.

"You know," she tells me, afterwards, "I don't think I ever really knew my brother."

"Do you think she's ever been laid?

My sister—"Annie Oakley"—again. She also wonders if Dorothy is, or has been, "a lez."

It sounds catty and lacking in all empathy (besides which, what's the point?) but my sister is fonder of Dorothy than anyone. They have a mysterious bond, an unspoken unity. Neither had married. They are (her word) "spinnies."

She's the one who came up with the idea of sending Sonias— peach-colored roses—to Dorothy on her birthday. The birthday is a major affair. If North Dakota were an oblast (province) in Russia, they'd be towing missiles through downtown Fargo for her. If North Dakota were in Spain somewhere, people would be jumping across the hoods of parked cars to escape raging bulls.

But the question, once raised, sort of sits there. Watching Dorothy toy distractedly with the sterling silver angel pinned to her jacket lapel (she believes angels are everywhere, a thought I later find articulated in Swedenborg's *Heaven and Hell*) or listening to her elaborate on the uses of shredded coconut in Jell-O recipes, it seems impossible that my aunt had ever touched a human being *down there*, let alone navigated the Sapphic channels. I glance around her apartment. Considering that she lived here all these years with my grandmother, where would she or they or, um, whoever...have done it?

Did she, at some point, have a wild side?

She offers few clues. Only this: Once, driving past the Fargo Theater, an art deco movie palace on Broadway, built in 1926, Dorothy mentions a date. The date was here, at this sumptuously restored venue, where, as the movie begins, an organ lodged beneath the stage emerges dramatically between the twin halves of a trap door, organist flailing at the keys.

Lunt and Fontaine were on the marquee the night in 1948 that a certain "Jewish salesman" took my aunt there.

"Oh, was Dorothy ever excited about that. You bet she was!"

I gather from her description that the opportunity to see Lunt and Fontaine (projecting "an animal vitality," according to their biographer, "a spirit of gaiety and intense pleasure...") mattered more than her date, the salesman, what they then called a "drummer." Who can say? What he sold, where he came from, whether there was dinner, sex, a sequel, about any of this Dorothy's not forthcoming. In those days salesmen traveled from town to town by train. Did they meet at the rail station? Would they have repaired to his room at the Powers Hotel, up the street? (Picture, only a few years previous, straw-haired songbird Norma Egstrom—Miss Peggy Lee—wowing them, night after night, in the coffee shop.)

Dorothy, animated but vague, dances around the implications of all this. I don't press the point. There're some people you simply can't imagine in lusty mid-romp, let alone frisking their way through an orgy, without the entire edifice of who they are and what they mean crumbling into rubble and rebar. It'd be like walking into the bank and seeing the nun who taught you fourth grade English and math pointing a sawed-off shotgun at a teller.

Fargo went from being somewhere I knew by hearsay to a place where I not only didn't have to ask for directions but could reliably give them. At some point on the first or second day of October, I'd fly into the Twin Cities airport, rent a car and drive. By Interstate 94, the trip takes about four and a half hours, five with coffee stops. Count on seven if you take the two-lane roads. I always did.

There are three ways to go. The one with the most distance between towns is Route 10, heading north just above St. Cloud, and then, at Detroit Lakes, bearing west in an "as the crow flies" line straight for Fargo. Or, you could drive west on 212, through Hector, Olivia and Renville to Granite Falls, then north on Route 7, straddling the Minnesota River, to 75. I took that route once, and when I stopped to photograph a building of some architectural significance (a 1920 bank in Hector by Prairie School design team Purcell and Elmslie), I found myself being questioned by a local man, who, finally ascertaining my purpose, invited me to his house for dinner (which they call supper) where, after chicken, salad and roast potatoes, he and his wife retrieved the file they kept on the building's history, including blueprints, and spread it out on the living room floor. And then there's Route 12, to Willmar ("Wilmer"), where you swing north on 9 through Benson. A favorite. (Some relative of a relative had had a business there once, and on that basis Dorothy suggested I might want to "take a tur" of it.)

The towns had the same look, since they were all built around the same time of similar materials, and the same sort of feel, since they were all more or less consecrated to similar purpose, yet were imbued with the solid sense of their difference, one from the next. (High school football mascots expertly painted on water towers.) The towns in Minnesota and the Dakotas were built around the railroads, but now passenger travel by rail had dimmed to insignificance: a single daily route, running from Chicago to Seattle. The rail stations are still there, usually, and they are freight depots, if still in use, gleaming silos towering beside them, though the greater portion of farm products go to market by truck.

The larger towns had their IGA supermarkets and their Hardware Hank stores, their Carnegie libraries and their train stations awkwardly converted to other, more pedestrian, use. You'll see baseball fields in a place of any size, usually on a town's edge, and invariably featuring a clean, well-maintained, and unlocked restroom, a mercy for travelers and something you'd never find in the East.

The drive became its own kind of destination, a run-up to the visit, a mental briefing for it, and the trip back—less hurried, pausing from time to time to eat in some small-town cafe, or just get out and walk the streets—an opportunity to reflect. These were towns that the young left as soon as they could. "If you watched your Dad milking cows twice a day, every day, his whole life, you'd leave too," a man once explained, when I asked why he had moved to Minneapolis.

So, the towns were full of old people, or people of high school age or younger. The young went to college and seldom returned. The movie theaters were long closed, the mom-and-pop stores hung on, sometimes, but the opening of a nearby Wal-Mart usually signaled their doom. A year later you might drive through and see the two or three blocks of the shopping district pocked with empty storefronts, the stores that remained—curio shops, furniture stores, even photographers—more or less relics of another age. If they went out, the only type of retailer available to take their place was the sort of bottom-feeder that exists because there are little to no start-up costs. A thrift shop, let's say, or a tanning salon.

"You was in Fergus?" my uncle Red said, a little startled, when I told him where I'd stopped for lunch. He seemed to be remembering something about the name, Fergus Falls. "These small towns're dyin' on the vine," he said.

In the spring of her 87th year, somewhere between Chicago and St. Louis, aboard Amtrak's Texas Eagle, Dorothy's back went out. That's how she explained it to my mother. She couldn't walk, let alone sleep, and arrived in Fort Worth, paler than flour. It took an extra month, there, to recuperate. That ended her railroading days.

It was also around that time people important to her began to die. The first to go was the family's middle sister, Arloene. Cancer. Red, whose hands by this time shook with Parkinson's, followed. Then, months after Dorothy's 90th birthday—which in-flight vertigo prevented her from attending—my mother, 14 years her junior, left this world. In November a shoulder bone broke when she went to lift a typewriter. Osteoporosis. Six weeks later she was dead, of COPD, cancer, diverticulitis, everything.

"Just wait," said cousin Bob at the funeral, where, for the first time, I actually met him. "Arne'll be the last one left."

Among the unopened letters strewn across the coffee table beside the sofa that was my mother's final redoubt were two from Dorothy and three more bearing the return address of a home for veterans in Lisbon, ND, where Arne had landed. Stricken with diabetes, the doctors were debating whether or not to amputate all or some of his left leg.

My mother had been dead less than a month when I got a phone call from North Dakota with an unfamiliar Caller ID. "They've got me at Elim," Dorothy said.

Elim, it turned out, was a nursing home on the city's south side. "Why are you there?"

She'd been walking across the living room, my aunt explained, when her hip simply disintegrated. She crawled to the phone and dialed 911. After the hospital stapled her back together, she was dispatched to Elim for rehab.

"How are they treating you?"

"I've seen better."

She didn't know when she'd be out, but it had to be soon. Medicare coverage expired in days.

Could she walk?

"Oh, I'm trying."

Fargo in late March is hard and pale, a ghost town with traffic. Nothing moves except vehicles. Emptiness amplifies all sound. A closing car door sounds like cymbals crashing. Water trickling from a downspout sounds like a cistern boiling with melted snow.

I checked into the Scandia Hotel, a modest downtown establishment with three attractions: it's cheap, it's close and the coffee's free.

"Bob stayed there the last time he was in town," Dorothy said, on the phone. She'd be packed and ready to go at one the next day.

I pull up 20 minutes early. From a distance the place looks like an elementary school, divided into single-story wings. Once past the double doors, I hear cheeping.

The receptionist, staring into a computer screen, looks up. So does the mixed breed lab asleep beside the desk.

"Dorothy Brantseg?"

"Room 203."

An Irish setter totters up, sniffs, lifts its head to my hand. Three or four parakeets appear out of nowhere, whizz down the hall and land on a plastic Ficus, where they screech and chirp some more before finally flying off.

In the common area, just past the desk, seven or eight bodies in wheelchairs sit parked in front of a wall-mounted TV set. On the set a young man who looks like a model argues with a young woman who also looks like a model.

"I know you've been seeing Dale," says the male model.

"I thought you're the one who was interested in Dale," says the female model.

A parakeet lands on the shoulder of one of the bodies. Eyes bat, blink.

"Ack!"

41

An arm rises, swiping without aim. Other bodies, in other chairs, stir. Heads lift.

"Shhhhhh!" A chorus.

Squinting, mouth open, the one who'd motioned the bird away begins to speak, but changes his mind. A string dangling from lip to shirt makes a spreading spot where it pools in the fabric.

"Why didn't you pick me up yesterday?" someone says. The voice sounds like it's coming from immediately behind my head. I turn to find a woman in a hospital gown, inches from my face. "I told you three o'clock, Edward, and you weren't here!"

"Lillian, settle down," the receptionist yells. Then, to me: "She thinks every man that walks in here is her son." She rolls her eyes and re-directs her attention to the screen.

In 203, Dorothy sits parked in her own wheelchair, waiting.

"Oh, Judas Priest!"

Red felt hat with pheasant feathers, matching chiffon scarf, gloved hands resting in her lap. She looks like she's dressed for a shopping spree in the underworld. Meanwhile, seated on the other side of the room, a figure. The face, a rictus of chronic irritation, glares. We both look. Dorothy sighs.

"This," she says, in her most neutral tone, "is Dorothy."

"Good afternoon," I say, to Dorothy #2.

No answer.

"So," I turn to my aunt, "there are ...*two* Dorothys?"

"Yes," Dorothy says, nodding, no longer looking at her namesake. "Yes," she says, "there are two of us."

A tug. The handle of her suitcase emits its cerulean squeak. A pair of hatboxes, a portmanteau packed with make-up, two bags of shoes and, lastly, a forlorn walker, folded and almost forgotten on the bed. Two trips and it's all in the trunk.

"I'll bet you're glad to be out of there."

"Oh, you got that right."

In the Holiday Inn dining room, a glass of sherry and a chicken salad sandwich dispel the grim mood. We linger till they close. She is quiet. I can see her mentally turning the situation over and over. How to fend for herself in that apartment? How to get up and then

42

back down the five steps to the street? How to rearrange the space so it's something other than an obstacle course?

We spend the rest of the afternoon rigging the walker with pockets to stow her wallet, phone, keys, and a flashlight in case the power goes out. We—she directs, I push/pull—move the furniture into more convenient, accessible locations.

The next morning, she hands me a 4-page single-spaced shopping list. Across the top, in capitals: NO SUBSTITUTES.

There're names. *Seniors. The elderly. Advanced years.* Euphemisms. They don't begin to hint at what it's like to be 80, 85, let alone in your '90s. They're terms a marketing department would come up with. Amorphous. Generalized. Polite. To be old is to be sideswiped, daily and hourly, by an ever-accelerating present. It is to suddenly find yourself on the one hand stranded by history, and on the other hand an artifact without a history anyone else would care to know about. You were you and now you're not. Everything's changed, and rarely in any good way. The strange outweighs the familiar. At 83 or 93 getting up and moving the day forward—making breakfast (or simply eating it), combing your hair, getting dressed, anything— is every bit as weird as it was when you were three, except that it's not weird in the sense of wonderful, but weird in the sense of alien. You've become your own other. The discoveries you make are more apt to be painful than pleasant. That's even truer if your memory's intact—Dorothy's never faltered—while the body's unraveling, one limb, organ or digit at a time. When, for instance, I offer to set up a laptop, and arrange an Internet connection, so she can send email, she doesn't argue or discuss, she just holds up, as an answer, her right hand. It's crabbed and stiff with arthritis. It looks like a piece of driftwood.

Still, she manages to move a pen with this claw. A letter arrives, a month or so later, in which she describes her routines. She "tries to get out every day," to the bank, the drugstore or The Frying Pan. Someone named Bess cleans every other week.

43

From time to time a friend collects her clothes and brings them back, washed and folded.

Money is short, an unspoken concern—out of pocket prescription costs are more than her rent, the usual American racket—but when I return six months later, on her birthday—91—a miracle has occurred.

"Judas Priest! Will you get a load of that?" she says, whistling. She holds a slip of paper to the overhead light and squints at the signature. A nephew.

The check is for $5,000.

Such a completely unpredicted and highly favorable turn of events calls for celebration.

"We'll go for 'spagett,'" she says.

"Where?"

"The Frying Pan."

In minutes she's dressed and ready to go.

"Can you make it up those stairs?" I say, closing her door behind me.

I'm starting to see the world through her eyes, a series of impediments, inconveniences, and embarrassments.

"Oh, you better bet."

She's out the door, with her walker. She folds it with a practiced snap, grasps the rail, drags it five steps to the landing, claps it shut. A moment later she's out the door and leans on the car, waiting.

But once seated in her favorite booth, Dorothy hardly touches her food.

"You know," I say, "you're looking a little thin."

"Jim, that place"—Elim—"just took my appetite away."

A note from Dorothy, wanting to know if I'm coming for her 93rd birthday. She's reserved a private room at the Holiday Inn in Fargo. I have reason to defer—home repairs underway on a house I just bought—so I call to say that maybe we should plan a major event for her 95th.

"Oh no," she says. "Better come for this one."

There were two dozen people in the dining room. Dorothy talking voluminously. From a journal, Oct. 5, 2003:

Holiday Inn, Fargo, and D.'s night to shine. She held forth on many subjects, including some of her favorites - her career ("What did you do before you retired, Aunt Dorothy?" a great-niece asks. "I was a stenographer, dear." "Oh, what's that?" "It's a job that doesn't exist anymore."), her mother's piano lessons (gave her first recital at 75), etc. She is—or seems—indefatigable. Wearing dark green corduroy pantsuit & brown beret with patriotic pins attached. Thinner now. Squints as she talks, for emphasis. You get the sense from the way people address her that she is regarded as the village eccentric, a role she is aware of & clearly relishes...

When the dessert plates are cleared, Dorothy digs through her purse for the newly issued MasterCard in her wallet.

I drive her back to her apartment and tell her I'll be over the next day to take her for a ride. She wanted, she'd said, to drive to Detroit Lakes, have lunch at the Holiday Inn on the water there, and see "the color."

Driving east, into Minnesota, the trees grow in clumps and clusters or are planted in lines separating swaths of farmland, much of it, that day, freshly turned, to root out sugar beets. Corn harvesters spit bits of stalk, split and ribbony leaves, across the fields.

From the journal, Oct. 6, 2003:

Nielsen symphonies on the CD player en route to Detroit Lakes but Dorothy couldn't actually sit back & listen, instead keeping up a steady stream of chatter.

Suddenly she's not hungry.

"Let's just look at the color," she says.

The wind kicks up. It's gusting, blowing tricycles and loose lawn chairs across the road. A plastic bag, someone's ghost, lifts, jerks, rises, whips across the sky and disappears. We go on this way for 15 minutes. A half hour passes. She stares out the window, quiet.

"You remember that time we went out looking at the leaves, when you lived in Connecticut?"

"Umhmmm," I said. I had hoped she'd forgotten that. But here she is, bringing it up, 40 years later.

"And you kept saying, 'Gorgeous,'" she said.

"What? Me?"

"Yes, you. You thought everything was gorgeous." She paused. "You were what, nine years old?"

She stares at the trees, the fields, the barns, a tractor, kids in a yard.

It's the middle of the afternoon. We stop for gas. We stop for Cokes. Dorothy would like a chocolate-covered donut, so we stop at an IGA and buy a box. She eats half of one.

At some point we hit something. Not an animal, but an object, though from the sound it seems like something large. A hubcap?

"Did you hear that?" Dorothy says. She draws a deep breath. "I thought we might break down."

We're circling the lake now and the lake's not small. The farms are gone and the roads have no names. My aunt is looking at the road, not the trees or the fields. The sky was as blue as I've ever seen it.

"Is this a good car?" she says suddenly.

"I think it's okay." I am hesitating, because I don't know and also because I hear fear in her voice.

"It won't break down will it?"

She pauses, considering.

"We came out here years ago," she says, "Mom and I. We were going to have dinner at the cottage of my boss. Mom drove Arne's car. On the way home, we got lost."

She stares out the window, considering.

"Maybe we should be heading back," she says.

I left the next day. A week later I get a call from Bob. She has fallen, fractured her vertebrae in three places. She's back at Elim. He says she will not be returning to the apartment.

"What do you do all day?"

"Oh, I sleep a lot," she said, from the phone by her bed there.

I call after that but the phone rings and rings. Someone tells me she's had it disconnected. "She won't eat and she hardly ever wakes up," a cousin says. It's like a nap that lasts for months. They attribute it to medication.

The second floor of St. Mark's Lutheran, in Fargo, filled early. There was the problem of getting Arne and his wheelchair up a narrow flight of stairs. Five of us, nephews and cousins, discuss possible solutions. Someone suggests we lift the chair and its occupant up the steps. Arne glares into some unfocused distance. I wonder if he even hears the conversation. We crouch and grapple and start to lift but the stairs aren't wide enough.

"Arne, can you hop?" Bob says.

Everyone laughs.

Arne doesn't laugh.

No particle of memory contains the image of Dorothy in a coffin. Where did it go? I didn't pay a lot of attention to the body. A glance, and it seemed exactly like what it was—a cadaver in a dress—and who can be interested in that? Afterwards, we drive from Fargo to Sisseton, South Dakota, where the family plot is. Arne in a van—for the wheelchair—all others in the caravan that follows. A long drive—an hour and a half—or at least it seems endless. It's May, it's warm, it's sunny and a breeze is blowing. Every now and then the hearse disappears then reappears and when it does all the cars and the van get in line behind it again.

The grave, freshly dug, clods piled all around, lays waiting. Right next to it, another plot, marked out.

"Oh, Arne, look at that," says a cousin, pointing toward the hole. "That's where we're going to put you."

With no trace of irony, she pushes Arne and his chair toward the grave so he can get a better view of his future. Arne's not looking. He isn't talking. His face says there is no possible interest left in anything anyone else can do or say.

Most of us are unimportant, except to ourselves and a handful of others, if that. Absent wealth or fame—the twin engines of social success—we're anonymous, faceless outside our own circle, however large or small. We fade away before death and stop living well before life is over. At some point we find ourselves receding into the background of everything that came before, until we're indistinguishable from it and no closer to understanding anything, really, since to understand something, you must understand its absence, nothing, and in a culture that exists to endlessly consume goods and services, there is always a reason for it, nothing, not to be there, never to be understood.

It's our insignificance we can't accept, the fact that our love leaves no record, our sorrows no remorse, our rage no heat. "It's hard to make a dent," a famous artist once told me, explaining the limited impact he had had on the post-War Pop Art scene, a tantalizing minor fame that owed to the accident of a single image, rendered first in metal, as sculpture, then paint. This was what people talked about when you brought up his name, so that his fame had transformed him into something like one of those 19th century actors who take the stage as the same character in the same play so often—Eugene O'Neill's father in *The Count of Monte Cristo*— that audiences become incapable of seeing them as anyone else.

Was it fame Dorothy was seeking when, several decades before, she had written a short story and mailed it to *Redbook*? She was shocked, she related, when the manuscript came back accompanied by "a personal letter" ("Can you beat that?") outlining ways in which her work could be brought up to some publishable level and encouraging her to write and submit more of them. She never did. She lived in the proverbial moment and the moment was speech, sound, syllables, a glance. Her gift was to convert experience into her own kind of verbal music, into the riffs—a word I'm sure she never knew, and one that likely would've mystified her—from which she would make conversation.

Maybe she talked to feel good, a low-grade enzymatic rush that just kept pumping as her vocal cords worked, or maybe it was because the world made her nervous, or afraid. With talkers there's often nerves in it. Maybe she was obeying some compulsion to articulate a vision only she was witness to. Maybe there were elements of all these. I don't know. She poured her billions of words into the void, and created, for a few of us, something that was, at times, strangely fascinating, at times even compelling.

Yet in all that volubility, Dorothy was also among the most guarded people I've known. As if there were secrets and talk kept them safe. She sought no confidences, nor offered any. And if someone were to say that I knew her only in the most superficial way, that we were, for instance, long-distance acquaintances united by the accident of family and circumstance, and that time had performed the trick of simply switching places as life went on—she being someone who visited occasionally, me taking on that role as she aged—I concede that that's true.

On the other hand, isn't that the way we know most people? They blunder into our lives or we into theirs and they stay, for however long, then they go. How many of them actually make for good company?

My aunt thought about other people in a way, it seems to me, few ever do. She was eager in a world where most hesitate. She had that quality—enthusiasm—that Ralph Waldo Emerson so often cites as essential and that he so valued.

Years went by and I never returned to Fargo, feeling, I suppose, that I had no reason to. The place, like the person I associate with it, went out of my life as suddenly as it appeared.

One day, on her birthday, I woke, remembered being there, and realized a dozen years had gone by. The sense of scale changes as life lengthens, and so does value, that is, what is meaningful or who is important, and what's not or isn't. I read my aunt not as a small town provincial, treading through the banality of her days, but as someone who made the most and the best possible use of her circumstances; unflappable in the dignity she inhabited and the independence she insisted on, enviable in the energy she brought to all occasion.

A last anecdote. She lived long enough to have seen her favorite item of clothing go completely out of fashion, and because these were no longer even available for sale, she was forced to manufacture her own headgear, a challenge which cluttered her apartment somewhat but one which she rose to with relish. She relayed, on the occasion of one of my visits, in tones that mixed self-satisfaction with annoyance, how she had once called for a cab in the middle of a snowstorm. The taxi sat in the street in front of her apartment, mid-blizzard, and after she'd emerged, tromped through a foot of snow, and landed in the back, she looked up to notice the driver's eyes in the rear-view mirror, fixed at a point located somewhere between horror and disbelief.

"Lady," he said, "that's some kinda hat!"

It was on that same visit that one of the cousins told me, laying it on rather thick, that everyone in Fargo agreed that the way Dorothy was able to coordinate her hat, shoes, dress, blouse, jacket and handbag had resulted in a style all her own, something unique. I repeated this to my aunt, thinking she'd cherish the compliment. She did not.

"They wouldn't know me from a loada hay," she said, and changed the subject.

ARE BIRDS SPIES?

It's about two hours since we left Chicago and Amtrak steward Julio casts a cold eye on the *Field Guide to Birds, Western Region*. The section on flycatchers is open on the foldout table in front of me.

"You like birds?" Julio says, leaning in, scratch pad in hand, to take the dinner reservation.

I tell him I do and explain that I'm headed for Silver City, New Mexico, specifically to look for some.

He glances around the roomette, notes the one small bag.

"By yourself?"

I nod.

I can see his mind turning questions over: why would anyone spend time walking around looking for birds, and moreover travel 2,000 miles to do that? I'm imagining that he's imagining what might make it an okay way to spend some time. I ask how long he's worked for Amtrak. He tells me he's been a steward on the Southwest Chief for 22 years, which I suppose is another way to say he's seen and heard everything at some point somewhere between Chicago and Los Angeles. The solitary birdwatcher in Room 5 of Car 0331 is minor fare compared to the geeks and freaks that come through.

"Birds, that is interesting," he says in the way that indicates he believes it could actually be interesting but only with a lot of work.

Now, he says, smile resuming, back from this mental detour, will that dinner reservation be for 5:30, 6:30 or 7:30?

In the bird world males stand out. That mostly means they're larger and/or more colorful. It enables them to attract a mate. Females are frequently drab. That's so they go unnoticed on the nest.

Paging through the *Field Guide to Birds, Western Region*, pausing at 521, it occurs to me that while there are numerous exceptions, the rule generally holds true and that things get radical when you're talking about certain species such as the vermillion flycatcher, found in Southwest Texas and New Mexico. The head and breast of the male is a one-of-a-kind shade of red, with blackish brown on the wing and a masking band of identical black extending from the bill to back behind the eyes. The female has the same brown on head, wings and back with a white breast brightening to buff, occasionally even a flash of red, on the belly. Unless you knew what to look for, you could mistake her for a lot of things. A male vermillion, on the other hand, can't be anything else.

Would I see some?

I came close on my first day. Early that afternoon I pulled the rented SUV into the parking lot of the visitor's center for Sevilleta National Wildlife Refuge, an hour south of Albuquerque. Outside, what looked like high-powered bumblebees flitted and whirred around a vertical red feeder suspended from the roof. Inside, using a glossy New Mexico Transportation map and a topographical display of the state set up as an exhibit, a woman named Elise runs me through a list of all the places I need to be in eight days.

"Start with the Bosque Del Apache," says Elise. She points to a green spot on the Transportation map. "It's right down the Interstate. The Bosque Del Apache has more birds than anywhere else in New Mexico. Of course you could also run into cougars. I wouldn't worry about that."

Elise would give a cougar pause. She is short, solidly built, with brown hair a shade that matches her glasses. She's probably in her 50s but the spirit is more along the lines of someone mentally flown in from the hippie era. Now, having given it more extensive thought, she proceeds to name, one after another, what she feels are the best parks in the state. She has, she says, sacked out in the cab of her truck in the parking lots of most of them.

"They got elk here," she says, pointing to a location on the Transportation map. She looks up.

"Elk!"

I nod and ask about the hummingbirds outside. Elise glances toward the window.

"Black-throated," she says. "Very aggressive."

I scribble away. Elise follows as my eyes wander to the raptor on the wall with its wings spread.

"Swenson's hawk. They live on prairie dogs. They used to be everywhere. Now there's hardly any. But they're bringing back the prairie dog and that'll bring the hawks back."

She launches into a description of the prairie dog reintroduction program, now underway in the state. Lots of detail about burrows, reproductive habits, predators besides Swenson's hawk (coyotes, etc.). She explains that if I've got extra time they have a list of the 200 best trails in the area at the public library at Show Low, an hour's drive into Arizona. It's worth the visit, in spite of the town having become "yuppiefied."

When I was in my 20s and 30s, I paid little more than polite attention to what anyone told me about anything. Not that I wasn't curious. I just assumed there was some motive for their wanting to be helpful—attention, sex, a favor—or that such information, when volunteered, came with a condescending smack.

Besides, how could they know what I didn't?

What changed that was a visit to a poet from Indiana. I happened to be in Indianapolis for work and called. He invited me over to talk about poetry. We soon wandered onto other topics. Two in particular: Prairie School architecture and Utopian communities. This poet, whose name is Jared Carter, knew the state's history, geography, geology, architecture and assorted hot spots and had written a handsome coffee table book titled simply: *Indiana*. He suggested the Eugene Debs Museum in Terre Haute, the faux-Louis Sullivan bank in Poseyville, French Lick for a view of the ballroom at the famous French Lick Resort Hotel, and sundry other places.

I jotted it all down, climbed in my rental car and drove north, south, east, and west, from Evansville to Lafayette and back. It was everything he promised.

I excuse myself and ask to use the restroom. The last thing I see as I climb into the car is Elise directing nectar through the spout of a watering can into the top of the hummingbird feeder—in effect, pouring the drinks—while 20 tiny birds watch and wait.

Bosque Del Apache Wildlife Refuge, down the Interstate maybe 45 minutes, sits in the center of New Mexico, a vast wetland penetrated and encircled by dirt roads. The ranger running the Visitor's Center hands me a map. "Somebody's seen vermillion flycatchers right about here," he says. Does he possess psychic powers or did Elise call ahead? He X's a spot in ballpoint on the paper map. "There's supposed to be a nest."

The Bosque attracts thousands of bird people in the course of a year. Its draw is mostly waterfowl and wading birds, including such lovelies as the white-faced ibis, the American avocet and the stilt, which is everything the name implies. Of course, to a visitor, the vermillion flycatcher makes any of these seem mere names on a checklist.

According to livescience.com, 60 million Americans identify themselves as birdwatchers and "birding" is among the most popular forms of outdoor activity. Of course if 60 million people were out in the woods with binoculars and spotter scopes, places like the Bosque Del Apache would feel like the Mall of America the week before Christmas. And that'd be the end of it for me.

Who or what exactly is a birdwatcher depends on your definition of the term. Most self-described birdwatchers conduct their observations from the vicinity of a feeder near the kitchen window where the political dynamics can fascinate—all the dominance behaviors you might've imagined as purely human are on display—but it's like fishing an overstocked trout pond.

Serious birders make up a small fraction of the 60 million. They tend to be pilgrims and they're almost always alone. Like David, the guy in a ranger suit and hat I met in Lassen National Park, in Northern California, a few years back. He comes marching up the trail with a tripod and scope on his shoulder, eyes darting back and forth from trail to trees, trees to trail.

"See anything interesting?"

"White-headed woodpecker."

That pushed a button.

"Seriously? I've been trying to see those for a week," he says. "I even played their call." He whips a phone from his vest pocket and plays it.

Chid-it-it! Chid-it-it!

"Nothing?"

"Nothing."

David's not actually a ranger. He's a retired middle-school science teacher who volunteers to talk about birds at public parks in different Western states.

I ask about warblers. He's seen two species in Lassen: the yellow-rumped and the hermit.

What does the hermit look like?

"The males have yellow heads and black throats."

Suddenly he squints at some willow shrubs on the bank of a creek emptying into the lake we're standing 50 feet away from.

"There's one now!"

David unlimbers his scope and has got it on the bird in about 10 seconds. I can't even get it into my binoculars.

"They're shy," he says, as we part ways. "That's why they call 'em 'hermit warblers.'"

In the woods looking and waiting are pretty much the same thing. You look, waiting for something to happen, you wait, and while you wait, you look. When something does happen, the moment's all that matters and getting to that moment is what all the energy's about.

This state of mind is the common property of bird people. Encounter another bird person on a trail and mention that you've just seen a hooded merganser or an American Dipper and watch the nervous system dial itself up a few notches. A bird person suddenly given that kind of information can look exactly like someone who's just found a forgotten $20 bill in his pocket and can't figure out what to do about it.

Who goes to the woods to socialize? If anything, you're there for the exact opposite reason—to get away from people—or, like Thoreau, to meet yourself. But when you do encounter one of these out on a trail, it's often like walking up to a mirror. Chances are they're your age, your sex, wearing clothes lifted from your closet. Or if they're not any of that, it doesn't matter. They know what you know and they're out there trying to find out more. Mention to even that most taciturn bird person that hummingbird nest you saw plastered to a branch or the eagle that snatched a fresh-caught trout from an osprey's talons—a mid-air theft over a lake I witnessed at Lassen—and they'll be chittering like sparrows.

There are also the few who, passed on a trail, can barely bring themselves to nod as well as the type who get all competitive about sightings and especially about their equipment, as if the more they spent on that scope, those hiking boots, these binoculars, the more seriously they're entitled to be taken.

Sometimes the types overlap. I'm thinking of the guy who, one April, set up a scope to watch baby great horned owls in an abandoned squirrel's nest behind a pond at Tinicum, a wildlife refuge across I-95 from the Philadelphia Airport. He had what looked like the Hubble Telescope set up on a tripod maybe 75 feet from the nest and a stone's throw from the trail. Let gravel rattle or a stick snap and he'd whirl, index to lips. *Shhhsssssssshhhhhh!* Even if you came through without making a sound, the look was not friendly. Meanwhile Big Daddy owl was up there on a branch above the nest, waiting to descend on anyone who got close. Seventy-five feet was pushing it. You get the sense that no matter where he is or what he's doing, this guy's always pushing it. The world is his, not ours. He's in control. I had a brief wish that a rotting tree limb might descend and take out the telescope, but I walked on to leave him scowling into his viewfinder for all the pleasure he might take there.

Back at the Bosque vehicles appear through a cloud of road dust. A mirage? Getting closer, it looks like the gentile side of the parking lot at an Amish mud sale: RVs, SUVs, Honda Accords, Toyotas, a pickup truck or two, parked shoulder to shoulder. So are the people. They've fanned out on the rise just before the water's edge. It's Picket's Charge with spotter scopes. There are enough already so that newcomers merit barely a quick, hard glance.

I get out, scan branches, and turn to inspect the birder army. All I could see from where I stood, to crib a famous line from Edna Millay, was white males in fishing vests and camouflage jackets. Is this the very picture of much-vaunted privilege or just a bunch of guys with time on their hands? Both. What I notice is the headgear. Half sport baseball caps, the rest are in this floppy khaki item shaped like something you'd wear while skippering a lobster boat.

I try to imagine myself in one. It's a strange thing the way that, at 15 let's say, you see some item everyone's wearing—example: desert boots, circa 1968—and it's almost as if not having them will cause the world to end in whatever kind of colony collapse it eventually will end in. Fifty years on, the temptation to rush right out and order something like one of these lobster hats does not exist. Experience teaches you need to be at least as careful about what you put on your head as you are about what you put in it. After 50 you can pretty much tromp around with your feet in old shoeboxes, like Howard Hughes, wear twine for a belt or, like an older gentleman I saw on the sidewalk in Philadelphia recently, stroll along in an accordion-pleated checkerboard skirt. No one's likely to pay much attention. But they will notice a hat.

The point was brought home once when I happened to overhear a conversation two middle-aged co-workers were having just over the cubicle wall at an office where I worked. It was 8:45 and they'd been going on animatedly for a few minutes when the conversation suddenly halted.

Fifteen seconds went by.

Then: "*What* is that *thing* on her *head?*"

I stood up to see, fast disappearing along the corridor, what had clearly begun as a beret but was now oversized, puffy and spangled in a manner that aspired to chic but failed, this perched on the head of a new hire anxious that her distinct fashion sense be made known.

Someone I once knew pointed out to me that you should never wear a hat that has more personality than you do and he proceeded to prove it by never wearing one at all.

But here in the Bosque today they had flycatchers, not fashion, on their minds. They peered into scopes and scanned the canopy. Not seeing color, nor movement, they scowled and scanned again. The scanning and scowling went on and after about an hour I began to pick up that vibe whereby collective impatience transforms itself into low-level hysteria. Once a crowd gets worked up, things can pretty much go anywhere and that's never a good direction.

One autumn a few years back in Cape May, New Jersey, I came on a gathering smaller in number but similar in spirit. They stood poised on the boardwalk, a dozen strong, ten or twenty thousand dollars worth of cameras, scopes and binoculars aimed at a single exhausted pine warbler. The bird was trying to down as many seeds as its stomach could hold before the next leg of its transcontinental migration trip. The birders, meanwhile, moved in like meth-addled paparazzi. They grimaced and leaned, strained and snapped. *Click! Click! Click!*

What, I am thinking, if these Bosque birders locate the vermillion flycatchers? Imagine the sudden stampede for choice observation spots, the lemming-like rush into swamp water? Shouting matches erupt and escalate into shoving matches. In some people birds bring out the inner landlord, in others the Black Friday shopper.

Elise had circled a spot on the map that's about 30 miles west of Silver City and right before you get to a nowhere little town called Cliff, NM. The way she described it, someone had shoehorned a wildlife refuge into the space between two ranches along land bisecting the Gila River.

A day later I'm driving down first one gravel road and then another and turn onto what is not so much a road as an unnecessarily wide path. No gravel left, just dust. I follow it along the Gila River to a donut turnaround shaded by willows. A gate that resembles something used to control the movement of cattle in a slaughterhouse provides admission. This device has two parallel chutes, with room for one person to pass. I think: this must be to keep people from grazing animals back here. Every rule has a reason.

Past the gate there's a meadow opening right on the river's edge, complete with raccoon tracks. It's April. The temperature's warm one day, cold the next. The trees have yet to fully leaf out, leaving a window of two or three weeks in which birds in spring plumage are easily viewed.

I spot movement and direct the binocs to a tree on the edge of the parking area. As I focus what comes into view is an undistinguished medium-sized bird with brownish markings that seem vaguely familiar. There appears to be a line extending back from the eye, as with a waxwing. I watch this generic something-or-other for a minute or two and resume walking.

The trail picks up about 50 feet past the turnout and runs along the left of the river, between the Gila—moving deep and green over rocks and logs at this bend—and a canyon wall, then into dense woods. The air smells of mud, boxwood and the river. There are shrubs and knee-high flowering weeds. A thick stalk lifts a thistle bloom a few inches higher than the rest and a mourning cloak, then a black swallowtail, rest on the flower. Color: magenta. Its texture calls to mind an HIV virus photographed under an electron microscope displayed in the examining room of my doctor's office. It went up on the wall one day two decades ago, in the middle of the AIDS epidemic, and never came down.

A mile or so in and it occurs to me that it'd be damned difficult to scramble up that canyon wall if something threatening appears. I'm not talking about a pissed-off rancher bearing arms or the local *squadristi*. If it's close enough, a black bear encountered in the woods feels like someone's pointing a Glock at you. Everything else becomes instantly irrelevant. You may think a bear's just an overgrown setter until you encounter one when there's no one else around.

And then there're lions. I scan the top of the canyon wall thinking: what if I see a cougar's face up there staring back? In fact,

I'd be lucky to see the cat before it landed on my neck.

Right now I'd almost, just this once, welcome the loud, dumbed-down drone of some *homo sapien* voices. But no one's here. And suddenly, so suddenly I damn near step in it, there's scat, right in the middle of the trail, a big nasty pile topped with berry seeds like some kind of Dairy Queen for coprophagics. It could be a cow flop, if cows could get past that gate and the barbed wire. More likely, given the seeds, this mess is everything that was on yesterday's black bear menu.

Okay, that's it.

The SUV sits under the willow where I parked it, take-out coffee in the cup holder. Cold, but a kick. A spotted brown horse at the top of the hill shakes its tail and neighs. Time to leave?

In the naked branches a stone's throw from the rental car something moves. I get the binoculars on it and recognize the same bird I saw coming in. Black eye and bill, gray head and back, yellow underparts. Same bird, though now I notice a slash of vague red on the belly. The bird launches itself into the air, executes several hairpin turns and lands on the same place on the same branch. Fly wings twitch from its bill. It launches again, snagging a second mayfly. *Vermillion?*

Field guides can add another pound to the bird bag but there always comes a point when you need to know. If she's here, an hour after I parked, that means there's a nest. And if there's a nest, there's a mate. A swift adjustment of binoculars brings a separate portion of the tree into focus. Ten feet away from her, glowing like a tiny meteor, the red-and-black jewel.

I came back the next day to find the bank littered with 30 smashed beer cans. It didn't matter. I was able to spend an entire afternoon, alone, watching the pair of them feed.

When you see a bird you know, and you're seeing it for the first time, nerves you weren't aware you had start to sputter. It's like celebrity spotting in a bathhouse. Oh my God, can you believe it? "Hope is the thing with feathers," Dickenson wrote, invoking one of her greatest metaphors and, for all her fellow bird people, something that's literally true as well. The idea of bird watching is predicated on hope, which is belief married to a wish.

On the other hand, if you don't know a yellow warbler from a loose canary, all it is is yellow. It could be any kind of anything.

Taking an adult who knows nothing about the woods into the woods is like dragging a 10-year-old who can't stand music to hear *Gotterdammerung*. The most you can hope for is polite attention. But I wouldn't count on it.

On a road trip I once suggested to a friend from Queens that we stop at a particular spot behind the State College, Pennsylvania, reservoir and go hiking. He was agreeable.

"Waxwings!" I said as a half-dozen flew into a tree overhead.

He gave them a quick glance.

"Mountain laurel," I said, as we passed thick clumps of the Pennsylvania state flower, then in bloom.

"Umhmmmm," he mumbled.

We climbed another hundred feet. Something that sounded like a snare drum stuffed with feathers exploded into the air and took off on a diagonal.

"Ruffed grouse!"

He nodded, not looking.

In 45 minutes, the face was bored and the pace lagging. We went back to the car.

Native Americans understood the woods as a universe bristling with information. We descendants of the people who degraded their cultures and drove them from their lands come into a forest to amuse ourselves, when we come at all. We come mostly like the tourist who knows enough to know that it's worth his while to be there, but not much more than that.

What does the tourist do?

He hunts for souvenirs.

"Did you get good photos?"

That's one of the two questions people almost always ask when I tell them where I've been. When I say that no, that I've never carried a camera into the woods, they look at me as if I'm hopeless. They can imagine being there, but failing to make a record of some kind seems pointless. Though for me, that is the point.

I explain that I can barely manage binoculars, forget any kind of high-tech camera, and that if I dragged a $2000 Leica or $3000 spotter scope along with me, these'd be broken, lost, or destroyed in about three hours.

In truth I have no desire to photograph what I see. Beyond writing a bird's name in a pocket notebook, the idea of documenting what I've been lucky enough to stumble on seems gratuitous. Looking at pictures or video is interesting but not like chancing on birds in the wild. Photography only tells me what someone else has seen. The experience of finding something you suspect might be there and happen upon only by chance is its own reward and to photograph birds is a separate and more deliberate procedure.

Besides, there's something in the compulsion to photograph nature that reduces the experience to a commodity. What were all those bird people in the Bosque hoping to come away with? An award-winning picture of a male vermillion flycatcher? Suppose they did? Then what?

The picture you take is essentially a souvenir and like most sooner or later gets thrown out. The image recorded in the brain somewhere stays put.

Kenneth Rexroth captures the way that image fastens hold in his poem, "GIC-to-HAR." That title would mystify many today, when printed encyclopedia have been relegated to thrift shop basements. Years ago, it was in that way that the 32 volumes of the Encyclopedia Britannica was alphabetically organized.

In the poem Rexroth recalls "Coming home from swimming/ In Ten Mile Creek" on an early summer evening, age unstated but implied to be about 12, when

> in a sycamore in front of a ruined farmhouse...
> a song of incredible purity and joy,
> My first rose-breasted grosbeak...

That gets it exactly right. You're immobilized, enthralled, frantic to take it in.

I encountered the same bird, at about the same age. There was, first, the song: a rolling series of figures in short notes, organized in beginning/middle/end form. This casual but earnest piece of communication burst suddenly from among all the familiar swamp sounds of the day—wind, water, ducks, red-winged blackbirds— and leaped immediately to distinction. I looked around. There it perched, 30 feet away, in the only tree that grew from a small, mossy island enveloped by streams. The roseate shield of the breast, the pale, oversized bill resembling garden shears, the black on white patterning, all of it vivid, all familiar. I knew it from the shabby mimicry on the second floor of the Stamford Museum and Nature Center, located in display cases featuring glass-eyed cadavers set in dioramas consisting of painted backdrops or three-dimensional props (marshy muskrat den, shellacked tree trunk featuring woodpecker hole). Someone 40 would quickly have spotted the bobcat's buckshot-nibbled ear, the mountain goat's missing hoof, etc. and dismissed this spurious tableau. On the other hand, if you were ten, these were anything but dull and dusty baubles locked behind glass. They were a Promised Land.

Fifteen years after that sighting, I saw my second. This was in Pennsylvania's Pocono Mountains. I was out on a trail with a friend who'd heard, probably more than one time in that long inebriated weekend, my rose-breasted grosbeak story.

"Jim, do you think we'll see one?" he said.

Extremely unlikely, I told Brian.

"Look!" he said, an instant later.

I was so sure he was pulling my leg that for a moment I refused to. Then I did. There on a birch branch, almost right over our heads, was the triangular pink shield. Black head cocked, the bird gave us the once-over for a good thirty seconds and flew.

People have looked at, wondered about, and named birds for as long as written records exist, and surely before that. The Romans looked at birds enough to have a term for those considered uncommon—*rara avis*. They named them and studied their movements, specifically flight patterns, and sounds, to discern divine messaging. This was known as "taking the auspices" of the gods, something that came down through various Mediterranean cultures in the figure of Calchas, a seer who reportedly received his gift for interpreting bird flight from Apollo.

If the gods exist, the Stoics argued, they care about humans and if they care, they communicate. Birds were the medium. Some—ravens, crows and owls—transmitted divine omens by their cries. Others (vultures and eagles) by movements. A few, including what the Romans called *picus martius*—the black woodpecker—provided information by both their sound and movements. According to legend, Picus, the genus for woodpecker, was the name of a handsome Latin king who spurned the love of Circe. The vindictive goddess of magic turned him into a woodpecker.

It required a legend for the Romans to explain *picus martius*, i.e. the black woodpecker known to ornithology as *Dryocupus martius*. It ranges across Europe, including Italy and Spain. The bird has a North American cousin, the Pileated Woodpecker, *Dryocupus pileatus*. They're both about 20-in. long. A pileated woodpecker landed on an elm in our yard when I was growing up. Duck-sized and all business, it hammered and slashed at the trunk, ignoring the clutch of little primates that watched. My sister felt an uncontrollable urge to contact the Audubon Society with her discovery and the call, once placed, calmed her.

Fast-forward two decades to a time—mid-30s—when, in my life, the field of interest had shifted. My fascination with birds seemed to have faded. Now architecture and utopian communities obsessed. A friend pointed me toward a book called *The Communistic Societies of America* by the 19th century American journalist Charles Nordhoff (published in 1876 and still in print). I wanted to know what had become of the Communistic Societies. I set off to find out.

Not long after, I was taking a walk one morning in New Harmony, Indiana, making notes and soaking up the Utopian vibe when right about in the center of a good-sized lawn I noticed something unusual. About every 30 seconds an object, vividly red and shaped like a detached mustache, rose a few inches above the ground line and then disappeared back into the grass. Back and forth flashed the red mustache.

It could only be one thing.

A crest. In Latin: *pileatus*.

I came closer. The crest reemerged, swinging like a clock pendulum. At 35 feet I realized why the bird didn't simply fly away. Greed inspires its own special bravery. The woodpecker was tearing into a stump. Cut to ground level and left to rot, the stump was alive with panicking carpenter ants. The bird was trying to get as many down as it could before my presence became an actual threat.

The head came up again and paused. A single yellow eye with black in its center took my measure. After a few long seconds the stabbing and smashing and tongue-flicking orgy resumed. If birds are the messengers of the gods, perhaps they have other duties in addition. Soon enough, my trips to the woods resumed.

In the mid-60s Allen Ginsberg and Gregory Corso went to visit W.H. Auden at Oxford.

"Are birds spies?" Corso asked the senior poet.

"Of course not," Auden insisted. "Who would they report to?"

"To the trees, of course," Ginsberg said.

Birds are spies. They don't report to the trees but to each other. It's why the first thing you learn in the woods, if you hope to see birds or anything else, is silence. Watching from branch and treetop, they know everything that goes on there, much like the residents of any crowded block of Philly row homes where "the street has eyes."

Watching is a kind of control. In a way, bird watching is a metaphorical two-way mirror: we think we're watching the birds while birds are watching us. You can feel their attention to your movements. And you may think that the motivation for each action is easily separated: we watch from curiosity, they watch to apprehend danger. But their motives are never that cut-and-dried, are often complex, and only explainable, on one level, by a fact we often refuse to acknowledge: every creature among the higher orders of animals has a personality which includes a range of characteristics, some more pronounced than others.

In the woods most birds stay safely out of the way of human trespassers but sometimes they're interested in the fact that you're interested. Walking a trail north of Lake Superior once a gray jay alighted on a branch an arm's distance, made some frantic kind of noise and stared. Up there they call it the "camp robber" for its habit of snatching campsite scraps. A guess is my gray jay expected a handout.

I have had a loggerhead shrike trail me through the Southern California desert, saguaro by saguaro, like a store detective. I have had a yellow-rumped warbler, male, fly from tree to tree to get my attention, until suddenly landing in the dirt at my feet to perform, in Scheherazade style, a series of elaborate tail-dragged-in-the-dust dances, whether to distract me from a nearby nest or merely to entertain, I have no clue.

I thought, and books tell me so, that the only sound a cardinal makes is its crude "chip! chip!" noise, but I was proved wrong in a Florida forest when a male followed me for a mile or so. Where the trail emerged into a clearing, the bird opened up with a rhapsody, complex and of considerable length. For exactly whose benefit I wonder?

Sometimes motives are clearer. In Arizona once I stopped to get a better view of the single black-and-white form I had just seen moving in undulant flight across the road and when I got out to see where it went what confronted me was a crew of five acorn woodpeckers, perched on the cross beam of a telephone pole. They watched for about 10 seconds before sending up an enraged and hysterical cacophony.

GET THE FUCK OUT!

I did. Not because I was afraid of them but because I respect what they are and where they are. I'm the intruder, but a polite intruder.

On hearing that I was going to be in Nevada, a contractor named Ed who was fitting out a room on top of my house with cabinets and a closet, immediately suggested a trip to the Great Basin for the specific purpose of viewing the Bristlecone pines, among the oldest living things on earth.

The like-minded Ed is forever taking off for remote Western locations. It's not so much about birds as simply being there. And when I got back and explained where I'd been, people would ask, for instance:

"What's there?"

"Bristlecone pines."

"Is that rare or something?"

"Actually they're the oldest living trees."

"I see."

Pause.

"Did you go by yourself?"

That's the other question people always ask. The answer will confirm the received notion that esoteric interests and an anti-social temperament are inextricable. Maybe they are?

No one I know or have met who goes to the woods looking for birds, or just to be there, ever asks that question. Either they assume I went alone, or that if someone came along, that was not the point of the trip and hardly worth discussing.

Ed, for instance, would never have asked. He goes hiking alone all the time and knows what's worth seeing.

The bristlecone pines, on some otherwise bereft ridges in northern Nevada, east of Elko, huddle up there like a lot of lost, large-scale driftwood. Gnarled, growing up out of ground that looks as if it hasn't tasted water since the 49ers went through on their way to the Gold Rush. They grow so slowly they actually look dead. They flourish at just below the tree line, that place on the trail where most of the vegetation is already behind you and the sound of the wind, roaming without impediment, is an eerie and continuous whistle, solitude's one-note sonata.

Going alone means traveling in the best possible company. Two reasons. The first is that there's no one pulling all your energies into small talk, gratuitous observations, worries about whether or not the car will be broken into, etc. Solo, there's the chance I can focus on nothing but the here-and-now. Solo, my unaccompanied thoughts arrive in places they would otherwise not venture. Solo I know my limitations, and more especially my strengths.

The second is that separate and apart from your knowledge of what goes on there, wilderness exerts a dynamic pull on the spirit, guiding it toward some more happy and humble place. What we most often think of as 'silence' is the absence of human noise and in the woods silence has a permanence interrupted only occasionally by a thunderstorm, a limb falling, a bird cry. The woods are a theater, a show that rolls on forever. Its silence has a way of placating old demons by assuring the hiker that the concerns of the human world—whether the break-up you're in the middle of or the military coup somewhere on the other side of the planet—are ephemeral. The smells in that place assure me that decay itself has benign purpose. Why else would it be so fragrant?

But the greatest reward lies not in finding what you came to see but in seeing what you never expected to find. The most extraordinary things appear without warning. On that same trip to New Mexico, I was moving on a trail that took me into the higher reaches of a rocky plateau and then down again, following a stream through a boulder-strewn rock bed. Something small and dark moved among the lower branches of the pines, descended branch to branch via strange miniature acrobatics, flitted to the ground and, after no more than five seconds, zipped back up into the shrubbery.

A warbler of some kind, the shape of which, with its long tail, looked a lot like a redstart, but the coloration of which—black, white and rose-colored red—was nothing like an American redstart and...

And I whipped the *Field Guide to Birds, Western Region* out of the bird bag and was able to quickly identify the painted redstart. The vermillion flycatcher I knew of. The painted redstart? Total stranger.

The long double-decker train lumbered up to the Albuquerque train station right on schedule, which is to say at about 11:45, shuddered a time or two and halted. Doors slid open and small steel steps dropped to the platform. Julio in Amtrak hat, white shirt and Navy pants, a suitcase gripped in each hand, stepped briskly down and onto the platform, set the suitcases on the pavement and turned to offer an arm to an old woman with a cane. There weren't many getting off. He didn't appear to remember me when I showed him my ticket but in a minute I stowed my big bag in the luggage rack by the bathrooms and climbed the narrow stairs to the sleeping car's second floor.

It's hard to imagine any room smaller than what Amtrak calls a "roomette." Even with only a duffel bag and a cloth sack of snacks it's tight. Of course space takes on a different value when you have so little. If you're in there by yourself, the sense of privacy makes it seem like a room at the Plaza. You can draw a curtain across the door, fasten it with Velcro, and be completely alone to watch the world pass.

A moment later the knock came.

"So, my friend, how are the birds in New Mexico?"

It's always hard to know if people are taking a polite interest in what you do because it's their job to be personable or because they're genuinely curious. I'm past the point of caring either way, but I didn't want to blow Julio off, so I pulled out my notebook which, I told him, listed 22 species I'd never seen before in the eight days since I'd originally arrived in Albuquerque. That seemed to intrigue him so I flipped open the *Field Guide to Birds, Western Region* to point out, among the color plates, the vermillion flycatcher, the painted redstart, the red crossbill, and the stilt. I leave it at that because I can tell by the way he nods that this is just about the right amount of information either way. Oh, he says, what time would you like to eat: 5:30, 6:30 or 7:30?

In early May, moving east on the rails in Colorado, the sun sets in the hour and a half between Trinidad and La Junta, which is when many people choose to have dinner. Once it does Julio comes by preparing the beds. In the corridors you can hear compartment doors rolling back and forth continuously. He tells the people who ask that he likes to get the beds made up early so that he can be in bed and asleep no later than 10:15, a subtle signal that after that hour he is not looking to be disturbed.

With the beds made up passengers draw the curtains and soon enough the car is dark. They're done for the day and done for the night. The only sound is the rhythm of the train moving on tracks, a not overly loud mechanical rolling and shaking that anyone soon gets used to and which induces the most prolonged and restful sleep. When the lights in the roomette snap out, the dark outside is darker than the dark inside. What you see from the window is wholly black, impenetrable. Soon enough the eye adjusts. Two or three lights in a distant farmhouse wink, blink and disappear. Now the edge of some town, which then becomes Main Street, storefronts under streetlights, silhouettes receding. The moon emerges from behind clouds and follows the train for a good long while.

A few years ago I was climbing up a rocky canyon on a trail to an oasis in the Southern California desert. I was more interested in seeing what an actual oasis looked like than anything else, including birds, though if I spotted something more exotic than a cactus wren moving among boulders, that would've been the icing. Getting there, however, was harder than it appeared on the map, though it was often downhill. In the distance I could see the oasis, and it looked, well, just like an oasis. Towering date palms rising up off a rock-strewn slope wedged between denuded hills, a small, clear stream, its edges lush with vegetation, somehow flowing through a few hundred feet of rock before disappearing back into the earth. Coming back was harder than getting in and at a certain point you stop looking—for lizards or birds or anything—and focus on lifting first one leg, then the next, and on breathing. Up one slope, then down, then up again. Suddenly the question: how much longer can I do this? In five years will I be able to climb 7,000 feet without having a heart attack? In ten years will I lose my balance jumping across rocks and fall, breaking a leg? There may be ten good years left, I think, or there may be two. It could all end tomorrow.

Exactly then, approaching from the other direction, heading for the oasis, came two people who, to judge by the look of them, had to be in their late 70s, perhaps even their early 80s. Their movements, however, belied their appearance. In each hand was one of those poles that look like ski poles, a slender metal walking stick, and using these the octogenarians propelled themselves along rather rapidly. A good word for the way they moved would be striding. I stepped aside and they greeted me and waved as they whipped past on their way to the date palms and the water. "You will do this as long as you want to do it," I thought. It is in the nature of a question to contain its own answer.

WHO'S VLADIMIR HOROWITZ?

The rented...Taurus?...whips along a mountain highway somewhere west of Charlotte. Sun up and not another car in sight. It's fall. Late fall. Leaves mostly gone.

I lower the window an inch and snap the radio on. Out here in Billy Graham Land it's a roll of the dice. Conway Twitty? Loretta Lynn? Still, I want sound and I'll settle for just about anything.

But on this particular morning how many years ago the dice produce a result that conditional probability and all its various outcomes could hardly have predicted: a classical music station, attached to a local liberal arts college I didn't know existed. And just as I'm inwardly celebrating, prepared to revel in whatever comes next—bang!—the opening chords of Chopin's "Ballade in G Minor" sound.

Of perfect moments life offers few, a handful at most, which might be why we call them that. X conjoins with Y, Y with Z, each seemingly unrelated yet all coming for some nerve-curling instant into alignment, what Jung called "acausal parallelism." This, I suppose, explains how I met Brian.

The word Allegro means "brisk pace," but in this case it's the name of a bar, long gone, where many went to get drunk and dance in that order. The exact circumstances I would give if I could but to extract specifics from the murk of too many beers and bourbon shots makes this not possible. Suffice it to say that after chatting Brian and I ended up in that room with the blue paneling and cardboard chandelier that I, in those wanton days, had the effrontery to call my apartment.

There we fall into the eager gab of two who know there's going to be sex but are hoping for something more, something better. Coincidence piles on. We both come from families of eight. Check. These eight consist of five males and three females. Check. We are both... middle children. Check. And before he leaves, this Brian, we tumble onto that gray felt sofa on which I made love to all the strangers who followed me home and as was my wont, somewhere in the middle of all that, I pass out, and he leaves.

In the weeks immediately after there are other nights that end similarly and somewhere at some point this Brian decides he's going to "save" me. I know this because he told me so years later. I knew, even then, that saving drunks was a losing proposition. To be always drunk is to be delusional and I didn't see myself as much in need of saving. He suggests we move in together. I immediately agree. I don't love him, but it seems an easy thing to learn how to do. Meanwhile he'll cook, clean, sew, run for beer, call in sick on top of my hangovers, and haul my clothes home from the cleaner.

We find a two-bedroom walkthrough at 10th and Pine, which Brian decorates with Ficus trees, a species he admired from having seen some at parties where he's bartending for a catering firm.

Once installed, of course, we fight night and day.

"Jesus Christ, it's Tuesday!"

"So."

"So? *So?* So, you're drinking!?"

"I'm just having a few beers."

Glance at the trash basket piled with empty cans.

"A few beers?"

Brian was a nice blond working-class boy with a wide face and a big heart. The high point of our romance was the time we both were asleep and each of us dreamed he was having sex with the other. When we woke up, we were.

"Jim, wasn't that strange?"

I agreed it was and fell back to sleep.

I had a job I didn't like and when I wasn't there, I drank. Or tried to. Sneaking drinks if you live with someone who doesn't is a mess. Unless they'll look the other way. Brian wouldn't.

"I can tell," he once said, "by the tone of your voice if you've had even one beer."

Oh Christ.

Of course, all I really wanted was to get drunk and pass out in peace. And every time it looked like that might be possible, some wretched eruption would shatter the household tranquility.

"WHAT THE FUCK?!?" I heard him scream one night from the bathroom.

I guessed, correctly, that he'd found the label-less fifth of Old Granddad stashed in the toilet tank.

Whether it was forgetting four loads of our clothes at U Do It, staggering home tipsy or disappearing for an evening only to appear at three reeking of beer and bad sex, I kept it up and Brian kept losing his shit. Sometimes he'd yell. ("I CAN'T LIVE LIKE THIS!") Sometimes he'd weep. Sometimes he'd hurl an ashtray at the wall. Once even a bottle of his precious designer cologne. (The bedroom stank for weeks.) Sometimes he'd dump a drawer of my sweaters on the floor and drop kick a pile or two across the room for good measure.

Once I came home to find the locks changed. The neighbors had a blast with that.

I looked for ways to save this relationship. How could I be his hero?

One day I happened to read in the newspaper that Vladimir Horowitz was appearing at the Academy of Music. It looked like my chance. I'd introduce him to culture. He'd grow, acquire taste, sophistication, and I, of course, would get the credit.

"Brian," I said, "look at this. Vladimir Horowitz is coming to Philadelphia!"'

I knew he didn't know Horowitz from Ho Chi Minh, but I was determined to get him juiced, or at least curious.

Of course, he'd learned that the slightest expression of enthusiasm for one of my projects amounted to giving me permission to drink.

"Who's Vladimir Horowitz?" he said.

"WHO'S VLADIMIR HOROWITZ?"

Upstairs a window slammed.

I told him that Horowitz had retired three times—most recently from 1969 to 1974—and three times come back to the stage. I said that he was famously fearful of audiences. I retailed at some length that old chestnut about how Horowitz had arrived once dressed to play but in an onset of stage fright told his manager he was too sick to go on at which point the manager suggested that that was fine with him but that he, Horowitz, would need to go out and explain to the people that their tickets would be refunded.

Guess how that turned out.

The next morning the line wound from the front doors and all the way to the rear of the Academy of Music. I stood or sat for four hours. But what seats. Sixth row back from the stage.

Then I blew it. The night before the recital—a Saturday—I happened to run into one of my old bar tricks named Timmy on Spruce Street. This Timmy had an amazing ass and knew it and, pining for old times, we ducked into the Westbury or Roscoe's, maybe even the Allegro, soon proceeding to his apartment, where I woke at 4:43 in the morning to notice a fifth of Old Granddad on the nightstand. I chugged whatever remained, dressed and—Ta ta, Timmy!— headed home.

"Brian?" I said, pushing the bedroom door open.

He was awake but pretended not to be.

It's hard working your way back from a fuck-up that big. I tried. I scrubbed the tub.

Silence.

I washed the day's dishes.

Silence.

Three o'clock rolled around. I pulled a suit out of the closet and laid it on the bed.

"Brian," I said, pawing through drawers for a matching tie, "what are you wearing?"

"I'm not wearing anything."

Uh-oh.

"Whadda you mean, you're not wearing anything?"

"I mean I'm not going, asshole."

He said this quietly. Quietly was worse than shrieking. It meant there was a lifespan attached.

"Not going? Are you insane? It's Horowitz!"

I've always had this knack for saying the obvious and self-defeating thing exactly at the point where I shouldn't. I suppose that's a talent of some kind.

The steps in front of the Academy look like a church letting out, filmed in reverse. Spiffy haberdashers, Rittenhouse ladies in pearls, piano students from hundreds of miles around, the whole desperate mass battling its way up and in. In the center of the stage sat a massive piano.

The concert was scheduled to start at four. At 3:45 the hall was packed. I folded my cashmere topcoat and set it in the only empty seat in the house.

Four o'clock.

Five after four.

Ten after four.

Spssss, spssss, spssss, spssss.

I could feel people preparing themselves for disappointment. It was as if they'd gotten out a brush and dustpan and were already mentally sweeping up their busted hopes. Me, I was wondering how the whole fraud would play out in the papers the next day.

At sixteen minutes after four, Horowitz appeared, stage left. Barely visible at first, he blinked from the wings, hesitated a moment, then loped forward into the lights.

A hush.

Watching the maestro in bow tie and jacket it occurred to me for the first but not the last time that loneliness comes in as many forms as there are people but that there is no loneliness that compares to that of the stage performer.

Horowitz cocked his head at the 5,000 lb. chandelier. He peered at the boxes flanking the wings. Was he, a Jew born under Russia's last (notoriously anti-Semitic) Tsar, thinking that those boxes were the sort of place a Tsar might sit? Now his eye alights on the piano. It was his own instrument, trucked down from New York, by terms of his contract. He stares as if he'd never seen one before.

The audience looked on indulgently. Suddenly from the top pocket of his jacket Horowitz extracted a folded handkerchief and flicked it open. He started with the music shelf, moved to the fallboard, the sidearm, the cumbrous but majestic lid.

Somehow, he was able to polish keys without making a sound—the first of the afternoon's miracles—after which he wiped down the bench.

Titters changed to laughter, the laughter that issues when hapless people are observed doing something ridiculous.

When the tension had reached a point where at any moment someone was sure to scream, he struck his first notes.

The program, including Schumann, Chopin and Rachmaninov, opened with Muzio Clementi's "Sonata in C Major," Opus 33, Number 3. Horowitz, who resurrected Clementi from a century of neglect, described him once as the "father of modern pianism." The appeal is evident. Clementi has the competence and some of the ingenuity of Mozart, lacking only the sparkling wit. Of course, no pianist starts with a blockbuster. That would be like handing out the best present first on Christmas.

Clementi gave me my first sense of the Horowitz sound. Its difference was instantly apparent. How to describe? Tender but restrained, mellifluous without a hint of corn. In performance as in creation, taste is everything. Each note belonged to him and only him.

My hunch is that most pianists are carried onstage in a cage of nerves. The exceptions are those unflappable artists—Yefim Bronfman, for instance, also a Russian Jew—who love to perform and would play through a nuclear strike and return for an encore. (A cell phone went off once while he was playing and Bronfman casually concluded the second movement of a Brahms' sonata, glanced into the crowd and said, smiling: "Eez that for me?")

Also obvious was the absence of coughing, sniffling, purse opening, program rattling, butt-shuffling, throat-clearing, etc. the racket that signals a performer's failure to fully connect. Silence enveloped the hall, the silence of 2,508 people concentrating on the same thing at the same time.

Soon enough it no longer mattered that I was alone, since, essentially, I was not.

Note by note, Horowitz cast his spell. Some pianists make a point of appearing enraptured with the sounds they produce. They sing, sway, grin, stare upward, shake their heads. It's a way to guide the audience toward what it should be feeling. This musician, on the other hand, was out to enthrall. Watching that face, mostly immobile but for the eyes, those fingers longer than piano keys pressing and plunging, it was clear that every note had been weighed and tested to correspond with a fully formed sense of the score. Every effect was intention rather than accident.

This truth became evident with the "Ballade in G Minor."

Chopin called this his "dearest" work. It begins, literally, with a bang before alternating between passages of somber reflection and explosive keyboard runs, like something remembered again and again, each time with greater mental violence.

With a face that looked as if he were performing an operation rather than making music, Horowitz stepped up the tempo just slightly, plucking notes in the slower passages so that they seemed to expand, echo, and take on shade.

It was at some midpoint in the work's roughly nine-and-a-half-minute length that I heard something I'd never heard in the Academy of Music before nor in any concert hall since. Somewhere off to my right, a woman began sobbing. More weeping erupted a moment later to my left and then, from behind, out-and-out bawling.

I started to wonder if I was at a piano recital or a funeral. I wondered, too, if these responses were a regular feature of Horowitz performances and whether it was possible that the pianist was hamming in some sly way? The bashful lateness, the handkerchief, the piano polishing, could it be a shtick? How much of this was showmanship, how much the expression of an essentially timid man called to greatness by the scope of his talent?

Soon enough the smiling bow, an exit, further bows, another exit, etc. The audience remained on its feet a good quarter hour. And when they knew that that was all they were going to get, they grabbed their coats and jackets, filing out in the same deathly quiet that had surrounded the music.

I was still up when Brian got back from wherever he'd been.

"Brian," I said, "it was amazing."

Silence.

It took a week for me to fully dry out and about that long for him to speak to me. Back and forth, for a year, it went like that. When I finally quit drinking the relationship died like an unwatered Ficus. But Brian found another lover, a Mathew. This Mathew, a bartender at the Venture Inn, a pub for old queens, would taxi out to the apartment we shared in West Philly, arriving a half hour after the bars closed.

DING DONG!

The landlady, Eleanor, and her boyfriend, another Mathew—so many!—lived on the first and second floors. If the doorbell didn't wake them, the sozzled stomp of Brian's Mathew up the stairs to the third floor was guaranteed to.

Door closes. Battle begins.

"I don't believe this, you're drunk?"

"No I'm not!"

"WHAT'S WRONG WITH YOU?"

Etc.

Eleanor might've put a stop to all this, except that her moral authority was considerably undermined given that she was known for moaning and howling during sex, keeping everyone in the neighborhood up. "FUCK ME YOU ANIMAL!" she'd scream, while her Mathew presumably did all he could to accommodate this request.

One floor up, my ear's to the wall listening to Brian and *his* Mathew get the festivities underway.

"WHY CAN'T YOU STOP DRINKING?"

A book hits the wall, followed by a shoe.

"I just worked a full shift. Leave me the fuck alone!"

On a good night their histrionics ended in sex. On a bad one, Brian ordered Mathew out or harassed him to the point where he'd leave in a huff.

"CALL ME A CAB!"

"CALL YOUR OWN FUCKING CAB!"

Slam! went the windows.

Brian drove off for good in a U-Haul one sultry Fourth of July. It was his birthday and rather humid. I went back upstairs and turned the air conditioner on.

I saw him intermittently in the next dozen years. He got a degree in nursing. He was working as a nurse. There was money in his pockets. I was glad. A grudge is just a wound with a long lease. Meanwhile suddenly he has yet another boyfriend, also named Jim.

Jims, Brians, Mathews, that was the world for me then.

Brian and I would run into each other on the street from time to time.

"I see where Horowitz died," he says to me, on one such occasion.

The obit had appeared the week before in the *Inquirer*. Why, I wondered, would it mean anything to him?

"I should've gone with you that time," he said suddenly.

"Yes," I said, "you should've."

It takes only a pinch of salt to make dead things edible.

"It's amazing how many people die," a friend said the other day, genuinely shocked by this fact, which reminded me of something that happened a few years after Horowitz departed this world. I was on the phone one night when suddenly a third party, with the operator's permission, burst into the conversation to tell me I had to get off right away. I was, said this third party, about to get an important phone call.

"From who?" I said. "About what?"

"Just hang up."

Seconds later the phone rang. It was Brian's boyfriend, Jim #2. He was combing through Brian's address book, calling us all to say Brian had died of pancreatitis the month before. Diagnosed one day, dead three weeks later.

"He had HIV," he said.

"Thanks for calling," I said.

I dreamed about him for a few years. There were three dreams, really. The most frequent involved blond sex, sometimes on red velvet. I'd wake with a throbbing hard-on, usually alone. In another we're exchanging Christmas gifts. I tear through wrapping paper, magenta bound in gold ribbon, to find the brand of cologne that he wore and wanted me to wear and which, of course, I refused to do, telling him it was strictly for pissy queens. The third dream has me stranded on a chandelier, in panic, calling for Brian to get help. "I wanted to save you," he said, once and only once, and I remembered it because of the way he said it, which was as if he were saying it to himself, a private thought that had somehow escaped.

"You saw Horowitz?" someone will say, frowning, when talk turns to the subject of the piano. "What year was that?"

WHAT MAKES A QUEEN A QUEEN?

Some months back, an older gentleman at the center of a wide circle of friends his own age and younger died. A week after the funeral a text arrives from a fellow mourner:

"I miss that queen."

I do too. But it occurred to me that had that message shown up on someone else's phone, the digital equivalent of a wrong number, it would almost certainly have mystified the receiver.

Queen? What queen? Whose?

Queen was once a term not fully understood outside the subculture in which it originated, i.e. gay bars. Gay men have always owned it. But today its use is creeping into mainstream vernacular via the corrupting touch of—what else?—marketing.

A friend sends a text saying simply "Nap Queen." I text back that it's not yet noon and that he's showing his age, at which point a photo of a pillow positioned in a window display at Marshalls pops on the screen. *Nap Queen* reads the pillow. A crown hovering over the words is part of the logo. An online search reveals that *Nap Queen* is a brand. *Nap Queen* mugs, t-shirts, sweatshirts, dorm decor and hoodies, all available. Buy one and proclaim your need to prioritize rest.

There is even a San Francisco-based business called Bitter Queens which "started as a spirited hobby amongst a duo of cocktail enthusiasts" and now retails, via mail order, "unique bitters flavors of superb quality destined for cocktail dens."

Please allow 1-2 weeks for delivery.

Marketing seizes words to sell things. It can turn transgression into toothpaste, attitude into cocktails. Is it possible to believe the geniuses appropriating *Nap Queen* haven't the slightest idea what's implied? That is, a geriatric homosexual.

Elsewhere in the culture, you wonder if this infinitely elastic word, queen—pejorative or term of endearment, take your pick—is going the way too many news reports tell us gay bars are going. That is, out of business. "From Indianapolis to London: Are gay bars going extinct?" asks a recent story in the *Chicago Tribune,* about Indianapolis, citing the uncomfortable but by no means shocking statistic that five of Indy's (once) ten gay bars closed in 2015, done in by dating apps and the respectable visibility of what was once a marginalized and underground community.

Let's hope not.

But you have to wonder: as gay bars close, will the lexicon they spawned similarly vanish, its picked-over pieces monetized by marketers? Will queen end up consigned to the same linguistic graveyard where "Mary" now lies buried?

Anyone under 40 would be utterly mystified to be called Mary but Mary was once the all-purpose form of address that doubled as a sly dressing down. Mary reminded you of your place. You didn't need to be in a dress to be addressed as Mary. You didn't even need to be out, since, I have no doubt, many were outed when summarily addressed by that term, like a friend of mine who had never discussed the issue of same-sex sexuality with his high school football coach/ex-Marine father, the father who, dying, would not allow his wife or either of his two other sons near him.

One morning at breakfast, he asked dad whether there was any milk left.

"It's in the refrigerator, Mary," the father replied.

After that he sort of felt they didn't need to "have that talk."

"What makes a king a king?" This rhetorical question, launched by Bert Lahr as The Cowardly Lion in *The Wizard of Oz* (if the single word answer doesn't pop in your head, watch the movie again for the 158th time) is intended to establish motive. This timid lion's about to grow a pair. Rhetorical questions have their uses, to be sure, so let's put Lahr's line to a different one by excising a single word and replacing that word with its opposite. Suppose instead he'd asked: *What makes a queen a queen?*

Start with Wikipedia: "'Queen' (slang)...a flamboyant or effeminate gay man."

Well, that's one version, though there's a want of serious consideration in it. It omits the element of self-mockery, the acknowledgment of marginalization implicit in the term. Every gay man is a queen, even if not yet actualized. But queen also offers verbal refuge from oppression. It's a subculture's safe house. And it contains a certain regal component that's essential, an element of calculation without which no truly great queen—Catherine the Great, of Russia, say—ever got anywhere. Queens must survive in a world where masculinity is power and to do that you need craft and cunning. These are as essential to being a queen as they are to winning at chess.

I cite as evidence the first actual queen I ever knew, apart from myself.

Time: early '70s. Place: the East Halls dormitories at Penn State, where residents are freshman and 99 percent, at least, white. Casual conversation centers on frats, food, football, parties, and pussy. Pussy, for our purposes, is not set in quotes, because that's exactly the way it was used.

In this pale adolescent world of hash pipes and thumb-smudged King Crimson albums, Darren Fairy was the standout. Of milk chocolate complexion, androgynous, even femme, in appearance, with a name gayer than he was, if that's possible. (I have replaced the original with its aural equivalent.) In dorm rooms and dining halls he drew quizzical looks, testosterone-fueled scowls.

Why Darren Fairy wasn't at some point set upon by football's finest, or at least subjected to the virulent harassment that precedes violence—neither unknown in that place at that time—became evident within about a month of his moving in. He had a posse or, more aptly, a suite (definition #4: "a group of people in attendance on a monarch or other person of high rank"), as proper queens must. Fairy's consisted of a dozen or so white guys, demonstrably working class who, it turned out, all lived on his dorm floor. In the mornings this jocular troupe headed off to First Period together.

In the evenings Fairy and his retinue similarly arrived en masse at the dining hall, advancing toward the chow line while scouts were dispatched to claim a table as the rest were filling their trays.

No sooner were they seated than you heard the voice. It was unmistakably fey and just as unmistakably contained within it the honed steel of a well-tested confidence. This voice stabbed at the air and came down like a snapping blade and the sound it made—only a few of his words, at most, discernable—was almost immediately muffled in yucks, titters, guffaws, hee-haws and sometimes by great crimson-faced peels of laugher.

Another remark, more mirth. Then again. And again. And so it went while the rest of the room, full at certain times to the point of crowded, looked on, glum, not quite knowing what to think. Clearly entertainment of the highest order was on offer at that table and only these—Fairy's consorts and protectors—had access.

Years later I read John Malcolm Brinnin's memoir of Truman Capote at Yaddo where a similar performance is recorded taking place in that venerable institution's dining room, various guests competing to sit at Truman's table, to join in the uproar his stories typically resulted in, leaving the others to glower with resentment. This is queen territory, ladies and gentlemen, as distinct from merely queer, which is only one of its many components.

The others? Well, we've already named a few. But add to these wit, eccentricity, and a thoroughly obsessive nature. Any real queen possesses all these and more in some measure. The "flamboyance" and "effeminacy" in Wikipedia's sterile definition are hats so old they belong in a box, to be kept there.

I've always thought the idea of Queer Studies earnest to the point of tedium. Why not Queen Studies? A PhD in it might include seminars on how to properly mix a Harvey Wallbanger (or bitters), lectures on orchid raising and (for Gin and Judy Queens) dissertations on that marvelous five minute-or-so take in *A Star is Born* when Judy Garland responds to a question from the dubiously sober James Mason (along the lines of: "What did you do at the studio today?") by singing and dancing her answer, a star turn that eliminates any question, ever, about the scope of her talent as artist and entertainer. *The night is bitter./The stars have lost their glitter.*

Queen can evoke whole ontologies. It's specific, but almost infinitely malleable.

Attach it to a trait, to sexual behaviors, to objects or fetishes, and watch it morph into a category, even if just, for the moment, a category of one. If there's one, there are, implicitly, more. You just have yet to meet them.

I'm thinking of the Christmas Queen in my building, whose studio apartment contains 284 Santas, in addition to three artificial trees lighted and fully decorated year round; or the Salt-and-Pepper Queen I was introduced to many years ago, whose living room furniture had been evicted to make way for three glass display cases big enough to cage a kangaroo and filled with condiment dispensers; or the clutch of Doll Queens I once met at an otherwise innocent-seeming dinner party. One bragged of owning 132 Raggedy Anns while another regaled us with tales of his exploits at Kewpiesta in Branson, Missouri, a gathering of similars to swap and sell Kewpie dolls. (That year's theme? "Further along the Kewpie Trail.") When I left, they were jousting over the merits of their respective collections.

Simple equation: Gay man + his obsession/fetish = queen. It's a way of calling attention to the fact of eccentricity as a commonplace. Queen can denote a mindset (Control Queen), a sexual predilection (Chicken Queen, Leather Queen, Scat Queen), a passion (Disco Queen), an occupation (Petal Queen = florist) or a hobby (China Queen). It can be an object—those kewpie dolls—or an activity. For decades it included all those in-group racial pejoratives—Dinge Queen, Rice Queen, Curry Queen—leveled at white men who dared to date outside their race (usually by queens lacking courage, consumed with envy, or both). A queen without envy is a cake that hasn't been baked yet. Though in our time the casual use of any of those terms would drop the temperature of a conversation about 300 degrees Fahrenheit. You'd suddenly find yourself moored on one of Jupiter's 67 moons.

But queen as a style endures. Sweater Queens, for instance. (A subject requiring its own separate course in Queen Studies.) Department stores were once ridden with them, gliding up and down escalators on Sunday afternoons, fanning away vodka hangovers.

"What's a sweater queen?" a woman at the office once asked, completely bewildered, while I was narrating the tale of my previous Saturday evening at the bar.

I tried to conjure for her the image of four or five 30-something gay men with loose cashmere limbs draped and knotted—bunched almost—directly above the solar plexus. She shook her head, still not quite getting it.

Size Queen?

That she got, no problem.

And then there's the Dish Queen. To dish is not just to pass along gossip but to do so in a purposefully destructive way. That deadly verb goes back to at least the '20s, if not before. Lorenz Hart—a major queen—uses it in a line in one of his best songs. ("Won't dish the dirt with the rest of the girls/That's why the lady is a tramp.") Not coincidentally, the noun 'queen' can be tracked back to that decade—which must've been a doozy.

Dish queens you will always have with you, Jesus said. Or something along those lines. My best guess is that dish queens always have been with us. "Trippers and askers surround me," Walt Whitman reports, in "Song of Myself," and it isn't hard to imagine a passel of dish queens in some corner of Pfaff's, on Broadway, *spsss spsss spsssing* away ("*Leaves of Grass*! Who does she think *she* is?") while the bard sits, sipping sherry and trying to catch the barkeep's eye. Dish is rage, power or recognition denied. Dish queens don't go for nobodies if there's a somebody in the room.

Picture three or four of them going at it just loudly enough that only the truly curious—which would be everyone else—can hear. What's left of the victim(s) could be scraped up, broiled and served between two halves of a small bun. Did you ever wonder why people in a gay bar where you've ever spent any time know more about your life than you do, or will?

But forgive me if I deliver the impression that dish queens gather in covens. Actually, the type operates more effectively when solo, preparing the intimate setting to disgorge his/her trove of gossip in the hope of collecting a confidence or two, which is then cycled back into the database. Capote made a career of it. Dish queens are the pollinators of invidious information. Any Queen Studies program worth its salts would have a whole course just on that subject.

But even if my co-worker had grasped the sweater queen concept, how to explain that the types intersect? A sweater queen can easily become a dish queen when presented with suitable opportunity. (Is a sweater queen simply a dish queen in cashmere?) Sweater queens pre-date written history, human language and probably *homo sapien*. Picture mastodon robes flung languidly across Neanderthal shoulders (even as those shoulders are busily engaged rendering cave drawings on rock). And sweater queens will survive global warming and every other apocalypse. Ralph Lauren is the archetype: Style's safest cuts and colors a stand-in for WASP assumptions and ruling class pastimes. (See "golfing," "yacht," "golden retriever," "single malt Scotch," "*Wall Street Journal* subscription.")

There once, it seemed, were an inexhaustible number of queens and types of queens to help give life the spice it needs, and these included the only two that seem to have crossed cultural bounds to become concepts the broad American public is instantly familiar with. One is the Drag Queen, lovingly sent up in a John Wallowitch song titled "Bruce" that was a set piece for the late cabaret performer/jazz singer and somewhat mercurial personality Blossom Dearie:

> *Bruce, you've got to reduce.*
> *Spruce up that caboose, Bruce,*
> *Or wear something loose, Bruce,*
> *You're lacking allure.*

The other is the Drama Queen. A signature type: the gay man not just prone to hysteria but requiring it to the point that he can be counted on to manufacture a full-on crisis where none exists. We've all had friends like these. For a while. The term captures the sense of an overriding instability. The drama queen's need for attention is breathtaking. Entire atmospheres disappear in its presence. Their tantrums can abduct any conversation in an instant. A scene-stealer's got nothing on a drama queen. Drama queens don't abscond with scenes, they create them.

You wonder if there's a genetic component. Are these the babies that hurl oatmeal and howl at the sight of disappointing toys?

Meanwhile 'drama queen' has been transformed via vernacular American speech into a term that means anyone inclined to view things in an, um, overly emotional way. It's gone generic. Women dismiss other women as drama queens. I've heard straight guys refer to another straight guy as a drama queen, and seen it used this way in, ahem, the *New York Times*. I thought: don't they get it? You need to *be* a queen—a gay man—to be a *queen*. Otherwise, it's word candy. Inclusion is the permission that gives you the right to use it. Whoever has that permission can, with a modicum of invention, apply 'queen' effectively and endlessly. It compresses a cloud of knowledge into the raindrop of an image, like the briefest poems are required to do. Speaking of which, I once asked a certain poet about a party he'd been to sometime the week prior. He shook his head and sighed.

"Real estate queens," he said.

We moved on.

WAITING FOR JANIS

A few years back I'm at a party chatting with Paul, poet and serious music fan, when the topic defaults to Memorable Concert Experiences.

"You *saw* Janis?" he asks.

"Uh, yeah."

"What was she like?"

Hell, I was hoping he wasn't going to ask that. Any answer would be somewhat complicated by the fact of my having been, on that particular day, cruising "comfortably in the neighborhood of 70,000 feet off the ground," to quote "Everything you could ever want to know about flying the U-2 spy plane." You know, the one the Russians shot down in 1962, capturing the pilot, Gary Powers, and nearly precipitating a diplomatic rupture?

Seventy thousand feet is thirteen miles up, and at various points on August 5, 1970, the day Janis Joplin performed at the Ravinia Theater in Highland Park, Illinois, it felt like I was tuning in from the stratosphere.

If you take enough of them, or the right kind, drugs can do that. A friend and I once climbed a tower some Explorer Scouts had built in the woods. Solidly constructed of cut branches, fastened with nails, the joints reinforced with twine, it rose about forty feet. We didn't ask ourselves why it was there. It just was, and since it was and since we were fifteen at the time, it seemed like a hashish picnic on the platform at the top was called for.

One problem. Once we were wasted we had no idea how to get down.

We sat there for a few hashish minutes, staring at the ground, which appeared at least as far away as Siberia must've looked to Gary Powers.

"We're fucked!" I said.

Kevin nodded, wide-eyed. He made to speak. A broken syllable, a grunt that wanted to be a word and changed its mind, came out.

Being in a problematic situation is one thing but having to manage someone seriously scared can make it truly fraught. Add to this a substantial dose of cannabis paranoia. What if the fasteners separate? What if Kevin panics and jumps? What if, after sundown, searchlights begin combing the dark from police car windows? What if the wind accelerates and bends the tower far enough so that it...

Each of these thoughts made the ground seem that much farther away and, as if cued to that last one, the wind intensified. It was early spring and a cold wind, strong enough so that branches were bending and waving.

Waiting is rarely the choice made when there're options, but ultimately we concluded that we could only get down by coming down, which happened a few hours later.

It's easy to get into an altered state, sometimes it's not so easy to manage one. You find yourself transformed into the plaything of whatever happens. You climbed to the top, then forgot how to climb down. Like smoking a chunk of dementia.

So with altered states the order of the day, the answer to the question—*What was she like?*—could not be a straightforward one.

Five of us sit on the grass. What looks like a white twig, moist at the mouth end, an ember at the other, makes the rounds.

It's early afternoon on a weekday in July 1970, in Lake Ellyn Park, Illinois. Brian has the floor.

Brian's the youngest in our high school pothead intelligentsia band. He's also the most political, the most culturally attuned. He quotes Allen Ginsberg, Nietzsche, Joyce, and William Carlos Williams, usually without attribution. He despises buckskin, bangs, and bellbottoms, the hippie accouterment of the moment. He combs his black hair straight back from the hairline and wears shoes with about two-dozen eyelets for laces. The shoes somehow curl upward at the tips, like clogs, which works with the big, baggy trousers he refers to as his "pimp pants."

Wherever we go, people look.

Brian holds forth on "pigs," pot deals, arson as a necessary and legitimate political tactic, and on the book he's reading. The book is on the ground beside him: *Selected Poems of Ezra Pound.* Today he's saving the best for last.

"I've got acid," he says, taking as big a pull as lungs permit and holding it.

His eyes get huge.

"And... " releasing the bluish vapor into summer's torpid air, "... Janis is coming."

Stoned expressions become startled ones.

"What?"

"Janis?"

"Did Brian say 'Janis'?"

"Yeah, Janis."

"Far out, man," says Far Out. He nods, grinning.

Far Out is the anomaly here. Rolling beard, shoulder-length hair, maybe eight years older than the rest of us. No one knows where he's from or, for that matter, what his given name is, except Brian, who met him buying drugs in Wheaton, one town over, and Brian pretends not to know.

"Where?" Lev asks.

Brian passes Peggy the joint and inserts a plastic fork into a box packed with pork fried rice.

"Ravinia."

"Far out," says Far Out.

Located twenty-five miles north of the Loop, Ravinia Park, a thirty-six-acre wooded tract that includes a performance space, is just that for five people without a car. How to get there?

It must be done. This is *Janis*. Janis Joplin. In addition to the pleasures certain to accrue from her performance, just being there comes with considerable countercultural cachet.

Still, the challenges appear formidable. Besides transportation, there's money. Peggy and Lev will be at Grinnell College in two weeks. They're not working. Far Out deals weed, but he's somehow always broke.

A seed pops.

"I've always wanted to see her," Peggy gasps, passing the joint to Lev.

In the distance, a commuter train rumbles past.

"It could be…interesting," Lev says, studying the object as if we were all anthropologists on a dig and he lucked on a pottery shard.

"When is that?" says Far Out.

"When is what?" everyone at the same time asks.

Far Out's expression is that of someone forced to switch languages in mid-conversation. It takes him thirty seconds to relocate the trail.

"When is she coming?" he says.

"First week, next month," Brian says. "The fifth." He clamps the roach between bobby pin tips.

"Wow," says Far Out. "That's *too* fucking far out."

Strategies are formulated, plans laid. Peggy lines up her father's car. I take a two-week job washing dishes in a pizza joint to help finance admission and the bottle of whiskey Brian insists we bring. With our pooled funds Lev buys the tickets, negotiating for cheap seating on Ravinia's lawn. Brian's contribution is the vaunted acid stash.

The evening starts at 8 o'clock. We'll meet at "the commune," a house in Wheaton Far Out shares with a half dozen other hippies.

Since Peggy's driving, we all agree she shouldn't trip, which is fine with her. She regards the counterculture scene with bemused detachment. So, in his way, does Brian. His oft-expressed distaste is rebellion for its own sake, a defiant nihilism. Lev? His first interest is philosophy, his second, politics, his third art and music. He's the resident Spinoza, more interested in the Isaac Deutscher biography of Trotsky he's reading than in Rock & Roll, though Janis's Bad Girl image and hippie celebrity definitely intrigue.

And Far Out?

A soul in druggy free fall.

Two weeks elapse. Invariably, complications arise. Janis is advertised in the papers. DJs are talking about her on the radio. But in the summer of 1970, things have a way of changing, suddenly and for the worse. Politicians and the press raise concerns and make threatening noises. By late July, the prospect of her appearance arouses controversy. She'll whip up a drug-fueled frenzy. The hippies will burn Ravinia down.

Not likely. Janis occasionally appears, for free, at concerts to raise money for the peace movement. Mother Bloor, she's not. She's a blues singer who's usually introducing the next song when she's not singing, though she sometimes delivers a quasi-political rap from the stage. Her concerts are all about inspiring the audience to get loose, party, and dance.

Then, a little more than two weeks before her gig, a free concert by Sly and the Family Stone, in downtown Chicago, becomes a melee. The Grant Park audience swarms the stage and can't be persuaded to leave. Sly refuses to go on. Furious, the crowd streams onto Michigan Avenue. Rocks and bottles fly. More than a hundred people are treated for injuries, at least 150 arrested. "Several thousand Negro and white youths, hurling rocks, battled the police for more than six hours tonight," reports *The New York Times*. "They roamed into the Loop business district and smashed windows."

A rumor makes the rounds that Janis will cancel her Ravinia gig. Another has it that Ravinia will cancel Janis. Highland Park's police chief, Michael Bonamarte, tells the *Chicago Tribune* he is "waiting for a riot."

"They'll be patting people down on the way in," Lev says.

We're back in Lake Ellyn Park, passing a joint, pooling cash for a run to Luck Chow House.

"The motherfuckers wouldn't dare," Brian says.

The rest of us aren't so sure. A few weeks earlier, at a Traffic concert at the Aragon Ballroom in Uptown, word spread that the cops were waiting outside to frisk all who exited. "Pigs are busting people," the guy next to me shouted, handing me a half empty bottle of red wine. I tilted it back—*glug, glug*—passed it to the stranger on my right and fished in my back pocket for the dime bag of weed I'd brought.

Dear Mr. Fantasy, play us a tune
Something to make us all happy

When the last sounds faded and the lights came up, baggies of pot and prescription bottles litter the floor.

"Are you feeling it?"

Lev asks this question as if he were talking to one person instead of a roomful. He's not putting us on. If anything, he's being earnest, as in the manner of important scientific inquiry.

There's a pause—that split second before a bomb goes off—and the room breaks up.

I guess we are. Feeling it.

Imagine having a car battery wired to your hippocampus for eight hours. There are other dimensions to LSD but the first is a kind of internal glow, as if someone had switched on some unknown energy source, purring away without a governor switch.

You can be tripping and appear mentally intact, even while on the cusp of full-on hysteria. It's a state of mind some learn to love.

I had a friend who would drop acid in the morning and wander around Philadelphia looking at things all day.

"What did you see?" I'd ask.

"Swan champagne," he'd say, grinning maniacally.

"Really?"

Had some chic new beverage hit the market? Had ornithologists discovered a new species of swan somewhere and broken out the bubbly?

A few months later it occurred to me he was describing the fountain in Logan Circle, here in Philadelphia, where patinaed cygnets joyously spout.

Two points: 1) on acid the mind defaults to absurdity at the first invitation, and, 2) acidified brains move in sync, like murmurating starlings.

Imagine reading aloud to a room full of people, as if sacred text, the instruction booklet for assembling a stereo.

Someone claps.

Now the whole room's laughing and applauding.

Triggers come out of nowhere. Why, I think, as we sit in Far Out's living room, are Lev's socks blue? Shouldn't they be...yellow? Or red? Why not yellow *and* red? What is the point of socks at all?

"Lev," I say. "Why are there socks?"

Lev smiles one of those rare smiles that could genuinely be called 'beatific.' It's as if he knows the reason but because it's rooted in some incredibly detailed historical explanation having to do with the invention of sandals, then shoes, then boots, with a detour, maybe, for mukluks, and for the very reason that it's just complicated and none other, he will do me the favor of declining to respond.

It's two in the afternoon. The acid kicked in half an hour ago. I've tripped a dozen times but never in daytime and never quite like this.

How high are we?

Think Gary Powers.

Furniture breathes. Voices cast shadows and the shadows dissolve at a touch.

On the other side of the room, Brian scowls, reading book titles.

"What are you looking at?" Peggy asks.

"*One Flew Over The Cuckoo's Nest,*" Brian, glancing up, replies.

HAHAHAHAHAHA

"Far out," says Far Out, when, a quarter hour later, it all stops.

We're spread out on two or three cat-clawed sofas and chairs, staring at the ceiling, or gazing outside. An old rag rug lies in the center of the floor. Is it purple or gray? Are they the same? Suddenly, we're all leaning forward at once, keen to catch the sounds everyone's just noticing, which is Joplin's *Kozmic Blues* spinning on the turntable:

Time keeps movin' on
Friends they turn away
I keep movin' on
But I never found out why

Why? I think. *What an odd word. Why is the room shaped like a rectangle when a triangle would work just as well? Maybe better. Fewer corners. Why is...*

THUNK.

A strange noise.

Where?

Heads turn right to left.

What made that sound?

Brian vaults from a sofa. The screen door bangs shut. He returns, strips the green rubber band away and drops the *Chicago Tribune*'s afternoon edition, open, onto the rug.

RFK Jr. BUSTED FOR POT

"Far out."

Once triggered, the laughter has no end point. It leaps body-to-body, some crazy contagion for which there is no vaccine, its symptoms this blubbering, rib-clutching, head-shaking seizure, complete with back-and-forth, up-and-down rocking motions. It's a laughter that paralyzes all functions so that you can't do anything but huff, pant, bawl and finally cry. Any stranger entering the room would've immediately phoned for a priest. Only Peggy holds back, wearing a DaVinci-esque smile while the rest of us gasp and shriek from halfway inside some other dimension. Was she regretting her decision not to trip, or congratulating herself for avoiding this Kodachrome squalor?

Brian looks down at the turntable and the motionless record. Where did this silence come from?

"Who's hungry?" he says.

The Dairy Queen is Lev's idea. Lev wants a banana split. No one asks why, fearing an extended dissertation on fruit farming in Honduras or a discourse on the evolution of human taste buds.

We push and tumble past the door, yipping like spring coyotes.

The glitzy franchise is take-out, mostly, with four black tables set against glass walls. Two cash registers are mounted on the counter and a few feet behind it a stainless steel thing like a Strong Box as big as a refrigerator, complete with some weird gearshift, flanked by stacks of ice cream cones. Over the counter floats a menu.

A kid no older than us, white smock, leans forward on the counter. We stand, staring. I hear him clear his throat.

Now someone with a salt-and-pepper brush cut, pencil wedged behind the ear, steps out from around back. Same mad scientist smock, which must be the reigning drag here, except that his has *General Manager* embroidered in red above the pocket. His eyes take us in. It's the old up-and-down, the Fuck You look-over that starts at the feet and inches upwards, pausing at a missed belt loop, a grease stain, last week's unhealed zit.

In old age you view youth as just another opportunity lost along a long trail fairly littered with them. You might even sympathize with its follies. Middle age is another matter. What does *General Manager* see in a pack of longhairs, loud and crazed, pupils dark and blazing?

The eyes move up and over Brian first, the most obvious spectacle, then Lev, with his *Out Now!* and *Stop The War* buttons, craggy Semitic nose, red-blond goatee. They widen at the sight of Far Out, a werewolf in search of adulthood, and finally alight on me. When you're a teenager in the closet, all scrutiny comes with a hefty dose of fear. I'm just starting to figure out how this works. For instance, if your friends carefully steer all conversation away from the subject of homosexuality, that says they know.

Only Peggy, the calmest person in the room, is spared.

"What do you want?" General Manager hisses.

We look at each other. It's not like we're touring the Vatican. It's a fucking *Dairy Queen*, for Christ's sakes. We're trying to read the overhead menu board. Lev giggles.

"I'll have a Dilly Bar," Peggy says to the kid at the counter.

She's getting the ducklings in line, trying to guide us back to the safety of the pond.

"That it?"

She nods. And just when things seem to have settled down, Brian turns to the group and asks, in his most mock-innocent: "Who's Mr. Misty?"

Everyone—the kid, General Manager, us—looks at Brian as if he'd just materialized out of thin air into our midst. His eyes gleam. The energy rolls off him in waves. He's all lit up like a casino.

"Is Mr. Misty the owner?" Lev asks, picking up the thread, but it's not a put-on, he's just that blitzed and seriously trying to get his mind around it, the source of this name.

Peggy shakes her head.

"Brian, what flavor do you want?" she asks, firmly.

"Lime."

"Far out."

Far Out also wants a Dilly Bar.

"I'll have a banana split," Lev announces, remembering why we're there.

The minion peels a banana, slices it in long halves, sets the halves on opposite sides of a black plastic dish and—*splut! splut! splut!*—releases from that big churning Strong Box three twisty dollops of soft serve on each of which he ladles separate syrupy toppings. General Manager, arms crossed, watches. The pineapple chunks look like a fistful of melting yellow dice. The chocolate I can taste just by looking at it.

Now that tongue-twisting Mister Misty mixer slams into action. It sounds like a chipper shredder eating a skyscraper, grinding ice, mixing it with sugar and dye, whipping it into a frosty green blend in a tall paper cup. Brian stares into his, as if waiting for the face inside to say something.

The parfait I've ordered is a curious thing, like valentines slathered in frozen cream tucked in a plastic glass.

We carry it all to a table.

Lev spears a strawberry, peers, pops it in his mouth.

"Far out," says Far Out

Far Out lifts his Dilly Bar like a scepter for us to admire.

I feel a gut-buster start up inside. It's working its way forward, one ticklish inch at a time.

Out of nowhere, General Manager looms tableside.

"*What the fuck's going on here?*" he says.

Silence for thirty seconds or so until Peggy says:

"We're on our way to a concert."

It's not the answer he's expecting because he's not expecting any answer.

That trick again.

"It's Janis Joplin," Lev says, as if he's introducing her onstage.

A titter. A cackle. Now it's impossible to stop. We're roaring. The table shakes.

"GET OUT OR I'M CALLING THE COPS!!"

General Manager turns. He disappears behind the counter.

Ten minutes later, from a broken sofa on Far Out's front porch, we watch a cop car speed toward downtown Wheaton, lights flashing.

It'd be far easier to describe what Janis was like at Ravinia if we'd been in the box seats, near the stage, me with notebook in hand, listening with unimpeded concentration. On the contrary, we were, as they say, ripped to the tits—all except Peggy—and comporting on some blankets she'd had the good sense to bring. Maybe 200 feet from the stage, we wait: Peggy vigilant, Lev curious, Far Out buzzing like a transformer, Brian and I banging back Jim Beam.

Whiskey and acid sounds like a recipe for epic social disaster, but combining them, I discovered, contains a certain logic. The booze has little or no visible effect—no staggering, stumbling, slurring—except to keep the acid from reaching the flat-out cuckoo stage. It's like pouring water on moving lava. Meanwhile LSD's inherent caution, that sense of setting foot on a strange planet for the first time, puts a brake on the jackass behavior typically associated with whiskey. It all works.

Good enough, since Ravinia, once we step past the gates, is alive with blue. Four or five cops gathered anywhere you look. Meanwhile something like 18,000 fans have assembled and, assuming safety in numbers, a few light up joints while the cops look the other way.

A country rock band from Indiana called Mason Proffit in buckskin, fringe and round Mountie hats, opens and is off soon enough. Figures appear, yank cords, lift equipment. It's Janis's crew, setting up for her band, Full Tilt Boogie. A frenzy takes hold. The congregation awaits its priestess.

What was she like? Concentration was compromised that evening, so if it's analogy you're after, an image in the form of quick and painless comparison, she was like a fire seen burning at some great distance.

The night we went to see Janis at Ravinia, my—to date—half-century of active concert-going was in its infant stages. I discovered music the way I discovered sex: something that starts out as one of life's fringe benefits and goes on to become almost a defining purpose. Except that it always gets better and lasts till the end.

For those who love it, music becomes a kind of timeline for life. The great performances we were lucky enough to be at, or the albums we played several times a day every day for six months, the single we absolutely loathed on the radio that came to be a favorite song, these pin experience to a time and place, creating small monuments within memory. The end of 1968, for instance, was when the Beatles' *White Album* came out. Someone bought a copy—there was a line at the store, and it sold out in minutes—brought it back to some den in which ten thoroughly stoned teenagers waited, unwrapped it and gingerly set the first disk of this telegram from the divine onto the turntable.

That was an early moment. Another is from 1973, the year Seiji Ozawa conducted the New Japan Philharmonic in Berlioz' *Symphonie Fantastique* in a tour that included Penn State, where I heard the ensemble with no small enthusiasm. Later that same night, quite by chance, I encountered the Maestro in a State College bistro seated alone with a glass of wine. I complimented him on the concert. He seemed surprised to be recognized and invited me to join him. We ended up talking for an hour and a half about Berlioz and French music.

Ravinia that night was another lucky accident. Who knew she had two months to live? I owned her three albums and played *Cheap Thrills* till my mother got annoyed enough to question my sanity. ("Turn that goddamn thing down! Are you crazy?") So on the night I went to hear Janis, the only basis I had for evaluating what she did or how well she was doing it were those records. I could only compare Janis to Janis. And Janis in concert neither expected nor wanted her audience to sit in deepest concentration. She wasn't interested in being evaluated or analyzed. She wanted the crowd on its feet, dancing or at least grooving high. That was clear from the moment she arrived.

There are various ways for a star to make an appearance. Sun Ra's band would take the stage, launch into a number with multiple percussion instruments and all sorts of overlaid horns, while the keyboard bench stood empty. Sooner or later you'd think: where's Ra? And right about then he'd appear in the wings, discreetly make his way through and around people, instruments, and amplifiers to the piano, so that the effect of his first chords, struck in a way that seemed tentative, as if the thought behind them was still being worked out even as the sound was being made, was electric.

Janis is the opposite. Her entrance is unsubtle, unstoppable and unforgettable. She takes the stage whooping, hollering, and waving her microphone, which looked like a light sword, before movies made it a thing. Feathers appear and disappear in the kliegs, an effect lysergic acid renders luminous. No matter how far out you'd traveled, there's no ignoring this arrival, which affirms that her presence is the entire point of the evening.

Full Tilt Boogie kicks up. Janis grabs the mike stand and rocks back and forth. She stomps. She stamps. Her beads swing. Her passion and fury remind me of someone indignantly resisting arrest.

Given that I'd subjected my brain to relentless levels of uninvited stimuli over the previous, uh, eight or so hours, and that yet more stimulation would be forthcoming as the night wore on, it's probably no surprise that Janis, onstage, is recollected in mostly general terms with specifics coming in and out of focus as the trip wears down.

Meanwhile the lousy sound system is making things difficult.

"Can you hear me out there?" Janis yells.

"NO!"

The sound blares, wobbles, fades, and blares again but it isn't anything anyone's going to riot about.

That we got there and that the evening even happened at all seems a kind of victory, as any undertaking we'd never think twice about seems triumphant under the influence of substances. She's here, we're here, and—as the sun goes down—there appear, briefly and everywhere amidst clouds of marijuana smoke, fireflies timidly signaling about a foot off the ground to potential mates, Nature's assertion of its place in all this human vanity.

The thought of what this might look like in retrospect isn't even there. Who at sixteen thinks of posterity? What does that word even mean then? You can't get your mind around the idea in any meaningful way because if you did, that would indicate you understood what it's like not to exist anymore, to be dead, or at least old, which for many under twenty amounts to the same thing. It's way too much for the average teenage imagination to engage.

What was she like? Well, if I'd been expecting a reprise of *Cheap Thrills*, ostensibly a live album that was studio-recorded except for one track, with the live effects (applause, catcalls, etc.) dubbed in later, it was not that. At another point in time, when I became a fan of symphonic music, I realized that when you go to hear an orchestra, the point of the performance is that it should resemble all others.

Standardization is the aim. With Janis, on the other hand, this instigator of Dionysian revels, everything is adjustable and anything could happen.

Her set mixes Janis standards with songs we've never heard, since they're on an album—*Pearl*—scheduled for release in two months. In fact, once she and her band get started, it's clear that Full Tilt

Boogie's arrangements of Joplin hits don't sound like Big Brother's except ("Piece of My Heart") when they need to. The arrangements are more polished, more rhythm-driven than anything she recorded in her acid rock days. They work with what she does, which is to stand behind a microphone and beg, shriek, wail, croon and plead in a vocal tone that registers as both playful and hard at the same time—a feat—and is dominated and defined by its gritty East Texas twang.

We're lying there listening and here comes that seventeen-note figure on electric guitar, which anyone alive and over the age of twelve in 1968 would recognize immediately (#12 on the pop chart) as the opening of Jerry Ragovoy and Bert Berns' "Piece of My Heart," a song since recorded by everybody from Dusty Springfield to Bryan Ferry and Melissa Etheridge:

> *Didn't I make you feel*
> *That you were the only man, yeah*

We're on our feet. Even Brian, the perennial non-participant in group displays of countercultural solidarity, even Brian stands, face transfixed, sweeping his raven hair back with the hand that isn't holding the Beam bottle.

Janis singing "Piece of My Heart," then and now, makes me think of the last stages of an impassioned argument between lovers, an argument that finally comes down to whether or not the love should exist at all. And if what she sings moves us it's because it reminds us that love never was or ever will be easy. She puts her own insistent spin on the song's blatant masochism, somehow transforming obeisance into defiance.

So, we're grooving high, temperature right about 70, zero precip. We've been pulled wholly and unthinkingly into the spell. Whatever you may have heard about the limits of her talent or of that talent having nowhere near enough time to mature, her act was as much presence as anything else, a force in whatever space she happened to occupy.

At some point—was it an encore?—Janis is talking about

someone named "Bobby McGee."

Lev wants to know who this is.

"She says it's a new song," Peggy says. "On her next album."

This song seems different. It's not a plea like "Piece of My Heart," or a romp like "Move On," but a reminiscence. It's also a showstopper. Or am I only remembering that because of the mega-hit it became?

A month or so after Ravinia, I got a job at a supermarket. When there were lines at checkout, I bagged. When there weren't, I collected carts.

The parking area sloped just enough that every few minutes one of those wire cages on wheels would suddenly roll toward the bottom of the lot, picking up speed and—WHAM!—slam into someone's Cadillac. The carts always made for expensive cars, never clunkers.

I'm out there one Sunday. It's about 3:30 in the afternoon and cool enough for a jacket. I chased a cart and snagged it. I jammed another cart inside it and grabbed a third. Six was as many as I could push back up the hill and into the store. On the baby seat of the last one someone had left an afternoon tabloid. Her picture filled the cover of the paper.

That winter, "Me and Bobby McGee" became a Number One hit. Her first, and only. On the radio, Janis's reading of Kris Kristofferson's tale of two drifters and their lost love felt like a valedictory:

Busted flat in Baton Rouge, waitin' for a train
And I's feelin' near as faded as my jeans

Artists, especially entertainers, rarely go out on a note of triumph. Often they falter, fail, or die some grisly public death that leaves the Philistines tsk-tsking. Why would people expend so much time, energy and anguish to risk ending up like that?

One reason, I think, is that artists, of every kind, are out to show us, in the beauty they create, the beautiful thing they know themselves to contain. When they succeed, the attention that results sometimes feeds a maniacal need for more. Some artists want to be loved not just by one person, or a loyal handful, but by everybody. What they make is the product of discipline's ability to bring the power of imagination momentarily under control. Still, we're drawn to this glamorous sorcery. We become a necessary part of it, the audience part, precisely because it allows us to imagine the chaos of our own inner worlds somehow tamed. We indulge in the fantasy that we could paint as well as Degas, write stories as brilliant as Chekhov's or sing about the love we want and need but aren't getting with the same conviction as Janis Joplin. The power to do that, however, comes with a certain risk.

In March of 1991 I went to hear trumpet player Red Rodney at the Jazz Showcase in Chicago. Red Rodney's appearance at that esteemed venue followed by maybe a year the release of a biopic on Charlie Parker called *Bird*. The film features a Red Rodney character, played by Michael Zelniker.

Red Rodney had been famous enough in his time. He toured with one of Parker's quintets, the only white musician in the ensemble, where he went by the name Albino Red and where this kid from Philly—his given name Robert Chudnik, his first trumpet a Bar Mitzvah gift—got seriously strung out on junk. Decades later he landed in a pit band in Vegas, suffering the kind of medical problems which in America quickly translate to bankruptcy. At one point in the '60s, he was jailed for passing bad checks.

After seeing *Bird*, I assumed Red Rodney was Dead Rodney. Then I noticed that he was on the bill at the Jazz Showcase in Chicago. I went, imagining a shell of a man blowing hackneyed solos while a crowd claps politely between drinks.

Nothing immediately displaced these expectations. At the mike stands a guy who could be the grandfather of anyone else onstage, except that he's white. He's also short and wide, and his head sports the reddest thatch of hair this side of Lucille Ball. A camp fire of a haircut. In blazer and slacks, he looks straight out of Miami Beach.

Red Rodney lifted his flugelhorn and blew into the microphone a single, dirge-like note, courtesy of Cole Porter, about 12 seconds long:

Every time we say goodbye,
I die a little.

You may've heard dozens of versions of that song. His, that night, was one you would not forget. By the second set, the place is standing room only.

Yet, even with the ability to turn in a performance at that level, who, a few decades later, remembers Red Rodney, except for a handful of jazz aficionados?

So why go through all that?

Red Rodney, it seems to me, had attained the satisfaction of knowing that he could do something no one else could: play that well, in that way, in front of a crowd who knew how good his playing was.

I am a fan and fandom is a whole made of parts, the parts being aesthetic enjoyment, intellectual curiosity, peer pressure, where you're at in your life, and the obsessive collector's need to have it all, own it all, be it all, inhabit it all. Oh, and did I forget bragging rights?

It was bragging rights, as much as anything, that got me to Janis's concert. Not only to have the experience but to say I'd had the experience. At the time, of course, I couldn't imagine I'd be talking about it 50 years later. Who could know her brief career would engrave a permanent place in cultural memory? An overnight sensation in the arts is often forgotten in just about the same amount of time. Al Jolson, for instance, was once known as The World's Greatest Entertainer—an actual title bestowed on this Russian-born tap dancer in blackface—but, unless you're a film historian, would you spend more than ten minutes watching his movies?

We live in an age when audio and video reproductions are readily created and transmitted, so that if you really want to know "what she was like" you can watch the famous clip from the late D.A. Pennebaker's *Monterey Pop*. The June 1967 performance recorded there so dazzled the San Francisco rock aristocracy that the image of Mama Cass's stunned mug has become at least as iconic as what she's watching, namely Janis's performance of "Ball and Chain."

A half-dozen videos of Janis on stage may convince you that in the three or so years she held our attention, she essentially reprised Monterey Pop again and again. But watching or listening to documents that record an experience is not the same thing as having the experience, even if, at the time you had it, you couldn't imagine you'd remember it at all a month or a half century later.

Janis Joplin became that permanent place in cultural memory called "Janis" for a few reasons. One is that she happened to have, at the time of her accidental death, an album almost ready for release, and her death—mortality is the ultimate marketing bonanza—propelled it to huge sales. *Pearl* sold four million copies, compared with *Cheap Thrills*, which at 1 million copies was among the best-selling albums of 1968.

So, there was a body of work. And there was, in addition, an image, a style, something emblematic—the bellbottoms, beads and boas—which perfectly accorded with, and encoded for historical and media purposes, the brief Bohemian heyday in which her star was ascendant.

Death secured the legend, and the legend, naturally, spawned imitators, some subtle, some fervent. If you want to experience something approximating Janis at the microphone, you could take in an act called Mary Bridget Davies and the Joplinaires, who reprise her biggest hits on stage. Davies moves and inflects in the Joplin manner to a degree that feels creepy in the same way that watching Janis's final interview and TV performance on Dick Cavett's show feels creepy. It's impossible not to know the outcome. In America, anything saleable sooner or later will be sold. One day long hair is a statement of social defiance, the next it's a Broadway musical and hit album.

And so, right around the time Janis checked out, rock and roll rolled into stadium-sized venues with louder and flashier performances for which audiences were charged twice or three times as much. You paid, for instance, five bucks to get into the Aragon Ballroom on the north side of Chicago to hear three hours of music, including headliners such as Muddy Waters or Jethro Tull. A year after Janis died, it costs twenty bucks to hear the same show in Philadelphia's Spectrum, capacity 18,000.

When I went to hear the great ladies of jazz, they were in the twilight of their careers. That brought urgency to the occasion. With Sarah Vaughan's performance at Philadelphia's Academy of Music, and most especially with Ella Fitzgerald's, at Radio City, in New York, there was the unspoken understanding that there might not (Sarah Vaughan) or would not (Ella) be another opportunity to hear them again. In each case, I remember little about what happened before or after the performance, only the performance.

Sarah Vaughn, for instance, whose menacing energy sometimes approximates Krakatoa ready to blow, sipped daintily from a water glass on a stool between mopping away copious quantities of sweat with tissues from a Kleenex box. When she opened her mouth, every song became like the great aria you're waiting to hear in the middle of, say, a Verdi or a Donizetti opera, hoping that whoever has the role will not only animate it in the way you already know it can be brought to life, but show you something you haven't seen, felt, or heard before. No one in Radio City Music Hall knew quite what to expect when, in her final performance there, May 2, 1992, Ella Fitzgerald, having lost a leg to diabetes, appeared onstage, age 80, in a wheelchair. As things moved along, the evening's unspoken question was just how long the show could last, given these disabilities. She worked her way through two full sets and sounded pretty much "like" she sounds on *Ella in Berlin*.

Those great singers were old then, the end of life's timeline as visible to them and to us as the last stop on a subway map. They'd worked long enough and hard enough that the artist was inseparable from the person and, as a consequence, they could deliver nothing less than a satisfactory performance.

Janis at 27 had no map and a talent she was still sorting out, still looking for ways to manage. She'd climbed to that high place with no idea that it might be hard getting back down.

What was she like? She was like the season's first snow, or a great lay, or seeing a bird you've never seen and were sure you'd never see, appear on a branch ten feet away. There was something evanescent about her, something fleeting, that was discernable even then. Otherwise seeing her blown-up tabloid photo with the headline JANIS JOPLIN DEAD would've felt like a shock. It didn't.

Three years, even three years of stardom, is not a lot of time. She blew through it not so much as if she believed there'd always be more, but as if nothing but the moment mattered. That element of the Joplin persona was something she flaunted, her recklessness part of the attraction. But it wouldn't have mattered without the other part, which is harder to pin down. Pathos and yearning, all the desperation of the abandoned, were in her voice and on her face.

People love the singer they believe sings for them, about them, from knowledge of their pain, which reduces, finally, to an absence of love. You have to know that absence to sing about it with authority, to sing about it in a way that's not just believable but convincing. It's something Janis Joplin was able to pull off literally to the end, that is, to the last track on her last album, *Pearl*, in a song that, in the face of life's brevity, urges us to "gamble on a little sorrow," which states the case as simply and directly as it's possible to do and may as well have appeared on her tombstone: "Get It While You Can."

ROMPING THROUGH THE SWAMP

This world, as a glorious apartment of the boundless palace of the
sovereign Creator, is furnished with an infinite variety of animated
scenes, inexpressibly beautiful and pleasing, equally free
to the inspection and enjoyment of all his creatures.

—William Bartram,
Travels Through North and South Carolina, Georgia, East and West Florida

"Do you know where the turtles are?"

The lady is 60ish. Her sweatshirt's lime green, a color
guaranteed to send anything sporting wings fleeing in the opposite
direction. She's heading up a column of seven-year-olds. The kids
stare, knowing their next move depends on my answer.

With the sun an hour from its zenith, the turtles are where they
always are, piled on planks jutting up from the murk at low angles.
So many they pile up on top of each other.

What is it about a turtle that never fails to arouse interest?
Their fortitude would be my first guess, that way of plodding on,
oblivious to discouragement. I once watched a box turtle I kept as
a pet scale four feet of chicken wire. It hoisted itself over the top of
the fence, landed on its back, extended its two left limbs, righted
itself and plodded off without a moment's self-pity or rage.

Or perhaps it's the face, an expression of perpetual
consideration. Or their knack for getting into difficult situations
and extricating themselves from same. Or the confidence displayed

when a turtle, knocked upside down, rocks back and forth on the ridge of its carapace until, legs stretched, claws straining, it gains sufficient leverage to right itself.

"See where the trail forks?"

She nods.

"Hang a right over the bridge. They're out there in the middle. Quite a few, actually."

Turtles drew me to swamps, specifically the one behind our house north of Stamford, Connecticut. At ten the box turtle's strange yellow markings fascinated, the wood turtle's orangey inner skin, obvious intelligence and sudden spurts of speed made them prize pets, especially for racing purposes.

It takes about an hour by foot and train to get from downtown Philadelphia to Tinicum. Tinicum—from the Indian word "tinnachkonck" meaning "next to water"—also translates (from Lenni-Lenape) as "Islands in the Marsh" and it's how the people who regularly go to the John Heinz Wildlife Refuge usually refer to it. Tinicum. It occupies 1,200 acres of woods and wetlands opposite Philadelphia International Airport.

In 15 minutes or so, the airport train from Thirtieth Street Station in West Philly will take you past the rolling Woodlands Cemetery, factories of crumbling brick, a post office warehouse, and a parking lot full of trash trucks plastered with American flag decals, before dropping you trackside at Eastwick, where a half-hour walk, uphill, past a sprawling apartment complex, awaits.

If all that sounds like a lot of work, you'll know 30 feet past the gate that it's worth it. The smell alone tells you. In May, it's pollen spilling everywhere into the air, in July, plant life brought by the season to ferment, in October the tang of burning leaf somewhere.

Mud is its base element. The dark muck of Darby Creek—wide as a river when the tide's in—joins with odors prevalent, whatever they might be.

Rivers—in this case the Delaware—and lakes spawn swamps.

Like any geological formation, a swamp—forested wetlands—is a lucky accident, a confluence of climate and geology. Don't confuse it with a marsh, though they're synonyms. If nothing else, it's spooky and appears to breathe, a quality the painter Charles Burchfield (1893-1967) captured well.

Something there is that doesn't love a swamp, and that something would be *homo sapiens*. North America includes 22 major swamps, or did, since many are reduced, via draining for agriculture, to pitiful remnants. Ohio's Great Black Swamp, which sprawled outward from opposite sides of the Maumee River, was once so vast and dense that when in 1835 Ohio and Michigan deployed their respective militias and almost went to war—the Toledo War—in a boundary dispute, the impenetrable region made actual fighting impractical, and the states chose instead to resolve their various claims without firing a shot.

Tinicum's 1,200 acres define it as small compared to, say, the Great Swamp in Morris County, New Jersey, totaling 7,768 acres, an hour's drive north. It's a dot on the map compared to the Okefenokee Swamp that straddles the Georgia/Florida state line (438,000 acres). Still, Tinicum is just about big enough to get lost in and you can get there without a car. Its sensory pleasures begin, depending on the season, with odor, that least appreciated but most erotically beguiling of the five. But then there is the visual contrast of four-lane roads and acres of public housing with what you see once past the gate, where all predictable similarity gives way to, on one side, a wall of willows and aspens flanking a deep, wide creek and, on the other, what is known as "the impoundment," a somewhat self-important term for what is, essentially, a large pond that may debatably be a lake.

A yet more noticeable contrast is auditory. Bird song replaces the automobile's honking and chuffing. The red-winged blackbirds ("*saug-ur-teeeeez!*"), robins, catbirds, and others here year-round sing individually and randomly but the ear apprehends their sounds in concert, one where the conductor has yet to tip his baton, so that, on entry, at certain times of the year, the sound resembles woodwinds tuning; bassoons, flutes and oboes testing the density of the air while a rhythm section of clicks, clacks and caws formulates the beat. All art devolves from rhythm, and so, it turns out, do Nature's glorious mysteries.

"Seen any warblers?"

Walt, white hair and mustache, lugging a camera with a foot-long lens, nods.

"It's like starting over, every spring," he says.

He's been down a few times so far this year, seen redstarts and "some yellows." Meaning yellow warblers. It's the third week of May, migration is in full swing, and I know I'm late to the game. I ask if he remembers the prothonotary warbler from last year?

"I saw it stripping moss off a tree for the nest," Walt says. "It flew back and forth, right past me. Not at me, but past me. About knee level."

Warblers. In the first few days of May, give or take a week, these small, fitful birds of many hues arrive here in groups. Species after species, mixed or in sequence, they fly at night and touch down during the day en route to more northern climes. Their visit, brief, is not exactly R&R. They'll whiz, flit and bounce branch-to-branch, gobbling caterpillars, flushing and swallowing spiders and flies until, reenergized, the trek from Central or northern South America to Canada, resumes.

The 53 species occurring north of the Mexico border—about 27 here in Pennsylvania—include such beauties as the blackburnian, the black-throated blue, the magnolia, and the wellow warbler. Even those not normally inclined to notice will feel compelled to do so should, for instance, a warbler such as the aforementioned American redstart plop down on the sidewalk, as happened once at the corner of 21st and Locust in Center City, Philadelphia.

"Oh my God!" a woman behind me exclaimed. "What *is* that bird?"

One Saturday morning last year, for instance, a Tinicum regular—he leads groups on weekend photo walks—recorded seeing

18 different warbler species in the refuge. That kind of luck comes from knowing where you need to be to see what you're looking for, and knowing what it is when you see it.

Combining black, blues, oranges, reds and especially yellow in some of its most exquisite shades and gradations, the spring finery of male warblers shows us Nature thinking out loud and in color. You might see warblers in the fall, as they stagger back south to escape the northern winter, but the whole vibe's different then. The males, their vanity in tatters along with their finery, don't care much who's looking, for how long or why. In the spring they're horny, and horny means frisky. In the fall, they give every appearance of exhaustion. A posse of about 20 black-and-white warblers touched down in the old Pine Street churchyard where I was sitting one September afternoon. One was so whipped that he or she—they're one of the few warbler species in which the genders are nearly indistinguishable—alighted at the base of a crabapple and for about 5 minutes just stayed put, turning every now and then to regard with weariness the primate on the bench ten feet away.

Spring is when to see them. Their ground time—three or four weeks— is brief, and they're not easily observed. Bird people need not only knowledge and lucky weather but practiced binocular skills. Warblers move at a tempo midway between Frantic and Frenzied. They're like hyperactive kids without Ritalin. With a lifespan short even by bird standards (three to six years, depending on species) they don't waste time for the simple reason that there's none to waste.

So, while a snooty robin pauses to indignantly denounce your presence to all avian beings in the vicinity, a blue jay jeers from a low branch, a crow responds with a cranky avian expletive, warblers dart, disappear, reappear, land and less than a second later have moved yet again. They're not in proximity to our world long enough to notice much, let alone comment on, its comings and goings.

If anecdotal evidence suggests that every year there seem to be fewer, scientific research backs it up. In 2014, ornithologists working with the North American Bird Conservation Initiative identified 33 common bird species as "in steep decline." The list included the Cape May warbler, the blackpoll warbler and Wilson's warbler. The draining and disappearance of swamps is one big reason.

"I remember 40 years ago, when spring came, you'd see all these birds, these warblers, right in your back yard," Suzanne, a woman I encountered on the trail said to me, a few years back. She said it ruefully, letting her tone and the silence that followed imply what we both knew.

That said, there are still species like the yellow warbler and the magnolia warbler that you wouldn't have much trouble finding.

The prothonotary warbler? Unlikely. At least not in Pennsylvania.

One April a few years back someone posted a photograph of a male prothonotary warbler on the Facebook page of the John Heinz Wildlife Refuge group. Weeks later, four shots of the same bird appeared, with directions to the place where it had been spotted.

Many in the Facebook group of amateur naturalists and swamp lovers had never seen a prothonotary warbler. A few weeks later, its location had been pinpointed.

"Prothonotary warbler at the refuge!" reads a June 18 post, with photo. In close-up it looked like a fat fist of buttery feathers with lineal black accents and obsidian eyes.

"Who can get us a photo of his potential mate?????" someone demanded.

"I think at this point she is sitting on eggs," someone else wrote back. "The male was bringing nest material to the nest on Saturday. It seemed like a drop off as he didn't stay more than a few seconds."

If the bird in the photographs seems nervous, even wary, it may be his overnight Tinicum celebrity. If a creature several thousand times your size decided to follow you around pointing a camera at you, you'd be a bit rattled too.

And if you're wondering about the name "prothonotary," it is an odd one. Most warblers have names describing what they look like. The black-throated blue warbler, the chestnut-sided warbler, etc. Some take their name from behavior. The hermit warbler, for instance, a West Coast bird, for its shyness, or the worm-eating warbler for what's on its menu.

Prothonotary? It isn't even easy to say. Most people find those five rolling syllables something of a tongue twister.

The word originates in Greek (*protonotarius*, for "first scribe") then carries over into Medieval Latin. Notables of the Catholic church, the dominant institution of Europe's Middle Ages, not only wielded life and death power, but were, somewhat like horny male birds, prone to strut their stuff. *Protonotaries apostolic* were the highest class of Monsignor, with robes suitable to the dignity of their position. Bright yellow ones. The legend goes that French people who first began arriving on the Gulf Coast in 1699 soon noticed a bright, bouncing yellow bird, at times almost orange, whizzing around the swamps and bayous, and noting the resemblance between its plumage and the official robes worn by the *protonotarius*, or scribe, in ecclesiastical courts, awarded it the name. Though not everyone agrees on the name's origin.

The prothonotary warbler's egg yolk head, breast and belly makes you think about yellow. Yellow, says a website on color psychology," sits between orange and green on the color wheel. Being associated with the sun, it stands for optimism, joy, enlightenment, but also for duplicity, cowardice, betrayal. But what does it signify? That's something painters consider as they're feeling their way toward the composition of an image. Yellow's a color with connotations sometimes negative. Yellow fever. Yellow-bellied. Jaundice. CAUTION.

The prothonotary warbler's yellow is on the warmth, joy, and cheer side. And because juxtaposition is the device Nature uses to heighten color's effect, the gold head sets off a black bill the slightest bit longer than scale would seem to justify and molded to a point with a bit of a hook on the upper mandible, used to probe tree bark and other insect hideaways. The eye, blacker than a cave, would seem to belong more rightly to the insect world with which, given its diet, it bears a symbiotic relationship.

I thought I'd seen a prothonotary warbler once before. So certain was I that I soon fell to bragging about it. But looking at the Facebook pictures, I knew whatever I'd seen was not that warbler. When you see it, you see it. It can't be anything else.

Sometimes "seeing" a bird you want to see is more desire than valid observation. Wishful thinking can turn a pileated woodpecker (magnificent but common) into the superficially similar ivory-billed woodpecker (close to extinct, if not gone altogether), which is why a photograph, a video, a recording, feathers or other proof (at least two) are required to make any claim of a spotting credible.

No, I admitted to myself, I had in my eagerness likely mistaken a yellow warbler for a prothonotary warbler. But now one was two strolls and a train ride away. Still, the thought of that stray that landed in New York's Central Park about a decade or so back and, within a day or two, found itself followed tree-to-tree by several thousand human onlookers, did not appeal. Under those circumstances, looking at a bird is more like a sporting event or the French Revolution than a moment of intimate transcendence. I resolved to wait until the prothonotary warbler hysteria blew over before going back to the swamp for another look. Four days later, at 7 in the morning on a Saturday, I'm on the train, headed for Tinicum.

The trail into the woods starts on a dusty gravel road wrapping halfway around the 145-acre impoundment.

"It's about a quarter mile down the road," said one of two women, in boots, vests and binoculars. "Where the creek cuts over to the pond. You'll see nest boxes. He might be flying around. I saw him yesterday and last week. I was over there this morning, but I didn't see him."

There was the wooden nesting box, presumably for tree or barn swallows, planted on a pole in the water. I surveyed the bushes along the bank for movement.

"If you're looking for the prothonotary warbler, it just flew over there toward the observation deck," a man said, folding up the tripod of his spotter scope. I walked over and looked. Nothing. I came back. He was gone but a guy and a girl with lifted binoculars were pointing to the understory opposite. Something vividly yellow bobbed, bush to bush. Every now and then it snatched a piece of straw and made for the nest box or leaned back to release a stream of notes.

A beautiful bird going about the morning of its day seduces us much like a great painting will. Take Juan Gris' "The Checkerboard," in the Art Institute of Chicago. You're strolling through the galleries for the first time. You notice it immediately. A glance morphs into the decision to sit down. Soon the geometric arrangement of board, table and newspaper becomes evident; then a logic underlying the palette choice of green, black and brown. Your watch says 15 minutes have passed. You rise and rush to catch up with your friends. Somehow the painting calls you back. An hour later you're on the same bench. What are those two blue triangles doing there? Why is the heart of the picture framed in white, chalk-like lines? You eat lunch and return. Now the geometric pieces of the checkerboard have a shadow, which is black relative to the shadow of the table. Each time you look, a great picture relinquishes some portion of its mystery while promising that much more.

With a bird, the mystery is all behavior, often repeated, sometimes unique to that species. You could observe it for a few minutes and add the name to a life list. Or you could watch it feed, fetch nest materials, drive off competitors, warble. It's not only part of the swamp, it is the swamp.

Soon the couple left, and I was alone with my quarry. The bird landed repeatedly on the stalk of a lily pad, disappeared into thickets on the opposite bank, returned to catch its breath on a weathered feeder planted in the water. At one point it took off like a shot and swept right past my head. He was making little effort to avoid people.

There came moments when his appearance on a dead stick, say, brought him fully into view. He groomed himself, presumably for lice. A mother wood duck with a passel of ducklings sailed past and rounded the bank. I watched the nesting box, waiting for the female to emerge. Nothing. No matter. I could add prothonotary warbler to my "Life List," if I ever bother keeping one.

Ordinarily, Delaware (state) is about as far north as this species gets, though they have been seen even farther north still, like New York City's visitor. Was the auriferous interloper merely looking to break free of the flock, stake out a big, gorgeous swampy woodland he wouldn't have to share with others of his kind? Or, lacking migratory experience, did he follow the Delaware (river) too far, make a wrong turn at the Schuylkill and blunder on into Tinicum, assuming, in time, some female of the species would follow?

Could it be that global warming—where north is the new south and south is the new Sahara—has advanced the northern limits of its range?

Daily the parking lot filled. Bird People will ford freezing rivers, scale high mountains or divorce attractive spouses to get a glimpse of a species they've never seen.

This bird, though, the prothonotary warbler, holds observers in thrall. Even among the jeweled luminaries of the warbler clan it is, more than any, gorgeous, regal and a tad exotic.

Fascination with just this bird started the process that eventually landed Alger Hiss in the slammer. In 1948, House Un-American Activities Committee investigators, led by Congressman Richard Nixon of California, were looking to "expose" the ex-State Department (under Roosevelt) official as a clandestine Communist Party member who'd been passing state secrets to the USSR through couriers to Soviet embassy officials. Whitaker Chambers, an ex-Communist Party activist turned professional apostate turned stool pigeon turned perjurer, accused Hiss before the committee in closed session, then publicly. Hiss sued for libel, denying he'd ever known Chambers. Since the supposed espionage had taken place in the '30s, the statute of limitations ruled out charges. But the famously vindictive Nixon was not about to let Hiss slip away. HUAC set out to catch him lying under oath, to obtain a perjury indictment. To do that, they needed to be sure Chambers knew Hiss.

As the two traded testimony, HUAC investigators behind the scenes quizzed Chambers about any hobbies Hiss might have had. Hiss, Chambers informed them, was a "bird observer." Asked for details, he told them that Hiss had once expressed great pleasure on seeing a prothonotary warbler in some Maryland woods.

"Is your wife interested in ornithology?" Nixon asked Hiss.

"My wife is interested in ornithology, as I am, through my interest," Hiss replied. "Maybe I am using too big a word to say ornithologist because I am pretty amateur, but I have been interested in it since I was in Boston. I think anyone who knows me would know that."

Committee member John McDowell (R, PA), also a bird observer, immediately asked Hiss if he'd ever seen a prothonotary warbler? Without thinking, the suddenly enthused Hiss stepped in it:

"I have, right here on the Potomac."

McDowell responded by saying that he'd seen one in Arlington, Virginia.

"They come back and nest in those swamps," Hiss said. "Beautiful yellow head, a gorgeous bird."

After one hung jury, the government, at a second trial, managed to convict Hiss of perjury. He served 44 months in the Federal penitentiary at Lewisburg, Pennsylvania. He was released November 27, 1954, age 50 and died at 92, insisting on his innocence and still fascinated by birds.

When most people hear the word "swamp," they imagine squishy leeches and/or a sleepy-looking alligator ready to roar forward and drag them into the deep. If they've ever spent time in a swamp they might think of big, tobacco-like skunk cabbage leaves which, when torn, smell like a loaded ashtray doused with perfume. They imagine spongy, moss-covered islands rife with the treachery of a misplaced step that results—*aghhhhh!*—in tumbling into the kind of black muck bath you'd pay big dollars to take in, say, Calistoga, California, where the mud, of course, would be heated, and an attendant, when signaled, would push a drink with a straw in it right at your mouth.

Let the metaphors begin. Swamp = Nature at her most treacherous, discomforting or out-of-control. Sooner or later we're all overwhelmed by the multiple demands of work. I.e., swamped. "Draining the swamp," originally an anti-capitalist term, is co-opted by Ronald Reagan's speechwriters into an American conservative crowd-pleaser implying that those in Federal employ are just so many frogs and mosquitoes. Every synonym for the word—bog, slough, swale, morass, and quagmire—sounds like somewhere you wouldn't want to be. Try telling someone you're planning to spend the afternoon, or a week, in a swamp. They'll look at you like you've neglected to trim your nostril hairs for a decade.

Folk singer Peter Stampfel wrote a song called "Romping Through The Swamp," which fellow folk artist Dave Van Ronk recorded on his 1967 album, *Dave Van Ronk and the Hudson Dusters*. It's classic swamp-as-metaphor but put to opposite political purpose.

Critics, beginning with those journalists who'd been to Viet Nam and seen the corruption that surrounded a savage civil war along with the utter lack of any discernable purpose for American involvement, apart from imperial prerogative, reached into the bag of swamp synonyms for a suitable symbol: *the quagmire*.

A quagmire, by its second definition, is a predicament; it's also (the first) a swamp you're stuck in. Eventually, beginning with David Halberstam's *Vietnam, The Making of a Quagmire*, the "quagmire theory" developed to explain the war. American entry into Viet Nam's civil war began in the early '60s, and by 1967 it was clear to many that only the limitless flow of American money and men kept the conflict going. No political solution was sought, so long as it looked possible for the U.S. to, per Curtis LeMay's avowed promise, "bomb them back into the Stone Age" at some point. Senior commander William Westmoreland had returned from a tour of Viet Nam in 1967 predicting that the war would soon be over. Westmoreland said he could see the "light at the end of the tunnel." No matter. By then, plenty weren't buying it:

Throw away your pomp
Romping through the swamp
Romping through the swamp in the month of May
Wading through the slimy ooze
You can drive away your blues
Romping through the swamp

The lyrics work familiar tropes: ooze, goo, mud, alligators, slime, and quagmire. It all seems suitably silly until you hear bombs whistling through the air, then exploding, while Van Ronk's cheery growl belts out the refrain.

Of course, he was preaching to a choir of fellow folkies but the song's fun anyway, agit prop that evinces not so much outrage as absurdity. Young people in America used to believe that if government officials and/or the general populace could only be made to understand the folly of bad policy, the policy would change. Historians understand that policy changes only at the point where it becomes untenable or politically inconvenient.

Mud, snakes and bugs are essential to a swamp. But to those who choose to go there, the sensual discomfort of, say, a forearm branded by nettles, the ripped skin and trickling blood that results when you wander into a brier patch, or the distinctly unpleasant surprise of discovering a fat gray tick nestled in your groin a day or two after visiting, etc. etc., to say nothing of tripping over a tree root and landing in murky swamp water, are inconvenient but finally minor matters.

In April of 1773, the Colonial-era naturalist William Bartram departed Philadelphia by boat "to search the Floridas," which he did, at least some of "them," from March to November of 1774, recording various "vegetable productions" and other subjects in a report now known as Bartram's *Travels* but published then in an edition of 1,000 as *Travels Through North and South Carolina, Georgia, East and West Florida*.17 Among subscribers to the second edition: President George Washington, Vice President John Adams, and Secretary of State Thomas Jefferson.

Whatever dangers or inconveniences got in his way—alligators trying to topple his canoe, for instance, or bears stealing the trout he's set aside for dinner—you can tell by the tone of the writing that Bartram's having an amazing time. His enchantment in no way interferes with his efforts to record—via writing and drawing—all he encountered, which, in Florida, included a good many swamps. It seems like half the place was a swamp. At least then.

I first ventured into a swamp at 8, about 40 years before I ever heard of William Bartram and visited his father John's house here in Philadelphia. This one consisted of maybe 75 acres and was (and is) owned by the Stamford Museum and Nature Center, in Connecticut. It bordered our back yard. This wooded morass proved for more interesting than math class, religious dogma, television, or team sports. I explored it daily, usually in the company of the family dog, a lab named Amos.

I did not go unarmed. Buckled at the waist, a pair of silver cap guns sheathed in a cheap black holster belt, a parental birthday gift, provided fallback protection should water snakes (vicious when disturbed) or other creatures prove unruly. I carried my guns with me until, one day, a false step into the muck sent this otherwise intrepid explorer tumbling into a pool lined with black mud and decayed leaves. Off and away slipped my six-shooters. I pleaded for replacements but the answer, my father informed me, was no.

"That's coming out of your allowance."

One Saturday morning months later, I'm in the front yard with Dad raking leaves. I should say that I was raking, and my father was directing the raking. He's hollering something about sticks that had been left on the ground or leaf piles needing to be bagged etc. when Amos comes trotting down the driveway.

"What's that goddamned dog got in its mouth?"

One gun, gone. The other, mud caked, poked from the holster. It was covered with dried mud and literally crumbling. Amos carried it to the end of the drive, set it down in front of the garage and wagged his tail.

A swamp is an ecosystem of evident complexity and richness, the place where woods and water overlap to make of the shaded zone between a third and different kind of environment. You get the sense Bartram knew he'd landed, snakes and all, in a place as much like Eden as anywhere he was ever likely to get.

Most Tinicum visitors come to race-walk, jog, ride mountain bikes or fish for things that look prehistoric and which signs warn are toxic to eat. It's just somewhere else to go. Then there's the minority. For instance, the person I encountered after a long morning's walk around the impoundment, in July, with my buddy, Cort. After four hours strolling through woods and swamp, we were running low on gossip and snacks when we encountered a wraith-like being with dark, curly hair pulled back behind the ears. Sharon.

"Seen anything?" I said.

"Juvenile orioles," she said.

When you run into fellow—what to call them, bird observers? forest creatures?—the conversation always sounds like it's taking place between allies fighting on the same side of a war. A few more questions get Sharon talking about the rest of spring's list. Warblers top it. She tells us spring's weather caused warbler migrations to overlap this year. The different species piled in on top of each other like out-of-state relatives squabbling about sleeping arrangements at a family reunion. This, she says, gave her the opportunity to see some she'd never seen. She mentions the Canada warbler, Tennessee warbler, and townsend's warbler. None of the three are on the Life List I don't keep but, no matter, I'm teal with envy.

Suddenly Sharon wants to know whether we've ever wondered why there are no muskrats in the impoundment. Or Tinicum? She pauses.

"Minks!"

As she explains how minks make mincemeat of muskrats, her eyes blaze with the ferocity of a muscalid loosed in a henhouse.

I tell her that when I was nine, I encountered a mink in a zoo cage. Shaped like a stuffed kneesock, the creature loped, sniffed and whisker-twitched behind its mesh wall. For pure nervousness, it has any warbler beat. A sign: DO NOT PUT FINGERS IN MINK CAGE.

I pushed the tip of my index between wires. It took two fat wads of paper towels and 30 minutes to stop the bleeding.

In 1998, English animal rights activists snuck into a fur farm in Staffordshire. Using bolt cutters, they released 8,000 minks into the countryside. "All I could see were thousands and thousands of mink pouring out on to the road," *Guardian* correspondent Paul Brown quoted a local woman, Sheila Keeling, as saying. "It was the amount that was so frightening."

Sharon points out the site of a former saw-whet owl nest. Saw-whets are one of the smallest owls. An ability to remain motionless rather than fly off once alarmed often has them hiding in plain sight. One concealed in a fresh-cut and newly wrapped Christmas tree traveled 140 miles from upstate New York to New York City inside the Norway Spruce destined to be that year's Christmas Tree in Rockefeller Plaza. It arrived after three days, hungry and dehydrated. The owl survived.

Sharon tells us winter is her favorite time in Tinicum. That may seem strange. What goes on in a frozen waste? Dry leaves crackle with each step. Ash and willow creak and sway. Paw prints on snow offer evidence that, far from disappearing, all sorts of creatures abound despite cold temperatures. The demeanor of year-round standbys—woodpeckers, chickadees, mallards, scolding and self-righteous robins—resembles that of resort town residents watching the tourists pack up and go.

"I owe my sanity to this place," Sharon says. Her sentence has the force of declaration and the strangeness of non sequitur, and she makes it just before turning right onto another trail to disappear.

Something unfortunate happened with the prothonotary warbler the year it arrived in Tinicum. Let's call it a personality change. We watched the bird morph from this bright gold speck foraging in thickets to the bipolar neighbor you hope you never have. "The Tree Swallows are trying to care for their chicks and the warbler keeps interfering," wrote one Pamela Dimeler, in a statement accompanying the video she posted on Facebook. "We are hoping for successful nesting this season for the prothonotary warblers."

That was not to be. Moreover, the feud with the swallows got nastier. On July 9, 2017, on the Facebook site of John Heinz Wildlife Refuge, Scott Kemper posted five photos of the furious prothonotary descending on one of the tree boxes planted in mid-muck. The last ass-kicking shot showed him knocking two tree swallows off their perch with feathery judo jabs.

When male prothonotary warblers engage in nest building, they're not actually nest building. They're pretending to. It's a signal to nearby females that they're ready to mate.

Once hitched, it's the female who builds the working nest and sits on the eggs. The male's nest is a sop. Once mated, he may even build a few more as a decoy to distract potential predators. This one flew around, tussling with anybody that got in his way. Once he whizzed by, two or three inches past my shoulder. The preening and singing ceased. There was only he, the golden robed one, an embittered bachelor. Until one day he flew away.

Having circumvented the impoundment, the column in search of turtles marches up the trail. They halt. They're distracted, but excited. I ask the woman in the orange sweatshirt if they'd found the turtles. She says they'd seen a lot, but nobody knew what kind.

"Probably painted turtles and red-eared sliders," I say.

The kids spot more turtles in the Darby Creek on the other side of the trail and charge, screaming, in the direction of the bank.

Turtles scramble off rocks and logs.

"Are there snapping turtles?"

"You usually won't see them sunning. They stay in the water till they're ready to mate. Then they crawl around looking for somewhere to drop the eggs."

"You should be a guide here," she says.

She summons her charges and the column moves out.

In my late teens, I considered becoming a herpetologist. It's occurred to me since that it's fortunate I did not, since that would've meant spending a professional career studying species steadily erased by habitat destruction and the ravages of a warming climate. Now, like most of us, I take what I can get.

It was a good day but maybe that isn't saying so much since it's hard to have a bad day in Tinicum, or anywhere that contains a swamp. Middle age brings with it the discomfiting realization that bad days will soon outnumber good until, when you're undeniably decrepit, the good days are few enough. There's only so much you can do to hold off the inevitable health problems. Over morale, or spirit, you have far more control. I figured I was able to at least catch the tail end of the warbler migration. A stranger named Chuck, 60ish, told me the migration had a week left at most. Maybe.

"Blackpolls bringin' up the rear," he said. That very morning he'd heard them singing and "seen two females." I hoped he was wrong but at just that moment we both caught a flicker of movement in a bush 30 feet away and both turned and aimed our binoculars.

"Warbler?"

"That's no warbler, that's a yellow-throated vireo," declared Chuck.

Another bird for the Life List I don't keep.

At 12 there was nowhere as exciting as a swamp. And that was not just for the birds, bugs, reptiles, or mammals but for the place that contained them. By then I knew its details, every acre, including of course the location of various islets—a favorite William Bartram word—those mossy pearls of land with a tree, maybe, enveloped by opposite halves of a clear-flowing stream, where, like the painter Charles Burchfield, I would "divest myself of all my clothing" (that from his *Journals*) and the feeling of nakedness outdoors, one wholly different from, say, scampering around the bedroom in undies, was its own untoward joy. Into the stream I went. It was never deeper than four feet, so I soon emerged, scrambling onto some arm-thick root, for the pleasure of allowing the sun and wind to dry my body. I remember thinking, at one point: what if someone, somehow, happens along? But then I thought about what it would take for a person to navigate the thickets and streams, the meadows of muck lush with clumps of iris, ferns, or skunk cabbage. To do that you would have to want to. Mere curiosity was not enough to prompt a sweaty pricker-piercing, nettle-stinging expedition of that sort and if, I thought, as the mind began to assemble a rationale for the sex I would have to wait a few long years to have, to taste, to lose myself in, if such a person by some chance did appear, then what might happen? And with that thought, my "member" (curious word, member of what exactly?) swelled to the size and firmness of a ripe stick. Now what?

A decade later other venues—bars, concert halls, strange beds where I carried abandon to delicious extremes—took its place. All that got stale. Swamps never have, never will. Because a swamp consists of water and trees, is what Whitman (fond of clandestine nudity himself) called "the produced babe of the vegetation," because swamps constitute an organism, a universe made up of other organisms, a universe where all within it will pulse and breathe continuously and in ways vivid enough for the senses to apprehend. For this simple reason we see in what they are, briefly or under study, time moving past, sometimes at a rush, at other moments sluggishly, but always mortal, a feeling that can't help but inspire another, which is helplessness and finally, dread. Take the water away, say by draining, and the swamp immediately morphs into something other than it is or was. A meadow, say, or corn fields. Which came close to happening to the Okefenokee Swamp.

But though it is readily apprehended by the senses, a swamp

presents itself as something so wholly unfamiliar as to make it less than tempting to most artists. The pastoral tradition excludes it; painters and even poets typically ignore what goes on there, unless it's something like Mary Oliver's poem "Skunk Cabbage," for instance:

> ...*Appalling its rough*
> *green caves, and the thought*
> *of the thick root nested below, stubborn*
> *and powerful as instinct!*

its sensuality mostly on the surface, its message proclaimed in an exclamation point.

To get the solid sense of a swamp artistically depicted, little surpasses Burchfield's watercolors. In the series "Heat Waves in a Swamp," the Buffalo, NY, master produced dozens of pictures that capture both the Carboniferous feeling there—would you be surprised if a dragonfly the size of a hawk landed nearby?— and the concomitant moments, a Burchfield favorite, of the sun overwhelming a tree or cloud to flood the image with light and make everything vibrate with energy. Even if we stick to skunk cabbage this artist, the Blake of Buffalo, gives us upturned, purplish whorls pushing up through cold mud—their first phase—the tips narrowing to a nail point, the dark flesh blackening as it recedes into the little chamber that houses the plant's sexual equipment.

By the time those purple nubs sprout and unfold from their coils into large, flappy leaves, the rest of the joint is humming right along with them. The horny amphibious baying of Spring Peepers drowns an evening's silence but for swamp-lovers there's nothing like that one night of the year when spotted salamanders crawl from the woods toward the nearest water to mate and lay eggs. They leave behind, under its surface, gelatinous sacks cemented to twigs and rocks. You'd be fortunate to see the survivors of this ritual in the early morning, which I did en route to the bus stop—black with dots of cool sulfur—moist and squiggling, dragging their bodies back to from where they came, and near them those less fortunate, flattened by early morning tires.

But then there are the turtles. If all those kids want to do is see turtles, that strikes me as a thoroughly admirable ambition. Who could resist its charms when water and woods combine to make of a swamp and its pond a turtle heaven, if only for the sheer number of species you might see: mud, musk, map, spotted, painted turtles and sliders, snappers and soft shells, with the occasional land turtles— box turtles and wood turtles—occasionally slogging through.

No doubt some people find all this tedious. If you don't know what you're seeing, it all seems the same. Finding your way inside any body of knowledge requires an entry point. Direct the attention and it will happen. It might be action—two big-ass snapping turtles, gripped plastron to plastron and spinning in the water, making testudine whoopee—would throw a ray of light inside even the most calcified consciousness. Or it may be mere beauty taking us by surprise. Say, for instance, the sight, somewhere in the wood at a swamp's edges, of dogwood blooming not white but pink. Who knew?

WILD CHILDREN, SCREAMING MOMMY

On July 11, 1959, my mother wrote the following in her diary: "Usual day. Wild children, screaming Mommy."

We lived in Dallas then. In addition to minding five kids, ages four to ten, she's packing and prepping for a move to Connecticut. Fast forward five weeks. The propeller plane flight from Dallas to Idlewild, now John F. Kennedy International Airport, seemed endless. Engines deafened. Barf bags were distributed. Now, after a similarly tedious taxi ride from Queens, we stare from an upper floor of the Roger Smith Hotel on 47th and Lexington, where we're to live for the few weeks it will take the builder to complete the house in North Stamford. On September 2, 1959, settled in at last, she records "ironing and sorting school clothes."

I discovered the diary stashed under scrapbooks at the bottom of a box a dozen years after her death. Three hundred and sixty-five pages, each day of the year centered at the top, dates running down the left-hand margin, all of it secured in a binder covered in white faux leather. A few lines in red ball point, more in turquoise, most in blue.

I recognized the forcefully curled script. I glanced at it once or twice. What could be in there that I didn't already know? Should I chuck it? I'd stumbled on the diary because I was moving, and I was at that stage of moving where you're ready to dispose of everything but your own birth certificate.

I read a line. I read a few more. Then a page. The dates begin in 1938. Age 15. A hit-or-miss effort. By 1949, three years after she'd married and the same year she first gave birth, she's writing one line each day. One line and rarely more.

People confuse journal and diary in the same way they confuse envy and jealousy. The terms equate in some ways, yet differ substantially. The distinction centers on frequency and discretion. Writers pen journal entries when the spirit moves. Many create journals with an eye on eventual publication. Example: *The Journals of Andre Gide*. The diarist is another matter. Daily and in secret the diarist (from *diarium*, Latin for day) inscribes unguarded thoughts and feelings. She conceals her manuscript where none would think to look. Diaries tend to surface posthumously. Examples: *The Diary of Anne Frank. The Diary of Virginia Woolf.* My mother hid hers well enough that a houseful of kids given to eavesdropping on phone calls, reading each other's mail, and ransacking parental drawers, never found it.

It took two days to read. She writes about relatives and friends, projects, and ("P.G.," her euphemism) pregnancies, worries and longings. Her world, inner and outer, notated as the thought came. Housework overshadows much else. Example, October 20, 1964: "Hard at washing - nine loads today." She balances drudgery, ongoing, against what she feels, which is, at different times, rage, joy, loneliness, exasperation, and ardor. Limiting herself to a line a day precludes digression or analysis. Forget padding. With one sentence, you get right to the point. Even news items rarely gain notice. One of two is November 22, 1963, where she and my father are off on a much-needed vacation to Skytop Lodge, in the Poconos. "Just resting & resting - President Kennedy assassinated." The other, earlier, records her attendance at a Truman rally.

It takes a dozen or so pages to grasp the diary's practical purpose. She's using it to modify, adjust or direct her own attitude, to gain the right emotional wavelength, as needed. And it was often needed. On May 30, 1960, for instance—Memorial Day—she writes "Bed changing - not much of a holiday really." 'No rest for the weary' becomes the tonic key. Complaints, rarely verbalized, instead find their way here. Diary as confidante and confessor. Of course, an ongoing grievance list would quickly make for tedium. She varies what she records, noting birthdays, anniversaries, vacations, visits by relatives. Away, maybe, for a mother in her 30s to reassure herself that life, in the main, is predictable, manageable, and benevolent while understanding, on some level, just how much it's not.

Why keep a diary? Because life takes us to strange places, even when we're not in motion. My mother, born Olive Gayle Brantseg in Fargo, married for love but also to get out of North Dakota. Three of her four siblings never left the place. Romance was her ticket out. The year she steps up her entries, 1946, proves significant. June 15, 1946: "Don & I wed."

Don is an Army Air Core veteran who'd trained at the base, just north of Fargo, that's now Hector International Airport. At the base, rumors flew about the "hot blonde" running the record department at Daveau's Music Store. In addition to records, Daveau's sold sheet music and instruments, with lessons offered via the "Fargo Music Conservatory" on the third floor. He came in one morning, pretending to shop for records. They marry a year later at the Cathedral of St. Mary, in Fargo, the biggest and likely the only Catholic church in the city at the time, following her obligatory conversion from Lutheranism. They move to St. Paul, where he tries his hand at commercial carpet sales.

A salesman, Arthur Miller tells us, in his most famous play, is "out there in the blue, riding on a smile and a shoeshine." Then as now, sales success can be lucrative. The problem? Commission sales impose cult-like demands on practitioners. Big ticket selling is not just a job. You build a persona. The persona thrives on assertiveness, and is "characterized by or displaying certainty, acceptance, or affirmation." Of the product or service you're selling. It's a general attitude, embracing life itself; the pervasive optimism needed to subtly deflect whatever objections a prospect might raise. Sales gurus such as Zig Ziglar argue you can't pitch what you don't believe in but, conversely, your belief imposes the moral obligation to complete the sale. Believe in your product, and you can identify and remove whatever reservations stand in the way of that prospect signing that contract. *Today*.

My father believed, for a long time anyway, in "Those Heavenly Carpets by Lee's." At the time he started working there, Lee's was the second largest seller of commercial carpet in the U.S., after Mohawk. At Lee's he racked up awards, bonuses, and promotions. Promotions meant reassignment. Between 1949 and 1959, he and my mother packed up and moved from Minnesota to Oklahoma, Oklahoma to Illinois, Illinois to Texas and finally to the Connecticut suburbs of New York. Five states in ten years. For my mother, news of each move arrives like a jolt. Jan. 13, 1952: "Chicago called – Don got job – we are moving to Oklahoma." Between sorting, wrapping, boxing, and contacting utility companies and van lines, moving requires organizational skills. Moving with kids? Yet more of them. And the kids keep coming: Donnie (1949) Debbie (1950) Judy (1951) Jimmy (1953) and Richie (1955). My mother organized the first move, in 1950, with two children, the last, in 1959, with five.

Chores, recorded here, went where she went. It isn't the menial specifics she records, it's that there are always more of them. Feb. 8, 1962: "Cleaning up the pig pen." You'd think, from reading what she's recorded, that the whole place was on the verge of falling apart. In fact, she kept it spotless. On May 23, 1963: "Usual busy day – I can't get anything done." Done as in finished. She cleans, irons, makes beds, plants shrubs, vacuums floors, tests recipes, straightens up rooms. One task struck from the list, five more take its place. When you're trying to do everything, how does anything get done?

Chalk some of it up to stoicism, the ornery stubbornness she sometimes references as *my Swede*. As in: *Don't go getting my Swede up.* This *Swede* is the stubborn, slow-to-anger side of the family originating with her grandfather, Jonas P. Johnson (1839 – 1929), who'd arrived in the U.S. in 1858, age 18, and within three years was fighting in the Union army. The Swede—meaning one righteously pissed-off Scandinavian— emerges when necessary. Which is often. The vigor required to keep going in the face of the day's multiple demands seems so big, so unyielding, so consistent, so entirely out of proportion to the reward provided, as to constitute a counterpart to the salesperson's showmanship and perseverance. These two clearly add up to determination with a dash of crazy. He's away making the money. She's home and not happy about it. Jan. 18, 1958: "Don had to fly to Kansas City for day. It's always me and the kids." Yet, like a bird selecting by instinct or experience the high-energy foods that will propel the next leg of migratory flight, my mother finds what she needs to keep going. October 24, 1951: "Thank God for knitting."

Still, time and circumstance exact their price. Read forward to back, the diary communicates the sense of someone on the edge of a breakdown she'd spent her life rehearsing but never quite brought to the stage. Even holidays frazzle. Especially holidays. She not only cooks, cleans, bakes, and decorates, but serves as mastermind, facilitator and impresario, the Sol Hurok of Christmas. This invariably leaves her "in shreds," to wit: January 1, 1965: "Ugh I'm tired - took tree down." Overseeing this brood of, by then, seven kids, plus a house and yard, encompasses everything from toilet training to carpooling, laundry to pet supervision. "A million things to do," she writes, on July 21, 1962. Tasks, as notated here—ironing, cooking, cleaning, sewing—outnumber all else. Unpaid, it goes without saying. In the face of it all, she's given to bouts of a melancholy that often shades over into fatalism. On August 8, 1964: "I wonder if I'll ever catch up."

This, her life, is multi-tasking before it had a name. It proceeds mostly without complaint. Mostly. Frustration, when expressed, took the form of head shaking, drawer slamming, great heaving sighs.

"Uh-oh, Mom's mad," someone would whisper. Meaning it was wise to stay out of her way, if not disappear altogether.

Occasionally, the Swede surfaces.

Good Good, Mert! she'd scream.

A broken snow shovel, abandoned in a snowbank. A carton of Camels, concealed behind the wheelbarrow in the garage. A turkey drumstick with a single bite from its pinkish-gray center, pushed to a remote corner of the fridge.

Who, I remember thinking, is Mert, or Murt, or Mirt?

Meret, research indicates, was the token wife given to Hapi, god of the Nile and personification of natural fertility. How my mother, who never went to college and had little time to read, might invoke this figure from Egyptian mythology, remains a puzzle. She often said or did things that seemed out of character, except that in their total want of precedent, or connective logic, or of any ability to be anticipated, they proved completely authentic. Being out of character was in character. Besides, divine assistance—Meret's or otherwise—was much needed in that household. She typically wasn't getting a lot of help from other quarters. Watching her engaged in a half-dozen projects, we kept our distance until, prompted by guilt or fear of retribution, someone would volunteer to wipe the kitchen table or empty the dishwasher.

Don't knock yourself out!

Of all her responsibilities, preparing meals delivered the least emotional return for time spent. You can get a week's worth of clean from the shower stall you just scrubbed, six months of steady foot traffic from the floor you just waxed. Ferry five kids to school, they're out of your hair for six hours. By 1966 there are 10 in the house. Cooking for 10 every night? Forget it. In the first place, it often took half an afternoon. And if, on occasion, she looked for relief, well, there was no one to hand it off to. My mother was the only person in the family, then, anyway, who knew how to do much more in a kitchen than turn the oven on. Since the reward in preparing food for others is gratitude, she probably hoped for plaudits. In that house, fishing for compliments was like tossing your line in the Dead Sea.

Marriage left her no choice but to teach herself kitchen skills.

People without the ability to combine a dozen ingredients into soup or bake a credible lasagna consider such competence frivolous right up to the moment the food arrives at the table. Then they're experts.

"These dumplings seem to need more salt."

It's right there on the table, buster.

If my father was home, my mother might bake a ham and whip up a side of mashed potatoes and gravy. Or she'd slide a raft of beef into the oven, piled with carrots and celery and drowning in Campbell's onion soup. If he wasn't, and five days out of seven he wasn't, she defaulted to something uncomplicated. TV dinners, for instance. In 1953, Swanson brothers Gilbert and W. Clarke, sons of founder Carl A. Swanson—a Swedish immigrant from Nebraska— introduced a cheap alternative to cooking. But cheap isn't always fast. In the days before microwaves became common, it took hours for those frosty rectangles to cook to some edible temperature, longer when curious hands opened the oven door every five minutes to check progress.

Christ Almighty, what are you doing? CLOSE THAT NOW!!

More often, she'd whip up something quick that could be produced in mass quantity. Swedish meatballs, fried chicken, spaghetti, scalloped potatoes, tuna casserole, and the inevitable hotdish. Hotdish—an Upper Midwest confection—can be put together out of just about anything in the refrigerator since definitions of exactly what it is vary. My mother's consisted of macaroni, canned tomatoes, ground beef, chopped onions, and an indeterminate spice or two off the rack. Of all her production line meals, the favorite was Chili Mac. Five cans of Hormel's Chili ("with beans") sitting on the kitchen counter said loud and clear what dinner would be. Heat, pour on boiled macaroni, add grated cheese.

Once or twice a month, so strapped for time or energy that even Chili Mac was pushing it, she'd load the crew into her Ford Country Squire—a truncated hearse in wood laminate, seating 9—and head for downtown. July 17, 1965: "Went to Roger Smith for dinner — busy day." This Roger Smith, the original in the (at one time) 8-unit hotel chain, opened in Stamford in 1928, added a "motor court" in the 60s and survived until demolished in 1981. We might've gone to the Parkway Diner, on High Ridge Road, and sometimes did, but the Roger Smith and its restaurant possessed a tattered elegance that put us on our best behavior, which was not, in any case, exemplary. It probably reminded my mother of the old Powers Hotel, in Fargo, built in 1914, still standing but converted to apartments. There, when both were in high school, she went to hear an older classmate, Norma Egstrom—soon to be known as Miss Peggy Lee—sing in the coffee shop.

Though we were at pains to appear civilized, it took assertiveness to manage this little posse through a meal in the dining room of a hotel. My mother let us know the outings were something of an extravagance. She also knew from experience to expect at least some kind of idiot behavior and how to put her foot down, even with the waitress tapping a pencil on the order pad.

"I'll have the surf 'n turf."

The hell you will.

"Um, in that case, I'll get the steak."

No, he's not having the steak.

"But…"

Just shut up. I said you're not getting the steak. Order something else.

The trips to the Roger Smith were infrequent enough to make them worth recording in her diary. Mostly we ate at home. A project. With seven, eight or, finally, ten, it's not just the cooking and clean-up, it's the logistics she had to manage.

"Do you eat in shifts?" a fellow fifth grader asked. She belonged to another large family—15 kids, including two sets of twins, and of course they all looked alike—and I think she was casting around for seating solutions. I said no, because our meals were consumed at a long table running nearly the length of the kitchen, with highchairs adjacent and everyone somehow squeezed in. Proximity made for wisecracks, sniping, swift unseen kicks and outbursts of parental rage, occasionally resulting in banishment. Stalin's late-night suppers in the Kremlin come to mind.

Her day's biggest challenge was to get the meal on every night.

Sometimes, pulled in other directions, utterly strapped, she'd resort to bacon-and-eggs, peanut butter-and-jelly sandwiches, or something quickly whipped up via skillet or waffle iron.

"Pancakes? For dinner?" someone would ask, spotting the pale green bowl of batter.

That's what's on the menu, buster. Take it or leave it!

Preparing the meal constituted only half the job. Managing table deportment was the other. It began with a collective Catholic mumble ("Bless us our Lord, and these thy gifts..."), with Donnie, the eldest, by then a teen, staring sullenly away. Prayers complete, reaching and grabbing—the emboldened frenzy of tourists swarming a hotel buffet—commenced. Sometimes greed prevailed over protocol, and someone lunged for a platter before prayers.

You wait for us like one pig waits for another!

The offending hand swiftly withdrawn.

Only Donnie argued. One night he ventured to baiting. We'd reached the dessert stage. He glanced at what was coming in feigned disbelief.

"Ice cream? In January?"

In an instant they were at it. Insults and accusations mounted in viciousness and intensity, until my mother reached for a glass. An instant later, milk dripped from my brother's nose and black hair. The Swede, evidently, summoned.

The compliments she managed to receive arrived as watered-down afterthoughts, manifestly obsequious, ever short on sincerity.

"Mom, this is good!"

Few as they were, and lame as they were, they nonetheless generated evident satisfaction. And nothing was more likely to produce accolades than Christmas cookies. On December 13, 1951, she's "knitting fast & furious"— Afghan after Afghan—"& making Xmas cookies." December 1, 1958: "Working on Xmas cookies — slow job." Indeed. Five days later (Dec. 5): "More Xmas cookies done — I'm sure tired."

There stands my mother's aproned form, whisking flour, salt, and baking powder into a metal bowl, emptying the mix into a separate receptacle of butter and sugar, whisking the result for a minute or two, adding milk and eggs, beating the thing some more. She kneaded all this into a formless mass, yellow-white, and rolled it out in soft, flat membranes from which an assortment of cookie cutters stamped out shapes.

Sheet after sheet was yanked from the oven and once cooled, decorated sparingly, with sanded sugar or sprinkles in red and green. Forget the gooey icing favored by some. It would've overwhelmed the subtle taste of these biscuits. Her signature confection was the Russian tea cake, with bits of ground walnut distributed through the dough, and once baked, rolled in powdered sugar.

She made no announcement before commencing this multi-day effort. Nor did she enlist assistants. The discordant bang and clang of mixing bowls and cookie sheets signaled it had started. The smell—sweet-scented and redolent of all first pleasure—dispatched an unmistakable second signal. Baking had commenced. It's difficult to say which delighted more, the dough or what the dough became when heat hit it. In the doorway, stragglers hovered.

Get your goddamned mitts out of that bowl right now or I'll slap you silly!

A dozen varieties issued. Last to go were her gingerbread men, with their bulging silver eyes. The balls rolled of mashed dates and shredded coconut similarly lingered. On the other hand, her sugar cookies in eight configurations (trees, bells, stars, angels, wreaths, canes, stockings, and the crudest approximation of a snowflake) disappeared on sight, and the Russian tea cakes were hardly out of the oven before scheming to get the lion's share began.

She extracted trays, set them to cool, layered the finished product into cans, separated the layers with sheets of waxed paper. Then came the greatest challenge: hiding them. It demanded all the thought and imagination that might be spent, say, concealing a murdered body. Slid under attic floorboards, tucked into trunks, buried in boxes beneath mounds of old toys and summer clothes, the treasure waited, only to be, like the tombs of Amenhotep or

Hatshepsut, plundered. One year on Christmas Eve several cans, retrieved from under a stack of suitcases at the bottom of a closet, contained only crumbs, crumpled paper, and gingerbread limbs.

God damn it, which one of you jackasses got into these Christmas cookies?
Silence.

Besides keeping a diary, my mother assembled 12 volumes of photos. They begin in 1946 with black-and-white prints and morph to color, in the early 60s. Like going from Kansas to Oz. The volumes look fragile yet proved sturdy. They're made to be handled and passed around. "Photo corners," tape or laminate hold the images in place. Above and below each, typed in all-caps, she pasted labels: "GAYLE IN FARGO, 1985." Etc.

In the photos my mother beams from sofa or easy chair, models a new dress, waves beside a blooming rhododendron. She appears without worry or care. What the pictures don't show is someone tucking in sheets, basting turkeys, scrubbing shower stalls, or folding ten people's clothes, hot from the dryer. Why record that? Since no one noticed how much my mother accomplished in a day, none of us had any idea how exhausting it might be nor how essential to the household she was, the pin that held this sprawling contraption together. Not much got done unless she did it.

Cleaning, for instance. My mother cleaned with concentration and organization, with buoyancy and verve. She swept and polished floors, vacuumed sofas, rubbed sinks to raw steel, washed walls, wiped down cabinets inside and out, spritzed glass with Windex, and dusted lamps and end tables with New Improved Pledge.

Jesus Jenny, if it's not one goddamned thing, it's another!
Not for her the faux cleaning that aims for an appearance of tidiness. This was the mad, Ajax-sprinkling, Easy-Off spraying, Tuffy-wielding kind, driven by fierce resolve.

The temporary nature of the result mattered not. It's cleaning-as-catharsis, all in the here and now. That bedroom, bathroom or den will soon enough return to their natural state—*Christ Almighty, look at this goddamned pigsty*! —but that's beside the point. The hard-core cleaner scours harder.

"A million things to do," she writes, on July 21, 1962. Ancillary tasks such as mending ripped clothes, hemming skirts, making curtains and drapes, shopping (school supplies, groceries, clothes), running errands, "knitting mittens" (January 4, 1959), tending the sick, these and many more appear again and again in the diary's pages. January 9, 1952: "Donnie has the flu so up most of nite."

The workload escalates over the years. Take laundry. She started out washing two people's clothes. In 1949, two becomes three. "Oh, for a drier (sp)," she writes, in 1951, at which point there are five in the family. Divine intervention—Meret's? — dispatched said dryer. No more baskets of moist shirts. No more mouthfuls of clothespins. Of course, pants and shirts require pressing and what, for sheer tedium, exceeds an afternoon at the ironing board? Fast forward fifteen years and all day long clothes whoosh through the chute on the second floor, bound for that dismal mound in the basement, a few inches higher each time she looks.

She dreams about vanishing for good. April 24, 1964: "Some days I would love to walk out of this all." Two years later, the reverie returns. She imagines her slipping away would be to our benefit. April 8, 1966: "Sometimes I feel like all would be better if I would leave."

The choice, to her, was flee or persevere. She persevered.

"Keep plugging along — no one will ever know how much," she writes, on February 2, 1966. The diaries show her soldiering on from chore to chore, crisis to crisis. A kid falls out a window and breaks an arm. Two more set the woods on fire. Feuding neighbors call the cops for "trespassing" when one of us steps on their property. Sibling squabbles erupt multiple times a day. She referees. December 2, 1958: "Richy & Jim just fight all the time."

She searches for shortcuts, efficiencies, as the path opening out of this trap. "I must try to figure out a way to get things done," she writes, on August 25, 1966. A line she could've written in 1960, even 1950, and something to serve as an epitaph on the tombstone that otherwise includes no information apart from her name and dates.

Hired help seemed the obvious way to offload. The various "cleaning ladies" my father employed over the course of 11 years, all African American, left their own large families for the day to assist her in managing this one. They stuck around for anywhere from one year to three; cooking, cleaning, and ironing for not a lot of money. Corine, in Dallas, for instance. That gentle spirit who hummed to herself while ironing, forbore while five wild white kids ran, screamed, dirtied piles of dishes and staggered into the house with muddy hair and soaked clothes after falling in the creek. Becca, who took the train in from Harlem, established her no-bullshit authority via her sometimes-bristling demeanor and the well-timed scowl. When she had an hour to spare, she prepared a pungent, tomato-strewn meatloaf we begged for.

Maids were a half-measure at best. "Not much freedom even with Corine here," my mother writes, on July 14, 1959, while packing and preparing the move to Connecticut. She longed for two days a week with assistance. It never happened. Besides which, Corine excepted, all the cleaning ladies—Dena, Pearl, Thomasina et al—sooner or later got fed up and quit.

With the older kids now anywhere from 10 to 16, another strategy deployed: enlist offspring. June 3, 1965: "These kids are going to have to help more." Requests become demands, demands dictates, dictates formally assigned chores. Basement, attic, garage, and driveway cleaning. Bathtub scrubbing. Lawn mowing. This also had its limits.

One October morning, for instance, she marched four of us to the garage, lifted rakes off the wall and distributed them like rifles to volunteers in a city under siege.

Now get out there and get busy!

Toward noon she opened the front door to a half-swept lawn and four rakes lying among piles of leaves.

God damn it! I give up!

The default solution was to expend ever more of her own time and energy, at that midpoint in life when both begin to wane. This produced the inevitable result. On Oct. 14, 1965, she writes: "I am so tired of giving to this family."

Tired is not a single, readily defined feeling-state. It's physical, mental, spiritual. "Just plain busy & tired," she writes, on July 11, 1949, with one kid in the crib and a second on the way. On April 16, 1950: "Sure am always tired."

Hers was the tired you wake up with and fall asleep to, the tired that's a second self, riding piggyback.

Tired, of course, makes for more tired. November 21, 1957: "I wish I could get over this tired feeling." Wherever she went, tired followed. "Finished wallpaper in bath - I'm tired," she writes on November 27, 1960. As the 60s wore on, with my father away, her tired is of the ready-to-drop variety. Dead tired. Dog tired. Bone tired.

It wasn't just fatigue; it was the being alone in it.

On October 11, 1954, with, at that point, four kids running, screaming, crying or in need of diaper changing, she writes: "Water in basement & nothing I can do. Always when Don's gone." Even when my father was home, there was no guaranteeing his availability. July 15, 1961: "Don golfed — I fought with kids all day." Two years later, September 8, 1963: "Don golfing — I ironed and ironed — never ends."

One afternoon, 15, my high school friends and I walk into a five-and-dime called Kresge's. A middle-aged woman, blonde, sat by herself at a far corner table. Her back was to the entrance. A white vinyl cigarette case, metal snap at the top, and a coffee cup with scarlet-smudged rim sat in front of her. She sighed, stared, tapped an ash, and blew a long column of smoke at the ceiling. It took a few seconds to realize who it was.

Nothing lifted or sustained her spirits—well, almost nothing— quite like the products of the Philip Morris Tobacco Co.

She started, in the 50s, with Commanders, the company's

signature brand. Commanders consisted of acrid leaf shreddings tucked in a paper cylinder three and a third inches long; non-filtered, mysteriously crispy, and always so dry that to slide one back and forth between thumb and index produced, in the ear, an ominous rustling sound. In the 70s she switched to Merit—Meret?— also a Philip Morris product, albeit filtered. It was one of the "light" cigarettes marketed by the world's largest seller of tobacco. "There was little evidence to suggest that filter cigarettes were any healthier than regular cigarettes, and the tobacco companies' own researchers knew this to be the case," notes Tara Parker-Pope, in "'Safer' Cigarettes: A History."

Honey, would you get me my cigarettes? They're in my purse.

Who didn't know where they were? We raided her pack when opportunity permitted, something she blithely overlooked. She bought a carton a week, stowed in a kitchen drawer. The pack-and-a-half a day went with Maxwell House coffee, until she switched to Sanka. A Philip Morris Commander also proved the perfect complement to bourbon, with 6 o'clock the official cocktail hour, at least during the diary period. Later—I'm Fast Forwarding again— cocktail hour arrived ever earlier and regardless of whether my father, a gin-and-tonic man, planned to be home. She sat at the kitchen table, sipping from a tumbler big enough to water a horse. The Texas Jigger. Her speech thickened. She'd stow sweaty highballs in cupboards for backups. On the phone she repeated herself. My father stared at the Jigger and shook his head, as if the dollar had collapsed.

Then, as abruptly as it started, it stopped. The infamous Jigger vanished. The bourbon disappeared. No Twelve Steps, no rehab, not so much as an announcement. She is possibly the only person I've known to pull this off. Nor did she ever once discuss it.

Cigarettes proved more formidable. The diary shows she quit once, but only once. March 7, 1957: "Nerves are sure shaky since I quit smoking." On March 20 of that year: "Still no cigs - hope I can keep it up." She did, for a little more than a year, then lapsed. April 18, 1958: "Started smoking again - darn it no will power."

It wasn't about will power, it was about anxiety and depression.

"At first nicotine improves mood and concentration, decreases anger and stress, relaxes muscles and reduces appetite," notes the Mental Health Foundation of the U.K. "Some people smoke as 'self-medication' to ease feelings of stress. However, research has shown that smoking actually increases anxiety and tension."

Sometimes cigarettes weren't enough. Only an afternoon nap resuscitated nerve cells stretched to the snapping point. She'd settle on the living room sofa, oblivious to all the squalling racket, close her eyes and doze. Once out, an asteroid the size of Rhode Island striking Earth couldn't wake her. She'd come to 45 minutes later, head for the kitchen, set a lighted Phillip Morris in the ashtray, empty the dishwasher, and start dinner.

For the most part, she kept her anguish concealed, understandable in a household of high-strung personalities whose kneejerk response to adversity was ridicule. There, if you tumbled off a ladder, whacked your finger with a hammer, received an electrical shock, got hit with hot grease from a pan or tripped and somersaulted down the stairs, it was funny. If you bled, broke a toe or finger, got the wind knocked out of you, or were hobbled or otherwise rendered unable to move, it was really funny. Third party accounts accomplished similar. Hearing a gleeful description of someone flying from a bicycle onto asphalt, falling backwards into a pond, swatting madly while fleeing a yellowjacket ambush—stranger, friend, or family member, it didn't matter—produced red-faced, sobbing, stomach-clutching helplessness. The tale of some poor fool slipping, sliding, grabbing for what wasn't there, flying into the air and landing, ass first, on wet ice, provided marquee entertainment. After some particularly embarrassing smash-up or spill, someone in the family would perform an impression—for example, the high school principal sailing into a snowbank—with skills such as mimicry and pantomime coming expertly into play.

In all this my mother stood as sole exception. The occasional slight shake of her head, the amused smile, indicated she couldn't believe the sort of assholes she'd raised.

You sickies!

Her nature inclined toward the sympathetic. She hosted slumber parties, baked brownies, groped and grappled her way through someone's algebra homework, and transported us to and from the homes of friends. Never late. God forbid a no-show.

Rigorously maintained calendars and schedules ensured on-time arrival at every doctor or dental appointment. Miss a birthday? Unthinkable. October 1, 1955: "Judy's birthday — she was so excited she couldn't eat." September 7, 1957: "Had Jim's party — 17 kids — need I say more?"

That fourth birthday stirs no recollection, but I can't imagine how holidays would've passed as anything other than some tedious exile except for her thought and planning. She assembled and distributed Easter baskets, organized Fourth of July beach outings, advised on and adjusted Halloween costume selections, and, on Thanksgiving, stirred and whipped, broiled and boiled, till she tottered. As the year slid toward its final month, the big one approached. Thanksgiving was only two days past when she writes, on November 24, 1962: "Did some errands — Xmas is getting closer." Two years later, November 20, 1964: "So much to do - wish Xmas were behind us."

Xmas—never referred to as anything else—doubled her obligations. December 10, 1956: "Trying to get beds changed & catch up on work." Seven years later, December 10, 1963: "So many things on my mind with Xmas." So many it daunted. On December 6, 1966, she writes: "When I think of Xmas I shudder."

Cookies, cards, decorating, shopping, wrapping, all suddenly thrown on the pile. It started months before. October 27, 1952: "Downtown doing more Xmas shopping." On the same day, in 1959: "Wrote letters - must get going on Xmas." November 2, 1953: "Dentist - lesson & downtown - did lots of Xmas shopping." November 18, 1954: "Trying to catch up on letters - wrapping Xmas gifts." November 30, 1958: "Took kids to church — worked on Xmas cards."

Each piece consumed days. December 3, 1964: "Boy I wish

Xmas were over. Don't know when I'll get done." The card project alone should've entitled her to secretarial assistance and a pension. She mailed out about 150, often more, and drew up lists with charts, snapped in a three-ring binder, to track who responded, and when. Meanwhile baking, not yet commenced, cried out for attention. Dec. 11, 1951: "Started Xmas cookies. Always something extra." When the cookies got stowed away, she drove the family to Caldor, Bloomingdale's, Brambert's 5&10 or the Stamford Record Shop to buy presents. Her own gift buying commenced in early October so that boxes bound for Texas, Minnesota, North Dakota, and points beyond could ship. Dec. 12, 1966: "Getting Xmas packages mailed – so much to do."

On December 17, 1963, my mother wrote: "There must be an easier way for Xmas." Anyone else would've converted to Islam or crawled in the deepest closet in the house and remained there till supplies ran out. The diary suggests she siphoned up energy for all this from the considerable frenzy created. December 24, 1961: "Boy these kids are wild."

Kids proved a mixed blessing. Between 1949 and 1967, dates that roughly bookend daily diary entries, my mother was pregnant ten times. She gave birth to eight: Donnie (1949), Debbie (1950), Judy (1951), Jimmy (1953), Richie (1955), Peter (1960), Stephen (1964) and Kathleen (1966). Ecstasy greeted the arrival of the first. "Donnie in playpen," she writes on May 27, 1949, not quite able to believe it. With the second-born came second thoughts. "I sure feel huge and uncomfortable," she writes, January 3, 1950. A wrenching birth followed.

She never got used to the weight and strain of pregnancy. Timing didn't help. Nativities drag on across hot summers. August 29, 1953: "Usual rough day – if only this baby would come." By the time "this baby" did—#4, me—enthusiasm gives way to anxiety, anxiety to dread. On March 9, 1955, she writes: "Am honestly afraid we might have No. 5 and I'll never survive it." This fear grows with time. July 29, 1961: "I am afraid No. 7 will be my luck – boy I don't know." A prescient thought. On Feb. 3, 1963: "Rushed to hospital – had a miscarriage."

Now 40, there was no rest for this baby machine. On August 23, 1964, again with child, she writes: "Boy I never want to be pregnant again." A week passes. September 3, 1964: "Just struggling along. Seems like I've been P.G. forever." Five weeks later, it's all she can think about. October 12, 1964: "Golly I wish it were over." On October 31, 1964, it is. She gives birth to a 7-pound, 14 oz. boy. Six months after that, it resumes. "No doubt in my mind that I am P.G. again," she writes, in May of 1965.

Incaution? Erotic excess? Apparently not. My father, an active Catholic, waved away her plea for "family planning," i.e., abstinence during the fertility phase. May 13, 1965: "Wish I could make Don see things my way – but it is too late now!"

It was. The baby arrives February 5, 1966. To the entry on that event, she appends a sarcastic note. "Boy I feel weak – Kathleen born at 5:29 – 7 lbs. 9 oz. Whee."

A year later, my father's notified he's being transferred. This time to Detroit. Why move a 50-year-old man with a family of ten? No one asks. My mother takes it in stride. March 21, 1967: "What with moving – I have so much to get at." A day later, March 22, 1967, she's pregnant and appalled. "I feel so horrible – Dear God it can't be," she writes. Two days after that, March 24, 1967, hers is the desperation of not knowing who to turn to: "Went to Stations [of the Cross] – I must be P.G. Lord I don't know what to do." A few months later, May 27, 1967, she announces her situation to the family: "Had to tell kids I was P.G. — mixed emotions."

Why had all this not ended years before, if only out of concern for her physical and emotional state? On June 16, 1967, she writes: "Just know something is wrong with this pregnancy." On June 20, 1967: "Went to the hospital about 7:30 — lost the baby — such an ordeal."

She sews, gardens, occasionally finishes reading a book. She teaches herself guitar. These, taken together, consume a small fraction of the time given to housework and child-rearing. Then, on March 13, 1963, something different pops up. "Just never stops here – had 2ⁿᵈ art lesson," she writes. Two months later (May 6, 1963): "Changing beds – worked some on my art."

The paint box I recall as pigment-splotched outside, tidy within. The canvasses she produced, invariably student work. She needed to learn. "Started a painting but didn't get far," she writes on Feb. 27, 1964. A year later, January 20, 1965, she begins again: "Started on art class with Mr. Otto."

Time holds her back. More specifically, the lack of it. A month into Otto's classes, Feb. 24, 1965, she jots down the following: "Not much time to paint for art class." To work, think, concentrate, make and absorb mistakes, requires hours, mornings, afternoons. To develop proficiency, years. In March of 1964, she longs for time to paint. Ten months later, January 11, 1965, in the run-up to Otto's class, she writes: "Wish I had time to do some oil painting." On Feb. 2, 1965, her diary reads: "Worked on my painting – wish I had more time for it." Three weeks later, Feb. 24, 1965: "Not much time to paint for art class."

The last mention of painting comes six months later. On August 11, 1966: "Spent day painting & completed a picture – loved doing it." Then this passion vanishes as completely as if it had never materialized.

She longed for quiet, to relax somewhere. "If I could only have a day to call my own," she writes, on July 22, 1961. She also wanted my father home, to help. "Don out again – sometimes I get tired of being alone so much," she writes, July 7, 1953. After a while her loneliness feels, to this reader, like a slap. Stuck in a crowd of kids, she couldn't wait to get us out of her hair. Sept. 1, 1959: "Won't be long – the kids will be in school." Aug. 28, 1962: "Rainy day – be glad when school starts." Aug. 24, 1965: "Boy this is a wild household –

oh for school."

Only my father could've relieved it. "Hate when Don's gone – so lonely in evenings," she writes, June 11, 1963. She waited near the phone. "Thought sure Don would call tonight," she writes, on December 3, 1956. He arrived, to her, like an emotional rescue expedition. January 12, 1959: "So excited about Don coming home – couldn't sleep."

In the 60s, as he moved ever higher through management, his responsibilities increased. For a while my father came home every other weekend. Then, since he spent so much time in New York City, he and two other executives arranged to share an apartment there. "Hate weekends alone – Don called," she writes, January 7, 1962, like someone with all the time in the world and no time at all.

The diary begins to falter in the mid-60s. June 23, 1966: "Just too busy to keep up with diary." She's reprioritizing an attention already pulled in too many other directions. Entries are already intermittent by the time we arrive in Detroit in 1967—a move the whole family dreaded. Our arrival coincides within a day or two of the rioting that began July 23, 1967. The slow-motion plumes of smoke rising over Woodward Ave. in the Motor City seem, in retrospect, a portent. Two more moves follow. A decade later, financial reverses—my father fired; their savings obliterated in a disastrous business venture—compel my mother, mid-50s, to return to work. For minimum wage, she stocks shelves and operates the register at a Hallmark card store in Wayne, PA. Within a year she was running it.

The end happened the way ends do. One day, everything changed. The 30-something doctor who'd taken over the practice of a guy she'd been seeing for decades asks my mother how much she smokes. She tries to laugh it off. The X-rays he orders show jagged lines crisscrossing the lungs. Emphysema. What it didn't show was the mass forming on her kidney. She stopped smoking that day. Daily rounds of medical appointments commenced. It was the first week of December.

I'm so far behind, she said, as we drove to one of them. *I haven't even started the Christmas cookies yet.*

What I hadn't figured out was that she possessed neither the stamina nor the strength to stand for the hours it'd take to pull that off.

"Well," I said, "there's always next year."

The look on her face told me she knew there wasn't going to be a next year.

It took a while to figure out who the people were. A contingent from the senior condo complex. Customers she'd sold cards to. Townspeople she gossiped with at the Rexall lunch counter. The drugstore owner, Sam. The haberdasher's son, Dave. The jeweler, another Sam, once an orphan and the only one in his family to survive after the Germans invaded Lithuania. They stood under umbrellas in a January rain. The most bereaved was my older brother. He'd flown in from the other side of the continent. He seemed shattered, alone and slightly bewildered. I had no idea why until, ten years later, when I found the diary. "Poor Donnie," she writes, in 1963. He was 14 and in the throes of adolescent confusion. "Wish he could find happiness."

Why, in the 30 years she lived after penning her final entry, did she not destroy the diary pages?

Perhaps, it occurs to me, she planned, at some point, to re-read them.

But the thought seems less than credible. Why revisit 20 years weariness and disappointment?

Maybe the diary survives because she forgot it was there?

On the other hand, my mother was someone who forgot nothing.

Did she preserve it hoping one of us would find and read these pages? She offers the occasional hint to that effect. November 10, 1963: "No one will ever know what I am going through."

What argues against that is that the diary went forever unmentioned. No note called attention to its existence.

Why she wrote it, why she saved it, remain ambiguous.

"Trying to get back to normal," she wrote, on January 3, 1962, after the madness of that year's holidays. "If there is such a thing."

WHY IS THAT GODDAMNED RADIO ON?

At the tender age of 10, my mother variously employed threats, sarcasm, coercion, and a policy of no negotiations, to get me promptly off to bed:

"Alright buster, it's 9:30."

"So?"

"What do you mean, 'so'? "

"*Bonanza*'s not over."

"It's over for you. Up to bed. Now."

"But can't I..."

"No, you can't. It's bedtime."

"But I need to stay up for the weather report."

"The *weather report?*"

"So I'll know what to wear tomorrow."

"GOD DAMN IT, GET MOVING!"

Delaying tactics proved futile. Eight children left my parents with zero tolerance for fibs, lies, prevarication, equivocation, or deceit. The survival tools of childhood. Up I went. That dark and silent room may as well have been a cage, albeit one with heat, light and toys. Nothing to do but wait for the first tenuous faltering of consciousness.

Then, something changed. At 6:45 PM, I'd cast a casual glance at my Timex, slide off the sofa and saunter toward the stairs.

"Where are you going, buster?"

"To bed."

"A little early, isn't it?"

"I'm tired."

"Tired? From what?"

I shrugged, as if to say they—all adults—were beyond the reach of emotional communication. It took them about a week to figure out these disappearances had to do with something my mother gave me for my birthday.

No, not the watch.

Situated on the nightstand, a foot from the headboard and its piled pillows, sat a rectangular box of not cardboard, nor wood, but plastic. Color? Honey Beige. Those in need of a drag name, take note. Best described as a jaundiced off-white, the color, as I recall it now, seems more suited to a psychiatric hospital or the bandage on a wound that's draining. On the right, the larger of its two dials, for tuning. On the left, the On/Off knob, which also controls volume. Under the tuning dial, the words GENERAL ELECTRIC. The model—a GE T-126B—is, like most low-cost tabletop radios then, an A/C-powered, five-tube superheterodyne receiver and AM only. AM stands for amplitude modulation, which has the ring of an upscale Weight Loss program but is instead the original method for moving sound on electromagnetic waves toward a receiver device.

In the daytime, silently sitting, my radio faded into the room's drab furnishings. The radios housed in wood or Bakelite decades earlier are, some of them, Art Deco gems, coveted and collected. Mine? Total Plain Jane. But to its lack of visual pizzazz, I was happily oblivious. It's not what this small, squat appliance looked like. What matters is what issues from the speaker once I turn it on. A twist of the knob and, 30 seconds later, tangerine-colored threads take shape in the thumb-sized glass tubes behind the panel. A burst of static. Voices blare, go silent, blare again. More static, louder. I imagine Zeros descending on Pearl Harbor. Then, miraculous clarity. A girl group, the Dixie Cups, crooning their smash hit single, "Chapel of Love:"

Spring is here, the sky is blue, whoa-oh-oh
Birds all sing as if they knew

Today's the day we'll say I do
And we'll never be lonely anymore

"Chapel of Love" reached #1 on Billboard's Hot 100 list on June 6, 1964. (2) Approaching 11, it's that time of life when your hearing's as sharp as a cat's and preadolescent nerves become overwrought for no discernible reason. Except, in retrospect, the dismal prospect of having to become an adult at some point. In the meantime, this electrified box supplies divertissement. A minute after slipping between the sheets, nimble fingers work the tuning dial like a safecracker manipulating a pin tumbler lock. I spin the dial back and forth from 55 to 160, keeping the sound reasonably low. Frequencies selected belong to three stations: WMCA (57AM), WABC (77AM) and WINS (101AM).

At 7 PM sharp:

"LADIES AND GENTLEMEN, IT'S MURRAY THE K AND HIS SWINGIN' SOIREE!"

The reach is local—the New York metro area—and the fan base fervid. Between songs, the evening's DJs—Murray the K on WINS, Dan Ingram or Bruce Morrow (on-air moniker: "Cousin Brucie") on WABC, 'Dandy Dan' Daniel on WMHA—talk like they're auctioning off farm equipment at a county fair. How can a mouth move that fast? In between contests and commercials, they issue rapid-fire cracks, quips, and puns, all of it engaging. But then there's the music.

Night after night I snapped it on. Parental suspicion becomes paternal annoyance. My father issues an edict. I'm informed my radio is strictly for daytime use. And because this struck me as selfish, unfair, irrational, mean-spirited and morally on par with whipping dogs, I responded in the only possible way I could think of. By ignoring it. Or him. As—*click!*—the GE T-126B purred to life,

I sought that mysterious volume level where lyrics are discernable to me but inaudible to the rest of the house. Yet, no matter how adroitly I manipulate the volume knob, at some point in the evening the door at the foot of the stairs is yanked open. A male voice, bristling with impatience:

"WHAT'S GOING ON UP THERE?"

To the left went the On/Off knob.

"Nothing."

"DON'T TELL ME 'NOTHING.' (pause) "WHY IS THAT GODDAMNED RADIO ON?"

"It's not!"

"THEN HOW COME I'M HEARING IT?"

"Hearing what?"

"YOU'RE A GODDAMNED LIAR!"

And with that—SLAM!—the door would shut.

Soon, decibel by decibel, the volume creeps upward. Now, twisting the tuning dial left, it's back to Bruce Morrow on WABC, where disembodied voices, sounding like lost ghosts seeking directions, chant: *Cousin Brucie! Cousin Brucie!* Soon, I'm spending my entire weekly one-dollar allowance on records. This starts with 45 RPMs (cost, 66 cents, first disc purchased, what else, "Chapel of Love"), and moving swiftly on to LP's, beginning with *The Shirelles Greatest Hits* which, at nearly three bucks, is not so much a king's ransom as a fool's.

That AM radio was alive and thriving in the 60s owed more to accident than intention. Fifteen years prior, industry oracles pronounced the medium doomed. TV, they suggested, would soon supplant it. In 2014, Michigan DJ Dick Kernen told *The Detroit News* that when he landed his first job on the air, in 1956, his father congratulated him, then, a moment later, took it back. "Radio is dead," the father told him. "Who wants to listen to *The Lone Ranger* when you can watch it on television?"

That seemed, at the time, a consensus. In the 50s, driven by consumer demand and the rapidly multiplying number of television stations, TV overtook radio as the biggest broadcast medium in the U.S. TV's rise mimicked that of radio 30 years prior. "In 1946, there were only ten thousand sets in American homes," notes Ben Fong-Torres, in *The Hits Just Keep On Coming*, his history of AM radio's revival. "Three years later, there were a million, and by 1952, some twenty-seven million receivers were aglow." By 1957, there were forty million television sets in use in over eighty percent of America's homes. Media scholar Stephen Mitchell notes that "No new invention entered American homes faster than black and white television sets; by 1955 half of all U.S. homes had one." Manufacturers proliferated. At least 150 television manufacturers entered the market. Top brands included Admiral, Zenith, Philco, and General Electric. Initially, television sets were not cheap. The $279.50 paid for a Magnavox in 1948 would cost $3,346 in 2023 dollars. The color set Westinghouse offered for $1,295 when it entered the market in March of 1954 would be priced at a little more than $14,000 today. In the beginning, at least, television was not for the casual buyer. That changed. Throughout the 50s, prices tumbled, pushing the product into the realm of affordability for working- and middle-class families. In 1964, I don't recall a house in the neighborhood without a TV. Yet, far from disappearing, AM radio's popularity grew, bit by bit, year on year.

Later, I wondered what I might've said had my father's question been a serious rather than a rhetorical one. Why *is* that goddamned radio on? Various answers come to mind, depending on the angle of approach. It's on, more than anything, for the music. You could hum, lip sync, move to, sing, or otherwise just get altogether lost in rock and roll music. That music arrived for AM radio in the nick of time. "The Beatles were a light in the night to save our industry," a late life Cousin Brucie recollected to interviewer Jay French in *Goldmine* magazine. The octogenarian DJ, still on the air at the time of the interview, also confided that the Beatles reinvigorated pop music just when its energies seemed to him, Bruce Morrow, spent. Another reason it was on? Demographics. In 1965, there were nearly 19 million people in the U.S. between 10 and 14, and another 17 million between 15 and 19. Overnight there sprang into existence a potential new audience for radio, meaning AM radio. They wanted not soap operas, sports, news, talk or, God forbid, religious proselytizing, but music. Pop music. And while that music was available on TV in the 60s, via musical variety shows *Shindig*, *Hootenanny* and *Hullabaloo*, I soon found that watching-while-listening provided diminished thrills relative to listening, alone in a dark room. Seeing the Rolling Stones perform "Satisfaction" on Ed Sullivan's Sunday night TV show (February 13, 1966) resonated for a day or two. Hearing the first eight notes of "Satisfaction" leap from a radio speaker every half hour, on the other hand, set off a frenzied urge to dance, or, if you didn't know how to dance, and I didn't, made you resolve to learn and fast. The spontaneity and seeming randomness of Top 40 radio play made you want to hear that song again. Which, soon enough, you would. Rock and roll brought quality and sprawling stylistic range to pop music. Long before the word "diversity" gained traction, rock and roll offered an ever-changing and continuously rotating assortment of hits catering to the broadest possible gamut of teenage tastes. Its reach touched all races and most classes. Included on the same Top 40 countdown were British Invasion bands (i.e., Herman's Hermits, The Dave Clark Five, Gerry and the Pacemakers, Freddy and Dreamers and of course The Beatles), Motown, Folk Rock, Surf Rock, Doo Wop, Girl Groups (the aforementioned Dixie Cups, for example) and the appropriately named Supremes—of such excellence they deserve a category all their own—as well as throwback crooners from earlier decades (Dean Martin, Frank Sinatra, Louis Armstrong) and occasional outliers sporting novelty tracks, such as "They're Coming To Take Me Away," a 1966 hit by producer/songwriter and One Hit Wonder Jerold Laurence Samuels, styling himself Napoleon XIV. When his dog runs away, our faux Napoleon descends into madness, anticipating his imminent trip...

To the funny farm
Where Life is Beautiful all the time
And I'll be happy to see
Those Nice Young Men
In their Clean White Coats
And they're coming to take me AWAY,
HEE HEE HA HAAAAA

Record sales boomed. The Beatles, alone, sold 15 million singles and LPs in 1964, the $25 million in sales that generated equivalent to almost a quarter billion dollars today.

Rock and roll radio spread from market to market, thanks to an Omaha, NE, station owner named Todd Storz. Legend has it Storz, owner of KOWH, the last and least of the city's seven stations, was sitting in a diner one night in 1953. Suddenly he noticed the non-stop activity around the jukebox. He jotted down which songs got played and how often. Out of that experience he created the Top 40 format, a list of hits, rotating weekly, based on record sales. Within the year, KOWH rocketed from last and least to Number One. AM stations around the country began to replicate Storz's programming approach. Top 40—short songs spun multiple times through the day—provided the medium with its perfect musical template. Meanwhile, as Storz's formula caught on, DJs evolved from record spinners to on-air personalities, their patter and chatter, jokes, one-liners, and general frenzy the music's ideal complement. They were stars, some of them. In 1964, for instance, Murray Kaufman, AKA Murray the K, the top-rated radio host in New York City, greeted the Beatles on arrival at JFK Airport and escorted them to their suite at the Plaza, where he proceeded to do a live broadcast. He was 41, a promoter, talent-spotter, escort, tag-along, cheer leader, you name it. Anything and everything but an artist. His celebrity was tethered to the acts he promoted. Afterwards, in a feat of shameless glomming, he of the turtleneck shirt and porkpie hat proclaimed himself the "Fifth Beatle." That left on-air rivals fuming. (The Beatles reportedly weren't thrilled about it either.) It helped that Murray the K was as entertaining on the air as he was ruthless off it. With a DJ serving as manic musical concierge and propelled by an attitude just beginning to dabble in defiance, rock and roll liberated AM radio, opening it up to the aesthetic preferences of a new generation. The tunes were catchy and fun, so much so that even adults—well, some adults—could listen.

My father's intrusions left me feeling as if something intimate and pleasurable—sex with myself, for instance—had been ruined by vandals. His oft-reiterated question was, of course, intended to induce silence rather than an answer. *SLAM!* To him, it was all noise. But with the door once more closed, and further parental reconnaissance unlikely that evening, I'd snap it back on. Decibel by decibel, the volume climbed. Why is that goddamned radio on? Because I turned it on. And I turned it on because it was there. And it was there because my mother bought it for me at a regional discount department store chain as a birthday gift. It's on because, even at 10, I've developed the type of obsessive personality readily channeled into fandom. And so on down the line. But why does this object, this appliance called 'a radio,' exist at all? Why is it part of our world? Who thought of it? How did it end up on the shelves at Caldor in Norwalk, CT? Consider that, as recently as a century prior, anyone suggesting the possibility of a mechanical device issuing music, speech, sports, contests, and commercials by pulling all that out of the air would be likely to find himself on the same ward as Napoleon XIV, hee-hee ha-ha.

Radio is all about electricity. It arises via a process of discovery and invention drawn out across 90 or so years, involving scientists from England, France, Germany, Italy, the U.S., Russia, Canada, and India. These include mathematicians, chemists, physicists, and electrical engineers. For much of that time, a box with voices and music coming out of it was inconceivable, let alone anyone's goal. Their intention was to extend and deepen human understanding by explaining how matter and energy interact. All those computations, formulae, theorems, experiments, and papers presented at academic conferences or published in scientific or philosophic journals constitute the theoretical underpinnings of electrical physics. Without which, no radio. Radio seems like something both inconceivable and inevitable. It represents the genius of modern science distilled into a single product. Ninety years is an instant, relative to the 100,000 to 200,000 years *homo sapiens* have existed, but it's long enough, or large enough, to contain the enormous technological and scientific advances of the 19th century, each following in the wake of its predecessor. Electricity, for the scientific community, initially proved a stumper. How to understand and explain something you can't see most of the time? Throughout human history, people observed its manifestations without much idea where it came from or how it worked. Something, somehow, produced a charge. The most obvious evidence was that huge, jagged spark in the sky that could split a tree in half or set a field on fire. Until modern science developed, people often attributed such phenomenon to deities. To the early Greeks, for instance, those lightning bolts Zeus hurled at his enemies were the ultimate weapon in the gods' formidable arsenal.

That science began with the investigative methodology first elaborated by philosopher and statesman Sir Francis Bacon (1561-1626). Bacon argued that a hypothesis—proposition, theory, or suggestion—becomes valid only at the point where empirically verifiable, i.e., measurable, data confirm the logic or process on which it rests. In the 17th century physicist/philosophe Sir Isaac Newton (1642-1726), who, with Gottfried Wilhelm Leibnitz, is credited with having invented calculus, further expanded the parameters of scientific investigation by working out mathematical formulations central to the research process. He elaborated his famous Laws of Motion and laid the groundwork for what became modern physics. There remained, of course, the challenge of figuring out what this force, electricity, was, and where it came from, a puzzle with few clues available. Not that people didn't try. Via kite, string and key, Benjamin Franklin (1706-1790) coaxed that force to earth in a thunderstorm and got a slight shock in the process. It probably felt like pulling crackling clothes from a dryer. But what makes electricity happen? Under what circumstances does it originate? (Note: electricity is "the movement of electrons between atoms.) But how does this force move between and among objects? It's not like studying pine trees, pine warblers, or pine martens, material phenomenon readily observed. Here was something non-tactile, mostly unseen, to be evaluated and understood by observing and generalizing from the way it acts or behaves under controlled conditions, such as those in a lab.

Its mystery deepened once the role of magnetism factored in. From his experiments, which demonstrated that electric currents produce a magnetic field, Danish physicist Hans Christian Oersted (1777-1851), concluded earth itself was a magnet, though he couldn't know that its core of molten iron and nickel is what made that a fact. Something another Danish scientist, Inga Lehman, only chanced upon in 1936 by analyzing seismic waves and the planet's magnetic field. But, returning to the matter at hand, Oersted's research made use of a voltaic cell that stored electricity, said battery newly invented in 1800 by Italian physicist and chemist Alessandro Volta (1745-1827). In the first decades of the 19th century, more and more scientists debated the apparent relationship between electricity and magnetism. Initially skeptical, French physicist Andre-Marie Ampere (1775-1836), the "Newton of Electricity," built on Oersted's work to elaborate a method of measuring electrical energy and a law, Ampere's Law, that explains how magnetic force arises between electrical currents. It states: "The magnetic field created by an electric current is proportional to the size of that electric current with a constant of proportionality equal to the permeability of free space." The International Exposition of Electricity, held in Paris from August to November of 1881, declared the ampere to be a standard unit for measuring electricity, along with watts (named for Scottish steam engine inventor James Watt), volts (named for Volta), and ohms, named for German physicist Georg Simon Ohms ((1789-1854), who developed a formula fundamental to understanding the interaction between voltage, current and resistance in an electrical circuit and explained it in his 1827 book, *The Galvanic Circuit Investigated Mathematically.*

So why is that goddamned radio on? Science supplied the context, genius the catalyst. British physicist/philosopher William Gilbert (1544-1603) coined the word *electricity* around 1600. He, like Oersted, concluded earth was a magnet. Enter, in 1831, Michael Faraday (1791-1867). The computations of this English physicist, a blacksmith's son and largely self-taught, theorized that electrical current produces a magnetic field around it, that electricity, as a form of electromagnetic radiation, moves in waves, and that said waves were both positive and negative. Ampere, after rejecting the idea of electromagnetism, revised his views and became the first scientist to measure electrical current, i.e., the number of electrons flowing through a circuit, via a device, the Ampere meter, that tracked the flow of that current through a coil. Building off Faraday, Scottish physicist James Clerk Maxwell (1831-1879) theorized that electricity, magnetism, and light were "all part of the same phenomenon." His death at 48 of abdominal cancer left it to a young German, Heinrich Hertz (1857-1894), to prove the efficacy of the four famous theorems that crowned Maxwell's research. He did that in 1894 by building devices, the Oscillator and the Resonator to both transmit and receive electromagnetic waves ("Hertzian waves") and testing these in his lab. High on the list of the many discoveries rendered by this extraordinary man was his confirmation of Maxwell's suggestion that electromagnetic waves have the same properties as light. Even that late in the 19th century, neither he nor others imagined such waves carrying news and music across oceans and continents. Let alone—fast forward 60 years— into deep space. Let alone Murray the K and his Swingin' Soiree.

Radio, like anything, required a reason to exist. That reason began to be elaborated in 1844, when American inventor Samuel Morse (1791-1872) used his newly patented electric telegraph to dispatch, by means of wires strung between poles, the first message from a station in Washington, DC, to a station in Baltimore. As more telegraph lines got built, telegraph enabled messaging in Morse Code dots and dashes across ever widening distances. Less than 20 years later, in October of 1861, messages moved coast to coast, courtesy of Western Union. Limitations, however, soon proved formidable. For one thing, the telegraph stayed where you put it. It could not be transported. Besides which, telegraph was person-to-person communication, not mass communication, i.e., broadcasting, a message to many, as with newspaper publishing after the 1830s, when steam-driven printing presses changed the cost equation of newspaper production. Then there was the expense. Building telegraph lines or laying undersea cable proved labor intense, thus costly. What evolved into radio was born in the effort to dispatch those signals station-to-station without the overhead of building and maintaining poles and wires. The solution was something called wireless telegraphy, soon expanded to include wireless telephony. Telegraphy or radiotelegraphy equals signals dispatched without wires. Telephony, arriving not too much after, delivers an actual voice, or music. Both, of course, transmitted signal via radio waves through the ether. Use of either term today would leave most people stumped. Telegraphy? Telephony? Though *wireless telephony* is mysterious only until you extract the cell phone from your pocket to take a call. Without, of course, having to think about just why you're able to do that.

"Didn't Marconi invent the radio?" someone asks. In 1895, the young nobleman from Bologna, fascinated by electromagnetism as a teen, built devices to transmit and receive signals via electromagnetic waves. His experiments, however, were not confined to the lab. Only 20 when his quest began, electrical engineer and inventor Guglielmo Marconi (1874-1937) initiated a series of demonstrations that proved the efficacy of wireless telegraphy over successively greater distances, a story well-told by Susan J. Douglas in her *Inventing American Broadcasting 1899-1922*. Naysayers, such as British scientist Oliver Lodge, pointed out that earth's curvature effectively prevented signals from traveling more than 100 to 200 miles. Marconi responded to the objection by disproving it. In 1902, aboard the *USS Philadelphia*, he picked up signals from distances of 700 miles by day, 2,000 miles at night. Soon, with his butler serving as lab assistant, Marconi created and patented apparatus—a magnetic detector and a horizontal directional aerial—which so improved transmission and reception that, within 20 years, radio was no longer a scientific hobby horse but an industry. But as much as his name is linked to radio as its inventor, Marconi's work, however original and ingenious, would scarcely have been possible without the (by then) extensive body of theoretical writing and research in electrical physics, that came before him. Many scientists and engineers contributed at each stage to its development, up to the final outcome of radio broadcasting primarily for purposes of entertainment, beginning in the 20s. Marconi changed the outcome by assembling radio into an integrated system of components and pointing wireless telegraphy, which is what it still was when he began his experiments, away from one-on-one messaging toward mass communication. His aim? To monetize it. In 1898, for instance, he opened the world's first radio factory 42 miles from London in Chelmsford, England, to manufacture wireless receivers. (It closed in 2008.) The year after that, on March 27, he transmitted signals 36 miles across the English Channel from Wimereux, France, to South Foreland Lighthouse, England. Trans-oceanic transmission followed. In 1909 the Nobel

Committee awarded Marconi the Nobel Prize for Physics, which he shared with Karl Ferdinand Braun, founder of Telefunken, the German electronics manufacturer, and inventor of the Cathode Ray Tube.

An invention is "a process or device" that at some point owes its existence to a thought, logical or intuitive. Some inventions—the nail or the candle, for instance—seem simple and straightforward, necessity the obvious parent. But every object made by humans tells a story. More than two thousand years ago, a Roman, perhaps inspired by the tent peg, conceived of the nail to speed building. Fast forward to 1790 and nails are still banged out, one by one, courtesy of the village blacksmith or your local naylor. After 1800 they're apt to be mass-produced as semi-finished goods in factories called slitting mills. The candle goes back further, at least 5,000 years. The National Candle Association states it originated when the Egyptians began soaking the core of a reed in melted animal fat, also known as tallow. The Romans added a wick. In the Middle Ages, chandlers (candle makers) developed the beeswax candle. Fast forward to the 19th Century and spermaceti, extracted from slaughtered leviathans, becomes widely used in candle production. The light bulb, patented by Thomas Edison in 1880, should've been the end of chandlers. It wasn't any more than radio meant the end of newspapers or television meant the end of radio. Events, including human discovery and invention, often unfold simultaneously and in combination, with many historical variables of different weight in play, each (or all) interacting to produce other than linear outcomes. Why are candles still manufactured and sold? Candles are romantic and romance never dies. What was once needed is now merely wanted. But that's enough to sustain the candle's appeal well into the age of electric light and power. Radio? Far from fading into oblivion, listening to the radio remains something Americans do weekly. "About eight-in-ten Americans ages 12 and older listen to terrestrial radio in a given week," according to Neilson Media

Research data published by the Radio Advertising Bureau.

Marconi wasn't the only one to claim radio as his invention. For instance, around the time Marconi began manufacturing receiver sets, scientists such as the Bengali polymath Jagadish Chandra Bose and the (like Faraday) largely self-taught Russian physicist Oleg Vladimirovich Losev, began using crystals to detect (receive) radio waves. A technology pioneered by Braun. Crystal sets—a type of radio receiver consisting of a tuning coil, a crystal detector, and headphones—came on the market before the First World War. In those early years, say around 1915, if you mentioned the word radio, it was assumed a crystal set is what you meant. Or owned. Crystal set receivers—such as the Aeriola Jr. made and marketed by Westinghouse in 1921—required an antenna to pick up signal and a headset to hear the sound that signal was converted into. Still one-to-one communication. The next big breakthrough, the invention by the "Father of the Radio," Dr. Lee de Forest (1876-1961), of the audion, or tube amplifier, came quickly, in 1906 (patented 1907). Dr. de Forest's contribution obviated the need for headphones and transformed the nature of the listening experience.

While Marconi was the first to transmit signals long distance, including across the Atlantic, it was another Marconi competitor, the Canadian Reginald Fessenden (1866-1932), who, making use of the amplitude modulation technology he created, broadcast the human voice—his own—live, for the first time, on Christmas Eve, 1906. The broadcast issued from a 420-foot tower in Brant Rock, MA, and was heard as far away as Jamaica. This engaging electronics pioneer—a reproduction of his demonstration can be found on YouTube—read a Bible passage and wished listeners Merry Christmas. Then Fessenden, the self-proclaimed "Father of Voice Radio," picked up his violin and played first Handel, then Adolph

Adame's carol, "O Holy Night." Fessenden closed the program with a sacred song by Charles Gounod, "Adore and Be Still." Only radio operators along the East Coast could tune in to Fessenden's broadcast.

By 1920 radio receivers using vacuum tubes to pick up signals and amplify sound began displacing crystal sets. The popularity of tube radios launched the radio craze of the 1920s. Anyone who could afford a set had to have one. Formerly written off as a fad, at least in some quarters, radio suddenly appeared as a market of seemingly limitless potential. Big corporations and daily newspapers jumped in the game. In 1920, Westinghouse was not only manufacturing receiver sets, but operating KDKA, a pioneering radio station in Pittsburgh (still on the air). It was also in that year—August 20, 1920—the *Detroit News* launched its radio station, WWJ, 95 on the AM dial, also still on the air, as a 24-hour news station). One estimate suggests that, at some point, 10 percent of all U.S. radio stations were owned by newspapers. Some gave away free crystal sets to new (print) subscribers. While in Europe governments tended to own, control, and operate such stations (the BBC, for example), the U.S. business model followed that used since the appearance of the Penny Press in the 1830's, meaning revenue generated primarily via advertising—airtime—sales.

With technology enhanced, and fortunes to be made, events moved at an ever-accelerating pace. The Commerce Department issued slightly more than 100 commercial radio licenses in 1920. As radio ownership increased, so did the number of radio stations. Between 1923 and 1930, 60 percent of American families purchased radios. In 1922 there were roughly 570 licensed stations. By 1928, there were 677. In 1920, one percent of U.S. households owned a radio receiver. By 1937, 75 percent had one.

To extend its reach and achieve economies of scale, NBC in 1926 launched separate Red and Blue networks of stations to distribute programming and extend the network's broadcast reach to the Rockies and beyond. Within a year, a network called CBS followed.

The first generation of radio receivers were typically housed in a wooden cabinet or console that rested on the floor. Tabletop models also used wood or plastic housing. During World War 2, tabletop radios became the industry's major seller, accounting for two-thirds of retail sales. By 1950, most radios were tabletop appliances.

My GE T-126B contains a political as well as industrial history. At some point between 1961 and 1963, the years General Electric manufactured the T-126B, and likely toward the end of its production run, my radio rolled down the assembly line in a building on Boston Street in the east side of Bridgeport, CT, one of two company plants (the other in Schenectady, NY) where GE made the product. The electrical giant, founded by Thomas Edison, bought the Bridgeport plant from Remington Arms in the spring of 1920 for $7 million. When Remington operated it, the factory filled orders for, among others, Russia's last Czar. Nicholas II—Nicholas the Bloody, to political opponents—ordered a million rifles for the Russian army. Apparently not enough to save his 300-year-old dynasty. Meanwhile GE expanded the complex, which ultimately consisted of 13 interconnected 5-story buildings on 77 acres, equal to 58 football fields. In 1935, 6,000 people worked there but in its post-War heyday the by then 20,000 people employed at GE's Bridgeport plant made electric coffee percolators, electric fans, irons, mixers, toasters, washing machines, and...until July 1987, when GE, citing "unrelenting Japanese competition," exited the market for electronics manufacturing, i.e., tabletop radios. Before May of 1950, most workers at the plant, management excepted of course, belonged to the United Electrical (UE) Workers Local 203. The post-War anti-communist witch hunt resulted in the Congress of Industrial Organizations (CIO) ejecting 11 unions, including the UE, claiming Communist Party supporters dominated the leadership. The CIO expelled, in total, roughly one million of its members. In electrical appliance manufacture, the federation hoped to replace UE locals with those of the politically sanitized IUE, the International Union of Electrical, Radio and Machine Workers. So, on May 25, 1950, the IUE 203 replaced UE Local 203. But even before the change in bargaining representation, the UE 203— a year after the vehemently anti-labor Taft-Hartley Act passed in 1948—expelled 26 members "for being alleged communists" and demanded all Bridgeport plant shop stewards sign affidavits stating that they weren't Communist Party members. So much for the First Amendment.

Piece by piece, an IUE member assembled my radio while, at the end of the line, another Local 203 member packed it in a box and sent it on to the shipping department, from whence to the regional (New York/Southern New England) discount department store founded in 1951 by Carl and Dorothy Bennett, headquartered in Norwalk, CT, situated midway between Bridgeport and Stamford. My mother bought the GE T-126B at Caldor's Norwalk store sometime in September 1963. The Bennetts proclaimed their chain the "Bloomingdale's of discounting" and marketed around the slogan: "Where shopping is always a pleasure." Caldor once operated 145 stores. It closed forever on May 15, 1999. Twenty-some years later, GE's Bridgeport plant, too, shuttered. According to WSHU's Morning Edition, what now remains on those 76 acres are "two brick guardhouses and a short stretch of wall."

As irritating as my father considered the music, his displeasure had more to do with rules being flouted. His rules. Maybe *that's* why that goddamned radio was on. Because he wanted it off. An unconscious act of rebellion springing up right out of Sigmund Freud's Father Complex, a nexus of behaviors the good doctor found most resistant to therapy. Add one more reason to the pile. Of course, it was also on because I was bored. Or lonely. Yes, there it is. When you're ten, eleven or twelve—life's sweet spot—radio easily becomes a night's companion, the first lover and one who'll never dictate clothing options, quibble with menu choices, or demand an account of your whereabouts the previous evening. The songs seemed to me sexy, though I had little clue as to what the word meant. It sounded right. Here I am, or there I was, in that body that is this body, but isn't, just past the age of pajamas with fire trucks on them, clad now in Fruit of the Loom underwear ("briefs," a term that succeeds in being both erotic and creepy) waiting for something to happen. That something was sound, not sex nor sleep. Sound that put all curiosity about ass, cocks, cunts, tits, and kisses on some shelf in some mental corner. Why worry about what has yet to arrive? Though that, of course, is what worry is all about.

Curious, I once removed the pressed wood backer board from the rear of my radio. The act felt weird, transgressive but pointless and inconvenient, like shoplifting a cucumber. What mystery did I think would be explained? Affixed to a panel were rectifier tubes, cylinders and what looked like an overgrown matchbox wrapped in red hair. That would've been copper wire, wound around the power output transformer. Thumb-sized tubes glowed. Two green wires connected the receiving mechanism to a small speaker which converted signal into sound. Four more wires—red, yellow, green, and black—connected the apparatus, mounted at a slant inside its housing, to the tuning knob. The mechanism resembled a tiny ship festooned by strings of orange Halloween lights, sunk at the bottom of an aquarium.

Night after night I listened, hours at a stretch, falling asleep, usually, as the clock approached midnight. The pleasures afforded made clandestine listening worth every risk. Whether it was silly ("Shirley, Shirley, Bo Birley, Bonana fanna fo Firley, Fee fy mo Mirley...Shirley!"), agonizingly confessional ("A'breakin' rocks in the hot sun/I fought the law and the law won..."), or inspiring, the music engaged, sometimes entranced. It was, above all, romantic. Romance—current, incipient, or only a daydream—powered the song output. Love was in the air, or on the airwaves. Like the Great American Songbook writers of the 20s and 30s—Johnny Mercer, Duke Ellington, Billy Strayhorn, Rogers and Hart, George and Ira Gershwin—rock and roll songwriters made desire the center of their lyrics. An evidently inexhaustible subject, for musicians and their audience. (A study cited by Casey Daly, a writer for the *Illini*, the student newspaper at U. of Southern Illinois, claims 67 percent of AM radio songs since the 60s are about love, with "money, partying and depression" as "close seconds." Songs often employed familiar amorous tropes, to wit: *I love her/she's mine* (See the Dave Clark Five, "Glad All Over"); *I admire her from afar and want her desperately* (see The Four Seasons "Can't Take My Eyes Off Of You"); *we broke up and I feel like a chump* (see Smokey Robinson, "Tracks of my Tears," Peter and Gordon, "A World Without Love," or...all-time favorite, "Don't Walk Away, Renee," by the brilliant but unfortunately short-lived Left Banke); *I don't know her but I sure as hell want to* (see The Hollies, "Bus Stop"); *I've lost her, and I'll do anything to get her back* (see Herman's Hermits, "Mrs. Brown, you've got a lovely daughter."). Top 40 songs tracked the course of romantic love from initial cluelessness ("She Loves You") to unhappy aftermath ("You've Lost That Loving Feeling") and bitter, dispirited complaint. Titles tell it all. "When a Man Loves a Woman." "Love Is All Around." "Will You Still Love Me Tomorrow?" "Love Is Here, And Now It's Gone." Gene Pitney's 1964 Top Ten Hit, "It Hurts To Be in Love,"—written by Howard Greenfield and Helen Miller—sums up its spirit.

> *Day and night, night and day.*
> *It hurts to be in love this way-ay.*

Immersed in this furtive glamour, I succumbed, bit by bit, to the idea love would find me, sooner or later. A picturesque notion, twin to the blundering naivete of 12. I gathered that, as much as love hurt, it healed. (See The Beatles, "All You Need Is Love.") I still had little idea what a man and woman did in bed, except that what it was might, sometime later, require fresh sheets. That was partly the fault of a Catholic education—which presumed to obliterate the subject of sex by rigorously ignoring it—and partly my own fault, as the notion aroused nothing in the way of curiosity. Soon enough, the boy-loves-girl thing ushered to the fore the realization of an undeniable (to me) sexual difference, one deeply rooted and non-negotiable. How could I fall in love when the feminine beauty songwriters, singers, and bands endlessly celebrated left me, um, erotically uninspired? Love, AM radio assured me, was evidently everywhere...

I feel it in my fingers
I feel it in my toes
Love that's all around me
And so the feeling grows

"Love Is All Around You," The Troggs

...but to me, then, the love I longed for seemed as invisible as the electromagnetic waves that brought signal and sound to the box on my nightstand. In supplying the word on how, why, and when desire arrives, the music communicated to this 12-year-old, via an implication reinforced at every point by social mores, that boy-loves-girl was the only valid kind of desire, certainly the only type to elicit adult approval and the only one any person could talk, write, or sing about. The implication was clear. Guard closely all talk of Eros. In any event, these desires turned out to be more real than radio itself, because when I snapped my GE T-126B off and fell asleep, the inevitable erotic dreams, like my waking thoughts of the day when they dared to venture there, contained not men and women locked in passionate embrace but my body and that of some other guy feeling and fumbling our way toward orgasm, at which point the dream collapsed and I woke in its sticky ruins.

My AM radio days, or nights, ended at 14, when I defected to FM (frequency modulation) stations without looking back. It wasn't just me. By the late 70s, FM radio—offering smooth, static-free sound; long-playing records; and the casual conversation of a somewhat spirited dinner date—overtook AM in listener share of market. By 1982, FM held the premier position among radio listeners—70 percent—and 84 percent of the 18-24 demographic. Sometimes you go with the flow without even knowing it. What had seemed, at 10 or 12, a sanctuary, at 20 struck me as either obnoxious or lacking sophistication. Probably both. It wasn't only because, when I tuned in, the songs were at that point unfamiliar and the DJs unknown. The medium had lost its charm. Yet, when from time to time the dial on my rent-a-car radio located an Oldies station, where I was guaranteed to know two out of every three songs, the music seemed like nostalgia without the trimmings. Even the DJs bugged me. Later I realized the DJs hadn't changed, I had. Was I hearing the music now through my father's ears? No, I'd replaced pop music with classical and jazz. What accounted for this abrupt change I couldn't explain. It seems a natural transition, to go where feeling takes you. Yet when I thought, later, of my magnetic (electromagnetic?) attraction to AM radio in those first furtive months of listening, it occurred to me why a parting of the ways was inevitable. I outgrew it, like you outgrow dolls, toy soldiers or a BB gun. From the vantage of 10 or 15 years I looked back on it as cheerful fluff. What had I gained for the few thousand hours I spent in its thrall, besides involuntarily memorizing the lyrics to dozens, if not hundreds, of songs? It was all a way to pass time, and seemed, then, anything but formative. But what's formative often appears only in the rear-view mirror of experience. I had learned to keep myself company. I had learned that the world outside house and school was the world that mattered. I learned that it was exactly the songs that aroused antagonism, the ones I despised on first hearing, that became the ones I liked most and best remembered.

What I gathered soon enough was that what I wanted to know was not to be found in the textbooks at St. Cecilia's School, where the sisters, when not hurling erasers at note-passers or thrashing malcontents with a pointer, retailed stories about devils under the bed, just waiting to drag those who refused to pray, or forgot to, into hell's scorching depths. A year or two into my AM radio period, age around 12, I abandoned Catholic dogma and all it stood for to become first a pot-smoker and delinquent, then a socialist. "Not till we are lost, in other words not till we have lost the world, do we begin to find ourselves, and realize where we are and the infinite extent of our relations," Thoreau writes, in "The Village" section of *Walden*. But finding takes time and the rewards are subtle ones. Tuning in was tuning out. Tuning out bellicose nuns. Tuning out my inability to catch a football, swing a bat or, God forbid, dribble. Tuning out the nattering, cheerless, dismissive voices of those bent on steering me toward the Great Gray World of respectability, conformity, and commerce. "LADIES AND GENTLEMEN, IT'S MURRAY THE K AND HIS SWINGIN' SOIREE!"

Had I attempted to explain any of this to my father, his attention would've evaporated in seconds. There was, after all, a lawn to be mowed, a garage to be swept, homework to be done. All else he considered slacking. He regarded rock and roll radio as vulgar, frivolous, and unnecessary. I see now he wasn't completely wrong. Taste, however ongoing, is a barometer for where you are in life. When I look around the concert hall where a Beethoven string quartet is underway, what I see is mostly a room of gray heads, a few of them nodding. My father hadn't the least interest in Beethoven but his disdain for rock and roll's spirited vulgarity makes sense.

For him at least. That was a good portion of its appeal. Rock and roll radio soothed a mind made fidgety by the intuition that my obvious indifference regarding those pursuits I was supposed to be interested in—money, basketball, and sex with girls—could only result, once its source became clear, in the most withering ostracism.

What we most often encounter in the day-to-day are products manufactured to enable our comfort and convenience. Being long separated from the thought, skill and toil involved in making what we use, we submit to the definition of ourselves as "consumers" who exist to unthinkingly absorb all this detritus by paying for it. Non-stop marketing drives our purchase behavior. One consequence is that we rarely consider how everything we own, or use, contains a history. How did bar soap, the spatula, the fork, the comb, the vacuum cleaner, roll-on deodorant, or half an aisle of laxative products in the drugstore this afternoon, come to be? Each deserves its own history. They're like folk song, the product of many minds time reduces, in its final iteration, to anonymity. Often enough, to conceive of that history requires only imagination. The car is a cart without a horse, the rifle a gussied-up crossbow plus gunpowder, the lawnmower two scythes whirling beneath a gasoline engine. Each, like the radio, speaks to human ingenuity in action. We acquire all this to ensconce ourselves in a world of our own supposed creation, though, being consumers, we hardly consider what becomes of the objects when they break, warp, wear out, burn up or fade away. We just buy more. Thus, on arriving home from college one summer, I found my radio had disappeared, discarded in a general cleanout. When I inquired of my father where it was or may have gone to, he changed the subject. I imagine this humble, innocuous object sitting in a thrift shop window, circa 1975, the power cord in the back bundled with a rubber band, a sign in black felt Magic Marker taped to the top. "Do Not Plug In. Ask Clerk For Assistance."

BIBLIOGRAPHY

Balk, Alfred. *The Rise of Radio, from Marconi through the Golden Age*. McFarland & Company, Inc., 2006.

Douglas, Susan J. *Inventing American Broadcasting 1899-1922*. The Johns Hopkins University Press, 1989.

Fatherley, Richard W. and MacFarland, David T. *The Birth of Top 40 Radio: The Storz Stations' Revolution of the 1950s and 1960s*. McFarland & Company, Inc., 2014.

Fong-Torres, Ben. *The Hits Just Keep On Coming: The History of Top 40 Radio*. Backbeat Books, 2001.

Garay, Ronald. *Gordon McLendon: The Maverick of Radio*. Greenwood Press, 1992.

Garratt, G.R.M. *The Early History of Radio: From Faraday to Marconi*. The Institute of Engineering and Technology, 1994.

DATE

It was late Friday afternoon and snow was falling. A feathery scrim of it lay on the limbs of the sycamore tree in the park outside Martin Bair's window. His orange cat leaped on the bed and forcefully thrust its head under Martin's limp hand.

"Oh my God, you again," he said, stroking the greedy head and maneuvering to create space between his arm and torso, into which the cat swiftly wedged itself.

Martin lifted the remote, changed channels and pressed Mute. A middle-aged woman was standing on the boardwalk of a New Jersey beach town, mike in one hand, umbrella in the other. She seemed tense, struggling to maintain control of the umbrella, and shouting into the microphone. A banner across the top of the screen read: Winter's Last Blast.

Some people regard a late winter storm as supremely inconveniencing. For Martin, it was one of those gifts fate occasionally sent his way, unasked for and unearned. The office had shut down early. The fridge and pantry were well-stocked. Now he could sit in the bedroom of his third floor apartment, drink coffee and watch the snow.

Actually, Martin felt relieved. He had a date tonight. Now, the date would no doubt cancel, which, he thought, was just as well.

Martin had made the date as part of a 'program' put together by his friend and confidant, Arthur, seven months prior. That is, shortly after he, Martin, had involuntarily become single.

Darling, you may be 42, but you're still a catch, Arthur said. *Just be aware that nobody's going to do any catching unless you put yourself out there. Buy some roller blades. Join a gym. If worse comes to worst, hit the bars. They've hardly changed since our ill-starred youth. You'll see some of the same—albeit superannuated—faces. And as long as I'm dishing out gratuitous advice, let me suggest this: Go on at least two dates a month. And remember to smile.*

The phone rang.

"How's it looking?"

Martin blinked.

"Um, Fred?"

"None other."

"It's, uh, looking like a snowstorm."

My God, he thought, that sounds banal.

"It certainly is," said Fred.

"Actually," Martin drummed his fingers on the headboard, "I think it might be better if we postponed our, uh, outing."

"Why?"

"Well, for one thing there's a blizzard going on, and I'd feel terrible if you had an accident driving into the city or something."

"I'm not anticipating any difficulty," Fred said. He paused. "I just got new snow tires. Michelins. And . . . ahem . . . I can work a stick shift with the best of 'em."

Martin heard a lascivious grunt on the other end of the line and cursed himself for failing to prepare a fallback. Fred would be there in an hour and the apartment was untidy, meaning he'd have to at least do the dishes.

Martin had met Fred exactly one week before, on a Friday night at Woody's. The noise was industrial, the crowd shoulder to shoulder, the air dense with fumes. He'd squeezed his way to the bar through a phalanx of sweater queens, snagged a Corona and relocated to a shadowy niche along the wall, where, surveying the room, he'd had time to reflect on a warning received from Arthur to the effect that Woody's on a weekend evening was an unlikely place to meet someone sane, let alone potential soulmates.

Dregsy, darling. Bottom of the barrel. What's left when everything else is consumed. Get the picture? No, you don't. Can't. You've been away from the scene too long. All right, this is what you'll find there. Freelance go-go boys . . .

"That sounds pretty hot, actually."

Hot? Cold. As in cash. They'll express interest. A bit too forward, but you'll be floored by your luck. Then, ten feet out the door, they'll turn and matter of factly state a price. Counting, naturally, on the element of surprise. And since you've been cursed for whatever reason with a complete inability to say no, I say to you: no no a go-go. Get it?

"But . . . "

Woody's on a weekend evening is filled with unemployed clairvoyants, vacationing proctologists, D.A.s on the down low, Philadelphia cops so deeply in the closet it would take a bathysphere to find and retrieve them, and the occasional mortician or two eager for the rare company of a body that actually breathes.

"How would I know they're morticians?"

Formaldehyde, darling. It's in their veins...and on their breath. Oh, and under no circumstances are you to go home with a hairdresser.

"Why? I've seen some cute ones."

Life's greatest traps are baited with butt. Haven't you learned that yet? The problem with hairdressers is they all want a relationship. And being in a relationship with a hairdresser is like being an indentured servant to hell's surliest fry cook. They'll dress you, cut your hair, and provide you with unlimited decorating advice. Which, by the way, you could use. Then, little by little, they'll turn your ego into a petting zoo. They're self-esteem burglars. Peace of mind pickpockets.

Arthur sighed.

And never fuck a priest. Even a minister. In fact, Protestants are actually worse.

"I've never seen a priest in a gay bar."

You've seen hundreds and simply never recognized them. It's not as if they put on clerical drag to go cruising. Who'd get near them if they did, except for some poor pansy with an altar boy complex? You'll meet one eventually. And do yourself a favor, leave it at the bar. Don't even think about getting involved.

"Why?"

That strident, self-righteous tone you used to hear on the other side of the confessional screen? You'll be hearing it over dinner. And in bed? Ugh. They have all the imagination of a baptismal font. Until it comes to their own little peccadilloes. Like diddling skateboard boys in the men's room at the mall. Or manning the glory holes of Gap Tooth County, where they're certain not to be seen going down on a similarly straying truckdriver or two.

Or three.

Actually, Arthur had been called on to console him a scant six weeks previously, the morning after Martin had met an impossibly ravishing creature named Nevin. (*Nevin?* Arthur said. *Right there mother would've smelled the rodent. Where do they get these names, Masterpiece Theatre? Darling, please, next time ask for i.d.*) He'd bought Nevin a gin-and-tonic. One round later, this was reciprocated. At that point Nevin suggested they repair to his place, across the river, in Collingswood.

Martin and his consort made their way out the door, then, just past it, through the gauntlet of smokers that stood warily eyeing all who entered, left, or lingered. He felt a hundred hard eyes at his back. Jealous queens, he thought, let them stare. Nevin led him halfway down the block to a yellow Mustang parked beneath a streetlight. Motioning toward the passenger's seat, he unlocked the door on the driver's side and slipped behind the wheel. The car started. Martin heard taunts, whistles, catcalls. He glanced toward the bar, where smokers looked on with evident mirth. An unease he recognized as incipient panic began its slow burn. He tried the car door. Locked. He waved, signaling that the door should be opened. The Mustang backed up a foot, rolled forward at an angle, and backed up again, forcing Martin to step away. Suddenly, with one hard swerve, the vehicle slipped from its parking space into 13th Street traffic where it sped away without acknowledgment or pause.

"Well, what was I supposed to do? Who could even imagine that someone . . ."

Darling, would you like some whine with your cheese?

Martin heard a refrigerator door open and close on the other end of the line. *Look, I tried to warn you. Dating's not for sissies. Well, perhaps that was poorly put. Anyway, there are monsters out there. Sociopaths in supermodel clothing. You're probably wishing you were back in that sinkhole with whatzisname, am I right?*

Martin blinked.

All mother's saying is that you need to be a little more discriminating when it comes to men. Or at least to the men you pick up at Woody's. I mean, basically, there're three types: misfits, misanthropes, and miscreants.

188

"Which was Nevin?"

Probably a misanthrope, but with misfit traits. The types intersect. That would explain the fake name. It's no doubt Bob, Bill, Allen or something similarly mundane. God, what people won't do to make themselves interesting. I had one who introduced himself to me as Seamus O'Somethingorother with an Irish brogue straight out of County Mayo and on my way back from the men's room someone I know pointed him out and said, Oh, I see you met Mark Capiello? We graduated from Northeast Catholic together.

"What if I see him again?"

Who?

"Nevin."

How far can you throw a drink and still hit someone in the face?

A week later, from nearly the same location along the wall, Martin spotted a reasonably attractive gentleman standing shy-eyed, eager and alone on the opposite side of the room. The individual was short, with straight blond-brown hair combed forward in bangs, ears slightly out of scale on the large side and a somewhat simian face. Passably cute but unprepossessing enough to be harmless. Martin followed his prey to the bathroom. He was at the sink pretending to wash his hands when the face reappeared in the mirror.

"Martin," said Martin, remembering to smile.

"Fred," said the face.

"Alone and unguarded?"

"I will be for five more minutes," Fred said. "Then it's off to a party." Numbers scratched on ATM slips traded hands.

You know what they do with those, don't you?

"Oh c'mon, Arthur, you're such a cynic."

They tack them to bulletin boards. Make collages out of them. Then, when it all gets scruffy, consign them to the flames.

"You're making that up."

I knew this queen who did it. He'd pin his phone numbers to cork and gaze on them as if they were telegrams from the underworld. Then he'd take the whole batch and toast them on a Hibachi.

Fred arrived at 7:30 wearing a large black and green Chinese military hat with flaps akimbo. Melting snow covered hat and shoulders. Once past the threshold, he made a show of looking Martin up and down, smiling as his eyes reached crotch level. He reared back on the balls of his feet, lifted himself on tiptoes, and left a wet peck on Martin's cheek.

"You're even sexier than I remember, big boy."

Fred pulled off his hat. A set of damp, dark curls sprung forth.

"How do you like my hair? Just had it permed."

"Uh . . . striking," Martin said. "Something to drink?"

"Scotch and soda."

"Actually, I don't have any hard liquor in the house. I've got Pepsi, Sprite, Snapple and cranberry juice. Oh," he said, "and there's Corona in the fridge."

"Beer is to beverages what tartar sauce is to condiments," Fred said. He smiled, much like a performer awaiting applause.

"I'm not making the connection," Martin said.

"Strictly working class, you see." Fred glanced around the living room, visibly taking in the thrift shop coffee table and trash-picked rug, the sprawling stack of magazines beside the easy chair, the battered floor lamps.

"I'll have a spot of tea, then," he said, brows rising like small, renegade wings.

"Herbal or the real stuff?"

"Earl Grey, if you please."

"I think we'll have to make do with Tetley."

"Tetley? Oh, *Tetley*."

Fred sighed, draping his hat and coat across the sofa.

Momo approached, nose poised and sniffing.

"Hello, kitties."

"That's Momo," Martin said. "He's very friendly. Sometimes a little too friendly."

Martin had just finished filling the tea kettle when he heard what sounded like a hiss, followed by a feline cry of pain. He returned to the living room a minute later to find Fred on the sofa, studying a book on the slave trade.

"Where's Momo?"

"Oh." Fred glanced up, startled. "I guess he must be hiding or something."

The restaurant, which specialized in Eastern European fare, was packed.

Martin congratulated himself for having made a reservation. A votive candle threw shadow across the table, making it feel close, almost cozy, and inspiring the hope that this date might have some sort of positive outcome and, who knew, perhaps even a sequel. After all, he didn't really know Fred, and had no right to judge him.

"I'm Emily, and I'll be your server," said Emily. "Could we start you off with something from the bar?"

Fred looked up, smiling.

"Do you have any single grain malts?"

Emily looked from Fred to Martin and back.

"I'm kind of new here," she said, "but as far as I know, we don't serve anything like milkshakes."

Fred sighed.

"I'm referring to Scotch, my dear."

"Oh."

"That's a type of whisky distilled in Scotland from malted barley."

"I see. Well, I'm sure we must have several kinds."

"Nothing likely to impress connoisseurs, I would wager. I suppose I shall have to make do with something pedestrian. Let's try Johnnie Walker Black. You do have that, I trust? Any tappy in Fishtown would."

"I'll see if we . . ."

"On the rocks, if you please."

Martin ordered a Corona.

"Will you excuse me?" Fred said. "That tea went right through me. I've got to visit the Gents."

Martin watched the hat-flattened curls and broad corduroy backside descend toward the restroom. This was not going well. Or, more to the point, it wasn't going anywhere at all. It had stopped before starting. They often did. Some greedy little gesture, some fumble or misstep, and suddenly an entire psychic history in vine-covered ruins was revealed, after which sincerity was vanquished and in its stead there arose, beneath the patina of pleasantness and strained wit, a desire to part company as quickly as possible without being uncivil. Mysteriously, the drinks had appeared.

"Well," Fred said, settling into his chair. He lifted the tumbler, sniffed, frowned, and swallowed. "Who would've imagined, a mere week ago, that we'd be sitting here in the midst of a raging blizzard?"

"Winter's Last Blast," Martin said.

Fred drew a deep breath and exhaled. "I just love the sticky white stuff," he said, winking. "So what do you do in real life, Martin? When you're not stalking the hallowed halls of Woody's, that is?"

"I'm a social worker. For the city."

"A social worker? How lovely. I'm sure that provides all sorts of grist for the mill. What exactly is involved? I mean, do you run around finding adoptive parents for incest survivors or . . ."

Martin felt a flash of annoyance and dismissed it with the thought that most people believed they understood what social workers did, but few had any real knowledge.

"I manage a caseload. I help people get food stamps. I sign them up for welfare. I find Section 8 housing, if they haven't got a place to live."

"Well, aren't you a regular Dorothy Day."

"It gets old fast if you're not careful. How about you? What do you do?"

"What would you guess?"

"Hmmmm." Martin smiled again, imagining Fred as the petulant manager of a condo complex inhabited by widows addicted to bridge.

"Actually, I'm a priest."

"In the Catholic Church?"

"Ah, something tells me you've had some experience with that venerable institution?"

Martin nodded.

"No, I'm an Episcopal priest."

"What's the difference?"

"Apart from the fact that the Pope's not at all in the picture, it's a matter of degree. The incense is stronger and the vestments more expensive. My parish is high, high Anglican. Oh, and we're not bound to celibacy. Thank God. No pun intended."

"Yeah, but, what do they think about clergymen going to gay bars and, you know, dating men?"

"It's a job. I mean, you have a job, she has a job . . ." he said, nodding toward the waitress, ". . . of sorts. Anyway, we all do something to make ends meet, you see."

Martin granted the point.

"What's the hardest part of being a priest?"

Fred's brows dipped down and back.

"The sermon," he said.

"Well, they say public speaking is the thing people fear the most. Maybe you could take a course? What's that called, Toastmasters?"

The brows rose.

"The delivery is altogether first rate, if I must say so myself. Polished to perfection in 13 years of practice, you see."

"That's how long you've been a priest?"

Fred nodded.

"Then what's the problem?"

"The problem is that I spend at least six hours on Saturday composing my text. Unfortunately, however inspired and erudite it may be, my parishioners seem to care not one whit. It goes right over their empty heads. I could be reciting the Koran in Mandarin or Li Po in Arabic, for all they notice."

"Maybe you could make it more relevant?"

"Relevant?"

Fred snorted and shook the ice in his glass.

"Now there's a word I believed long banished from our modern lexicon. Relevant?"

"I mean, you know, accessible."

"Better, but not by much. So, I should, say, make it entertaining? Throw in a few jokes? Season it with a pun or two?"

"No, that's not exactly what I meant."

Martin blinked.

"Maybe we should just drop the subject?" he said.

"Yes," Fred said, staring at his glass with a slight smile, "perhaps we should. Miss! Oh, miss!!"

The hand he waved was small, chubby, child-like.

What did you do then? Call for a droshky, I hope.

"What's a droshky?"

Oh, c'mon! You've read Chekhov. A cab, darling. A horse-drawn sleigh. That's what mother would've done. Left that cloying cleric, that misogynist minister, that vituperative vicar, that . . .

"OK, OK."

. . . in the lurch. If you tell me you picked up that check, I swear I'll never speak to you again.

"We split it," Martin lied.

Moisture fell in clumps the size of ping pong balls. The sound of boots crunching packed snow reverberated in the frosty air. Carefully they picked their way through the foot-wide paths shoveled or trampled out along sidewalks.

"Well," Martin said, as they arrived at the doors of his apartment building. This was the moment he always dreaded. Goodbyes were bad enough, but when goodbye isn't good, only bye, what to say?

"Drive safely."

Fred cleared his throat.

"I've probably had one more Scotch than I should have. I'm thinking I may perhaps need to use the Gents, if that's alright."

"The what? Oh."

So you invited him up?

"It was the polite thing to do."

Polite is frequently synonymous with stupid. Naturally, once inside the apartment he gave no indication of leaving. Am I right?

"How did you know?"

Mother's been around, darling. And around. And around.

Sure enough, Fred doffed his coat and hat before closing the bathroom door. On reappearing, he indicated no intention of putting them back on.

The passing minutes gathered weight.

"Uh, would you like something to drink? Maybe something warm for the drive home?"

"Tea," Fred said, sighing. "Yes, some tea would be lovely."

Martin went into the kitchen and put the gas on under the kettle. He squatted, watching blue flames fan out across the bottom.

"Lemon and Sweet-N-Low, in case you forgot," Fred shouted.

Martin returned, with a mug of tea.

"That's strange, I haven't seen Momo?"

"The kitty? Must be off chasing a mouse somewhere," Fred said. He glanced around the room, as if observing it for the first time. "Have you lived here long?"

"About four years. I moved in with a boyfriend and after he left, I sort of inherited the apartment."

"Happens quite frequently, I suppose. So, what sort of hobbies have you, Martin, if I may be so bold as to ask?"

"Hobbies? That word always makes me think of model airplanes, and stamp collecting."

"Childhood passions, I take it?"

"Airplanes, yes, stamps, no."

"I've dabbled in philatelic myself now and then. And rare books. Signed first editions are my specialty."

"Collecting can be fun."

"Great fun, provided the objects collected are in suitable taste." Fred paused.

"You've got a fair number of CDs over there."

"I've always been a music lover."

"Pop, and that sort of thing?"

"Actually, I'm a big fan of classical music. I have been for 20 years. Most of my CDs are in cabinets."

"Ummmm. Do you play something?"

"I took piano lessons as a kid. To tell you the truth," Martin said, feeling a sudden need to confess, "one of my biggest regrets is that I never learned to master an instrument."

"I hope that doesn't include the skin flute."

Fred chuckled, rose, and strode toward the window.

"You know," he said, "I would imagine that, even with snow tires, driving in this is going to be rather difficult."

Martin blinked.

"I really think it might be better if I didn't."

"Are you saying . . . you want to stay here?"

"Assuming that's convenient."

"I don't know. I mean, I guess you could sack out there."

Martin nodded toward the sofa.

"That doesn't sound very romantic, now does it?" Fred said, smiling.

Inviting yourself up is bad enough. Insisting on sex is tantamount to rape.

"What could I do? He wasn't taking no for an answer."

You could've directed Reverend Manrammer to the Rittenhouse Sheraton, for starters. I'm sure they have rooms . . . and single grain malts. Or at least locked yourself in the bedroom. Though that type is known to dematerialize and slip beneath doors. Believe me, there is no force in nature more relentless than a horny priest. At the very least, you could've dosed his tea with Valium, something to quell the liturgical libido. Instead . . .

"I know," Martin said. "I know, I know, I know, I know."

The digital clock read nine minutes past midnight. Fred stepped free of one dubious trouser leg, then the next. Thighs swelled against the gray, stained briefs. Button by button, the shirt cleaved into halves that resembled weary flags. Off came the T-shirt, freeing sandbag breasts and football-sized love handles. Tucked between sheets and blankets, Martin watched his guest balance himself with one hand against the wall while unsheathing a sock with the other. How, he thought. Why?

"I made a New Year's resolution to lose weight," Fred said, as he reached for the light switch. "Obviously I haven't gotten around to it yet."

Bedsprings groaned. The mattress dipped. Now a warm paw stroked his chest, the fingers fumbling for a nipple. He felt a second extremity moving in serpentine fashion between his legs. Something warm and moist, then sharp, visited his neck. Meanwhile the member, feverish and diligent, pressed at his back. He twisted in the creature's grip. There was growling. The situation presented only one solution: Mutual masturbation. He reached for the gluey knob. Eighteen minutes later, Fred lay, exhaling great, wet, Scotchscented snores.

Martin woke to see branches laid bare by a low wind. Gingerly he extended an arm, then a leg, over the inert, still-snoring form.

The coffee maker gasped and sputtered. With a whisk, he beat eggs, evaporated milk, and a sprinkling of Parmesan cheese into a mixing bowl. He emptied the mix in a pan from which the smell of just-melted butter simmered. He slid four slices of bread into the toaster oven, folded and re-folded the eggs. From the bedroom he heard a series of gagging wheezes and faint but audible chirps, which called to mind some large, prehistoric bird resting from the labors of extended flight. Hmmmm, Martin thought, his guest would be gone soon. In the meantime, Momo had not reappeared. Alarming. He recalled a recent piece of gossip wherein a repairman had kicked his neighbor's cat, Cleo, after which the cloying Cleo had acted wildly fearful, then vicious, and eventually had to be put down.

"Coffee or tea?" he shouted, startled at the no-nonsense tone in his voice.

They ate in silence. Unshaven, Fred looked as if he'd tumbled from a train.

"What time is it?"

"Ten o'clock."

"Is it still snowing?"

"Stopped hours ago."

Fred, nodding, lifted the mug and closed his eyes. Martin watched the throat bob, the mug resume its place on the table.

"So, Martin, what are your plans for today?"

"I have quite a number of things to do," Martin said, for two or three seconds profoundly regretting his inability to lie with finesse, then reveling in the obviousness of this untruth, with all its dismissive implications. "This morning, for instance, I need to get to the post office."

"Will they be open?"

"It's Saturday. They're open till two."

"What about the weather?"

"Everything's open, Fred. This isn't the suburbs."

"I see."

Fred looked around.

"How far is it? Perhaps I could give you a ride?"

And with the thought that freedom was less than an hour away, Martin agreed to this arrangement.

The cars lining each side of the street were indistinguishable under a foot of wet snow. The city was quiet, except for the occasional shovel scraping, the relentless, rattling drip of moisture from roofs and gutters, and, every now and then, the gunning of an engine and the whine and whir of tires spinning for traction.

"This is it," Fred said, swiping a thick layer of snow off the trunk.

"You're sure?"

"Fairly. Though," he stepped back from the car and frowned, "I think it may take a bit of time to get it out."

Martin glanced at his watch.

"It can't take too long, because I need to be somewhere by noon."

They started. Martin pushed armfuls of snow off the hood. He found the windshield more difficult to clear, as the snow closest to the glass had warmed and re-frozen to a half-inch thick crust. Lifting away the last dripping chunk, he saw something large and white hovering beneath the glass. A sign, resting on the dashboard. *CLERGY.*

Fred started the car, a maroon Buick LeSabre. They dug for 15 more minutes to free the tires, then climbed in.

"Isn't this distracting?" Martin said, nodding to the sign on the dashboard. "Where do you want me to put it?"

"Leave it right there," Fred said. "That's my parking ticket prevention placard."

"Your what?"

"As long as it's visible, I never get a ticket. Well, let's just say it's extremely rare."

The tires made a crunching sound as the Buick pulled away. Gripping the steering wheel with small, bloated hands, Fred peered ahead. The streets were slick with packed-down snow, ice melting on top of it. Two blocks from the post office, a problem of some sort caused a half dozen cars to back up, effectively halting their progress.

"Oh, for Christ's sakes, look at this," Fred said.

A white van, marred with graffiti, sat in the middle of the intersection. Three men, one in front and two in the rear, struggled to rock the vehicle free of its rut in the ice.

"This is ridiculous," Fred said. "I don't fucking believe it."

Martin looked away.

"What's there to believe?" he said. "There's ice on the road and they're stuck."

Thirty seconds passed. Fred flicked the window button.

"HURRY UP, YOU MORONS!"

"Fred, for God's sakes, shut up."

Martin watched as the window slid back into place.

"They're doing the best they can," he said, quietly.

"Oh, I forgot. I have a bleeding-heart social worker in the car."

"Well, you won't much longer, because I'm getting out."

"What?"

"I said I'm getting out, *asshole*."

Martin pushed the door open. Turning, he snatched the placard off the dashboard, stepped from the car and whipped it into the air. The sign landed on a sidewalk, where an obliging gust lifted it into a mound of shoveled snow.

The cat, famished for attention, was waiting by the door when Martin returned.

"Alright, Momo, alright," he said. He stroked the animal's head and scooped a can of Fancy Feast into a bowl. For the rest of the day his body afforded him a rare and empowering energy, which he put to use alphabetizing CDs, then cleaning the apartment. On the nightstand, he found a strange wristwatch, gold with straps of alligator hide. Well, he thought, turning it over, he could package it up and mail it back.

So you think you've seen the last of Pastor Priapus?

"He won't be calling again."

Don't be so sure, darling. If I were you, I'd go right down to the hardware store and buy the biggest can of Rid-A-Queen they have.

"Arthur, I made it abundantly clear that under no circumstances

. . ."

Such a naif. Rejection only feeds their frenzy. Now you're a challenge. A challenge invariably becomes a project, and a project requires strategy and perseverance.

"That's insane."

Try to make it fun. Think of it as your own personal horror movie.

Martin came home late on Sunday afternoon to find the red light on his answering machine blinking.

"Martin, it's your mother. I'm calling to remind you to pick up a card for your father. You know he's got a . . ."

Click.

Arthur, darling. Just back from Tower Records with this amazing recording of Khovanschina, *performed live at the Bolshoi . . .*

Click.

"It's Fred."

Pause.

"I have to say, our little tiff, was most unfortunate."

Pause.

"However, I just wanted to let you know that in spite of it, I had a marvelous time Friday night and . . ."

Click.

"Fred again. Listen, did you happen to find a watch somewhere? I believe I set it on the nightstand and just forgot to retrieve it. It's rather expensive, a Phillipe Patek with gold facing and . . ."

Click.

"Martin, Fred. I'm wondering if we can get together next weekend for dinner or a movie? That way you can return my watch to me and . . ."

Click.

"It's Fred. I hope you don't think I'm being a pest, but I just wanted to say I think your cum is extremely yummy and . . ."

Click.

Martin erased the last three messages without playing them. He felt exhausted and went into the bedroom to lie down. He got up 20 minutes later, dropped the watch in the wastebasket and put on a recording of Prokofiev's piano sonatas.

Later that evening, at just after midnight, he was asleep and dreaming when the phone rang.

"Martin?"

"Yes."

"This is Fred. I hope you don't mind my calling this late but I . . ."

"Uh, frankly, I do mind."

"Oh?"

"Yes, I mind very much, as a matter of fact. And if you ever call here again, even once, I'll be paying a visit to the parishioners, where we can all have a splendid little chat about the relevance and erudition of your sermons, as they relate to cocksucking, ass licking, semen guzzling, and other matters of the soul. Is that clear, Fred?"

Martin heard breath released, then a click. He put the phone down. At the end of the bed, the cat stirred and sighed. Martin shifted his legs to avoid disturbing it. Now I'll never get to sleep, he thought. Self-fulfilling prophecy, he thought. Put the light on and read for a while, he thought.

Failing to do anything, his mind flipped through the usual catalog of fear and regret, inevitably returning to an identical point: That what had once seemed theoretical and remote—a life without intimacy—now stood in the immediate foreground, a solid possibility that would grow plainer and more painful with every year that passed. Oh, fuck it, he thought. As he began to drop away, he found himself hoping to return to the dream he'd been having, a dream that found him stranded but serene on remote Arctic shores, where blue-green water lapped at black rock and fissures opened in glacial fields of snow.

THE RISE AND FALL OF MALIBU BARBIE

"Darling," said my friend Richard on the phone one day, for that is how the now-deceased Richard always began and sometimes even ended his conversations, "I've decided to join that new gym that opened on Spruce Street."

He paused, leaning into the silence of my non-response.

"You haven't been there yet?" he said.

I hadn't. Worse, I wasn't even aware it had opened.

"Whaaaaaaaaaat?" he howled. "What *are* you waiting for? *Everyone's* joining!"

Richard fancied himself cutting edge. He was cutting, and there certainly was an edge, but his enthusiasms flowered and blew away as regularly as anything in a rose bed. Hence my somewhat tepid response.

"What exactly is so special about a gym," I said, anxious that the subject be dropped. "I mean, it's a room, right?"

Silence.

"Full of mirrors, mats and weights, right?"

Silence.

"And a bunch of posturing sissies in spandex?"

I heard a growl I chose to interpret as throat clearing. The silence lengthened. I readied myself for the *click* he was quite capable of.

"Honey," Richard finally said, "you're just showing your ignorance. You and the rest of those intellectual queens know nothing about bodybuilding." He paused. "Maybe you ought to go over there and have a look before shooting your mouth off about it. I'll have you know some very hot men work out at that gym, to judge by the, um, outdoor advertising. And, by the way," he paused to take aim before tossing the bait, "you could probably do with a few muscles yourself."

The year was 1982, and bodybuilding among men was beginning

to evolve from an eccentric cult-like activity confined to a coterie of vengeful and isolated misfits into a genuine mass market attracting mostly vengeful, vain, and socially extroverted misfits.

Frankly, I could've cared less. I hadn't set foot in a gym since college and considered myself fortunate. Richard, ever the trendsetter, had belonged to three in as many years.

About an hour later I happened to be strolling in the vicinity of 11th and Spruce streets here in the City of Brotherly Love when curiosity got the better of me. I figured I'd give Richard's latest enthusiasm a quick look-see, if only for the purpose of further baiting him.

He was right about the advertising. A ten-foot panel of glass separated weights, mirrors, and mats from the street and sidewalk. I stood there, watching a lone muscleman in green nylon jogging shorts and the clipped military mustaches of the period shoulder several hundred pounds of iron. I noticed, reflected in the glass, a man with carrot-colored hair standing behind me.

"You know," he said, in that disarming way people have of jumping right into a conversation as if it had a long and fascinating prologue, "I'm still trying to make up my mind about joining."

"What's stopping you?"

"Well, I'm afraid once I do, I'll come a few times and quit. I mean, who wants to waste all that money?"

I acknowledged the validity of this fear and together the carrot-haired gentleman and myself leaned into the window, squinting. More people halted. More people squinted. Soon a small throng had gathered, all male, all unabashedly admiring the bulging pecs and equine thighs of the man in the mustache.

When I entered to fill out an application for membership, I found the proprietor at his customary perch, behind a counter. Under the counter was a glass-walled cabinet filled with sweatshirts, locks, and jock straps. He wore a blue t-shirt faded from many washings, with the word Malibu on the upper left pocket. His eyes, gray-blue, came alive only at the moment when I handed him my credit card. Every now and then he'd look past me toward the sidewalk and the street, like a performer peering discreetly from the wings as his audience gathers.

No one today can remember his name, except that it was one of those names—Bob, Mike, John, Ed—so common that everyone knows at least three of them. When he first arrived in town, all we knew about him was that he hailed from California. This was not exactly secret information, since he sprinkled his sentences with California placenames and every other item of clothing he wore referenced the Golden State. One day he'd don a fashionably faded Bear Flag Republic sweatshirt, the next a Castro Street tank top, the day after that it was a pair of shorts with UCLA printed on them and three days a week, the t-shirt with Malibu on the pocket.

"I want to look like that," Richard whispered one day as we both walked in, nodding to the owner. Calves bulged. Ropes of muscle ran along shoulders, back and arms. His abs were lumps of solid meat. At a time when such bodies were rare, it was a splendid conversation piece.

Bob, Mike, John, Ed or whoever told people he'd been a trainer at "the studios," implying, I suppose, the Hollywood studios. He dropped names: Schwarzenegger, Stallone. He let it be known he'd competed in certain Olympics and insinuated that medals had been awarded.

Within months the alchemy of gossip transformed these from bronze to silver, then from silver to gold.

I grant him this: from the standpoint of marketing, the location—in the heart of the gay community—was a stroke of genius. The sight of beefy guys pumping iron in public was advertising he couldn't have bought with ingots of gold. Hundreds, then hundreds more, applied for membership. Soon the gym, which in its first month harbored an occasional sullen Hercules or two, was packed to the dropped ceilings with bodybuilders and wannabes. Membership became a social necessity. No one noticed, or cared about, the overcrowding or the second-hand equipment.

In the next few months, and merely for having opened a business everyone was desperate to patronize, the owner of the gym became an icon. He was treated and feted, taken up and talked about, his bland pronouncements attended to as if he were Emerson discoursing on the relationship between thought and feeling.

"Darling." Richard said to me one day, on the phone. "We were at a dinner party at the home of____ on Saturday. You'll never guess who the guest of honor was?"

I mentioned the name of the owner of the gym.

"How did you know?" he shrieked.

Who couldn't know? He was on every A list in town. Various individuals mounted elaborate attempts at brown-nosing— extending invitations to dinners, seats in opera boxes, weekend jaunts to vacation homes—to get chummy with him. They sought him out on diets to follow and supplements to take. They asked about his preference in sportswear and equipment. They made a point of showing up at the restaurants and bars he patronized to be seen talking with him or even just waving at him from across a packed room.

It's hard to say exactly when this honeymoon began to fade. At some point the forever-kibitzing habitués of the gym began to find holes in the rickety structure of whatever story they'd pieced together on his behalf. Someone noticed, for instance, that the owner was not being completely forthcoming about his age. To one patron he volunteered it as 34, to another, 28, to a third, 30. Yet the map of faint lines across his face indicated either a life of dissipation or the fact that a decade added to any of these figures would've been fully believable.

"Twenty-eight?" Richard said, incredulous. "As in: year of birth?" He paused. "Honey, she was neck to neck with Jesse Owens in the Berlin Olympics. We're talking 1936. Hitler pinned those fucking medals on her chest."

This discrepancy opened the trail to others. Suddenly it was noticed that the owner's hair—which resembled spun strands of sunlight—was of a color which did not occur naturally among humans, at least after the age of six. Following that realization, all seemed open to skepticism.

"Darling," Richard whispered, glancing over at the proprietor one afternoon, between bench presses, "you just don't get a body like that without steroids!"

"What're steroids?" I said, wincing at the image of pulverized lamb fetuses sautéed in foul and noxious chemicals.

"Beef boosters! Magic muscles!" Richard intoned. "Honey, you are such a naïf!" His voice dropped to a stage whisper. "And that ain't the half. She's done drugs you and I have never heard of."

Around this time a discernible change in the owner's attitude began to be manifest. It was noticed, for instance, that he never offered to pick up any portion of a lunch or dinner tab. At the convenience store around the corner, I once saw him pause and wait, expecting a stranger to hold the door for him. And whether it was medication, mood swings, or a firmly resolved notion that some people merited courtesy while others did not, he began to be unfriendly to select customers. No attempt was made to disguise this. Someone he disliked or to whom he was indifferent would approach the desk.

Perfectly well aware of their presence, he'd let them stand a full minute before looking up with a quick, curt, "Yes?"

As membership soared, a decree came down in the form of a memo posted on the bulletin board. Henceforth the establishment on Spruce Street would be a place for "serious body builders" only. These, presumably, included not only the behemoths in their leather girdles, farting and howling ORRRKKKGGGG!!! and GRRRRAAAARRGGGHHH!! while hefting great elephantine loads, but the hot young numbers the owner met in afterhours clubs such as the DCA, who, rumor had it, were not only welcome but came for free. Frumps and fatsos, the scrawny, old, ungainly, ugly and—God forbid—effeminate, were all now carefully screened, their applications denied with the excuse that the gym was full and taking no new members.

Not content with this, the owner next moved to "disinvite" some who were already paid-in-full, including even a few who'd joined when the place was empty and untried. Such as, for instance, Lawrence B.

Lawrence B. was a chubby, helium-voiced individual with weedlike hairs extending from back and biceps, natural receptors of whatever electrical currents happened to be passing through the room. He worked as an instructor at a beauty school. Give Lawrence credit. He showed up just about every day. No amount of diligence, however, seemed to alter the essential physique, which resembled that of a sea mammal, minus tusks.

The owner, by now, was long in the habit of ignoring him. But one day Lawrence B., taking one of innumerable short breaks, was loudly gabbling by the water cooler. His voice, the upper registers of which could not only shatter glass but melt it, penetrated every ear and angle. The owner glanced up. He jerked his chin back, beckoning Lawrence B. to the desk.

"I am," he said, "revoking your membership, as of today."

"What?" said Lawrence B., who appeared not to understand.

"You heard what I said, you ridiculous queen, you're outta here," said the owner. "Now collect your things and go."

"What are you talking about?" said Lawrence B., "I just paid $1000 for a three-year membership!"

"What I'm talking about," said the owner, "is that I can't afford to have you as a member of this gym. The people I want to attract are not going to join, or stay, with a fat silly faggot like you prancing around."

This exchange caused the decibel level to drop to near-zero. It ended with a shell-shocked Lawrence B. disappearing into the locker room, from which he emerged moments later with his gym bag slung so low you'd have thought it contained bowling balls.

"Darling, did you hear?" Richard squealed. "The owner threw Lawrence B. out of the gym today! He gave him the gate!!"

"I not only heard about it," I said. "I was there to witness it."

"Whaaaaaaaaaat?!" he almost screamed. "Tell me all! EVERYTHING!!"

Lawrence B. was back the next day. He pushed the glass doors open and strode toward the desk with a prophet's blazing eye.

"I didn't particularly appreciate what you said to me yesterday, motherfucker," is how it started. The owner reared back, flashing his best blond sneer, prepared to take up where he'd left off. He didn't get far.

"You have no legal right to revoke my membership just because of who I am," Lawrence B. informed him.

"This is a private club," the owner snorted, "and I..."

"Yes it is a private club," interrupted Lawrence B., "and by engaging in discrimination you are in violation of city, state and Federal statutes. The lawsuit I'm going to file will close this dump in a week!"

At the sound of the dreaded word, the proprietor's self-assured belligerence vanished. "Calm down," he urged, "calm down." He took a long pull on his bottle of Evian. "Alright," he said, screwing the cap back on, "you can continue coming."

"Continue coming?" said Lawrence B. "You can go fuck yourself, Mary. You're going to write me a check for the full amount of my membership right now and then I hope and pray never to have to see your steroid-soaked, pill-popping, bottle-blond ass again in my life. *Fucking freak!*"

The spat with Lawrence B. proved a turning point. The next day the owner appeared at the usual time and in his usual attire, a pair of jeans and the blue t-shirt with Malibu printed on the pocket. But an undue quiet prevailed, signaling some reverse magic. "Hey," someone said, loud enough that all within 30 feet might share in the jibe, "did you hear how Malibu Barbie over there threw Lawrence B. out of the gym?"

Certain nasty nicknames stick. Others don't. Those which do require not only the adhesive of malice, but the gripping surface of deserved contempt. In this case, the analogy between the owner of the gym and the plastic form, excelsior hair and tabula rasa personality of a toy manufactured by the Mattel Company captured some previously undefined essence. It spread like coffee on mohair. A few droll wits among the bodybuilders began inserting it as a reference point in their conversations. "We saw Malibu Barbie at the Streisand concert," someone would say, between bench presses. Or: "Malibu Barbie was dancing at the DCA last night with..." someone would gasp, while undergoing self-torture sessions at the squat machine.

The damnable shirt was swiftly consigned to the rag bag. It made no difference. One afternoon a spray of roses arrived, addressed to a certain Malibu Barbie. A week after that the postman delivered an anonymously dispatched parcel containing the now-infamous namesake. Mischievous souls began calling the front desk to inquire whether or not they'd reached Malibu Barbie's Gym. Such calls caused the owner to slam down the phone and disappear into his office for what was variously rumored to be either nose candy or a nap.

He must've believed the derisive moniker would fade, like a California tan. On the contrary, time lent it permanence. This was signaled when, three months after the Lawrence B. episode, one of the cattier members, a florist the owner clearly didn't care for, approached the desk while a handful of confreres looked on. He stood there a minute or so while the proprietor paged through a protein supplements catalog, making no effort to acknowledge his presence. The gym was one giant ear.

"Um, excuse me," he said.

"Yes?"

"I think my meter's about to run out. Would you be a doll and give me change for a dollar?"

He cleared his throat.

"In quarters?"

I have never quite a seen a face that color before. From its natural shade—pale as the moon moving from white to yellow—it bloomed instantly to horizon's pinkest edge, deepening by the second from raspberry to vermilion to burgundy. Every blood cell rushed to the front. From the shoulders up Malibu Barbie was a bust of molten iron. You could feel the heat from across the room.

Finally, without replying, the owner drew a deep breath and, opening the change drawer, extracted four quarters, which he pushed across the counter as if they were flattened pellets of shit. The unfortunate nickname soon proved to be a minor problem, relative to the larger one of declining membership. Word was out that a bigger facility was opening a block away. The competitive gym would feature three levels filled with new equipment and classes in step and aerobics. No sooner did it open than the crop-topped hunks who'd arrived as pioneers began to desert the fort.

I remember overhearing a pair of them discussing this decision. These two were among the many who'd invited Malibu Barbie to their opera boxes, brunches, and beach homes.

"This place is so tired," said the one.

"I could faint just thinking about it," said the other.

"It's almost as tired as the owner," said the first.

"Nothing but death could be that tired," said the second.

Etc.

Suddenly rooms which had resembled a Saturday night disco equipped with weights appeared near-empty. And with cash flow difficulties came unpaid bills and missed payrolls, which led in turn to unscrubbed shower stalls, unchanged light bulbs, and a dozen other reminders of an evaporated prosperity.

"Oh dear," Richard sighed one afternoon. to no one in particular, "has anyone noticed this place is getting...icky?"

Indeed, it was. And a day or so later I happened to overhear Malibu Barbie on the phone, pleading with Bell of Pennsylvania for another week in which to scrape up the funds to pay his bill. "I'm a business," I heard him say. "Please don't shut me off."

They didn't. But the situation hardly improved. And now the hard core—those without the resources to simply pull up stakes and migrate to the next new thing around the corner—discovered that gym memberships and steroids weren't the only wares Malibu Barbie had to sell. At various times older gentlemen arrived, looking nervous and eager. To judge by their shape, and age, they weren't exactly power lifters. They would stand around the front desk chatting with the owner for a minute or two, then disappear into his office, where, from behind closed doors, grunts, groans, slurps, and sighs issued. The proprietor made no effort to rein in this little commotion. On the contrary, Malibu Barbie acted as if the knowledge that he could get paid for sex was another mode of one-upmanship.

"Darling," Richard said. "I was at the gym today and you'll never believe what happened?"

"What?" I said.

"Well, these two guys showed up. They looked like mafiosi on a fishing trip. They disappeared into the back room with the owner.

I was doing lats at the time, you understand, so I happened to be close to the office door and..." Here he cleared his throat... "I heard the distinct sounds of men having sex. Are you familiar with those sounds?"

"Um, somewhat."

"Then I won't need to describe them. Anyway..."

Somehow, in the space of six months, Malibu Barbie had gone from the toast of the town to burnt toast. Now, as he was about to go from burnt toast to bankruptcy, he hit on what appeared to be a solution to his problems. At least the financial ones.

The concept was not quite as ingenious as his original idea of locating on the ground floor behind plate glass. It was just crude. Crude but energetic.

Flyers appeared on telephone poles, bulletin boards, walls, windshields, everywhere, advertising bargain rate prices for membership. A single year—previously $500—dropped to $225. Three years, which once cost a grand, now ran $400. Eight hundred bucks bought lifetime rights to the place.

This produced the desired effect. The gym was almost crowded again. But these new members were not the power lifters of old. No, it looked as if an army of the flabby, skinny, outsized, desperate, and depraved had seized and occupied the facility. Art students with magenta hair fashioned into foot-long points hefted barbells. Bow-tied antique store proprietors, poodle owners, and dimestore pederasts posing as clergymen, all pumped iron. For the first time, women—in the form of a trio of motorcycle dykes—invaded the hallowed halls of masculinity. Now the toned and bulging Atlases who remained found themselves distinctly in the minority. Needless to say, the small crowds which had gathered outside to admire them were a thing of the past.

"Darling," Richard said, "I have been more loyal than a dog to its master. More loyal than Job to God. More loyal than anyone had a right to ask or expect. But there are limits. And this is an imposition beyond tolerance. It is too much!"

"Richard," I said, "what in God's name are you talking about?"

"Well, today I was at Malibu Barbie's gym and this creature with pink hair, thin enough to squeeze through a keyhole, informed me that I could use the squat machine if and when he, she or whatever it is was done with its sets."

"How long did you have to wait?"

"At least seven minutes!" He paused. "But that's not the point. The gym's gone totally to hell. Malibu Barbie's signed up all this riff raff. And that's not all. To quote Walt Whitman, there are real female women in there!"

"So?"

"*So?!?* So, I am joining that new place. As of today. You are welcome to accompany me, if you wish."

I demurred. But one morning about a month later as I was walking down Spruce Street I was surprised to come across a crowd gathered in front of the gym's windows. Ah, deja vu. But drawing closer, I noted that the contingent assembled there had a whole different look and feel than the peeping Toms of merely a year prior. Everyone carried a gym bag. They stared, blinked, babbled, and shook their heads. They looked like ghouls gracing an accident scene.

"They say he loaded it all up on a truck at 4 this morning," the man standing next to me said.

Inside, a single overhead light glowed. Every bench, mat, machine and iron plate was gone. The water cooler was gone. The counter and cabinet full of sweatshirts, protein pills and overpriced locks, gone. Dustbunnies breathed in the corners. "I bought a lifetime membership last week," I heard someone say. I turned. It was the carrot-haired man I'd talked with the day I came down to check the place out. "That prick," he said, to no one in particular.

"He got eight hundred dollars of my money!"

As a subject, Malibu Barbie's exit kept the bars, restaurants, and coffee shops of our little enclave in excellent gossip for at least two weeks. People who loathed each other suddenly found a subject they could discuss in perfect civility. But time has a way of leaving such things behind, and soon enough the members of the community moved to new topics and fell back on longstanding antipathies.

Maybe a year or so later, I was at a dinner party when someone—

the host, I believe—raised the subject of Malibu Barbie's abrupt departure. Indignation mixed with abjection as several guests who'd held on to the bitter end conceded they'd been taken in. Others—those who'd abandoned the gym for its competitor—righteously claimed to have smelled a rat from the get-go. Our host, just back from Palm Springs, waited until coffee and dessert had been served before asking to be excused. He returned with newspaper in hand. Before he'd even opened it I knew what I was going to see. There it was, a half-page ad with special introductory membership rates. A look of winsome guile graced the mug of Whatzisname. I recognized the bench he perched on by a familiar crack in the vinyl. Seeking The Serious Body Builder, read the line across the top.

"Oh my God," someone said. "Can you believe it?"

"That son of a bitch!"

"Shameless swine!"

"Call the police!"

"Fuck the police! CALL THE FBI!!"

Etc.

I felt as if I'd landed in the middle of a chiffon lynch mob. There were cries for Malibu Barbie's arrest, his imprisonment, exile, torture, execution, and corpse desecration. Having played the fool a few too many times, I held my tongue. So did our host, who leaned back, wearing the faintest of grins. I doubt he'd ever lifted anything heavier than a martini.

People come and go. It's been at least a decade since I last heard Richard's voice gushing on about the reservation he'd made for us at some new restaurant catering to the most arcane of palettes, or about that revival of *Fidelio* at the Met "that, no excuses, we simply cannot miss!" or describing the Iranian movie at the Ritz he'd just that afternoon returned from, "in Farsi, darling, with subtitles, of course." I think of him every few months or so. His splendid physique—at one point, he could bench press twice his own weight—was a source of great pride, until illness overcame him, at which point those muscles vanished like a costume on loan.

And every now and then, usually as I book a flight to California, I mentally trip across the image of Malibu Barbie. I still see those eyes—blue fading to gray—which I recall as hungry and hard, and which today I would recognize from nearly any distance as treachery's flag. Those who remember the episode speak of him as vicious, and a con. Who knows? It may be that the only talent he had was for painting himself into corners, and that he carried his corners with him from state to state. On a truck.

And only yesterday I caught sight of Lawrence B. sauntering along Spruce Street. It was that, in fact, which triggered these recollections. He was unshaved, slightly wider, with a baseball cap concealing his gleaming dome. His chin tilted upward, as if he were at one with tall buildings, and his mouth wore that slightly pursed expression of disappointment and defense I have come to recognize as habitual. He would've been, I'm sure, ready in a second to disgorge the latest indignities inflicted on him by the larger world, but for the moment he seemed perfectly comfortable and absorbed in the slightly smaller one of his own making, so I let him pass without acknowledgment, as I went about the business of my day.

DISH

In the middle of the 1980s, there used to gather in the corner booth of a certain diner a short block from Philadelphia's Rittenhouse Square a motley assemblage of debauched hairdressers, disgruntled waiters, testy ex-seminarians, disbarred attorneys and sundry other defamed and defrocked persons—in other words, the dispossessed of careers—joined from time to time by various individuals who'd never had careers to kill, though if they'd had, rest assured, these would've died an embarrassing and unseemly death.

Alcohol and its ravages brought these people together, for the group was a subset of something larger, that is, the Alcoholics Anonymous meeting which gathered daily in the basement of the church up the street.

The basement was a low, broad room interspersed with wide pillars where, on any given occasion, 75 to 100 people sat on folding wooden chairs facing a table on which a microphone rested. The arrangement divided seating into thirds—left, right and center—and in time it came to be that the rows immediately to the speaker's left attracted those of the homosexual persuasion, this being unofficially christened the 'Chiffon section.' Afterwards, a coterie of Chiffons drifted down the street toward the diner and its corner table, there to cackle and cluck and otherwise pass the time, which in those days moved as slowly as growing hair.

At the diner, before and after these meetings, discussion generally fell into one of two broad categories: addiction or gossip. The talk regarding addiction was full of party line pronouncements, pseudo-scientific theories, and grisly or mock-heroic drinking anecdotes. The gossip, on the other hand, focused on money, sex, and careers.

Failure cast its shadow over all these conversations. Who had lost his job and why, who'd been dumped by a lover and for what reason, who was being two-timed and by whom, who had embezzled how much from an employer, who had declared bankruptcy, who was being hounded by the IRS, and most especially who had resumed drinking and under what circumstances, the whole range of flaws and fetishes, mishaps and mistakes, provided an inexhaustible and often exhilarating fund of subject matter for the group. The coffee flowed and the adrenaline ran high. The atmosphere was raucous, defiant, and uncouth, erupting periodically into mocking laughter. Sometimes this mirth consisted of the reassuring roar that follows any well-formulated exercise of wit, but more often it seemed the hard and bitter ribaldry of the defeated, with sarcasm its catalyst and judgment its subtext.

Besides myself, some of the principals usually included in these impromptu assemblies were Robert Hatch, a former heroin user and aspiring poet, forever lugging with him the William Carlos Williams Reader, and Duncan Nesbitt, a waiter at one of the better restaurants on Spruce Street. Hatch's several eccentricities included his abhorrence of pets or plants, and his refusal, based on some unexplained principle, to reveal his age or shake anyone's hand. He never told the truth if he could help it, compulsive lying being one of the many "character defects" he was "working on." Nesbitt, in his early 30s and already rapidly balding, sometimes spoke in a squishy lisp. He typically limited his conversation to objections or complaints, chief among which was that the owner of the establishment where he'd worked for years refused to fire him for his many drunken and drug-addled escapades, only because, he insisted, she enjoyed it and wished to go on making his life a misery.

Other habitues included Thom McDuff and David Featherstone. McDuff was a one-time tax attorney who had drunk himself out of more jobs than boyfriends and now drove a cab. Featherstone, a hairdresser, occasionally impersonated Marilyn Monroe at a Center City club with no name in an alley that didn't deserve one. With his mood-wide face, moist brown eyes and yellow hair, he was easily mistaken for a sunflower.

Daniel Burnham and John Wood, who always showed up together and were fond of trading insider quips, often frequented the table. Burnham, a raven-haired beauty who worked for the company his parents owned, drove a jeep owned by that company, and lived in a house which the company also owned. The last chapter in Burnham's drinking career involved passing out in a locked bathroom aboard an Amtrak train, which necessitated the intervention of the Baltimore Police, whom conductors invited aboard at that city's Pennsylvania Station. The cops pried open the door and carried the bewildered Burnham out and off, to the cheers of passengers, exasperated by delay. Wood, a short, cute boy from the suburbs, was adept at firing off flippant bon mots. He liked to retail horror stories of his drinking days, as we all did, though his involved, often enough, waking up beside trolls with no recollection of where he'd met them. Cesar Birrato, a lanky ex-hustler from South Philly with hair the color of moist wheat, manned the Aramis counter at Wannamakers. He showed up everywhere reeking of scent, and was often in the company of Terry "Father" Mayo. Father Mayo was a former student of the priesthood at St. Charles Bartolomeo, where he claimed to have bedded a third of the faculty and half the graduating class, before being expelled for various sexcapades.

All these, including myself, gathered daily, nightly, and frequently in the afternoons at the corner table. Sometimes novices, stragglers and even jaded AA veterans joined the gathering. But the one figure that dominated the proceedings, who, for a little more than a year, it seemed, was always there, and always talking, and came to incarnate its very spirit, was Edgar Moffit.

It is characteristic of the provinces that a clamor for the company of newcomers arises should these have anything—beauty, charm or a perky ass—to offer. Edgar, equipped with all three, showed up one evening at the meeting and immediately turned heads. No sooner were the proceedings mumbled to a close than he was four deep in people scratching out phone numbers.

One of these people led him to the diner where, ensconced at the corner table, he quietly sized us all up. He was back the next day, voluble and assertive. Within a week he was appearing daily. In a month, Edgar ruled.

"My dears," he'd begin, rescuing us from one of those occasional moments of sullen silence, "is it my own hypersensitivity to aesthetic matters or did someone else notice that the hair on top of our speaker's head and the hair surrounding his ears are distinctly different colors? Or shall I say ...*shades* of a single color?"

"Talk about a cut rate dye job," said Featherstone.

"It's a wig, you idiot," said Burnham.

Wood looked away, rolling his eyes,

"Est-her!" said Cesar, holding his cup aloft that our diligent and overworked waitress, one of three old troupers working the tables, might refill it with the brown boiled acid that passed for coffee.

"And not a particularly expensive one, I would venture to say," Edgar continued, jerking his neck so as to toss back the six or so inches of sandy hair which had fallen across his forehead. "Certainly, an ambulance chaser like her should be able to swing something a little classier than that moth-eaten muff."

"I heard he dove in a pool in Key West and when he climbed out, it was floating on top of the water," said Hatch, pushing his cup across the table.

"Those queens must've thought a muskrat had gotten in," said Father Mayo, handing Esther his own cup.

"Or a manatee," said Wood.

Edgar dressed in faded green or maroon turtlenecks under plain or plaid wool sport coats with patched sleeves. His conversation mixed the occasional original insight with a repository of artistic anecdotes, appropriated witticisms, and mentally rehearsed gag lines. He was 32, with pale blue eyes in a face conventionally handsome till you arrived at the mouth, where a thin upper lip drew away at the corner in a curious kind of curl, as if, in the course of development, the body had outrun its supply of connective tissue, though what had happened is that the lip had merely outspent its muscular strength performing several million sneers.

If gossip was Edgar's forte, innuendo was his signature. What he didn't know about a person he imagined. Every inference became an assumption, each assumption a fact, every fact a body of them. What was remarkable was how accurate he could be in discerning, for instance, that so-and-so's emphatic defense of monogamy meant that the monogamist was preparing an out-of-wedlock tryst or had just one; or that someone's spirited denunciation of child molestation was all the proof anyone needed to confirm that he was either its victim or its perpetrator.

"My dears," he said one day, when Featherstone was absent, "is it an illusion on my part or has David at some point been the victim of a...funny uncle?"

"Odd you should ask," said McDuff, who proceeded to unburden himself of Featherstone's darker secrets, among which was an unpleasant episode involving the pre-pubescent David and a member of the Roman Catholic clergy, drawn out—at Edgar's prompting—in minute detail.

Edgar specialized in sniffing out falsehoods, concealed desires, and other evidence of sham. Closeted skeletons and physical flaws were a specialty. Somehow, he had come to know about X's L-shaped penis, Y's protuberant naval, about that Greenland-shaped birthmark on so-and-so's lower back, or the nasty case of eczema that _____ was at such pains to conceal. ("Have you ever seen her with a shirt off? Of course not! It's like fish scales on diaper rash...everywhere!"). Where and how he retrieved these tidbits was a mystery, to me at least.

"Look at that!" Wood said one day, as everyone turned to watch a stunning physique sheathed in designer jeans move at a brisk, confident pace up Spruce Street.

"Oh, that's Nathan Freed," Nesbitt said.

"Nathan who?" said Featherstone.

"Plays oboe in the Orchestra," offered McDuff, lifting his coffee.

"I believe he's also a composer of some renown," said Hatch.

"My God, what a body," said Father Mayo.

"I wish I could get a torso like that," said Cesar.

"I'd just as soon settle for borrowing his," said Wood. "At least for an evening."

Everyone stared.

"My dears," Edgar said, expelling a short puff of air, flicking bangs from his forehead, and drawing his upper lip back in what could've been either excitement or contempt, "I have it on good authority that the back of that particular body has more fur on it than a rug made from the skin of *ursus horribilus*, also known as the American grizzly."

Silence.

"No!" said Hatch, feigning horror.

"Appalling!" said Burnham.

"Ah was weak!" said Nesbitt, who had lived in the South for a time and there acquired a small repertoire of exclamations, often pronounced with a faint drawl.

"Yes," said Edgar, "which is why Nathan's last lover left him. And the one before that. And the one before that. To qualify for a date, you not only have to be a season subscriber, you need to own a hedge trimmer."

As for Edgar's history, or chronology, it blurred somewhat. He'd come to Philadelphia from Harrisburg, and to Harrisburg from Pittsburgh, and to Pittsburgh from somewhere else, which someone said was West Virginia, though nothing of the hills remained in his speech. He mentioned these places at AA meetings—he'd been sober for a little more than a year—but they were allusions, fragments disconnected to any larger whole. About specifics he tended to evade, and if someone tried to pin the larger picture of his story into place by asking where he'd grown up or gone to school or where his parents now lived, his response provided no real information and cut the line of questioning off altogether.

One day, a month or two after he came to town, I arrived at the diner immediately following the meeting to find only Edgar at the corner table. We sat in a stalemate of anxious silence, not really knowing each other, only about each other. He nodded, glanced around, and picked up the menu. I found myself wishing the others would arrive. Then—as if he'd stepped onto a stage and was therefore compelled to speak—he set the menu down and began talking. He told me he found Philadelphia far preferable to where he'd lived previously.

"Harrisburg?"

Edgar nodded.

"Did you come here for a job?"

No, he explained. He'd come to escape a violent and tyrannical lover.

"Esther!" he snapped, waving.

"Where'd you meet him?"

"At a bar. He was playing pinball. Asked if I wanted to play. I'd never played pinball in my life, but he was hot. Very."

"What was his name?"

"Alonzo."

"That's one I haven't heard."

"He was black," Edgar said.

"So, what happened?"

"I realized a few months after we moved in that he was using cocaine. Freebasing. Then he started cheating on me. We'd be coming down the street and he'd be looking at some guy walking past. I'd get pissed and say: you're cruising him, aren't you? And Alonzo would say: 'Forget it. It's just the drugs.' And finally I said: "You're right, it *is* the drugs. And he slapped me."

"On the street?"

"He loved drama. Lived for it. Who could blame him? The street is a theater that elevates to sublimity every banal emotion. And banal emotions were the only ones Alonzo knew. Then...we'd get home."

"Yeah."

"And he'd pick up where he left off."

"You mean..."

"Right. Black eyes, bloody nose, the whole thing. It usually ended in rape."

"Why'd you stay?"

"I was drinking, and Alonzo paid the rent," he said, with a shrug that implied I knew exactly what he was talking about and no further explanation was needed.

He tore open a packet of sugar, deposited the contents in his cup and turned back to me with eyes of tenderest regard.

"I stopped drinking, for a while," he continued. "Alonzo thought that was great. Then he changed his tune. Got really nasty. One day, while he was out—probably copping—I packed everything and fled.

"Does he know where you are?"

Edgar shook his head.

Pain is such an appealing dimension in others. It's not until you've seen people desperate and howling that they become fully human.

"So what about you, Eric?" he said. "You're a hot guy. I'm sure love's thrown a few curveballs in your direction?"

Edgar leaned forward on patched elbows, brows furrowed, while I hashed out the history of my self-thwarted pursuit of Eros. Just as it seemed we'd broken through to something, had entered some zone of enlightenment and understanding, the doors flew open and Nesbitt, Hatch, McDuff and the rest entered. Edgar scratched something on a piece of paper and slipped it in my hand. McDuff, ever vigilant, settled in next to me and without looking at Edgar, whispered: "Careful, honey. You can't take her anywhere."

The apartment to which he invited me two days later was a large studio fronting on Lombard east of Broad Street. The block was a shabby stretch of third-rate pizza parlors, bike repair shops and hippie jewelry establishments. In the foyer of Edgar's building, crinkled tape fastened withered strips of paper to mailboxes, pieces of paper on which the names of past tenants had been crossed out, and the names of new ones scratched in. It had a certain appealing squalor. Edgar lived on the third floor.

The place was furnished with thrift shop detritus, but among the knock-kneed end tables and cat clawed easy chairs, the chipped ashtrays and motel-era lamps, three items stood in relief. The first was a cabinet packed with Fiesta ware and Depression glass. The second, more intriguing, was a glass coffee table, cut in the shape of an open palm and mounted on delicately curved legs of hand-hewn cherry. The third was a chair the back of which consisted of one long slab of wood, planed and stained to perfection, set on a boxy frame of sawed poles, each painted a different color. Edgar, searching for Sanka, pretended nonchalance, and when I asked where he'd gotten the coffee table and chair, he explained he'd designed and built them himself. He was, he said, a great admirer of Frank Lloyd Wright and the Prairie School, which I imagined as some sort of Nebraska educational institution. He planned to apply to Penn to finish his architecture degree at some point. He'd saved $4,000 to that end.

Edgar kept his back to me as he trotted around the apartment in black jeans, I suppose to provide ample time for viewing the magnificent ass of which he was clearly all too aware. I had this idea it would begin with a long, passionate kiss and proceed from there. Instead, Edgar repaired to a closet and reappeared with what looked like a handful of belts, after which, poking around beneath the kitchen sink, he turned, cleared his throat, and tossed a length of clothesline at my feet.

"You know," he said, grinning, "you'd look really good in a leather harness."

This was so unexpected, and so completely in conflict with my own arcane notions of finding romance, that it was as if a plug had been pulled and desire, like an overheated appliance, wheezed to a halt. Not that soulmates can't or don't come in leather harnesses, or wound and knotted clothesline for that matter, but the suggestion seemed both wanton and calculated.

I was, I concede, tempted to give Edgar what he wanted: a good thrashing, followed by a deep, slow fuck. But then it occurred to me that this was about more than sex. Edgar had arranged our rendezvous not to launch a romance, but to assemble a dossier. So I told him I felt uncomfortable and thought it would be a good idea if we got to know each other more, and perhaps that could begin by going out to eat, as planned.

The restaurant Justine's was designed in someone's cocaine-fueled imagination to resemble a sheik's vast tent, cozy verging on claustrophobic. Parachutes draped the ceilings. In place of an actual harem, black and white photos of starlets, encased in Deco frames, covered all available surfaces. Period accoutrement prevailed. To add to the sense of willed eccentricity, every table, chair, and piece of silver- and flatware differed from the next, all of it providing a suitable context for some major attitude on the part of the waitstaff, for which the place was far more famed than its food.

A rasping debauchee I recognized from late nights-or should I say early mornings? —at the 247, a druggy after hours club, led us through several doorways to an inconspicuous table. After a moment Chip, his name, another fading veteran of Philadelphia nightlife, arrived with his pad. He introduced himself with a tortured sigh and stood waiting. Were we ready? Edgar shot him a look intended to both threaten and condemn, at which point we both ordered soup and other items I can't quite recall.

Edgar's spoon had no sooner dipped beneath the surface of the soup—cream of cauliflower with a tinge of tarragon—then a shadow crossed his face. He lifted, sipped, lifted, sipped, set the spoon on the plate, and stared at the bowl in disbelief. The corner of his lip rose.

"Something wrong?"

Without replying, he lifted the spoon, dug through the liquid, inspected the contents. What I saw was white cream with a fleck or two of herb.

"Is it...bad or something?"

Hand raised and fingers snapping, Edgar summoned Chip, who'd apparently been nipping vodka in the pantry, to judge by the odor.

"This soup has not been properly cooked."

"It's been on the stove all afternoon."

"Why, then, are there pieces of cauliflower in it?"

Edgar brandished his spoon, in which rested a ghostly sprig of undissolved coral.

Chip glanced and looked away.

"I don't know what the soup's like at Cracker Barrel, or wherever it is you're accustomed to dining," he said, "but that's what cream of cauliflower is supposed to be like. Would you care to see a recipe?"

I wondered for a moment if Edgar would hurl the soup in the waiter's face before the waiter had a chance to empty a nearby water pitcher over Edgar's head.

By now, of course, all within earshot had ceased dining and were making no effort whatever to be discreet about eavesdropping.

The maitre'd arrived and, clearly exasperated, demanded to

know if there was "a problem." Edgar and the waiter both began speaking at once, at which point waiter and maitre'd disappeared—likely for another hit of vodka—only to reappear in three minutes to announce that there would be no charge for the soup. Or, at least not for Edgar's.

I was prepared to write all this off as an accident, except that two days later, in Little Pete's, a greasy Greek spoon on 17th Street, Edgar got into a nasty tussle with the waitress over the freshness, or lack thereof, of the coffee, and then, a day after that, caused a similar commotion at Tony's Pizza on Pine Street when he vigorously disputed the quantity of pepperoni on the pie we'd ordered. He claimed to have been shorted. That nearly got us tossed out of the place.

"Didn't I tell you," McDuff said, when I ran into him on the street the next day. "He's the terror of every restaurant in Center City. Including Taco Bell and McDonald's."

"But he's never pulled that in the diner," I said.

"He tried once or twice but the owner put his foot down," McDuff said. "Told him if it happened one more time, he was barred."

All might have gone on as it had, the members of our little claque bitching, kvetching, squabbling, and back-biting as before, except that in April of that year a fresh face arrived at the meeting up the street, which shifted matters considerably.

For weeks, all anyone knew was that his name was Lionel, and the reason they knew that was because those who attended the meeting were required to introduce themselves by stating their given name. When someone—McDuff or Hatch, I think, though it may've been Father Mayo—finally ferreted out the information that Lionel's surname was Dove, that single syllable closing on a consonant as soft as slowly folded wings seemed eminently logical, since there was something avian about his person, though Hawk would've made more sense, as the diminutive Lionel had the large piercing eyes of a raptor and there could easily have been talons concealed in the $800 shoes he wore. In any event, the discovery of that one small piece of information launched a frenzy to find more.

Lionel Dove seemed in no way ordinary. To our meetings up the street he wore jeans washed and faded to precision with a cotton shirt of designer label, but elsewhere he dressed, as they say, to the nines: cashmere sweaters, linen shirts and slacks, footwear of thinly tanned leather with straps and unobtrusive buckles. Jewelry was a passion. Lionel sported ornamental rings—set with sapphires and emeralds—and neck chains and wrist bracelets of hammered gold. With that omnipresent and enigmatic smile, he looked as if he moved, or had moved, in circles where money was plentiful and easily made, among film stars, say, or record producers.

Lionel was sexy and knew it. Every early evening, he sat in the last row of the meeting, quite apart from the Chiffon section, though well within its view. There, eyes closed, he'd tilt his chair back, then lean forward on it, thrusting, then withdrawing, his ample crotch, as in some dreaming parody of the sexual act. It's difficult to say if this was unconscious—the sort of irrational rhythmic compulsion associated with milder forms of insanity—or an attempt to tantalize the Chiffons. But at any given moment in the meeting, many eyes were more likely to be focused on Lionel's blissfully seesawing crotch than the speaker.

The aura of danger, on the other hand, while present, was more oblique.

"Well," said Hatch one day, breathless with what he was about to suggest, "I heard Lionel has a black belt in martial arts."

"Judo," McDuff said.

"No, no, no. It's a green belt in karate," insisted Burnham.

"Ju-jitsu," said Wood, just to throw his two cents in.

"My dears," said Edgar, annoyed that Hatch had pre-empted this tidbit he'd eagerly anticipated presenting, "whatever it is, he certainly put it to use not two weeks ago at 21st and Spruce streets…"

"What?!"

"Stop!"

"…in a rather unpleasant altercation with a motorist."

"No!"

"Whah, I neveh!"

Edgar paused.

"He was crossing the street and some guy in a Buick Skylark, instead of braking, slowed down, honked and kept right on going. The car slammed Lionel into a news box and nearly broke his arm."

"I love it, a Skylark colliding with a Dove," said Wood.

"So what happened?" said McDuff.

"He chased it a block, caught up with it at a stop light, pulled the driver out and proceeded to beat the shit out of him."

"Where?"

"On the sidewalk."

"No!"

"Stop!"

Edgar then related how the driver of the car had had to be hospitalized, but that, following a conversation with Lionel's attorney, said driver had declined to press charges for assault.

This, of course, was delicious dish, but a bigger mystery remained. How did Lionel get by, with his apartment at the Dorchester and his lunches at the Four Seasons, despite having no job? Three theories circulated to explain it. The first, originating with Lionel himself, held that he was independently wealthy and lived off a trust fund. The second, that he dealt cocaine. The third, which evolved over time, began, as far as I know, with Edgar.

"Has anyone ever noticed those wrist chains he wears?" Hatch said one afternoon.

"So South Philly," said McDuff.

"South Jersey is more like it," said Cesar.

"Men who wear jewelry clearly have a gender confusion problem," Edgar stated, smirking. "On the other hand, those tacky bagatelles of his could be...gifts."

"From whom?" said McDuff.

"According to J. Anderson Black's *History of Jewelry*," said Edgar, "jewelry was given by men to women, as a way of subjugating them."

"So, what're you saying?"

"Yes, Edgar, what are you trying to tell us?"

"That sheesh a kept woman?"

A brief silence settled in.

"My dears," Edgar said, "I'm afraid *gigolo* would be the more accurate term."

How exactly Edgar and Lionel became friendly no one really knew. All I can tell you is that one day Hatch bounded into the diner like a cheetah, scarcely able to contain himself. He squeezed in the booth—where myself, McDuff, Nesbitt, Featherstone, Terry Mayo, Cesar Biratto, and Burnham and Wood had gathered—and without even waving for a cup of coffee, blurted out what he claimed to have seen: Edgar and Lionel sitting on a bench in Rittenhouse having a cordial, if not animated, conversation.

Everyone sat quiet.

"Sheesh hallucinating," said Nesbitt, after a minute had passed. "Acid flashbacks."

"Hitting the bottle, I'd say."

"Robert, have you been nipping?" said Burnham, who sniffed the air for traces.

Hatch simply beamed.

"You've got to be making this up," said McDuff.

But the claim was already too extravagant for fiction, and Hatch was in far too ebullient a mood to have invented it.

"Alright, Robert," said Nesbitt, "tell us exactly what you saw." "Yes, tell it!"

"What I saw," said Hatch, "was the two of them sitting on one of the wooden benches by the goat statue, chattering like magpies."

"Magpies?" Burnham said.

"Sounds more like doves," said Wood. "They're the ones that coo."

"Oh c'mon," Nesbitt said, "Edgar wouldn't have anything to do wish Lionel."

"He can't stand that queen."

"Loathes him!"

"It's preposterous, Hatch."

"Wait!" said McDuff, thoughtfully shaking his head. "I think Hatch is telling the truth."

The proof that this was no invention appeared not one moment later, when Edgar and Lionel came strolling up 19th Street, well within view of the corner table, whose occupants sat like yard ornaments—deer and dwarves, cast in concrete—utterly transfixed.

Except for Hatch, who smirked.

"Now I've seen it all," said McDuff. "Talk about strange bedfellows!"

"I wouldn't go to bed with either of them!" exclaimed Wood, who had, in fact, slept with both, and thought no one else knew.

Stranger still was the information received a few days later to the effect that the duo had been seen together at the opening of a major show on an important local architect at the Philadelphia Museum of Art.

"And they were skipping around the gallery doing everything but holding hands," reported Hatch, who knew someone who knew someone who was an assistant curator and had seen the whole thing.

"You mean, like boyfriends?" said Featherstone.

"It's called 'a date,'" Burnham said. "You now, Featherstone, boy meets boy? That sort of thing? Not that you've ever had one…"

"Eat shit, you tired queen, if I…"

"Hmmm," said McDuff, "sounds like something rather strange is abroad in the land."

"And," said Hatch, "from what I gather, Edgar has gone out and got himself a whole new outfit."

"What kind of outfit," said Nesbitt.

"You know, the levi/leather thing. Black vest, motorcycle boots, chaps."

"Chaps?" said Burnham, aghast.

"Her ass is too skinny for chaps," said Wood. "She'd have chap gap."

"What's chap gap?"

"You know, where there's too much fabric and not enough flesh. So the chaps flap around the buns?"

"How utterly unappealing."

"Whah, I neveh!"

"I have a hard time imagining that tightwad plunking down money for real leather."

"I jusht don't get it," said Nesbitt. "I mean, Edgar's so… intellectual. And Lionel's just a rich little cock teaser with a black belt."

"A black cock teaser with a black belt," said Burnham.

"A black cock teaser with a big black cock and a black belt," said Wood, a bit too eagerly.

"They have nothing in common," Nesbitt insisted.

"Oh, c'mon honey," said McDuff, "you're talking about gay men. There's really only one thing that matters. Well, two. Eight good inches and a hole to fuck. We're ruled by desire. It's all about cock."

"I'm glad you put it so romantically," Hatch said. "I mean, it's always nice to get laid but..." Here he sighed and with his straw vacuumed up what remained of his Coke. "Besides," he said, "Edgar's not stupid. Maybe he has other motives?"

At that point, I could only guess what sort of motives Edgar had, since he wasn't often around to expound on them. On those occasions when I did see him—such as at the meeting, which he still occasionally attended—he clung to Lionel in touchy-feely best friend fashion. And not only there. Ensconced in a box at the Academy of Music, they poked and prodded, whispered and giggled, fanning themselves with playbills throughout a performance of Verdi's *Macbeth*. One bright day that June, I watched them advancing up Sansom Street in the jewelry district, chummier than a pair of poodles. Edgar raced ahead to point at watches or bracelets. Lionel followed, sauntering up for a casual look.

"Let's face it, she's smitten," said Hatch, late one evening, with the chairs already stacked on tables.

"Obsheshed," said Nesbitt.

"New Beau Riche, is what I call it," said Wood.

"Well," said Featherstone, looking somewhat bewildered, "jewelry *is* rather expensive and..."

"Featherstone, for God's sakes, shut up," said Hatch. "And what else were they doing, Eric?"

I shrugged.

"Pricing rings is what it sounds like," said Cesar.

"The world is a wedding," said McDuff. "Or, excuse me, a commitment ceremony."

Outside, thunder rumbled, followed by a crack of lightning branched forth in jagged seams.

"The damned, dirty Judas," said Father Mayo.

"She thinks her shit don't stink," said Cesar.

"Who would've predicted?" said Nesbitt, sweeping a palm across the top of his head, to, I suppose, gauge the quantity of hair that remained.

Rain beat on hoods and windshields.

"Oh," said McDuff, shaking his head, "what won't we do for love?"

Everyone looked at him.

"We tell ourselves it's a con job. One of those phony free trips that comes in the mail. The bait for some time-share from hell."

"Who's *we?*" Hatch demanded, indignant.

"Every dumb jerk who believes his own lies," said McDuff, sighing. "We act like the only thing that really matters is turning ourselves into little models of self-sufficiency. No drinking, no drugs. Relationships, a no-no. Too dangerous to sobriety. The whole party line. Then let a boyfriend come along, or a lover, whatever they call it these days. And with it, hope. The hope of a hope. That's all it takes—*poof!*—gone. That's all any of us really wants, isn't it?" said McDuff.

But no one bothered to answer him as one by one we slipped on jackets, gathered umbrellas and headed for our solitary apartments.

Within a week I got a phone call from Edgar. He had the day off and wanted to get together.

I suggested the Square.

"I was thinking dinner," he said.

"Uh..."

We rendezvoused at a cafeteria called the Savoir Faire. My suggestion. Gone were the blond locks that fell over the forehead. In their place, a brush cut. Gone was the turtleneck and patched plaid sport coat. In their stead, a brown bomber jacket and stone-washed jeans. The oddest item in the lot was the slim stem of gold encircling Edgar's left wrist.

We moved down the line, selected food, found a table.

No sooner did I deposit the first slice of quiche in my mouth than I had the sense something was seriously awry and looked up to see Edgar staring in horror at an object on his tray that I guessed was the dessert.

"What's the matter, Edgar?"

"Notenoughstrawberries on this tart," he mumbled.

Before I could calm him, or attempt to negotiate the situation, Edgar'd snatched the offending pastry and, bounding past the bewildered cashier, made his way into the now crowded cafeteria line. One hand pointed to the tart, the other furiously waved at the hapless server. He gestured. He grimaced. He explained.

The server smiled and nodded, as she'd obviously been trained to do. But as this went on her demeanor changed. She drew a mental curtain down, directing her attention to the stream of would-be diners, ignoring the still gesticulating Edgar.

"What a gyp!" Edgar said, re-seating himself.

Then he started. He'd called, he informed me, because, out of "all those horrible queens" at the diner, I was the only one he could trust.

"I'm in love," he declared.

For a moment, I was stumped. How do you congratulate someone on an emotion?

"That's great," I said. "I'm happy for you, Edgar."

On that note Edgar launched into his paean to the beloved. This consisted of lush descriptions of Lionel's apartment, his white leather sofa, his closetful of Armani suits, the shopping trips he took to Paris and Rome and Milan, the fabulous lunches they had at the Four Seasons. Etc., etc., etc.

"The queens in this town think they know something about fashion?" Edgar said. "They dress like they're going to a Billy Graham rally. Look at McDuff! You could easily mistake him for a gas station attendant. And Nesbitt? Ugh! She ought to invest in some implants."

"So I take it you've slept with him?"

Edgar paused, frowning.

"Actually, not." He lifted a glassine slice of berry from the half-consumed tart. "We didn't want to just jump in the sack. That's not Lionel's style."

I nodded.

"We're still getting to know each other. The whole history of romantic love indicates that relationships which begin with sex are never about anything more than that."

I conceded the point.

"So where do things go from here?"

"We're moving to Paris," Edgar said.

"Do you know anyone there?"

Well, Edgar explained, he did not but Lionel's financial acumen and fashion contacts would provide entrée to all the smart circles. Meanwhile Edgar could master French and finish his degree in architecture. It sounded both practical and breathtakingly ambitious.

"Isn't Paris expensive?"

"Lionel's got money," he said. And he, Edgar, would find a job under the table. Moreover, he confided, he'd just transferred his savings to Lionel, whose prowess in the matter of investments was guaranteed to at least double it in six months, and quadruple it by the time they left, at the end of the year.

Two months later, word of a falling-out hit the diner like a streaking missile. Hatch, of course, launched it.

"Well," said Nesbitt, seeking to dispel one of those ennui-threatening moments of silence, "has anyone seen 'the couple' lately?"

Though he'd mastered discretion in the service of slander, Hatch couldn't resist an eyeball-rolling guffaw.

"It's over," he said, flatly. "You haven't heard?"

"Heard what!?" said McDuff, setting down a BLT as if he'd suddenly remembered he had a plane to catch.

"You've got to be kidding," said Burnham.

"I saw them together in the Square, frisking like two minks in the mud," said Wood. "That was…"

"When?"

"Not two weeks ago."

"You may very well have," said Hatch, "but if so, that's probably the *last* time you'll see them together."

"What happened?"

"Tell us, Robert."

"Do dish!"

Hatch lifted his glass, took the straw between his lips, and stared out the window for a period long enough to qualify as a catatonic seizure. He set the glass back down.

"Well, according to what I've heard, Lionel's been giving Edgar the cold shoulder," he said. "I mean, *glaciers*."

"Who's this Edgar?" said Chip, late of Justine's and fresh out of rehab.

"Oh, just someone we used to know," said Featherstone, batting his lashes.

"Well, that explains it," said Burnham. "I saw Edgar come up to him after the meeting and Lionel brushed him away like a cobweb."

"I knew it," Nesbitt said. "I'll bet she started acting out at the Four Seasons."

"Her shrimp fork hadn't been properly sterilized."

"No, the dessert spoon was unpolished."

"Actually, the water wasn't cold enough," Burnham said. "Edgar called the waiter to send it back to the kitchen."

"Ahem," said Hatch. "Apparently it had to do with money."

"Money?" McDuff said. "Whose? Edgar doesn't have a centime."

"Sondheim? I don't..."

"Shut up, Featherstone."

"Not anymore he doesn't," said Hatch, flashing a grin that came and went so fast it might've been either parody or illusion. He turned once again to the window for inspiration, meditation, or perhaps simply to catch a quick glimpse of himself. Everyone waited.

"Apparently," he continued, "Edgar at some point handed his savings over to Lionel, who was supposed to have invested it for him."

"In what, aftershave?"

"Lionel specified that he needed it in cash."

"No!"

"Stop!"

"Like to die!"

"And last week a friend of mine, well, a friend of a friend, actually…"

"Do you mean the acquaintance of a friend's friend, or someone acquainted with the friend of an acquaintance?" said Burnham.

"He means an ex-lover's ex-lover's ex-lover," said Wood.

"No, he means the acquaintance of an ex-lover's friend's friend," said Father Mayo.

"Look, you assholes. I'm not saying another fucking word if you don't shut up and let me finish."

Silence.

"In any event, on Saturday he happened to be at a certain coffee shop on 12th Street where 'the couple'…"

"Not!" said Wood.

"…where the couple," Hatch continued, clearing his throat, "happened to be sitting. And what he heard was Edgar vehemently demanding an accounting."

Silence.

"Exactly how much was involved?" said McDuff.

"Apparently $40,000."

"Oh, c'mon Hatch. Where would Edgar get money like that?"

"I don't know, but that one could sure squeeze the last sliver of silver out of a dime," said Cesar.

"What a cheapskate."

"World's worst tipper."

"We were in a cab once," McDuff related, "and he actually left the driver 35 cents. A quarter and two nickels."

We all shook our heads.

"And the driver turned around and handed it back and said…"— McDuff slipped into the reedy sing-song of the Caribbean—"Here, mon, you keep dis. You need it more den I do."

The Saturday night meeting in the basement up the street was thronged. I sat in the Chiffon section, wedged between McDuff and Nesbitt. In the last row, 20 or so feet from the Chiffons, Lionel tilted back and forth in his seat: rocking, dreaming, crotch-thrusting. The meeting's chairman, an axe-faced South Philly fireman, rested his elbows on the table and stared at the speaker. The speaker—an elderly professor of literature much given to long-winded anecdotes of chic Manhattan nightlife despoiled by the ravages of alcohol—was ten minutes into his talk. All this was going on when I felt a nudge at the knee. McDuff pointed his chin toward the doorway, where Edgar had just appeared.

He either didn't see us or, if he did, chose to ignore. We watched him look from left to right. Whatever he saw confirmed his need to be there. His face wore the slight snout I'd come to associate with spotty stemware and pound cake of questionable freshness.

In swift strides he made for a large pillar and vanished behind it. He reappeared, moving toward the next pillar. He disappeared again. Appeared, disappeared, reappeared. By this means he progressed almost unnoticed toward the assemblage, on the far side of the room, emerging ten or so feet from his quarry. At that point Edgar walked up behind Lionel and, hesitating only a second—I assume for the drama—let fly with a right that landed between ear and forehead. The blow sent Lionel sprawling to the floor.

Half the meeting was on its feet.

"Order!"

"First Aid!"

"Call the police!"

"No, don't!"

The speaker, his head jerking left to right and back again in the manner of a barnyard fowl alert to the possible presence of feed, snatched the tortoiseshell bifocals dangling from his neck and squinted into the chaos. "What the fuck is going on?" he said to the chairman, forgetting that the mike was still on. BANG! BANG! BANG! went the gavel. But by now almost the entire Chiffon section had already rushed forward, toppling chairs, spilling half-filled Styrofoam coffee cups, in a scramble to be the first to come to Lionel's aid. Meanwhile, having delivered that swift and single *coup de main*, Edgar had already turned tail and fled before anyone could think to stop him.

"I really didn't think Edgar needed to attack Lionel," said Nesbitt. "I mean, fishical violence. I consider that dishpicable."

"Vulgar, to say the least."

"Treacherous."

"Well, what other options were there?" Hatch said.

"He could've sued him."

"You mean to get the money back?"

"Apparently he told someone he was going to," said Featherstone.

"Actually," said Hatch, "he went to see an attorney—you know, that one in the program with the toupee?—who told him he had no case."

"No case?"

"Shocking."

"No documents, no case. There was nothing signed. No promissory note. Nothing on which to base a suit. It would've been his word against Lionel's. And apparently Lionel knows some aggressive and well-connected lawyers, if that's not redundant."

"Do you think he'll ever set foot in the meeting again?" Chip said.

McDuff chuckled and lifted his cup.

"He does and his ass is grass," said Cesar.

"Well," said Featherstone, "no one's ever really banned from a meeting, I mean..."

"But since Lionel vowed to kill him, I don't imagine he'll be back very soon," McDuff said.

"Murder seems like a rather stiff punishment."

"Do you doubt that he's capable of it?"

"That savage? Of course not."

"He didn't look all that savage squirming around on the floor," McDuff said.

"He almost sounded as if he was bawling," Featherstone said.

"Mortified at the prospect of getting his outfit dusty, I would imagine," sniffed Hatch.

"Creased jeans, can you stand it?"

"Probably raced right home and took everything to the dry cleaner," Burnham said.

"You know that's the first thing she did," said Wood.

"Besides take out a contract on Edgar."

"You mean trashing the apartment wasn't enough."

In fact, what happened in the immediate aftermath of 'the attack,' as it was now all but officially christened and universally known, was this: Lionel, his wits and balance restored, proceeded forthwith to Edgar's apartment. Equipped with a key, he entered, to find Edgar out, possibly celebrating. At that point, he began hurling and heaving through one of two front windows every object which could fit. First to go was the glass-topped coffee table. He dropped the base to the sidewalk, then tipped the palm-shaped top through the window. It burst into shards. The slant-backed chair with its multi-colored legs followed.

Down went the contents of Edgar's antiques cabinet, Fiesta ware and Depression glass shattering on the concrete. That was followed by everything in his cupboards, then the drawers. Silverware rained to the pavement. Painter's pants, jeans, t-shirts, and sport coats parachuted to earth. Record albums fell and cracked in their sleeves. The commotion attracted a small crowd of parking lot drunks from the 7-11 up the block, several of whom swiftly appropriated whatever looked appealing, especially the silverware and any intact record albums. Others—figuring the occupant of the apartment had lost his mind—began cheering each appearance of Lionel at the windows.

"More!" they chanted. "More! More! More!"

Lionel was quite happy to oblige his instant fan base.

He left, locking the door behind him, 30 seconds before the first squad car pulled up. While what was by now a small hoard picked through the debris, the cops stormed upstairs, broke the door in and completed the ransacking of Edgar's pad, helping themselves to whatever items of value Lionel had overlooked.

"Where is Edgar now?" said Chip.

"No one knows," said Burnham.

"The landlord evicted him after Lionel trashed the apartment," McDuff said. "He told him he understood it wasn't Edgar's fault, but he couldn't risk having it happen again."

For a while the dish on Edgar came fast and furious. But like a rara avis on the brink of extinction, the sightings were many, the facts few. He was, they said, 'out,' i.e., drinking. Someone had seen him at Woody's, Budweiser in hand, a year's sobriety vanished with the first devil-may-care sip. Someone else had seen him passed out on a bench in Rittenhouse Square at dawn. Drunk, he had supposedly invaded the lobby of Lionel's apartment building at 3AM, determined to set things right. When the doorman refused him entry, he unleashed a torrent of racial invective and fled. No, no, no, no, someone insisted. Edgar'd moved to South Philly, was still sober, and had been seen going to meetings at the 4th and Tasker clubhouse.

There were rumors he'd acquired a heroin habit, had finally broken a heroin habit, was recovering from a near-fatal skiing accident, was involved in the manufacture of LSD, had joined a circus and was learning to train tigers, or had fled to Australia. Someone insisted Edgar'd taken refuge in the top floor of a massive townhouse belonging to a rich old queen in Society Hill. In exchange for this Anne Frank hideaway, he was obliged to keep the house tidy, in addition to supplying his benefactor with sexual services on demand.

All this kept the corner table alive and alert, at least for a few months. In time the fascination extended its tentacles well beyond. Around that time, I was attending a dinner party at Nathan Freed's sumptuous Delancey Street townhouse. Twelve men had just sat down at the big well-polished ebony table in the front room. It was about 6:30 and soup was served. A man in a Navy trench coat with blond locks passed before the windows. His odd gait aroused such curiosity that everyone rose to watch. Ten swift steps and he swung his head to the right to determine whether or not he was being followed. Ten steps, glance. Ten steps, glance.

"That man looks possessed," someone said.

"Or at least in a very big hurry."

"I know I've seen him around," said a plump stockbroker, between sips of his third martini.

"Oh," said Nathan Freed, training his gaze on the steadily retreating figure. "That's Edgar Moffit.

"Edgar Moffit?" said a certain attorney, whose passion for dance was exceeded only by his appetite for dancers. "He came to our firm several months ago looking to file suit against a companion he claimed had defrauded him."

"And what became of that?" someone said.

"Oh, nothing," said the lawyer. "It was just a fantasy, I suppose."

"I hear he's flagged from Woody's"

"Didn't he break a chair over someone's head or something?"

"Threw a drink in a trick's face, is what I heard."

"Actually," said Nathan Freed, "he's rather harmless. And behind all his compulsions and little games, somewhat talented and even charming."

"Well, if you feel that way," said the stockbroker, "why didn't you invite him to dinner?"

I could almost see Nathan Freed mentally checking the stockbroker off all future guest lists.

"Because," said Nathan Freed, "he's also the biggest mess in this very messy town. Besides," he sniffled and cleared his throat, "whom I invite to my own home is my own business. Wouldn't you agree?"

This last remark should have settled it. It didn't. For the next 30 minutes, Edgar's situation was discussed, analyzed, probed, and penetrated in depth.

"Eric," said the stockbroker, working now on martini #4, "you're part of that AA, aren't you? Do you know this Edgar, what is it, Muffin?"

"It's Moffit, I believe," I said, feeling the blood rise. "And yes, I know him. Though I'm afraid there's not much I can add that hasn't been said before."

I encountered Edgar later, as I was leaving and he was coming back up the street.

Or, rather, I should say I saw a man halfway up the block in that same blue trench coat almost racewalking along the sidewalk.

"Edgar!" I shouted.

He whirled, then waited for me to catch up.

He certainly seemed sober. Though the closer I came, the more frightened his eyes appeared.

"Eric," he said. "Thank God it's you! Where are you coming from?"

I told him. Edgar's left lip began to rise.

"Nathan Freed?" he said. "That horrible queen? I suppose you were at one of his famous soirees." He paused. "And who supplied the toot for that little gathering? I can just guess. Lionel Dove, the biggest dealer in Center City. I've always wondered why the cops never interfered with his little import/export business. Maybe the proper authorities haven't been notified. By the way, are you aware that Nathan Freed likes to have sex with…"

"Wait," I said. "I wanted to ask…how you're doing?"

He told me he'd moved to Upper Darby, a working-class suburb on the Western fringe of the city. Edgar didn't say why, but he knew I knew. If Upper Dumpy, as it's known to some, possessed no other attractions, it was at least cheap, and a very unlikely place to encounter Lionel Dove.

Edgar went away. It was not a dramatic disappearance—no body found—nor were there any further incidents along the line of 'the attack.' The sightings became fewer and yet more speculative. At the corner table, the instances of his name being raised—in contexts invariably mingling derision and mock regret—dwindled to the extent that any mention of it would've required extended explanation. Edgar wasn't seen, Edgar wasn't talked about, and Edgar, by degrees, faded from collective consciousness.

His name surfaced about a year later when the corner table, AA and half of Center City Philadelphia was appalled or delighted—depending on who you asked—to see, on the evening news, Lionel Dove being led from the Dorchester in handcuffs. He was on his way to the Roundhouse to be booked for cocaine trafficking. "According to the police investigation, Mr. Dove supervised an operation which delivered 10 to 20 kilos per month" of high quality Bolivian nose candy to the City of Brotherly Love, said Channel 9's Mona Zorawski. Walking between detectives en route from the Dorchester's lobby to the waiting paddy wagon, he flashed that enigmatic smile that for so many months had been the key piece to the puzzle all of us were trying to assemble. Watching him, it at last occurred to me what it meant: Fuck You.

As for the action which flourished at the corner table, in

the next few years it came to seem like one of those plays which runs forever, a low-brow pseudo-mystery requiring frequent cast changes; a dramatic spectacle in which apprentice thespians might try out their skills and add some. Those who'd foresworn alcohol for a while or had fallen off the wagon and hence were unwelcome to return, were displaced by those taking their first tenuous steps into sobriety. Chip became a regular, as did Justine's maitre'd, who, on being introduced, turned out to have the innocuous name of Albert.

These were the years the plague was taking its frightful toll. Nesbitt, at 34 or so, was one of its first embittered casualties. Father Mayo followed shortly thereafter, then Cesar Biratto.

Wood contracted the HIV virus, but somehow hung on. His friendship with Daniel Burnham, however, did not. Burnham returned one summer from a trip to Europe with a new French lover in tow. Once ensconced in the company-owned house, and with Burnham's newly re-written will leaving him everything, Monsieur Guy-Michel Lambert set out to sever every connection between Daniel and any friend he'd ever made, starting with John Wood. He then proceeded to cook for, and feed, his boyfriend like a goose slated for the supper table, so that at last glance, the dark-haired beauty of the corner table days weighed so much he was compelled to move sideways while passing from one room to the next.

Featherstone opened a salon, called Hair Today, Gone Tomorrow, which flourished. You may see him in the window, all but unchanged in appearance, wielding the snips. McDuff began practicing law again, became quite successful, and bought a condo in those I.M. Pei designed towers on the Delaware, described by one wag as a housing project for homosexuals. Hatch, who briefly inherited the position of dominance Edgar had held, was the last to vanish from the corner table. The publication of poems in a number of small magazines led to the acquisition of a beautiful boyfriend. All this caused his head to swell considerably. Being dumped by the boyfriend brought the swelling down, but not enough. He ended up bankrupt and hooked on prescription drugs, the handful of poems all but forgotten in the image of Hatch wandering through Rittenhouse Square, shoeless and delirious in the snow.

The diner itself became a casualty as the decade drew toward its close. It had been built in the 50s, re-faced and remodeled again and again, each time with less insight, but always a diner with a counter and booths. One day a piece of scrap paper appeared, masking taped to the door, with the single word "Closed" scratched across it. Six months later a chic counterfeit debuted, a darkened spot-lit room of cocktail nooks and intimate marble-topped tables, the centerpiece of which was a bar with a countertop of cast concrete behind which an infinity of bottles stood racked and massed like some kind of shrine to booze. It was said the service was Neanderthal and the food distinctly second-rate.

The corner table clique, with not a single original member remaining, had meanwhile migrated to another spot, on the other side of Broad Street. There, I'm told, you'll find a similar group conversing in similar tones on similar subjects. Or objects. Of disaffection.

About a year after the diner was shuttered, in October as I recall, I happened to be in San Francisco. It was late, I was visiting friends near Dolores Park, and at some time after midnight, I left. I crossed the park and walked along Dolores to Market. Groups of people, mostly men, passed. I entered a sandwich shop at Market and Noe. It wasn't, of course, the notion of sprouts and avocado between slices of whole wheat toast which appealed so much as the prospect for a night's companion.

I settled into a booth by the window. A waitress—'Nancy'— wiped the table down and slipped a menu and silverware in front of me. She moved to the next booth, where two men were seated. The one facing me was a multi-pierced muscle stud in a wifebeater with a shark tattoo'd in fading blue green to one bicep. The other I couldn't see, except for the back of his blond head.

I was trying to decide between the bean sprout sandwich and the vegan Mexican chicken when I heard a voice.

"How long ago was this coffee made?"

I heard Nancy explain that it had been made on the previous shift and she was about to make a fresh pot and would bring another cup shortly.

"And another thing," said the voice. "See the black speck on this French fry? No, right there. See it? How long has it been since anyone back there changed the oil in your fryer. I refuse to..."

I glanced toward the window, where I saw, in silhouette, the mouth with its lip drawn up in a contemptuous curl. I set the menu down and rose. Without being noticed—feeling delightfully invisible—I slipped out the doorway, into the cool clean air and the California night.

AN IDEAL COUPLE

They met in a hustler bar the year Tom came out. The establishment, called Roscoe's, consisted of one windowless room in which there were to be found from mid-afternoon on a besotted assortment of middle-aged disability cheats, pocket-picking drag queens, trust fund drunks, and the skeeviest male prostitutes on Spruce Street, all of whom used it for a headquarters. It was the clientele, more than anything, that drew Tom. That and the cheap beer.

On the evening in question, Tom had just finished using the lady's room, which no female person had probably ever entered, and where a Quaalude or a small quantity of coke could be bartered for a hand job or a five-dollar bill. There he ingested a line of snowy powder and, conspicuous in gray flannel slacks, a blue cotton shirt, navy blazer and patterned red tie, was bustling toward the door, trailed by many eyes, some lustful, some venomous.

Tom was on his way to a concert. Halfway to the door, a hand closed on his shoulder. The hand tugged him, almost lifting, in the direction of the bar. A thrill of imminent adventure transcended the panicky millisecond of indignation he experienced. Tom found himself yielding. A pair of slightly protuberant eyes the color of seawater, under a shock of gray brown hair, stared into his own.

"BUY YA A DRINK?" the chubby apparition roared. It was a command as much as a question.

Whether it was the sheer brazenness of this maneuver—Tom had long since learned to deflect free drinks at Roscoe's—or because he really would've preferred getting drunk on top of the cocaine to squirming through another Philadelphia Orchestra concert in the far reaches of the leg-constricting Academy of Music, Tom acquiesced. "I'M STEVE," shouted the would-be benefactor, who raised a ten spot above his head and waved it back and forth like a gleeful child.

Two Budweiser appeared. They were off and running.

Tom, twenty-three, thought anyone older than twenty-six was not only over the hill but so far past it as to have disappeared beyond the horizon. Steve, he figured, was...forty-five? Fifty? Age alone ruled him out as a sex partner.

Tom lived at home with his parents in the suburbs. He told Steve all about Penn State and what he planned to do, which was get a job with an arts organization. Normally, Tom's discourse on ambition—thoroughly laced with an unselfconscious arrogance—bored people after three minutes. Steve actually paid attention. Not only that, he kept buying beers. At one point late in the evening, it occurred to Tom that politeness dictated he reciprocate. This gesture surprised and pleased Steve. It seemed to seal some kind of deal. When the mustachioed barkeep bellowed, "Last call!" at 1:49 A.M., the two of them were just getting started on the four extra Budweisers they'd had the "prescience" (Tom's word) to order.

"'Tis a pleasure to have many," Tom said, quoting Chaucer on the subject of books. Steve howled.

Tom woke the next morning on a sofa in the living room of a Center City, Philadelphia town house. His brain had morphed into a glutinous mass of frog's eggs. He felt some vital energy leaking away through an invisible orifice and stuck his fingers in his ears. He removed them a second later and opened an eye. "Ugh," he said. He heard water splash somewhere behind his head.

On the wall opposite the sofa, a handsome young man, maybe twenty-five, with blond-brown hair and startling green-blue eyes, stared down out of a large painting executed in accurate if splashy fashion. Tom peered at it through a filter of pained brain cells. It took a full minute to recognize the figure as Steve. Some wholly different incarnation gazed out from that canvas: radiant, preppy, thin.

Steve emerged from the kitchen in a blue terrycloth bathrobe, a glass in each hand.

"HAVE A BLOODY!" he said.

The glasses sprouted pale and slender celery stalks. Wedges of sliced lemon graced their brims. Tom squeezed the lemon over the texture red surface and took a big gulp of what tasted like textury raw vodka. He polished it off in five minutes.

Tom's visits to the town house on Juniper Street grew frequent. He and Steve became drinking buddies who cruised, or cruising buddies who drank. It wasn't quite clear which. The relationship seemed wholly uncharacteristic of Tom, who distrusted older people, especially men. Tom and Steve launched their weekend evenings with beers in Steve's living room before proceeding to the round of bars, which began and ended at Roscoe's. From Roscoe's they repaired once more to Steve's, where Tom took to sacking out on the sofa in the finished basement, one morning even emerging "naked as a jay bird" (Steve's description) with an overnight guest in tow, though that practice ended when Steve laid down the law. ("Tommy, you can crash here whenever you want. *But no numbers.*") Steve, it turned out, was finishing a long-delayed dissertation in psychology and working as a staff psychologist at a social-services agency. Tom, who'd majored in English, had settled for waiting tables and working in bookstores after trying, and failing, to land a white-collar job. He thought at some point he might return to school for a graduate degree.

They made an odd, if complimentary, pair. Steve enjoyed Tom's beer-fueled self-assurance and wit. He could see right through the smart-ass know-it-all-ism to the naivete underneath. He chalked Tom's little romantic dramas up to age. Tom liked it that Steve was open to being teased. In warm weather, for instance, Steve always wore extra-large shirts that he never tucked in. These masked a considerable, and growing, tummy. "I see you're wearing your muumuu," Tom would say. Or, "Been to the gynecologist lately?"

Steve would frown in mock annoyance, tap his cigarette at the ashtray and snicker, "Oh, fuck you."

Some evenings they would down an entire case of Budweiser while recalling exploits from their drinking careers. In Steve's case, the worst thing that had ever happened was the time he got fired from a teaching position at a local university for propositioning a student when drunk. The student, invited to Steve's for dinner, filed a complaint, insisting Steve had come on to *him*, that the whole thing had been—in one of two versions Tom would hear over the years—either a setup or a misunderstanding.

"Once his father got involved, I never had a chance," Steve said, stubbing out a Marlboro.

Fairly soon in their relationship, use of terms such as "blackout" and "dry drunk" caused Tom and Steve to realize they were both AA dropouts. Neither planned to stop drinking again. Steve genuinely preferred inebriation to sobriety, and Tom now had Steve to bail him out whenever his own drunken escapades resulted in disaster. As, increasingly, happened.

Like the night Tom, half in the bag, rolled his station wagon in a field. He crawled out of the car and saw a factory in the distance. Tom stumbled to the factory gate and knocked at the guardhouse door. "Call the police," he said. "There's been a terrible accident." He woke in a cell, wearing his Academy of Music finery minus tie, belt, and shoelaces. Released on his own recognizance, he took a bus to City Hall.

Steve was having a party that afternoon. Tom walked to the town house and knocked on the door.

"Can I come in?"

"Tommy! My God, what's happened to you?"

Steve filled the tub and brought Tom a Bloody. Two hours later, the party was on and Tom was the center of attention.

It's hard to say if they were like-minded spirits or similarly damaged souls. They never went to bed together, but the relationship grew to resemble that of lovers who evolve into genial, if sexless, companions. The difference in their ages—almost a generation—conferred on Steve the Grumpy Uncle role. When Tom moved to a small, studio apartment in Center City, Steve helped him furnish it. When he set out to take a graduate degree, in spite of having no savings, Steve wrote a check to pay the bursar.

They talked about everything, or it seemed that way to Tom. Parents, schools, siblings. Steve had grown up in New London, Connecticut, and still had family there. He especially liked to hear about Tom's love life. Tom was in and out of relationships large and small in search of the Ideal Mate. His Ideal Mate, he told Steve, "has a perfect ass and reads Pound and Plato." Steve, who'd never read either, was always anxious to hear about what Tom did in bed with these revolving-door boyfriends, but Steve never, as far as Tom could remember, talked about his own relationships.

When Tom finally "met someone"—a big-lipped blond named Brian—Steve seemed almost as excited as Tom. Steve liked Brian, though he didn't like the way Brian controlled Tom by nagging and, later, provoking arguments in public once Tom had a few under his belt.

About a year after Tom took up with Brian, Steve's sister died, and Steve moved from Philadelphia back to New London to be near his father. He bought an old apartment house a block from Ocean Beach Park. Steve invited Tom and Brian to New London for a long weekend. Brian, bored with their drinking, left Tom and Steve sitting in a bar called Frank's and went off to explore the town on his own. Tom and Steve ended up drinking all weekend.

Tom's relationship with Brian, fragile enough when Tom was going out and getting drunk every night, didn't survive his new-found sobriety. After he went back to AA and stopped drinking, Tom began standing up to Brian's nagging and corridor confrontations. They decided to end their relationship, and Brian quickly found another drunk to take up with. He continued living with Tom for a few months, and every night Tom heard, through the wall between bedrooms, Brian and his new lover, Michael, screaming and throwing things at each other. *It's like being an extra on the set of my previous relationship*, he thought. Finally, Brian moved out. Tom phoned Steve in New London to tell him the news. Steve told Tom that he, too, had quit drinking.

"I was getting started on the beer every morning around 10, Tommy," he explained. "The tenants knew if they wanted anything done, they had to get hold of me before noon. Otherwise, I'd be potted."

It reached the point, Steve told Tom, where one day he had found himself unable to urinate. The day stretched into a day and a night, then into the next day, at which point he became concerned. The doctor he went to see directed Steve to lie down on the examining table, then plugged a stethoscope in Steve's ears and set the opposite end of it to his stomach.

"Hear that sloshing around? That's all the fluid your body can't eliminate because your kidneys have shut down."

The doctor scratched out three prescriptions.

"If you'd come in here even twenty-four hours from now, it might've been too late," he said. "And here's a piece of advice, whether you want it or not. If you drink again, and I mean *at all*, it will be too late."

So Steve stopped drinking.

That year, Steve started teaching psychology at the University of Rhode Island. The next year he got a part-time job as a youth counselor at a social services agency, specializing in substance abuse and AIDS services. The year after that, he started buying real estate. He bought a duplex in New London and a house in Mystic. He took on mortgage after mortgage.

Tom came up to New London several times in the summer and fall, usually with his newest lover in tow.

"Tommy," Steve said, steering him aside on one such occasion—"I hope you're taking precautions."

"What do you mean?"

"Are you using condoms?"

"No."

"Can I ask you a question?"

"Go ahead."

"Do you want to die young?"

Tom started using condoms.

Tom and Steve, and whatever new lover Tom had in tow, would go out to dinner at a waterside restaurant, the kind serving cheeseburgers, French fries, or fried clams in greasy paper holders, to be consumed at splintery picnic tables by a dock. Once Steve signed them up for a riverboat excursion on the Thames, complete with Dixieland band. Steve liked playing social director. He took pictures and sent Tom copies. Even though Tom sometimes found these occasions a little too "gin and Judy," he went along without complaining.

Steve without booze seemed a bit strange at first, but then Tom realized it was because his friend was forced to fill up what had been his drinking time with other activities. He still loved going to bars and restaurants that served alcohol, where, as in the drinking days, he'd eyeball the crotches of all the young waiters passing by. That had amused Tom when, sodden and uproarious, they rolled from bar to bar in downtown Philadelphia. Now, however, he noticed Steve's lurid glances earning hateful looks from waiters, restaurant managers, and other customers.

One early evening, as they sat facing each other at a restaurant in Mystic, a hawk faced waiter with slicked-back blond hair emerged from the kitchen, balancing a loaded tray. Steve turned to his left, then swiveled to his right, in an effort to "check out the basket." He repeated this gesture when the waiter came out of the kitchen again.

Tom felt himself flush.

"Steve," he said, clearing his throat. "Work the mirrors."

"What?"

"Work the mirrors."

"What do you mean?"

"Okay. This mirror behind me?"

"Yeah."

"You can use it to see everything you need to see. And a lot more discreetly.

"Was I being too obvious?"

"Uh, let's put it this way: you were just about inside his pants."

Tom rotated his spoon in his hands. "If you want a good look without drawing attention to yourself," he said, "you gotta work the mirrors."

"What if there isn't a mirror?"

"There's always a mirror, Steve. There's a mirror behind the bottles on the bar. Use the windows; they reflect everything. Pull out your fucking compact, for Christ's sakes."

They both laughed and that was the end of it.

Steve talked about sex a lot. Driving through New London in his BMW, or the Jeep Cherokee he bought to replace it, he sometimes nearly steered into stop signs watching hot guys walk down the street. Being engaging, he often developed friendships with men far younger than himself. Sometimes they were current—or former—clients who'd been referred to him by a court on account of substance abuse problems. Some were guys he hired to cut lawns or paint. Some were young academics, who looked to Steve as an authority on adolescent psychology.

One day Steve called Tom to tell him about his latest piece of real estate, a condo in Provincetown. The two-bedroom third-floor apartment on Freeman Street overlooked the town library at the corner and had a view of the harbor.

Steve furnished the condo the way he furnished his house in New London: homey and haphazard. A chair and ottoman of tan-colored leather. An overstuffed cream-colored sofa bed. A colonial rocker. A fake bearskin rug. He placed his dining room table next to the window overlooking Commercial Street and the harbor. Post-it Notes ("Call Dad," "Pick up shoes," etc.) littered the surface. Mail sat stacked and unopened on the windowsill.

Tom became Steve's regular condo guest, coming up for a week at least twice a year. He had the room facing Provincetown Library and was free to come and go as he pleased. ("Just don't bring back any numbers.") On Tom's arrival, the two of them would drive to the A&P where they bought six-packs of Diet Coke, assorted pastries, Baby Ruth bars, ice cream and—Steve's one concession to a healthy diet—cantaloupes. A typical Steve breakfast consisted of a bowl of carefully sliced melon wedges speared with toothpicks stuck on miniature seashells, a cherry or apricot Danish glistening with sugar, and a pint of chocolate or strawberry ice cream, consumed between cigarette puffs.

Steve loved to watch the comings and goings on Commercial Street. He was especially enamored of a restaurant opposite the library call Big Walt's. He ate lunch there daily and grew chummy with the rotund Walt and his lover, Jason, who between them owned a half-dozen restaurants and considerable real estate in Provincetown. Tom and Steve would eat breakfast on the condo deck overlooking the library. Tom marveled at the dish Steve collected.

"See that guy?" Steve said one morning. "He got fired from the Gifford House."

A round-shouldered figure with a monk-like fringe of brown hair slouched down the street, hands in pockets.

"What for?"

"Didn't come in to work because he was drunk. Second time. So, they canned him."

The man halted, looked from right to left.

"Then," Steve continued, "the idiot phoned in a bomb threat."

"You're kidding?"

"No. He called up at about nine on a Sunday night and told whoever answered that there was a bomb in the building.

"What'd they do?"

"They evacuated. They have to."

"What happened?"

"The owner called the cops and the cops traced the number. Right now, he's out on bail, awaiting sentencing."

The figure glanced up at Tom and Steve, scowled, then hurried on.

It was early September and chilly. Steve wore a bathrobe, Tom an oversized gray sweatshirt. Steve lit a fresh cigarette. A brown-haired woman about thirty-five appeared, walking a golden retriever.

"Oh oh," Steve said, pushing the first spoon of Haagen-Dazs in his mouth, "there goes Liz."

"She doesn't look happy."

"That's because she's drunk and on coke every night."

"How do you know?"

"She lives on this street. I see her coming in at two in the morning.

He paused. "She had sex with her dog at a party."

"What?!"

Liz dug in her pocketbook for something while her pet lifted its leg at the library Dumpster.

"She was drunk and started making out with it."

"Oh, c'mon Steve. Where'd you hear that?"

"Jason. Him and Big Walt know everything that goes on in this town."

After breakfast, Tom would pack his knapsack and bike to the beach. Steve spent the day doing chores or sitting at the table by the window, smoking, punching numbers into a calculator, scratching notes to himself. At night the two of them would walk to the video-rental store on Commercial Street and rent a tape. Steve kept his eye out for live entertainment and two or three nights during Tom's visit they'd hit the Town House to catch a drag act or go to The Moors to hear a piano playing comedian named Lenny with whom Steve had gotten to be pals.

As the years passed, Steve spent more and more time at the condo, but went out less and less. Apart from lunch or dinner at Big Walt's, he rarely left the apartment. A recession had substantially reduced the value of his properties, and Steve was fending off banks and creditors. Instead of going out, he sat by the window shuffling through bills and mortgage statements. When he and Tom did venture forth, Steve would have to sit down and rest every other block. He'd gotten that big. The last time they went to the video store, Steve had had Tom call a taxi. After that, he simply sent Tom to get the movie. He'd also developed a racking, phlegmy cough.

Tom noticed a certain distance, an irritability, which he suspected wasn't limited to himself, and which he thought might be related to Steve's finances, or health. Steve became obsessed with his weight and started taking diuretics. Tom stopped kidding him about it. Steve also grew openly suspicious of people and their motives. If one of his houseguests offered to take him to lunch, it was because they were trying to maneuver him into buying them dinner. When Tom and the newest love of his life, Jeff, borrowed the condo for a weekend, they left behind a bag of French coffee with a thank-you note. Tom phoned later to ask if Steve liked the coffee. "Oh," Steve said, "I thought it was leftover coffee you didn't want anymore."

Steve also became quick to take offense, even cutting off people he'd known for years. When Glen, one of Steve's friends from college, came to visit with a new and much younger lover, Steve took them both to a well-known restaurant on the water.

"We'd only just been served," Steve recalled to Tom, a few weeks later, "and all of a sudden this fucking New York queen sort of tilts his head back and starts sniffing. "What's the matter?" I said. "He says..." Steve pursed his lips and tilted his chin a fraction of an inch. "Sewage." He paused. "Sewage," he repeated, rolling his eyes, and stamping out a cigarette. "You'd better believe they're not staying *here* again."

Tom began coming up once a year instead of two or three times a season. He did that for two years in a row. Steve was quiet a lot and seemed to have run out of funny stories to tell. The next year Tom decided to make it a four-day weekend instead of a week. Steve didn't say anything, but the atmosphere became strained. One afternoon during his visit, Tom stood at the sink scrubbing breakfast dishes. Steve came up behind him and screamed: "Tommy! YOU'RE WASHING THE DISHES WRONG!" Tom left a day early, with Steve in a sulk. They barely said good-bye. Six months later, when Steve called to invite him up, he told Steve he couldn't make it on account of a business trip.

The next summer, Tom and Jeff were staying up the Cape in Orleans, with Jeff's brother. Feeling guilty about turning down yet another invitation to visit Steve, Tom suggested they drive to Provincetown and take Steve to dinner. Surprised and pleased to get Tom's call, Steve said he'd be ready at 8:00. When Tom and Jeff arrived, there was no answer. They knocked again.

A light appeared. Steve opened the door, wiping his drained face with a washcloth.

"I'm sorry," he said. "I fell asleep."

It was Labor Day weekend. A line of people stood outside Big Walt's, waiting for tables to open. Steve complained to the waitress about lukewarm coffee, then to Jason about the waitress. He smoked nonstop and kept asking Tom questions about Orleans. Where were they staying? What were the good places to eat? When it was time to leave, he tried to persuade Tom not to leave a tip. Tom was happy and relieved to walk Steve back to the condo.

"When he answered the door I thought for a moment he was drinking again," Jeff said, when they were back in the car.

Tom agreed that Steve looked pretty bad.

"And his paranoia is completely out of control. It's just raging."

"Do you think so?"

"All those questions about where we were staying and what we were doing in Orleans. I mean, obviously he didn't believe we were in Orleans. He thought we'd been in Provincetown the whole week and just never called him."

"I don't think he's well, frankly."

"How could he be? He smokes constantly. He's at least a hundred pounds overweight. He can hardly get up those stairs. At some point he's just going to drop over."

Three months went by. Tom got a Christmas card from Steve but neglected to send one back. Then, in the early summer, one of Steve's hand-scrawled-in-ballpoint notes arrived. "Tom," it read. "Hate to be the bearer of bad news, but I've had to sell the condo. Health's not good. I need to rest a while + get my strength back. Steve."

Tom decided to phone.

"Steve," he said. "What's going on?"

"Tommy, is that you? Where are you?"

"Philadelphia. What's the matter with your health?"

"It's not good. I've got congestive heart failure."

"What does that mean?"

"I'm not sure, but they tell me it means my circulatory system is compromised. On a practical level, it means I can't walk across the room without having to sit down and catch my breath. I had to stop teaching. I'll probably have to give up my practice."

"Are you still smoking?"

"I'm cutting down," Steve said. "How're you doing? How's Jeff?"

"Jeff...left. He went to New York to take a PhD in social work."

"Well, scratch another one. How long were you two together?"

"Five years."

"I'm sorry," Steve said.

Tom didn't want to talk about Jeff with Steve. Jeff had been the one Tom was going to spend his life with. For three years, everything seemed fine. People described them as an ideal couple.

Then, strained by the need to hold down jobs they both hated, by the death of one of Tom's closest friends, by the terminal illness of Jeff's mother, and by what the therapist Tom finally engaged told him later was his own selfish and demanding nature, the relationship unraveled.

"The problem with you is that you don't know how to love anyone," Jeff said and started packing. Tom, furious, at first disbelieved Jeff would ever leave, then grew impatient for Jeff to be gone, then convinced himself Jeff would return. Months went by. The mornings he woke by himself in the bed they'd shared were the worst he'd ever had, not counting hangovers. He became convinced he was going out of his mind.

Six months later, in mid-August, Tom received a letter stamped with Steve's New London return address. His own name was inscribed in a blocky, unfamiliar hand. *Steve's dead*, he thought. He tore the letter open.

"Dear Folks," it began. "We are sorry to inform you that Steve has terminal lung cancer. It was diagnosed about a month ago and the prognosis was that he would live another year or so. However, on Friday, August 1, he was told that the cancer was rapidly spreading to other vital organs and that, barring divine intervention, he had maybe a week or two or three at most to live."

The letter was signed by Steve's cousin, Rick, and his wife, Sheila.

Tom reached Steve by phone at the hospital. Steve assured him the letter was "somewhat alarmist."

"Listen, Tommy," Steve said. "My cousin and his wife and some friends are taking me to Provincetown for my birthday. They're going to drive me up in an RV. I want you to come."

What in the world are they thinking? Tom thought. He considered the whole idea of the trip foolish and began rehearsing excuses not to go.

At the end of the week, Tom flew to the Cape and took a taxi to the Truro motel where Steve and his friends had made reservations. Steve's group hadn't arrived yet and he had a few hours to kill. He decided to rent a bike. He rode the bike into Provincetown, then back to the motel.

The RV arrived hours later. Steve lay in a foldout bed in the back, tethered to a canister of oxygen. He had lost about a third of his weight. His hair, now thoroughly white, stood out in tufts and cowlicks. *He looks like a corpse*, Tom thought. *Except for his eyes.* The eyes held all the life that seemed to have deserted the rest of his body. They also lacked the hard squint of suspicion.

"Tommy," he said, "get me my slippers, wouldya? And that walker!" It amazed Tom how quickly he fell back into doing Steve's bidding.

Using a special wood ramp he'd built, Tom's cousin, a contractor, unloaded from his pickup truck a three-wheeled scooter with a chair on it. Steve inched his way to the scooter with a walker and climbed into the seat. He started the motor, gripped the throttle, and glided across the parking lot toward the motel room door. Steve's New London friends—all staying in rooms above or next to Steve's—hooted and clapped. Steve waved to them before dismounting. Steve quickly made himself the center of attention, issuing orders and wisecracks from his gurney in the room. He directed Tom to wheel the gurney to the sliding glass doors, so he could see the water.

Later, Tom excused himself, mounted his bike, and rode into Provincetown for something to eat. He parked the bike in front of a pizza place. The late afternoon sun divided the patio out front into zones of light and shade. Tom bought two pieces of cheese pizza and sat on a bench to watch the crowds pass. It was mostly guys in their twenties and thirties. He was now forty-three, a few years older than Steve had been when they met. Middle-aged. He remembered watching men in their forties when he was in his twenties, trying to guess what they might've looked like when they were young, wondering what he'd be like at that age. Impossible.

After Jeff left, Tom thought of himself as ready to retire from dating and sex. Six months later, when he began going out again, he found he attracted a different kind of man. Or men, since there had already been several. They were mostly in their early to mid-thirties, looking for a strong, seasoned guy who took care of himself. *I guess*

I'm what they call a Daddy, he thought. He imagined Steve's mirth on hearing the term as applied to him but then considered that Steve had more pressing concerns. *Still,* Tom thought, *I'm back where I was in my twenties. That revolving door of dates and convenient little relationships. At some point I'll be too old even for that.*

Shirtless men in shorts or cutoffs walked past, some holding hands. Tom noted lots of couples, many dressed alike. Two guys went by in baggy khaki shorts, white socks and construction boots that looked as if they'd never seen a building site. Another couple, in their sixties, strolled along arm in arm. One of them was bald and had a thick, white mustache. The other wore glasses and marched along on spindly, hairless legs. Tom studied the legs, fascinated, thinking how odd it was that guys in their twenties shaved off the leg hair that guys in their sixties would kill not to lose.

Someone was sitting next to him, balancing a paper plate with pizza on it. Someone attractive.

"Hello," Tom said.

"Hi," said the guy, whose name was David. David worked in a jewelry store in New Jersey. He had dark hair and a great tan. It was David's first visit to Provincetown and he and his best friend, Anthony—"Ant"—were having a fabulous time. They'd been there a week and were leaving tomorrow, unfortunately.

"How about you?" David said.

"I'm just here for the weekend. I'm staying in a motel in Truro."

Tom heard a slow, thudding bass coming from down the street.

"How was tea dance?" he said.

"Kind of boring. I like the beach better."

Tom bit his crust in half and noted, out of the corner of his eye, David inspecting his crotch.

"Where are you staying?"

"Ant and I rented a condo."

"Where?"

"Freeman Street."

"Which building?"

"I don't know the number."

"Is it by the library?"

"Right across from it."

Steve must've sold the apartment furnished. Everything he'd had there—the overstuffed white couch, the brown leather chair with ottoman, the rocker, the VCR and TV, even the fake fur rug—remained. Brown bottles of tanning lotion and a pile of rainbow beach towels lay on the table by the window where Steve used to sit with his bills and his mortgage payments.

Ant emerged from the bathroom, toweling himself off. Unbelievably cute, Tom thought. Especially that rubbery butt that bounced to the back-and-forth swing of the towel. Tom and David disappeared into the room where Tom had always stayed.

David unbuttoned his blue-jean cutoffs and let them drop. A lime green Speedo glowed against his brown skin. "Ummmmm," Tom said, rolling the tip of his tongue across his lower lip. Barefooted, David kicked his shorts away. A long, slightly curved cock lay horizontally to the right of the crotch under the bathing suit. Tom walked over and drew two fingers along its length, pausing to caress the head, which took the shape of a fat acorn. He slipped a hand under the bathing suit and squeezed the whole plump package. David grinned as if there were not a thought or feeling inside him except that of anticipated pleasure, and Tom smiled back into David's smile, then pulled his own T-shirt off and flung it on a chair. He unbuttoned his khaki shorts, let them fall, kicked them away. Naked but for his boxers and black boots, he tugged David's Speedo down and his eyes closed, his mouth formed a perfect seal over David's and they breathed each other's air while tongues pushed, touching teeth, cheeks, gums, throats.

Tom heard the door creak slightly and opened his eyes. In the mirror above the dresser, he saw Ant, nude but for the strawberry-colored bath towel around his neck.

"Mind if I join you?"

When Tom got back to Truro he found Steve in his motel room alone, alert and watching CNN. Steve hit the mute button. "Rick and Sheila went to the A&P," he said.

Apart from the fact that his days were, literally, numbered, something seemed odd. Tom realized it was because Steve wasn't smoking, He couldn't remember fifteen minutes when Steve hadn't been lighting up, smoking, or stabbing out a cigarette.

"I gave it up right after they diagnosed the cancer," Steve said.

"Was it hard?"

"I just threw'em away, Tommy."

A giant dollar sign came on the screen next to a chart of some kind, both superimposed over a black-and-white photo of Wall Street.

"I went into therapy, too," he said.

"How come?"

"Lots of reasons. It's too much to go into." He paused. "Well, maybe not."

They sat without saying anything for a minute or so. Somewhere in Southeast Asia a ferry had capsized, spilling dozens of people to their deaths. A shot from a helicopter showed lifeboats struggling through rainy swells.

"You know," Steve said, "I was never good at relationships. That's my biggest regret. I never really had anybody in my life. Well..."—he thought about it—"...I had one relationship. With this guy, Gary. It lasted nine months."

"When was that?"

"In my twenties."

Steve looked from Tom toward the glass doors that opened right onto the beach. A woman trudged in the direction of the motel, tugging two blond boys with plastic pails. Tom thought of the portrait in the house on Juniper Street, that picture he'd seen the first morning he woke on Steve's sofa.

"Where'd you meet him?"

"In grad school. At UConn. He was a knockout, Tommy. But we fought all the time."

He paused. "I was drinking. He was still dating girls. I don't think it was meant to happen."

Then Steve changed the subject

"Tommy, I want you to know you're the first person named in my will. I'm leaving you some money. It's not that much. Five thousand dollars. Find some way to use it."

"Thanks, Steve, that's very generous of you."

Steve stared at the TV screen and frowned.

"All the other people I left money to told me I didn't really have to do that for them," he said.

"Well, I don't know what they said, but what I'm saying is thank you very much. You've always been generous."

"Oh, fuck you," Steve snorted. They both laughed. "Would you get me a Diet Coke? They're in the fridge."

Tom retrieved the cold can from the fridge under the sink, popped the top, and handed it to Steve.

"Steve," he said, "I had sex in your condo."

"Oh, c'mon, Tommy, that hardly matters now."

"No, I mean a half hour ago."

Steve rose on his back, almost jerking away the tube of oxygen clamped to his nostrils.

"What?! You're kidding me!"

"No, I met this guy and started talking to him, and he suggested we go back to his place. It turned out to be the condo on Freeman Street."

"So you finally got laid there?"

"I finally got laid there."

"Whore!"

Someone knocked and Steve's cousin and his wife came in with bags of groceries, including cantaloupes, cookies, pies, Baby Ruths, and Danish.

Later that night everyone went out to dinner. They used Rick's portable ramp to get Steve's scooter chair into Big Walt's, where Steve and his party occupied the premier table for an hour and a half. Then they loaded the chair into the truck and drove to The Moors, where Steve's friend Lenny was still the entertainer-in-residence. Steve was able to go down the ramp and into the bar, where Lenny kept throwing him jokes

Sunday afternoon, as they helped Steve into the RV, Tom hugged him goodbye.

The pilot pushed the throttle of the Fokker steadily forward as the aircraft approached the end of the runway. It hopped into the air, jerked, righted in a split second, and climbed. The plane ascended to what Tom assumed must be five or six thousand feet. At 6:47 A.M. the Cape's end was the sand-covered sliver of a dying moon, tufted with pine canopies and tied with strips of gray asphalt, the stone phallus of the Provincetown Monument rising above it.

I almost didn't go, Tom thought. *Imagine what you'd feel like if you hadn't gone.*

The plane leveled off over the broad, flat expanse of Cape Cod Bay. Someone behind him in the cramped nine-seater swung a camera at the window and clicked the shutter button. Someone rattled the pages of the day's *Boston Globe*. Most just stared out the window where, off to the right, a trawler spilled its foamy wake into the sea and, a little farther out, a pair of sailboats floated, seemingly motionless.

He probably wouldn't see Steve again. Steve had...weeks at most. Whatever he might think. Steve, he thought. *Moving back and forth between poles of generosity and bitterness. Expecting to be betrayed. Making the same mistakes again and again. How not to repeat them? Anyway, he, Tom, had made worse ones. What does that mean, that I'm flawed? Of course, you're flawed. Who isn't? I've done things that were so stupid, so selfish, so inconsiderate...*

Steve. Whose pleasures had killed him without providing any real enjoyment. Who used pleasure to displace time. Who filled up his time with anger. Killing it, really, with anger.

Then the thought came to Tom that Steve, who'd lived as if the act of living were a chore, and always by himself, who'd seemed so far from the reach of love, had loved him, Tom. Had always loved him. From the beginning. And had, somehow, chosen never to state it.

Why don't I ever think about love? Tom wondered. *I think about everything else except that. I think about money, work, sex, people I hate. I never think about love. You don't even know what it is. You've never even seriously thought about it.*

Was it, he wondered, something beyond his reach? No, in fact, he had loved. He couldn't define it, but he had felt it with some people. It was there or had been. Lately he had come to understand that it wasn't the instant attraction he'd believed in for so long, but something more subtle, something long term, a connection between two beings that was larger than either of them, that had to put down roots and grow. Jeff, for instance. Steve talking about someone named Gary, a name he'd never heard mentioned in twenty years. What held that in place? That mirage.

The plane made a wide turn over Boston Harbor and descended toward Logan Airport. Tom looked at his watch. The twenty-minute trip had passed in seconds. Wheels hit the runway. The craft slowed, braked, fell in behind a jet taxiing toward the concourse. Another small plane came up behind them.

"Please wait till the plane is safely parked at the gate before unfastening your seat belts," the pilot said, without turning around.

And then they were parked and Tom was lifting his bags off the carousel to get the airport bus for his flight to Philly.

The memorial service, in New London, took place two months later in a bar on the Thames River. Lenny officiated from the piano. Tom was supremely grateful for Steve's decision not to have it in a church. A church would've been so un-Steve. At one point, while Lenny pounded the keys, enacting some bawdy song, he saw, reflected in the wall of windows behind the piano, a submarine moving downstream toward Long Island Sound from its base farther up the Thames in Groton. *How odd*, he thought. *This is what happens when you work the mirrors.*

And laughed.

After Lenny finished, someone told a story about Steve's outrageous behavior in a New York bar. Tom liked hearing the stories people told, which were mostly about Steve's humor and kindness. They each seemed to know a different Steve, but nothing he heard that afternoon surprised him.

PUBLICATION ACKNOWLEDGMENTS

"Where's the Hotboy Going Tonight?": *Chelsea Station*, June 2018.

"Are Birds Spies?": *New Haven Review*, Issue 20, Summer 2017.

"Who's Vladimir Horowitz?": *Chelsea Station*, August 2019.

"What Makes a Queen a Queen?": *Gay & Lesbian Review Worldwide*, July-August 2017.

"Waiting for Janis": *New Haven Review*, Issue 24, Spring 2020, published as "What Was She Like?"

"Date": *Harrington Gay Men's Fiction Quarterly*, Vol. 7, #4, 2005.

"The Rise and Fall of Malibu Barbie": *Skidrow Penthouse*, Issue #4, Fall-Winter 2001.

"Dish": *Skidrow Penthouse*, Issue #7, Spring 2006.

"An Ideal Couple": *James White Review*, 1995. Republished in the anthology *Fresh Men 2*, edited by Donald Weise, 2005.

ABOUT THE AUTHOR

JIM CORY is the author of numerous chapbooks of poetry, including *Birds & Buildings* (Moonstone Press, 2019), *Wipers Float in the Neck of the Reservoir* (The Moron Channel, 2018) and *No Brainer Variations* (Rain Mountain Press, 2011). He has edited poetry selections by James Broughton (*Packing Up For Paradise*, Black Sparrow Press, 1997), Jonathan Williams (*Jubilant Thicket*, Copper Canyon Press, 2005), and Karl Tierney (*Have You Seen This Man?*, Sibling Rivalry Press, 2019). Cory's essays have appeared in *The Gay & Lesbian Review, New Haven Review, Chelsea Station*, and elsewhere. His poetry and fiction have appeared in *Skidrow Penthouse, Unarmed Journal, Bedfellows, Painted Bride Quarterly*, and many other venues. He has been the recipient of fellowships from the Pennsylvania Arts Council, Yaddo, and The MacDowell Colony. He lives in Philadelphia.

WWW.RADIATORPRESS.COM